SUCCUMBED

South Bay Billionaires
Book 3

ASHLEY JACOBS

S. S. RICH

ISBN 978-1-962441-05-6

A note on content

*To those who crave control—may you also discover
the beauty and pleasure in surrender.*

*And to our moms...
Skip this one.
Please.*

About the Bay

This series is set in a fictionalized version of Northern California called South Bay. You can think of it as our spicy contemporary romance take on Silicon Valley. Like Palo Alto, the fictional Bay is full of entrepreneurs, technology startups, and the people and companies that invest in them. It's a cutthroat environment, with different tech startups all clamoring for investment from the same venture capital (VC) firms and angel investors.

VCs are companies like Athena Ventures, the fictional business founded by Lex Livingston that connects most of the characters in the Bay. VCs seek out the most promising startups to invest in, with the goal of the company either being acquired or going public–both at considerable profit. It's a lucrative business, if you bet on the right startups.

Angel investors behave similarly, though they're typically single individuals providing funds/capital (like Preston Brooks did for Cami's Kitchen in *Reserved*) instead of companies.

Here, every conversation is an opportunity and the stakes are always high.

Welcome to the Bay, babes. Let's dive in, shall we?

Prologue

I could count on one hand the men who had earned my trust. My father threw me out for my ambition, my younger brother gladly took what was rightfully mine, and others had wronged me at every turn.

If they didn't underestimate and patronize me, they found me intimidating and were threatened by my success. As I grew my career, I buried the idea of romantic love in my ambition.

I set my boundaries, established my rules like a fortress around the truest parts of me, and approached romance as a transaction. For nearly two decades, I kept most men at arm's length.

But this man? This beautiful, raw human being with his heart in his hand and an apologetic smile on his lips?

This man isn't dismantling my barriers; he's setting them on fire and reveling in the flames. I don't know him as intimately as I do the other men I love, haven't made it far past the walls he's reinforced every step of our journey. But I see him.

I see how he thinks through a problem and stops at nothing until he solves it. How he gives his whole heart to what he believes in and fights fiercely for it without hesitation. How he's unstoppable when challenged, no matter how unlikely the odds.

I've watched him put the people he loves before himself, time and again, even when it tears us apart in the process.

But I don't mind a little pain with my pleasure.

Thanks to them, I crave it.

Chapter 1

Declan

The last time I saw her, I was a fool. A stupid, trusting fool who put my future in the hands of someone woefully undeserving. Seeing her striking face again brings it all back to the surface–the humiliation, the anger, the overwhelming need to tear it apart just to rebuild it better.

"Dec, are you watching this?" My brother's voice interrupts my rage-fueled thoughts as he saunters into the room, flipping his baseball hat around to sit backwards on his brown curls.

I look at the phone he thrusts toward me. There she is again, impeccable as I remember. The video is paused a few minutes before the version still playing in my earbud. Linc looks down at my screen and grunts, pocketing his phone as he plops next to me on the couch and peers over my shoulder.

"Shane!" he hollers, eyes glued to the interview. He knocks my shoulder with his. "Pause it for a sec, yeah? Maybe start it over."

My narrowed look goes unnoticed as he glances back over the couch and gestures urgently.

"C'mon, man, you gotta see this."

Shane, my best friend and business partner, rounds the

couch and takes the open spot beside me. His lean, muscled thigh bumps mine as he settles back on the couch, blue eyes piercing as he turns to me in question.

"Seriously?" I grunt, gesturing at the immense amount of space around me. "This fucking thing seats twelve. Why the hell are you two on my lap?"

"You're fine." Linc waves his hand at my phone. "Start it over, Dec."

"Here." Shane plucks the device from my fingers, ignoring my frustrated exclamation and tapping the screen.

Before I can ask him what the hell he's doing, the video appears on the television mounted across the room.

"God, does she even fucking age?" Linc reaches up to resettle his hat, his eyes trained on the screen. "She's even hotter now than she was three years ago."

He's not wrong. I immediately hate the thought, dismissing it as quickly as it appears.

"Have some respect, kid," Shane barks, reaching across me to back-hand my brother's chest.

I grunt, and try to make my wide frame smaller to get a modicum of distance, ready to tell them both off again. Laughter rings out from the television. We all still, watching the woman who tossed us out without remorse as she smirks.

"It's an honor to have you both here." The interviewer, Cass Thompson—startup and tech reporter for the Bayview Bulletin—smiles at the two women seated opposite her.

"Thanks for inviting us," Preston Brooks replies. She's a society darling and angel investor, well-known in the Bay. "I relish any opportunity to talk about the importance of women-led businesses."

Lex Livingston, owner of Athena Ventures and arguably one of the most successful businesswomen in the country, dips her chin. "Agreed. Empowering female founders, particularly in the male-dominated tech space, is something I'm fiercely passionate about."

Shane leans forward to rest his elbows on his knees, his hands clasped loosely in front of him and ice blue eyes laser-focused on Lex. She's radiant in a simple fitted suit the color of merlot, her blazer open over a loose-fitting black silk camisole. Even next to the modelesque Preston Brooks in her electric blue dress, Lex holds us all captive.

"That passion is well-documented, and a big reason why we're so pleased to have you and Preston co-hosting our annual Bay's Brightest luncheon to honor women in the startup community next week." Cass tilts her head to the side, her brows furrowing minutely. "Your own path to success has had its own share of challenges, hasn't it?"

Lex's bright green eyes flash with something unreadable, and my gut tightens in response.

"It certainly has," she answers smoothly, "And that's a big part of why I've invested my time, energy, and funds into causes like these. I don't want the next generation of female leaders to face similar hurdles."

"Could you share an example with us?"

Lex's lips twitch up at the corner as she glances down. "What I've always been most offended by, if I'm honest, are the women who climb up by stepping on others. While I'm not the type of person to preach sisterhood–"

Preston snorts, then covers her mouth with wide eyes as she holds back a laugh. Lex smirks and presses on.

"I do believe every woman who has a seat at the table should save one for another."

"Preach, sister," Preston agrees, raising one hand toward the ceiling.

Lex chuckles as she glances at her, then refocuses on their interviewer. "I'll share a specific example from several years ago.

My business partner, Van Costa, and I were waiting to hear a pitch from a promising young startup."

"Oh shit, here we go." The proximity of Linc's voice is jarring, and I flinch away as he eagerly leans in.

"Why the hell are you still on top of me?" I demand, shoving away from him only to find Shane still hovering by my other side. "Seriously, you two have zero fucking physical boundaries."

They glance at each other over my head, then shrug in unison.

"You're both impossible," I mutter, turning my attention back to the interview.

The three women are laughing, Preston's eyes shining as she looks between the other two. "Sorry, Lex, couldn't help it. Please, continue your story."

Lex inclines her head, then turns back to Cass. Her expression hardens as she speaks, her features sharpening. "One of the four startup founders was a woman who has since made quite a name for herself in this community. She waltzed into the conference room as Van and I stood to welcome them, but she went straight to Van."

Her eyes lose focus and she gazes into the distance, then huffs a laugh. "She shook his hand and introduced herself, then looked me dead in the eye and said, and this is a direct quote, 'I take my coffee black and a water would be great. We've got a lot to cover with Mr. Costa.'"

"The hell she did," Preston gasps, her expression murderous.

Cass clears her throat and shoots the mouthy brunette a pointed eyebrow. Preston winces in response.

Undeterred, Lex tucks a short lock of auburn hair behind her ear and continues. "She did. I'll never forget it."

"What did you do?" Cass asks.

The smile that settles slowly onto Lex's face is cold, calculating. Something stirs in the pit of my stomach in response.

"I got her a black coffee, then sat down with Van and listened to her pitch. Neither of us said a word."

"Oh, you're good," Preston praises. "You let her set up her own fall."

Lex's nonchalant shrug is impossibly elegant. "So to speak. When she finished, her business partners knew something was off, but she was too arrogant to notice."

"Tell me you eviscerated her." Preston leans forward.

"That chick is bloodthirsty," Linc laughs. "I fucking dig it."

"Shut up." Shane snaps his fingers, then points at Lincoln, his gaze never leaving the TV.

My brother's lips part, then draw into a frown as he crosses his arms and sits back against the couch with a pout. *I am surrounded by children.*

"I didn't eviscerate her, no. But I was honest. Their tech was promising–incredibly so–but they didn't have enough hard evidence to back up their claims. I was skeptical from the start, and shared that, but her failure to know her audience? That was unforgivable."

"Say more about that. Why was that your takeaway?"

"She and her business partners came to my firm to ask for my investment. It was their job to know us and what we cared about, and tailor their pitch accordingly. She should never have stepped foot in Athena without knowing who I was. Mistaking me for an assistant should've been an impossible error for her to make. The fact she made it?"

Lex tuts. "It was lazy. And if you're not willing to put in the effort, you're not worth my time. Because if it's easy, you're doing it wrong. I don't tolerate laziness or lack of preparedness because I've found both to be at the root of most avoidable failures."

"You should teach a masterclass, seriously."

Lex chuckles at Preston and shakes her head. "I don't have time for that. But I make time to coach every female founder on our roster."

"Sounds like she missed out on more than just your funding," Cass quips with a wry smile.

"She did, but I doubt she'll ever realize it. When someone is focused on their own success without consideration of others, their aperture becomes incredibly narrow. That's risky for the business and society because people making decisions from a narrow perspective rarely make the right choice. And one terrible decision can negatively affect us all, especially when it brings a magnifying glass to a group that is anything other than white and male—female founders in the tech startup world, for example."

Linc reaches out and slaps the back of his hand against my upper arm. "Dec, that's our sign. If we went back—"

"Quiet," I demand, refusing to look his way. I can't tear my eyes from the screen, and I'm not ready to entertain the suggestion I know is coming.

"What would you say to her if your paths crossed again?" Cass asks.

The answer is immediate.

"Not a word. If she approached me to make amends, I'd listen. Otherwise, there are other women in this industry who are far more deserving of my attention." She gestures toward Preston. "Take this brilliant young woman, for instance."

The brunette basks in her peer's praise for a moment, then grins at her. "Is this the part where I'm supposed to demure and say you're too kind?"

"I hope you don't. Own your brilliance, Ms. Brooks. It suits you."

Preston turns to Cass. "You've given her all the best lines!

It's really not a joint interview at this point. Don't get me wrong, I'm here for it. I'm basically president of the Lex Livingston fan club."

As the women laugh and Cass turns to question Preston, I lean back against the couch. I can feel Lincoln's eyes boring a hole into the side of my face, but I don't turn toward him. A few years ago, we fucked up. *I* fucked up. And I want nothing more than to make it right and restore our business and reputation. Well, that and one more thing.

"Linc's right, Dec. We should approach her." Shane's voice is steady and sure.

"I'm still not convinced."

"What more do you need, though? A flashing neon sign?" Lincoln throws a hand toward the television as the women chat, the young brunette talking animatedly. "You know we can't do this alone. We need help. We need *her*."

"Like fuck we do." I scowl at him.

"Don't be blinded by your pride," Shane intones.

I glance over at him, ready to defend myself. But he's the picture of relaxation, arm flung over the couch and legs up on the coffee table. *How is he always so goddamn calm?*

"I'll think about it." I stand, needing space from them and the reminder of past failures.

"Think quickly."

My eyebrows rise as I turn back to Shane. "What's your rush?"

His eyes flash to mine. "The backstabbing bitch is close to launching. She goes live before we make our move, and it's all for nothing." He looks back at the television. "Who knows how many lives are at risk. And over a decade of work, Dec. Gone."

I look back to the screen a final time. Lex is speaking again, but I tune out her words and study her face. Her light green eyes are fierce and glittering. Experience and knowledge are heavy in her gaze and in the intentional way she speaks. Frustration wells in me, and I huff, stalking from the room.

Time hasn't dulled the sting of betrayal or the weight of responsibility settled on my shoulders. I'm reluctant to trust anyone other than Lincoln and Shane with our business, but the need for retribution is a persistent drumbeat in my skull.

As much as I want to focus on building our business into what we envisioned, I can't ignore the siren song of revenge.

Chapter 2

Linc

"You need to check your attitude, Dec."

My brother, Declan, continues to stare out the windshield of his BMW i4, refusing to turn my way.

"Linc's right," Shane adds, his deep voice quiet and commanding. The rock of our family, we can always count on him to smooth things over and keep the peace.

My older brother ignores us. For all of Shane's talents as our fixer, even he couldn't rival Dec's stubbornness. Dec had gotten it in his head to resist outsiders at all costs, and it wasn't going to be easy to convince him otherwise.

I watch the tension filling his shoulders and straining the muscles in his neck as frustration wells, hot and prickly. I huff a sigh and flop back in my seat. Shane stares out the front passenger window, the only sign of his annoyance the light tap of his fingertips against the door.

"And you call us childish," I mutter. It's passive-aggressive and I'll hear about it from Declan later, but his only response is a clenched jaw.

"We discussed this," Shane rumbles. "We see it through. All of us."

I send a pointed look at my brother to drive our friend's point home, but Dec doesn't turn to see it. *Asshole.* Even though we'd all made mistakes in the last few years, Dec insisted on bearing the lion's share of the guilt. If things had gone according to plan, we would've launched a revolutionary product last year, instead of floundering to pick up the pieces after being betrayed.

Wincing internally as my thoughts stray to Anne-Marie, I give up on Dec. He'll either step up once we get to Athena Ventures for our pitch meeting, or he won't. Either way, I know Shane and I will make the most of the opportunity.

We'd visited the Athena offices before. I was shocked we'd secured a second meeting, given the way our first (and last) encounter ended. But when the 15-minute calendar appointment came through, I didn't question it.

As the top venture capital firm in the Bay, Athena can afford to be demanding. Startups they invest in have revolutionized entire industries. Athena has a reputation for being tough but fair, with a portfolio a mile deep. *And we deserve to be part of it, damnit.*

Three years ago, getting on Athena's roster was our main goal. I can still remember the disbelieving grin on Dec's face when he walked into the lab to tell us we'd booked a meeting with Athena's executive team. Shane had laughed in surprise as I jumped and hollered. We'd been so sure it meant a turning point for us, for the dream we'd started building as four young grad students. *Maybe we can salvage it now.*

We pull into a parking space and Dec exits without a word, the sound of his door slamming bringing my thoughts back to the present.

"Fuck's sake," I scoff as Shane and I follow after him.

"We'll be fine," Shane mutters, straightening the cuffs of his button-down as he rounds the back of the car.

Why he insists on hiding all that ink under business attire, I'll never know. Our friend was a juxtaposition in the flesh—quiet and unassuming in a crowd, but the most dominant motherfucker I'd ever met behind closed doors. He also wore business casual like a second skin most days, while I felt like an asshole imposter in my button down and slacks. *Can't wait to get back in my basketball shorts.*

I give Shane a nod and try to channel his endless calm, resisting the urge to reach for the ball cap I'm not wearing. We have a lot riding on the next thirty minutes, and I suspect Dec is too in his head to rally. His pride can't handle that we're walking back into Athena with our tails between our legs. But it's his damn dream we're chasing, and I refuse to watch it fail when we have a chance to turn everything around—even if that chance is slim to none.

"Welcome to Athena Ventures," a perky blonde at the front desk greets us as we enter the lobby. "Do you have an appointment?"

Dec remains silent, arms crossed as he gazes impassively at her. I step forward, a smile on my lips.

"We do. With Ms. Livingston."

Her eyes shift from Dec's stormy countenance to my friendly one. "Lovely! I'll let her office know you're here. What's the name?"

"Wilde. Lincoln Wilde."

"Alright, Mr. Wilde. Take a seat and someone will be with you shortly."

"Thank you."

I turn to find Dec standing by the plush chairs in the waiting area, arms still crossed. Shane folds himself into a chair facing the office, his watchful gaze tracking the few people we can see.

"This is a waste of time," Dec mutters, sharp green eyes meeting mine as I draw close.

"We don't know that," I retort, raising my eyebrows in a silent warning to *be nice for fuck's sake*.

He looks away with a scoff as I fight the urge to knock some sense into him. He might be the older one, but he's acting like a toddler.

"Mr. Wilde," a haughty voice calls.

I turn and smile at the slim, impeccably dressed man standing by the front desk. "That's me."

"On time, at least." He glances down and picks an imaginary bit of lint from his sleeve. "I'm Miles; I'll be taking you back. Ms. Livingston will meet you in the conference room. Do you need water? Coffee?"

His expression suggests it would be best if we did not, in fact, need anything.

"We're fine."

He simply arches a brow and turns on his heel. I glance over my shoulder to find Dec close behind me, Shane guiding him forward with a firm grip on his shoulder. We follow Miles down an eerily familiar series of turns, arriving at the same conference room we'd visited on the single other occasion we'd been at Athena.

"Make yourselves comfortable," Miles instructs as he opens the door. "Ms. Livingston will be along soon."

"Thank you." I slip past him and walk to the far wall to appreciate the view of the redwoods from the floor-to-ceiling windows.

It's surreal to be back in the same room. I can still feel the apprehension roiling in my gut when our former business partner, Anne-Marie, mouthed off to Lex. I'd known who Lex was the moment she walked into the room—her presence alone took my breath away. But misplaced trust in my friend and partner had kept my mouth shut, even as I worried Anne-Marie had delivered a killing blow to our pitch before it even began.

I start to comment on the view and distract myself from the past, but a soft noise makes the hairs on the back of my neck stand up. *She's here.* I turn slowly toward the doorway, my chest tight in anticipation.

"Well, this is unexpected."

Lex Livingston stands at the entrance to the conference room in a fitted white pantsuit and black heels that make her legs look a mile long. *Fuck, she's even more stunning in person.* Her energy alone commands the room, the three of us turning toward her like moths to a flame.

"I believe there's been a misunderstanding." She glances down at her watch, her light green eyes catching mine as they raise.

"No misunderstanding, Ms. Livingston." I step forward, my hand extended. "It's good to see you again."

One sculpted eyebrow arches as she searches my face for a moment, taking my hand in a brief, firm grip. "I wish I could say the same."

Her cool response lights a fire under my skin. *That's right, gorgeous. Never pull your punches, not even for me.* "That's fair. If you'll give us a few minutes, though, we have a proposition for you."

Her eyes flit to Shane, then Dec, before returning to mine. She seems as curious as she is wary.

"Very well."

She steps into the room and takes the seat at the head of the table, the door closing behind her. It's the same chair she sat in as Anne-Marie dug the proverbial grave for our fledgling startup.

"I'm Lincoln Wilde—"

"I know who you all are, Mr. Wilde. Yours aren't faces I'd soon forget." She leans back in her chair and crosses her ankles. "You have fifteen minutes. Don't waste them."

I tell my cock to simmer the fuck down as her eyes glint. "The last time we were here, things didn't go as planned."

A slight incline of her head is all I get in answer. Taking the seat nearest her, I press on. I can sense my brother and Shane settling around me, but I keep my eyes on her.

"We were idiots."

Her eyes widen, surprise flickering. "Go on."

My lips twitch, but I fight the smirk. "We should've stepped in when Anne-Marie, our *former* business partner, disrespected you. I own that mistake, and I apologize for it."

She studies me for a moment, then her gaze slips behind me. "It's been three years, gentlemen. As much as I appreciate the apology, I certainly hope it's not the reason you're here."

"It's not." Shane's deep voice fills the space.

Some of the tension leaves her as her gaze settles on him, waiting in silence for us to explain.

"Things have changed," I go on. "The three of us formed a new company: Solum Technologies. We've evolved the sustainable building material we pitched to you before, and we think you'll be pleased by the progress we've made."

She drags her attention from Shane back to me. "You're seeking investment for this new venture?"

"We are."

"Why Athena?"

"You're the best."

She scoffs. "Try again, Mr. Wilde."

"You, Ms. Livingston," Shane interjects, instantly drawing her attention. She turns toward him as he continues, "We're here because of *you*."

"What about me, Mr. Kelly?"

"Our former business partner is 'making a name for herself' in this community. Your words, from your recent interview for the Bulletin. We thought you, as an advocate for women in tech, might have a vested interest in her fate."

"One of you needs to spell it out for me." Her voice is hard, her expression fierce, and my desire flames. "I have little patience for games."

"She stole our original tech," I blurt, intent on getting her to see our side. "It's fatally flawed, but she ran with it, pitched the hell out of it, and got acquired. She's building that name for herself on false promises and she lacks the skill and knowledge to make it viable."

Lex is silent, considering, then turns her attention back to me. I try to ignore the pleasure that flushes through me, but there's no denying I want *her* as fiercely as I want Athena's funding.

"Why are you here, Mr. Wilde?"

Pushing everything else aside, I focus on what we came here for. If we can convince her to support our business, I can figure out what to do about my raging libido. "We want your help. To bring our product to market, yes–the real one, the one that works. But we also want to...stop her. Bring her down. However you want to say it."

I take a deep breath, gazing at Lex with what I hope is an open and earnest expression. "She's playing a dangerous game in a highly visible arena. If she fails, as we expect her to, it would be damaging for the industry, the startup community–"

"Female startup founders," Shane adds.

"Yes, exactly." I gesture toward him with an open hand, catching sight of my glowering asshole of a brother as I glance back. *Your silence isn't lost on me, shithead.* "Imagine what her highly visible public failure could cause. She's sold so many lies, attracted so much press. Hell, she's the poster child for female startup founders right now. It'll hurt more than just us if she isn't stopped."

Her gaze is assessing, but she doesn't acknowledge or validate our concerns. I admire her poker face; it's almost as strong as Shane's.

"You've brought updated data?" she asks, and I could fist pump I'm so happy she's not dismissing us. "I recall inconsistencies in your test results."

A derisive snort sounds behind me. *Goddamnit, Declan.* Lex's attention turns to my brother, her eyes narrowing.

"Yes," I interrupt, keeping her attention on our pitch and, if I'm honest, me. "We've refined the formula considerably since the last time we were here; the building material is far more stable across all normal-range weather conditions. Shane and I lead the research and development, but we've hit the point where our lab can't meet the testing needs for the next phase—extreme conditions."

Shane nods during my brief pause. Grateful I'm not the only adult in the room with Lex, I continue. "We need equipment to finalize the stress tests before we can ship a production-ready prototype. Declan's been running the business and operations side of things. He has all the forecast details, but the tech we need is...pricey."

"You're out of money."

"In short, yes."

She relaxes back in her chair, her elbows propped on the arms. "I see."

"I know we have no business being here and asking—"

"Stop, Mr. Wilde." She holds up a hand. "No platitudes. You're here. You've asked."

I'd never noticed a power imbalance in a room until the first time we sat in Lex's presence three years ago. Being before her again is a stark reminder that she wears power as easily as she wears her suit. Strength and command radiate from her relaxed body language, ring in her hard tone.

But something tells me she's a well of vulnerability under the armor she's crafted for her professional persona. I desperately want to peel that armor off her, bit by bit.

I bet she'd break so beautifully.

"What do you need from us?" Shane's voice cuts through the fog of lust surrounding me.

Her eyes move to him, energy sizzling between them. *Like recognizes like.* Shane can be a stoic, scary motherfucker, but he looks at her with nothing but respect. It's not something he gives easily, and it speaks volumes of his regard for her as both a professional and a person.

"Send me your data," Lex orders. "And your concerns about what will happen if your former business partner takes her flawed tech to market. I need to understand the possible damage."

Shane inclines his head. "We'll send it over by end of day."

Lex taps the table absently, eyes flitting between us again. She seems to settle something internally because she rises to her feet. "It's been...interesting, gentlemen. I'll be in touch."

"When?" Dec asks, voice flat. *Welcome to the fucking party, brother.*

"When I choose." She turns and walks to the door without a glance.

Lex pauses at the door and looks back at me. The moment of eye contact has my nerves singing, my body strung taut in response to her gravity.

"You can see yourselves out, I trust?"

"We can," I rasp, my voice belying my unprofessional thoughts.

Her lips tilt up ever so slightly as her eyes flick down and back up. I want to see her smile break free. But the hint of a grin is gone as quickly as it appeared, and she turns and vanishes down the hall before I can process what to do or say to stop her.

This was either my best idea ever, or my worst. I'm here for it, either way.

Chapter 3

Lex

"Miles, with me."

My assistant stands immediately, following on my heels as I sweep into my office. He closes the door behind us and makes a beeline to the bar cart in the corner.

"How did my last appointment get scheduled?"

He glances at me curiously as he hands over a tumbler with a generous pour of scotch. "They emailed requesting a second meeting. They were in the system under a different company name, but I assumed they had an update to share. Why?"

He elegantly drops onto my midnight blue couch, looking up at me with innocent eyes as he strokes the lush velvet.

"You watched the interview I did with Cass Thompson and Preston Brooks?"

He rolls his eyes. "Of course. The entire office has seen it no less than fifty times at this point."

"Lovely," I mutter, taking a long swallow of scotch. After years of benefiting from press coverage as I built my business as a newcomer to the Bay, I don't hate the spotlight, but I certainly don't love it. "Well, the story I told in that interview?"

Miles's brows crease. "Yes?"

"It was about Anne-Marie Townsend."

He blinks as his brows rise. "The golden child of Greenstar Labs?"

"The very same."

"You don't say…" Tutting, he shakes his head. "I have to be honest, Lex, I have no idea why she's the talk of the town. What does her big idea even do, exactly?"

I laugh. "She's claimed she can revolutionize commercial construction. She's developed a green building material that's lighter, more cost effective, and carbon neutral to use. Plus, it's produced without all the excess waste of typical milling and manufacturing processes–"

"Lex, honey. No. That's all Greek to me."

"Imagine you could build a school for 30% less, and it was more durable over time."

"Oh. Well, sounds nice, I guess?"

I grin. "And imagine you could do it without hacking down forests, wasting millions of gallons of water, mining, or otherwise destroying the face of the planet bit by bit."

"Wait, so you're saying traditional construction isn't green?" Miles smirks, cocking one perfectly sculpted brow. "I'm shocked."

It's my turn to roll my eyes. "You asked."

"As much as I love a lesson in green tech, why are we talking about the wicked bitch of the past?"

I take a long swallow of scotch. "The three men you put on my calendar are her former business partners."

He chokes, sitting forward abruptly. "Excuse me? The business partners from the story? The ones who just sat there while she made a complete fool of herself *and* them?"

I chuckle and swirl the amber liquid in the glass. "The very same."

"Fuck. Lex, I'm sorry. That whole thing happened before my time, but if I'd known, they'd never have gotten on your calendar–"

I wave him off. "It's fine, Miles. Not your fault; you followed protocol. I just wasn't prepared to see those particular faces waiting for me."

His grin turns salacious. "Those particularly delicious faces, you mean?"

My eyebrow rises as I glare at him over my glass. I had neither patience nor time for his suggestive shenanigans.

"Oh, come on, Lex," he chides. "Tell me you noticed how gorgeous they are? I can't decide who is hotter: the sexy, sullen one with all the muscles, or the tall one with the shaved head and the piercing blue eyes."

I snort internally at his spot-on description of Declan Wilde. *Sullen, indeed.* "Honestly, Miles, I didn't notice."

I wasn't lying. Much. Yes, the arresting blue-eyed gaze of Shane Kelly caught my attention. And Declan's imposing, brooding bulk. *But the attitude should be a huge fucking turn off.* Lincoln Wilde's messy curls and warm brown eyes, though...

None of those things matter because I'm a fucking professional.

"I believe you." His expression suggests he, in fact, does not believe me. *Stop reading me so well, Miles.* "Do I need to put them on the block list? Are they a waste of time?"

I shake my head. "No. They're sending over some materials, then I'll need to decide how to proceed."

His look is long and incredulous. "How to proceed? Lex, honey. You proceed by telling them to fuck right off. Your calendar is full, six in the morning to six at night, every day for the next three months. I should know; I scheduled most of it."

I hum in response as I click open my email inbox.

"Lex." The barest hint of a whine creeps into Miles's voice.

"You're not honestly considering taking them on. Hand them to Parker or another associate. Or something."

Glancing up at my meddling assistant, I smirk. "Perhaps you should grab Van for me. I could use his opinion."

Miles purses his lips. "Rude. I'll grab Mr. Grumpypants, but I'm not sticking around for the verbal beating he's sure to give me for simply existing."

I snort. "I'm sure you won't say anything inflammatory to him, either."

"Me!?" He throws a hand up to his throat in mock horror, his eyes glinting. "I'd never."

"Go," I wave a hand. "Incite your drama. Just make sure he ends up here before my next meeting."

Miles grins. "I'll try to only rile him a little."

"Good of you," I murmur, already distracted by the unread messages filling my screen.

He scoffs as he saunters out. "No promises, boss!"

Shaking my head with a quiet chuckle, I focus on answering the highest priority emails awaiting me. Miles was harmless, and with the exception of one incident when he'd pushed Van too far, their playful rivalry both entertained and steadied the office. There was comfort in the banal routine of their back-and-forth, particularly in an industry as tumultuous as ours.

My mind wanders back to the shock of seeing the three men of Procerus—now Solum—in my conference room. Our first encounter three years ago was memorable for all the wrong reasons, but I'd somehow forgotten how they drew me in despite their former partner's blunder.

They'd been quiet that day, had simply watched as Anne-Marie sealed their fate with a flourish and a thin smile. Hearing from Lincoln directly, seeing the passion and desire in his eyes, was something else. He was so earnest, his eyes warm and inviting as he made their presumptuous ask. And Shane? I shift in my chair as the memory of his deep, calming voice rolls over me. Even Declan, though he'd been little more than a silent, brooding shape in the back of the room, was striking.

"Next time, IM me." Van's surly tone breaks through my thoughts.

I smile sweetly up at my business partner as he closes my office door before heading straight for the bar cart.

"Where's the fun in that?" I tease.

"I fail to see the fun in your assistant's antagonistic attitude." He tosses me a glare as he finishes pouring his whiskey, but it lacks heat.

"You're the only one, my friend."

Van considers me as he sits on the couch like it's his personal throne. "Miles said you had something to discuss?"

I walk over to join him, settling in the chair opposite. "I had an unexpected meeting earlier, with the founders of Procerus."

"You're joking," he barks, expression darkening as he recalls the disastrous meeting.

"Not Ms. Townsend, just the other three. Miles put the meeting under Lincoln Wilde, and I didn't remember why that name rang a bell until I saw them all."

Some of the tension leaves his face. Like mine, most of his vitriol is reserved for Anne-Marie. "Why the fuck were they here?"

I explain our conversation, highlighting the concerns Lincoln and Shane shared about the faulty tech Anne-Marie stole.

"This sounds messy, Lex," Van sighs after a few moments. "I understand your desire to protect reputations and do what's right, but we have little reason to trust these three. Plus, Green-star is a big player in the space."

He isn't wrong. "I hear you. Rumor also has it P&L recently joined their board."

I can feel Van's eyes on me as I gaze down at the tumbler in my hands. Price & Livingston Capital, better known as P&L in the Bay, is the venture capital arm of my father's investment firm. My younger brother moved from the East Coast to launch P&L, and our few interactions since have been strained at best.

"Your gut is telling you something, isn't it?" His question is quiet, knowing.

My lungs fill on a deep inhale, and I meet his gaze. "It is."

"You're rarely wrong, Lex." He closes his eyes, steeling himself, then meets my gaze head on. "As much as I don't want to entertain this situation given the complexities...What's your gut telling you?"

"There's a shit ton we don't know, but I'd put good money on the three of them being genuine. They want to take their former partner down, yes, but they seem motivated by altruism more than revenge." I gaze out the window at the redwoods beyond, considering. "And their tech was promising, Van. I remember that much from their initial pitch, and they've had three years to refine it."

Van lets silence gather between us, waiting for me to continue. We both know I haven't shared a compelling reason to say yes.

"If they're right, and the tech she's peddling as the next revolution is faulty, the fallout would affect far more than the green tech industry. That woman has unprecedented visibility in tech circles right now. She's a media darling acting as the face of female startup founders in a competitive, male-dominated space."

I meet his intense gaze. "If she's full of shit and it all blows up, Van, it's going to reinforce the glass ceiling with rebar. Every woman with a startup is going to be scrutinized to a greater degree, regardless of industry. I've spent my entire career paving the way for more women to succeed in a cutthroat industry, and one stupid girl with delusions of grandeur could undo it all and set it back another decade. In a moment."

Van finishes his whiskey, setting the tumbler down on the coffee table as he leans forward, elbows on his knees. "It's not your responsibility to stop that from happening."

"I know." *Feels like it is, though.*

"You don't owe the startup world anything. You built Athena from the ground up, on your own, and have made it the most influential and successful VC firm in the country."

I can't stop my small smirk. "I know that, too."

"As long as you're doing this because it's something you want to do, and not something you feel obligated to do, I'm in. I've got your back. We can navigate whatever fallout happens with Greenstar and P&L, as long as you're confident this is the right thing for Athena to do."

Unspoken words sit between us. *You're not in this alone.* Emotion wells in my chest, warm and comforting. "Thank you, Van."

He nods sharply, settling back on the couch. "Of course. Put Parker on due diligence, he's been building a sustainability portfolio."

"Perfect. The guys at Solum owe me data; I'll send it to Parker as soon as it comes in."

"Solum?"

"Solum Technologies. They've started fresh with a new company name."

"Here's hoping they have better taste in business partners these days."

"That'll be one of my conditions."

His eyes brighten. "You're going to rake them over the coals with conditions, aren't you?"

"Of course." I smirk. "I deserve some fun."

Van's laugh is deep and loud, drawing an answering grin to my lips. "That you do. And they deserve a dose of humility after the shit they pulled."

I finish my scotch and stand, taking Van's empty glass back to the bar cart with mine.

"One thing, though, Lex."

I turn back to him.

"You're already burning the candle at both ends. How will you fit this in?" He cocks his head at me as he gets to his feet. "With how passionate you are about this, I take it you'll handle it personally?"

"I haven't decided to take it on. Yet."

"But if we do," he presses, knowing full well my mind is 95% made up.

"If we do...you're right. I won't hand it off."

"Promise me I won't find you sleeping in the fucking office again."

I lean away in surprise, my lips pursing. "Of course not. I haven't done that in years, Van. Not since I hired Miles to handle my calendar."

"Right," he drawls. "As long as you don't forget to take care of yourself, this will all work out just fine."

"I don't forget to take care of myself," I mutter, rolling my eyes.

"You do. Even Cami noticed. She brings you lunch every day now, whether you order or not."

I blink up at him. His wife owned a catering business and delivered lunch to the office daily. She also happens to be one of the sweetest people on the planet, so the suggestion isn't out of character. That doesn't stop me from denying his claim. "She does not."

"She does."

My lips purse. "Fine. If we do this, I'll work with Miles to make sure I get everything on the calendar so I don't forget." I wave my hand at him. "Now get out of here. I assume we're both late for something."

He chuckles as he leaves. "I'm sure we are."

Chapter 4

Shane

"Where is he?"

Linc looks over his shoulder. "Where do you think? Downstairs."

I scowl as he rolls his eyes and turns back to the game. Pulling my shirt over my head, I walk into the kitchen to grab a water bottle from the fridge. It's been three days with no word from Athena or Lex, and the tension in the house is palpable.

I met the Wilde boys in middle school. Declan walked up to me at recess and asked me to help him keep an eye on his little brother. I'd agreed immediately, knowing firsthand the class bully was a real shithead. Our playground understanding turned into friendship, then brotherhood, and the three of us have been inseparable ever since.

"He's been down there this whole time?"

"Yeah, he went down about three minutes after you started your run." Frustration is evident in his tone, as it has been for weeks, particularly about Dec.

I'm getting fucking sick of playing middleman.

"About the same time you sat your ass on the couch?"

Linc throws up a middle finger, not turning from the TV.

Shaking my head, I go to the basement stairs and jog down. The space is surprisingly quiet as I emerge onto the unfinished landing, the bare concrete cold under my feet.

"Dec?"

"In here."

I wander toward his voice, ducking the plastic sheeting hanging from the ceiling and skirting the tools strewn across the floor. We'd lived in the house in Los Altos Hills for three and a half years after moving to the Bay from Seattle. It was close to our facility, with just enough wrong with it to keep Dec mostly sane. Anything home improvement related was his preferred outlet for stress. Linc liked to yell at sports on TV, and I ran. *And we've all been using those outlets overtime this week.*

I find Declan standing by a makeshift table built with sawhorses and plywood. He has a pencil in hand and a notepad in front of him with a rough diagram of the next section of framing to build.

"You've made more progress in the last two weeks than the two months before," I observe. He ignores me. "I wonder why."

"You come down for a reason, Dr. Phil?"

I drop my shoulder and throw it into his. He stumbles to the side, then rounds on me. His temper has always been on a hair trigger, but it's only gotten worse since Anne-Marie blew up his dream. Dec's entire focus has always been on achieving something great—for himself, for the family we've created for the three of us. Any deviation from the path he's set in his head sends him into a tailspin before he recovers.

"This," I point to his scowling face, "is a shit look on you, you know."

Dec's eyes flare in annoyance before he blows out a harsh breath. "Stop baiting me."

"Take the bait and I will."

Declan had been in a foul mood since Anne-Marie pulled

her bullshit, but it had been decidedly worse since we'd all gathered to watch Lex's interview. His attitude and unwillingness to get on board put our chances with Athena in jeopardy. I know he feels guilty for not seeing Anne-Marie's duplicity, but it's misplaced. We all played a part in failing to recognize her selfish ambition. *But if he fucks this up, it's on him. And I'll fucking tell him so.*

Some of the fight leaves him. "Not today, Shane."

"Then when?"

"Excuse me?"

"When are you going to deal with all that guilt you're carrying?"

His eyes narrow. "I said not today."

"And I asked when."

"You pushing Linc like this, huh? Or am I the only lucky one?"

I ignore his sarcasm. "You're the boss."

He stills and his expression pinches.

"And yet," I continue, "the kid is the one who got us a second chance, then stepped up in the room to make the most of it."

"I'm aware," Dec growls. "But Athena isn't our only option."

My eyebrows raise. "What else you got?"

He's breathing heavily despite standing still, tension filling his limbs as he clutches the pencil so tightly I wonder if it'll snap.

"We could go to another VC."

He's grasping at straws, his pride getting in the way of admitting we're out of options. It's a familiar conversation. "None of them have reason to believe us about Anne-Marie. She's got quite the reputation now."

"Fuck that bitch," he scoffs. "We don't need to tell anyone about that. We can just pitch our product."

"Right, because no one is going to question why it sounds eerily similar to hers."

"Fine, we tell them. Make them sympathetic to our cause."

I understand his concern over trusting someone new after Anne-Marie fucked us over, but he's taking it too far.

"Right. I'm sure they'll believe her former business partners have no ulterior motives for bad-mouthing her."

His jaw clenches, the muscles flexing. "We go to Greenstar and tell them the whole story and take our files as proof."

I chuckle and his face goes red. "What reason do they have to believe us over her? Our files and the ones she pitched to them are nearly identical."

He throws his hand up. "Fine, let's just sell the house. Cut our losses and leave California."

"Yeah, okay, drama king. Homelessness sounds like a great option."

He groans, throwing his head back as he stares at the ceiling. "Goddamnit, Shane."

His chest heaves with a resigned sigh as he meets my gaze. I stare him down, arms crossed, stance wide and relaxed.

"Listen, Dec." My voice is calm, barely above a whisper, "You need to stop treating the rest of us like fucking opponents. No one has you on the ropes here; not Lex or Athena, and certainly not me and Linc."

He blows a sharp breath through his nose, nostrils flaring. *At least he hasn't told me to fuck off. Progress.*

"The more you face off with us, the more you're setting Anne-Marie up to succeed. And that's the last fucking thing any of us want."

"I get it, Shane. Believe me." His eyes close briefly as he runs a hand through his hair in frustration.

"Man, you've been acting like a cornered animal. To be honest, I'm tired of the defensiveness." I'm also tired of playing peacekeeper between him and Linc, but I'm not going down that road. *Yet.*

His brows draw together and his breathing evens out, his color returning to normal. "You that tired of me?"

I point at him, lips tipping up. "Don't put words in my mouth, asshole."

He huffs a laugh and looks away. "Yeah, okay. I hear you."

"Yeah?"

"Yeah, *asshole.*" His lips twitch into a broad smile.

I grin. Before I can invite him to come up and have a civil conversation with Linc, I hear footsteps rattling the stairs.

"Dec? Shane? You guys good?"

Dec's eyes close briefly before he answers. "Yeah, we're fine. Be right up."

The footsteps stop. There's a pause, then, "Okay. Well, we got an email from Miles, so...yeah."

The vein in Dec's forehead pops. I give him a pointed look as the redness reappears at his collar.

He waves me off, eyes rolling. "Go. I'll be up in a minute."

"Deep breath, man," I mutter, turning for the stairs.

It's never been this tense between the three of us. *I hate it.* If Declan was anyone else, I wouldn't tolerate his attitude, but I owe him and his family my life. They took me in when I had nothing to offer but friendship, then raised me like one of their own. Loyalty matters more than anything to me—I can give the man who adopted me as a brother some time to figure his shit out. *But I'm not above drastic measures if he doesn't get it together. Soon.*

Linc's in the kitchen when I get to the main floor, his back to me as he stands with his hands braced on either side of the sink, shoulders by his ears.

"What did Miles say?" I call, walking around the island.

He looks over his shoulder and turns, crossing his arms and slouching against the counter as he faces me. "Dec coming?"

Nodding, I slide onto one of the leather-upholstered barstools.

"He okay?"

Linc looks sideways at me, knowing Dec's more transparent for me. He takes his role as big brother far too seriously to let Linc see all the cracks in his armor. Always has.

"No."

"What are we going to do about that?"

I meet his gaze. "Keep going. He's either going to get on board or walk away."

"Dec doesn't walk away."

"I know." I incline my head.

The loaded pause is broken by Dec's heavy footfalls as he enters the room. He glances between us, a small crease forming between his brows. *Yes, we're talking about you.*

"What did Athena say?"

Linc straightens, matching his brother's tension. I push away the discomfort the strain between them causes, refusing to put words to my concerns for our dynamic. It feels fragile for the first time.

"It was a calendar invite. Dinner with Lex in two days."

Interesting. "Just Lex?"

Linc dips his chin. "The four of us."

Something about that phrase stirs a memory. I can picture the four of us around the table at Athena with perfect clarity; Declan across from me and Lincoln to my right, with Lex poised at the head of the room. *Felt right then and feels right now.*

Dec's fists clench, and I watch as he forces them to relax. "Okay. Did you accept?"

Annoyance flares in Linc's eyes, but he tamps it down. *Atta boy.* "Not yet. Wanted to make sure we were aligned."

"Thank you."

Linc flashes me a grateful look, then turns back to Declan. "Obviously, I think we should accept."

Declan swallows, then nods once. "Agreed."

Linc's eyebrows climb as he glances at me again, seeking confirmation he heard correctly.

"Same," I offer.

"Great." He pulls his phone from his pocket, his thumbs flying across the keyboard. As he finishes, he meets his brother's eyes. "Done."

"Good. I'm going to clean up, then let's talk strategy." Dec glances my way. "Pizza?"

I smile and duck my head as the last of Linc's tension leaves his body. "I'll call it in."

Dec grunts in thanks before turning on his heel and heading for the stairs. We watch him go, then Linc grins and reaches over for a high five. I chuckle and slap my hand against his, pulling my phone out to place our order. We're far from being back on track, but I'm counting the afternoon as a win. *One step at a time.*

Chapter 5

Lex

"You trust their data?"

Parker meets my gaze from across my desk, his expression thoughtful. "I do. They're thorough and have been diligent in their testing. From what they've shared, I can see they're close. But they need capital to rule out the weakness they identified in the version Greenstar is backing."

While there are few men in my life I trust fully, Parker has earned my faith over his years at Athena, growing from a senior associate to principal I rely on often. He does his homework, has great intuition, and is respected by his clients.

I have the due diligence summary he'd pulled together for Solum up on my laptop, and I scroll through it as Parker continues.

"Everything they sent over from the R&D perspective was immaculate, Lex. Their data is meticulous, and their product is one of the most innovative the industry has seen." He pauses, glancing at his notes. "I can see why you're considering giving them a second chance."

"So, R&D is strong. What about the business side of things?"

A small frown tugs at his mouth. "Those records are accurate as far as I can tell, but they sent over the bare minimum. They haven't been irresponsible by any means, but I don't have a lot of insight beyond verifying they need more investment to afford the equipment they've identified as critical."

"Hm. Shane and Lincoln run R&D while Declan manages the business and strategy. He was largely silent the other day."

"Sounds like he's less bought in. Could be a problem."

"That's an understatement," I mutter, scrolling ahead in the document.

"Lex?"

"Hm?" It takes me a moment to look up, and I find Parker's eyes on me when I do.

"What do you need to know to make the most of tonight?"

A soft smile curls my lips. *Good question, Brooks.* I lean back in my chair, propping my elbows on the arms and steepling my fingers. "Ultimately, I'm either going to wish them luck or offer a deal. Which would you do?"

He straightens in his seat. "Do I have a vested interest in any of them?"

I shake my head.

"But I *am* invested in the startup community.."

"You are. Very."

"And I'm concerned about the potential impact of the other party if they succeed under false pretenses."

I nod.

Parker grins. "And I've already got a deal drafted."

I laugh. "You do."

"I'd offer it." He doesn't hesitate. "I haven't been this excited about a possible green tech deal in a while.."

Parker flips to another slide on his laptop, turning it around so I can see. "If we target a launch at the Green Innovation Summit in Paris in May, these are my early projections for the end of year. Based on what they've shared about their manufacturing facility, they'll be well-equipped to meet initial demand. Plus, their product should be relatively inexpensive to produce, which means margins will be high."

The trend line went up and to the right at a steep angle, showing strong potential.

"How generous were your estimates?"

"They weren't. These are conservative."

"Looks promising," I murmur, studying the next slide Parker shares, which shows a five-year trend.

"And I probably underestimated the public sector. There are a few initiatives likely to be on the next ballot that could send state demand through the roof. Several proposed bills with decent early support will require more sustainability commitments from local governments, including for construction. Using Solum's materials for new government buildings like schools or low income housing would meet and exceed those requirements."

I regard him. He's leaning forward in his seat, eyes bright. "You're excited about this one."

Parker chuckles. "I am. I think they're the real deal."

"What's the news from Greenstar?"

He relaxes in his chair. "They haven't been forthcoming about the details, but they're making big claims. There are rumors they're meeting with a high-up official at the state's Department of General Services."

A lightbulb goes on in my brain. "The budget for new schools...." My voice trails off. The state had recently announced a nearly $1B investment toward school construction projects throughout California. I'd read an article written by my friend Cass about it earlier in the week.

"My thoughts exactly." Parker's mouth turns down. "Lex, if

they're right and Greenstar is using faulty data to pitch green building materials to the State..."

A chain reaction of potential catastrophic events flashes through my mind. "I know. I'm worried about it, too. Forget the impacts to the startup community, faulty school buildings would put too many lives at risk."

Silence falls between us. After a moment, I sigh. "Well, that's decided, then."

Parker can't quite fight his smile.

"I need to be hands on to start, but I'd like you to take over once we get past the Summit. You up for it?"

"Absolutely," he enthuses. "And whatever support you need between now and then, I'm your guy."

I chuckle. "I'll take you up on that."

———

I'm late. Only by five minutes, but still. *You have no reason to feel guilty, Lex.*

"Please excuse my tardiness, gentlemen." I step up to join the three men at their table.

Shane and Lincoln stand on my arrival, both dressed in smart suits–Shane with black on black, and Lincoln in navy blue over a white button down, open at the collar. I have to resist the urge to look them up and down, my eyes drawn to the bulge of Linc's bicep and the narrow taper of Shane's waist. Declan remains seated, though he still cuts an imposing figure in a simple black suit and white shirt. *His tailor deserves a raise. That coat looks painted on.*

Declan barely glances my way before his eyes fall to the glass of water in his hand. I remain standing, watching him while Shane and Lincoln watch me. After a minute, I break the tense silence.

"You came to me. Am I to assume you're no longer interested in my investment?"

Declan's fierce green eyes finally fly to mine. I feel the fire in them like a physical burn, and it stirs parts of me I shouldn't be noticing at a business dinner. *There's no denying his...intensity does something to me.*

"What do you mean?" he barks.

"Like most people, Mr. Wilde, I expect a modicum of respect from those I choose to work with. If you can't scrape together enough to acknowledge my presence, there's no reason for me to waste my time with you or your venture."

"Ms. Livingston, I assure—"

I hold up a hand, stopping Lincoln mid-sentence, my gaze still pinned to Declan. "While I appreciate your desire to smooth things over, Lincoln, I'm going to stop you there. I've dealt with far more difficult challenges than Declan Wilde, and I don't need anyone to speak for me. Stand down."

In my periphery, I see Lincoln settle back in his chair. A vein on Declan's forehead throbs and he swallows roughly before rising to his feet. He gives me a stiff nod.

"Perhaps I would've been more welcoming if you'd given us the respect of being on time." He mutters the last, as though saying it quietly could soften the insult.

"Declan—"

"Lincoln, if I may," I interrupt, shooting him a pointed look before turning back to his older brother. "Let me be clear, Mr. Wilde. I will not apologize for things beyond my control. If the support I can provide Solum Technologies is not worth five minutes of your time, then I'll take my leave. I came here tonight intending to have a very different conversation, but I will not tolerate your disrespect."

Declan's emerald eyes flash. In my peripheral vision, I see both Shane and Lincoln standing stock-still, their gazes flicking between us. As frustrated as I am with their partner, I'm inordinately pleased they both heeded my warning and are letting things between us play out without interference. Declan opens his mouth and Shane leans ever so slightly toward him, drawing his gaze.

"Mr. Wilde," I demand, refocusing his attention.

Tension eases from Declan's broad shoulders as he sighs, as though the weight of the world is on him. He slowly meets my gaze.

"Forgive me," he says tersely. "It's been a stressful week. We'd appreciate it if you'd join us, as planned."

I want to laugh in his face. In my experience, a woman's definition of 'stressful' can make a man's look like a goddamn spa day. But I don't feel like prolonging what is rapidly becoming the worst moment of my week, so I fight the urge.

"Fine."

The three men settle into their seats, then turn their eyes to me. It's a heady thing, being caught in their intense gazes. I clench my thighs and breathe deeply, pushing my arousal away. *Focus, Lex.*

"Here's how tonight is going to go," I announce. "I came with an offer. It is conditional, non-negotiable, and valid for twenty-four hours. The purpose of this conversation is to give you enough information to make a decision. We'll go over the details and you can ask any questions you have."

Lincoln's eyes light up and he leans forward, glancing excitedly toward Shane, then Declan.

"However," I continue, letting ice creep into my voice and gaze as I stare Declan down. "If I feel disrespected by you again, at any point, I will walk. Immediately and without hesitation. Do I make myself clear?"

The vein on Declan's forehead reappears. "Crystal," he

answers smoothly, though the redness flushing his neck belies his frustration.

"Good. I understand you were very recently betrayed and might find trust difficult." Declan's brows rise a fraction, and he shifts uncomfortably. "But I am not Anne-Marie and I do not deserve your vitriol. The fact we're both women does not give you license to be a dick. Got it?"

Declan clears his throat. "Got it," he rasps, dropping his gaze as he sips his water.

I take a steadying breath and lower myself to my seat. Lincoln goes to speak, eyes bright and eager, but Shane interrupts him.

"Let's order, then discuss business."

As it did in our meeting at Athena, Shane's deep voice captures my attention and I turn toward him. There's something striking about his focused gaze, something steady and calm in the way he carries himself that draws me in.

My answering smile is tight. "Let's."

Our server stops by a few moments later to collect our orders. As she walks away, I look up to find three intense pairs of eyes on me once more. Tingles prick along my skin, my breath catching at the weight of their attention. Ignoring the way the fine hairs on my nape rise in reaction, I draw the folder containing the offer from my bag. Lincoln reaches out a hand, but Shane gives him a warning look. Lincoln blinks and drops his hand, watching silently as Shane offers his instead. *Interesting.*

"This is a formal offer from Athena." I hand Shane the folder, who accepts it with a slight bow of his head before setting it on the table, his eyes never leaving mine. "We're offering twelve million dollars for a twenty-five percent stake in Solum Technologies."

I sense both Lincoln and Declan shift, as though gearing up to speak, but Shane holds up a hand. "Go on, Lex. Please."

His simple command of the table, which the Wilde brothers defer to without protest, is as sexy as it is unexpected. *I appreciate a confident man.* I fight the urge to smile, surprised by my reaction. Taking a sip of water, I give myself a moment.

"We all know there's more at stake here than just your product and professional future," I go on. "Given my personal investment in your success, I'll be handling your account myself. At least until launch."

"We'd be honored." Shane's voice is arresting. Both quiet and deep, it somehow fills the space. "Do you have a launch date in mind?"

"I do, and it's another condition. You'll launch at the Green Innovation Summit in Paris."

"That's only three months away," Lincoln cuts in.

I glance over as Shane casts him a stern glare. "It is indeed."

"We'll be ready," Shane affirms. "What else?"

The gentle dominance in his tone sends electricity skittering along my skin. I struggle to keep my expression passive as I answer.

"My availability is limited, but weekly in-person progress meetings will be necessary. We'll have to be creative with scheduling, including early mornings, late nights, weekends."

"Not a problem."

I tilt my head, trying to read his neutral expression. Declan was who I'd expected to lead negotiations, despite Lincoln driving our last conversation. In our first meeting years ago, Shane was silent, the quiet, though obviously brilliant, lead engineer. Now, I have the overwhelming feeling there's far more lurking beneath his surface.

"I might be handling your account to start, but this deal is with Athena. My team will have carte blanche access to your data, and I need a facilities tour within forty-eight hours of accepting the offer."

Shane's look turns thoughtful as he considers my words, and I look to Declan.

"And I need you to do the same with the business records. Don't think I missed that you've been less than forthcoming so far. You need to walk me through it, then provide me access to your files so our team can get up to speed."

Declan's eyes narrow briefly before darting to Shane. His jaw clenches in response to whatever look he receives before responding tightly. "Alright."

What the fuck is his deal? I return my focus to Shane, patience wearing dangerously thin.

"One thing working strongly in Anne-Marie's favor is her visibility. The press adores her. We need to be thoughtful in how we take Solum to market, but the business will need a consistent, reliable public face."

"Do you have someone in mind?" Shane's eyes glint knowingly.

"Declan."

Lincoln coughs in surprise, but I don't look his way. True surprise flickers across Declan's face for the first time, his surly mask slipping and giving way to incredulity.

"Me," he says.

"Yes," I confirm.

"You must be joking," Declan protests.

"Do I sound like I'm joking?" I tilt my head, daring him to argue.

His grumpy expression returns immediately, lips pursing in annoyance. As our server returns with our drinks, I bite back a smirk and turn to Shane. His eyes shine with amusement.

"Is there more?" Shane drawls as our server departs.

"One last thing." I pause and meet each of their eyes, ending with Shane. "I'm going out on a limb and trusting you all are as brilliant as the data and my team's forecast suggests. I expect you to be successful, because there's one type of business Athena refuses to back. Do you know what type that is, Mr. Kelly?"

"Failures."

"Precisely. So if we're going to do this, I expect each of you to put whatever baggage you're carrying aside." At my targeted glare, Declan swallows roughly and drinks deeply. I try to ignore the way his Adam's apple bobs behind his dark stubble. "We're going to dive in and work together to make your dream a reality. We have a short runway and plenty of opportunity for missteps, but failure is not an option."

"Agreed." Shane's gaze doesn't waver.

"Good." I settle back in my chair, holding a hand up to invite Shane to take the floor. "What questions do you have?"

His response is immediate. "You mentioned you'd handle our account until launch. What comes after?"

"You'll be transitioned to the head of our sustainability portfolio, Parker Brooks."

"And we'll no longer meet with you personally."

I shrug noncommittally. "I'm sure Parker will invite me to milestone meetings as a courtesy, but he'll be responsible for working directly with you and the team you'll build. He'll keep me apprised of your progress."

My eyes dart to Lincoln and I can't help a small smile. He looks so pleased with where the conversation is going, his expression open and a wide smile on his lips. He catches me looking and winks. My chest warms as I tuck my hair behind my ear.

"Thank you, Lex." Lincoln raises his glass, amber eyes twinkling.

I raise mine and tap it lightly to his. "You're welcome, Mr. Wilde."

"Linc. Please, call me Linc."

"Linc," I murmur through my smile before taking another sip.

"Ms. Livingston—"

"Lex," I interrupt Shane. "Just Lex."

I can see Linc's smile out of the corner of my eye. Shane's lips twitch as he inclines his head.

"First names, it is. Do you have connections with the Green Innovation Summit organizers?"

"I do. We've hosted launches there in the past. Parker and his team will ensure we get everything ready for a big splash at the Summit."

"I look forward to it." Shane nods thoughtfully. "You mentioned Anne-Marie earlier. We have no contact with her anymore."

"Smart. Keep it that way."

Shane's gaze holds mine. "We trusted her, Lex. Her betrayal was a surprise, but we're not motivated by revenge."

Declan makes a rough noise, but I ignore him. *I have no time for your bullshit, Wilde.*

"I'd hope not," I say. "There's true potential in what you've built. Potential that will have far more positive impact than the temporary satisfaction of bringing down someone who hurt you."

"I agree." He glances at Declan as he replies.

Our server returns, arms laden with a heavy tray. Our conversation pauses as she distributes plates to a chorus of "thank you" from each of us, even Declan. *At least he's not a total asshole, I guess.*

"Enjoy!" The upbeat brunette turns away with a smile as I

look back at Shane. He's leaning forward with his elbows on the table, blue eyes calculating.

"What other questions do you have?" I press.

He considers me. "Why?"

I pause, my fork halfway to my mouth. "Excuse me?"

"Why give us an offer?" He sits back in his chair, the curve of his lips more smirk than smile. "What's in it for you?"

I reach for my wine. "It's good business. We have goals around growing our sustainability portfolio." Taking a sip, I can see he's not satisfied by the partial truth. "Mostly, though, I abhor dishonesty, especially when it puts others at risk. There's enough evidence to suggest Greenstar may do exactly that if they launch, and it's not something I'm willing to overlook." *And there's something about the three of you that just won't let me say no.*

Shane watches me for a long moment, almost as though he can read my inner thoughts. I gaze back calmly, comfortable in the silence. Linc glances between us as he eats his steak while Declan is still. There's a comfort and ease between the three despite their differences, a familiarity in how they interact that speaks to years of close proximity. Being part of their dynamic, even briefly, is...intoxicating. *I don't hate being the center of their attention.*

"One more question."

I tilt my head, returning to my waiting bite. A slow smile curves Shane's lips, and I feel my core clench.

"Does five tomorrow evening work for that facility tour?"

Chapter 6

Declan

"**A**fter you, milady," Lincoln announces, bending at the waist and flourishing his hand through the air like an absolute buffoon as he holds the door open for Lex. *What is she doing to us?*

My brother could be a clown. As kids and in college, he was always the first with a joke or a laugh, loving any opportunity to rile a crowd. But I haven't seen him perform for someone in years, not since before...her. Before Anne-Marie.

Shane's voice, deep and gentle even in the cavernous warehouse, breaks through my thoughts. He's explaining our R&D equipment to Lex, walking her through the basics of what we have and what we need. She listens thoughtfully, asking intelligent questions along the way. She even poses some that give him pause, make him think. It's not often I see someone stump him, but I have the nagging suspicion she can. *Another reason not to trust her.*

She laughs at something Linc adds to Shane's explanation, and discomfort settles in my gut. There had been no laughter for the last hour as I walked her through my records, no smiles as I explained the financial data she'd demanded at dinner the night before. In fact, we'd both been hanging on by a thread when Linc stopped by my office to collect her for the tour.

"Why did you target these investors?"

Lex pointed to three line items in our early budget. All represented funding we'd secured from other sources after Athena had shown us the door.

"We needed funding from somewhere."

I didn't want to admit Anne-Marie was the reason. She'd been adamant about who we should pursue, but didn't explain why they were the right choice. We trusted her, so after asking a few questions, I didn't push. I knew now that was a mistake, but I had no desire to admit my failings to Lex.

She narrowed her eyes at me.

"There are thousands of options for funding sources, Declan. Why did you pitch them? They're big names, but have few resources in green tech or heavy manufacturing. They were ill-equipped to help you, unless there's an angle I'm missing."

"What's done is done," I dismissed her line of questioning, unwilling to dig at the open wound. "Do you want to tear our history apart bit by bit, or should we do something useful with this hour?"

Her eyebrows arched and her lip sneered slightly. "By all means, let's do something useful. Where do you suggest we start?"

She gave me enough leeway to damn myself by the end of the hour. Our books were in order, I'm meticulous about that, but she had too many questions I couldn't satisfactorily answer. I'm not willing to tell her how much we allowed Anne-Marie to dictate, how much I gave up to her control. Lex is frustratingly intelligent, and I suspect she saw right through me.

"I'll be honest, Declan. I expected a clearer vision from you."

She searched my gaze for a moment, the picture of calm professionalism while she cut my pride to shreds. We'd just finished reviewing my draft launch strategy for Solum after painstakingly combing through the financial statements from the last three years line-by-line. Lex didn't pull any punches, and I was more than ready to hand her off to Shane and Linc and watch her cut them down instead.

"I expected a different answer from you three years ago."

There was no use digging up the past, I knew that. But I couldn't resist the urge to steer her away from the raw wound left by Anne-Marie. It was more than my pride under threat, it was everything I thought of myself—as a leader, as a brother, as a businessman. I was the one responsible for everything, and I'd dropped the ball. It was hard enough to admit to myself, let alone allow someone as strikingly intelligent and beautiful as Lex see through me.

She scoffed and shook her head.

"I'm not sure why you're so defensive around me, but you need to let it go. If I remember correctly, this entire operation was your idea. You were the genesis of Procerus and now Solum."

She leaned a hip against a low cabinet along the far wall, facing me head-on across my office.

"So tell me, Declan, why you seem so disinterested in working with me now. We can't change the past, so why aren't you jumping at the opportunity to change your present and future? How long will you let the memory of Anne-Marie and her betrayal have a seat at the table?"

None of what she asked was out of bounds. Harsh, yes, but not unreasonable. And she wasn't wrong about any of it. I was letting Anne-Marie and her duplicity affect me; I hadn't been able to get her out of my head since she walked out the door with our plans in her desperate, selfish hands.

The man I was when I had the idea for Procerus was wildly different from the man I'd become. Recent graduate Declan was idealistic and trusting. He was analytical but took people at their word. He had ten years of challenges, failures, and betrayals awaiting him.

Lex laughs again, the sound arresting. *I hate how I can't walk away.* I scoff in response, loud enough for the three to hear. Lincoln turns to me, brows furrowed.

"You okay, man?"

I go to say something biting about how hard they're working, but catch Shane's warning look. I desperately want to tell my best friend to fuck right off, but I hold my tongue.

"Fine," I answer, waving a hand at him. "Don't let me interrupt your fun."

Shane tsks, his blue eyes sparking in challenge. He was playing middleman between me and Linc more than usual lately, and I knew he hated it. Something about my brother's enthusiasm sets me off, especially when it comes to our new investor.

"I'm surprised, Declan," Lex cuts in, the small smirk on her lips a warning. "I didn't think that word was in your vocabulary."

"What word?" I challenge.

She arches one elegant eyebrow, crossing her arms under her chest. "Fun."

Linc barks a laugh and Shane stifles a grin as I shift, discomfited by the ease of her banter. Something dark and ugly rises in my chest in response. I push it down, choosing not to engage, though I know my frustration is written all over me. *She's not Anne-Marie.*

"No biting comeback?" Lex presses, tilting her head. "Pity."

My brother chuckles and turns to settle the cover he'd lifted to show her some aspect of the equipment. Shane cocks a brow, either checking in or telling me to calm the fuck down. He was always doing one or the other lately. Lex holds my gaze for another beat, then dismisses me by turning back to Shane.

"What's next, then?"

Even her voice is different with them. Softer, lighter. Every question she'd asked me earlier felt like a blade—sharp, pointed, aimed for the heart. Like she knew where my weaknesses were and wanted to expose them.

The most frustrating part? I *want* to join their fun. I want to rise to her challenge with a snappy comeback, something to make her laugh or smile. The me from four months ago would've been bantering back and forth, not seething from the outside. *Feeling like a failure.* I shove my self-pitying thoughts into the box they belong in at the back of my mind, lock it up, and throw away the key. *I don't have time for that shit.*

I follow as Shane leads us around to the makeshift showroom he and Lincoln created. It features scale models built with our product, along with four full size prototypes of our green construction materials.

"Can I pick it up?" Lex asks, reaching for the nearest prototype.

"Of course!" Lincoln snatches up the piece and tosses it to her.

"Oh!" Lex gasps as she catches the brick, eyes wide. "Wow, it's so much lighter than I expected."

Shane nods. "One of the benefits from an installation and repair perspective. Still durable, though."

She turns the brick over in her hands, inspecting it from all sides. "And the temperature weakness?"

"We think we've solved for it," Linc chimes in. He reaches over and picks up another prototype, holding it out to her. "This is the latest one. It's passed all the testing we're capable of, but we need to get new equipment to be confident it'll hold up under extreme heat, cold, and wind."

Lex hands the first prototype back as she accepts the new one. "This seems denser. Still light, but it has more heft."

"That was part of the change, yes. We updated the composition slightly. Same ingredients, altered recipe."

As Shane goes into more detail about how he and Linc cracked our biggest development hurdle, I cross my arms and lean back to watch.

When she joined us, Anne-Marie fit seamlessly into the group. Lincoln introduced her to us, both of them bright-eyed with excitement for what the future could hold. Anne-Marie was as tenacious as she was exuberant, and she quickly became the public face of Procerus. *And now Lex wants me to take on that mantle.*

The conditions Lex shared at dinner last night weren't what I anticipated. Part of me expected her to rake us over the coals with a terrible valuation and unreasonable demands, expecting her to be as duplicitous as our former business partner. Contrary to my assumptions, everything she laid out made sense. It was almost overly generous of her to handle Solum personally, given her schedule and how in-demand Athena was.

I glance up as Lex hands the prototype back to Lincoln with a friendly smile. She isn't what I expected after our two meetings at Athena, either. Seeing her at dinner and here in our space, she's more relaxed and open. I can see Linc trying to charm her, see how he brightens at every positive reaction he gets. Everything I witness spells trouble. I don't know her angle, but I'm positive she has one. *We should've stuck to the plan and done this on our own.*

"Declan, anything you want to add before I head out?"

I look up to find three pairs of eyes on me, Lex's brow arcing in question.

"Did we scare you off sufficiently, then?" I taunt.

Linc widens his eyes, a "dude, what the fuck?" look on his face while Shane sighs. Lex just smiles, a harsh glint in her eyes.

"No, you didn't scare me off. Were you trying to?"

"Maybe."

She laughs, as though my terrible attitude has no effect on her whatsoever. The fact she can be so at ease when I want to crawl out of my skin in aggravation makes me want to hit something, or yell. And as I watch Shane and Linc smile in response to her laughter, visible relief on their faces, something sharp twists in my gut.

"So what now?" I sweep one arm out to the side in question.

"The analysts at Athena are going to pore over what you've shared, raise any questions or red flags they deem appropriate. Then it's off to the races."

She speaks nonchalantly, as though she doesn't hold our future in the palm of her perfectly manicured hand.

"And what have you done to prove we should trust you and your people?"

"Dec, take a beat." Lincoln holds a hand up, palm out, as though to calm me.

"I'm sorry, has something changed since last night?" Lex crosses her arms again, extending one leg to the side.

It's a power stance if I've ever seen one, and I answer with my own—feet planted, arms crossed.

"No change. I still don't trust you."

"It seems you keep forgetting *you* came to *me*."

"*They* came to you," I counter, jutting my chin out toward Shane and Lincoln, who stand together to her left.

"Last I checked, all three of you have a stake in this business. Or are you telling me I've walked into some kind of internal territory dispute?" She glance over to Lincoln and Shane. "I have to be honest, gentlemen, I don't have the patience or resources to handle internal turmoil on top of the drama with Anne-Marie and Greenstar."

"No, Lex, there's no issue—"

"Respectfully, Linc, take it up with your brother." She casts me a cold look, relaxing her arms. "I'm done here."

Lex turns on her ridiculous heel and stalks out of the warehouse. As she disappears down the hall toward my office, no doubt to gather her things, Shane rounds on me.

"My office. Now," he demands, thrusting a finger toward my face. He turns to Linc. "Go. Try to fix this."

"You got it." Linc turns and jogs after Lex without a backward glance.

"This is a waste of fucking time, Shane!" I growl, throwing a hand out. "We don't need her. Haven't we learned enough about the dangers of bringing in someone new?"

"Cut out the willful ignorance, Declan. She's not Anne-Marie and you fucking know it."

I run a hand through my hair, frustration rising. "I know she's not."

"Doesn't seem like it from here."

"I just—"

"I know what you *just*, Dec. You don't want to feel responsible for the next bad thing that happens."

My eyes fall closed as I blow out a low breath, my head dropping. His words are a gut punch. *I'm not ready to confess.* "I just have a bad feeling about this."

"I don't."

I look up, lips parting. Shane and I rarely disagreed, but he'd been adamant about supporting Lincoln's idea to go back to Athena from the start.

"I think you're off base on this one, Dec. And I need you to get back on track before you take us all down with you. Anne-Marie wasn't your fault." He sighs and scrubs a slow hand over his jaw before meeting my eyes. "Tanking this over your own unresolved guilt and fear would be."

Chapter 7

Lex

"Lex!"

I turn toward Linc's voice to find him emerging from the building, hand raised, and sigh. Crossing my arms, I lean one hip against my Maserati–a gift from Van when we hit our first billion–and wait for him to cross the parking lot. He offers a sheepish smile as he draws closer, shoving his hands into his pockets.

"He's an ass." I brush imaginary lint from the sleeve of my blazer, then look up at him.

Linc looks off into the distance. "Yeah. He is."

I scoff. "I thought you'd be defending him."

"Nah, not this time." He gives me a boyish grin, an irresistible dimple appearing in one cheek. "Our family's big on calling it like it is. He'd want me to be honest."

Smiling, I shake my head and inhale deeply. "He's a problem, Linc. And shaping up to be a big one."

"That's fair. I can see how you'd come to that conclusion." He glances down. "You rushing off somewhere?"

Checking my phone, I breathe a sigh of relief. "Looks like

my next call got canceled. So, no; no rushing off. I'm done for the night."

"Brilliant. Full transparency, Shane sent me out here for damage control." He grins, that dimple coming back out and making my stomach flip. *He's so fucking cute.* "Do you have spare kicks in your car? There's a trail we can get to out back. The fresh air might do us both some good?"

I study him for a long moment, considering. It's a kind offer, but it's also skirting the line between professional and personal. Linc's full of infectious energy, and I'd be lying through my teeth if I claimed to be immune to his flirtatious charm. He puts me at ease in a way few men can, his playfulness balancing the open want in his stolen glances. *Those bottomless brown eyes don't help, either.*

However, I'll be working closely with him and the others over the next few months, and building a solid relationship now will only make it easier. Making up my mind, I click the button on my key fob to pop the trunk and fish out my gym bag. *We're all adults, right?*

"If we're walking, I'm getting out of this." I motion to my fitted red skirt and oversized blazer.

His expression heats as his gaze dips to the black lace bodysuit peeking out from under my blazer, then snaps back to mine. "Hell yes, let's get you comfy. Come on, you can change inside."

"Somewhere we'll avoid your absolutely delightful older brother?"

Lincoln chuckles. "Yes, we'll avoid the asshole."

Ten minutes later, we're strolling away from Solum, a comfortable silence between us. True to Linc's word, we avoided seeing anyone else as he smuggled me into the bathroom and stashed my work clothes and heels at his desk. He led me out the back door as Shane and Declan's voices sounded down the hall, and we jogged to the trailhead to escape unseen.

The trail is narrow with lush growth on either side, so we walk closely, arms brushing. In my heels, we were almost eye-to-eye, but in my sneakers, Linc has a solid four inches on me. I look up to find him watching me, a small smirk on his lips.

"What's that look for?" I knock my shoulder lightly into his arm, feeling comfortable in the outdoor environment and my workout gear. *If I could work in yoga pants every day, I would.*

"You know that saying, 'you clean up good'?"

"Uh, yes?"

"You're like the opposite of that. You dress down real nice, Lex." He grins at his own ridiculousness and I can't stop my laugh.

"Why, thank you."

I preen teasingly, then snuggle my hands into the pockets of my fleece. I didn't miss the way Linc's eyes darkened when I emerged from the bathroom in my yoga pants and fitted jacket. That, and our sneaking around, went a long way toward easing the tension caused by his brother.

"As much as I'd rather just enjoy being out here with you, I do think I should share a bit." He flashes me a small smile. "About Dec."

"Might be helpful," I murmur as I look ahead.

Linc sighs. "I'll start at the beginning. Stop me if you have questions or get bored, yeah?"

"Sure." I smile softly in encouragement.

"It's always been the three of us. Met as kids, only got closer as the years went by. Dec's always been...proud of being the older brother."

I scoff quietly and he chuckles, looking down.

"Yeah, I'm sure that's not a surprise. He was the de facto leader of our little three-man gang for as long as I can remember. Being three years behind him and five behind Shane, I always felt like I had to work to catch up and be on their level. I didn't want to get left behind."

"You've definitely won in the emotional maturity department."

His surprise makes me chuckle. "What?" I lift a shoulder, my mouth turning up in one corner. "Just saying."

"I can't wait to hear what Shane says when I brag about that later." He winks at me before his gaze turns thoughtful. "Shane went to undergrad–Stanford–first, then Dec did the same, and I followed them. After they graduated, they went straight to grad school, then Shane got an engineering job at a chemtech startup. The two of them did a lot of volunteering while at school and after, and I joined them."

"What kind of volunteering?"

"Building houses, mostly. Locally, and we even did a few trips abroad."

"Makes sense." Some pieces start to fit together about them and how they found their way into the green building industry.

"Yeah. I loved working with my hands and learning new things, and we got to meet some awesome people." He shoves his hands deeper into his pockets and exhales, long and low. "That's where I met Anne-Marie."

I glance up at him. He's frowning, with a crease between his brows. I want to reach up and smooth it away. *What the fuck, Lex? Boundaries.*

"She was so enthusiastic, you know? We got to talking, and I shared some of what Dec and Shane were working on. She had a lot of ideas, and she'd studied sustainability with her business degree. It seemed like serendipity, like we'd met because she had the missing piece we needed. Dec had big ideas, Shane had the science and tech expertise to make them real, and my engineering skills could turn his lab experiments into something scalable."

The sky darkened as we walked. It won't be long before the path is hard to see, but Linc's story holds me captive.

"I introduced her to the guys, and everything clicked into place. We started working together immediately." He reaches a hand up to grip the back of his neck. "Then our parents died."

I suck in a harsh breath and lay a hand on Lincoln's arm. "I'm so sorry."

He casts me a small smile. "Thanks. It's been years, but it was a shock. Car accident." Linc peers into the distance, his expression tight. "Declan...he took on a lot of responsibility after that. All of it, really. They were our only family, so when they were gone, it was just us three. Four, with Anne-Marie. Declan was determined to make things happen for us though, to turn my parents' legacy into something new and impactful."

"Their legacy?"

"Yeah. My dad owned a construction company in Seattle. We sold it to invest in Procerus, and now Solum."

My eyebrows rise. "Wow, that's quite the leap of faith." *And a shit ton of pressure.*

He chuckles. "You can say that again. But we were all in, you know? Ready to make it happen. And Anne-Marie told such a good story. She started booking meetings for us left and right, getting us in front of investors and press."

My heart aches at the hurt in his voice, the dejected slope of his shoulders. This girl, this ambitious, selfish person, clearly did a number on them when she made off with their formulas. My fingers flex in my pockets and I shift minutely closer, our shoulders touching, a small attempt to offer comfort.

"She's not the one who reached out to Athena, though," I muse.

"I wondered if you knew." He glances over at me, his smile tinged with pride. "That was all Dec. Early on, we talked about our big goals. Investment from Athena was definitely one of them. We all challenged each other to get out of our comfort zones; reaching out to Athena on our behalf was one of those things for Dec."

"And then Anne-Marie botched it."

"And then Anne-Marie botched everything, Lex. Shortly after that first meeting with you, we had our first blowout fight. We wanted to go back to the lab, focus on solving the issues causing people like you to question investing in us." He looks over with a self-deprecating grin. "You were right to be skeptical. The more we pressure-tested the product, the more we realized we needed to reset. But Anne-Marie was adamant we forge ahead."

"So, it wasn't Declan who chose which VCs to approach for your first seed round." The story came together, suspicions forming about the true cause behind Declan's defensiveness.

"No, Athena was the only investor he specifically targeted. The rest was Anne-Marie. She used her connections, and, as you've seen since she got picked up by Greenstar, her identity as a woman in tech to get her foot in any door she could. We were on board with it until she started lying."

We round a bend on the trail and head back toward the facility. It's a good thing, because it's nearly dark.

"At first it was little things, stuff we could chalk up to a simple mistake. Then she started making claims we couldn't substantiate, suggesting we pitch to high-profile firms and projects without disclosing the flaws. She and Dec were constantly at each other's throats. He was listening to me and

Shane, recognizing we needed to focus on R&D before we made any more promises we couldn't fulfill. She didn't want to hear any of it. Just shut us out and kept taking meetings."

"How did it all fall apart?"

He laughs, but it's an ugly, bitter sound. "She called me. It was fitting, honestly, because she wouldn't have even been involved if I hadn't brought her in. She told me she was sorry, but she couldn't let us hold her back anymore. Said our tech had too much potential and we were fools to get bogged down in the details."

"She was the fool," I mutter, frustration on Lincoln's behalf welling in me.

"She was. Is, if we're honest. Anyway, she told me she didn't need us anymore and thanked me for introducing her to her destiny. Two days later, Greenstar announced their partnership. So who knows how long she'd peddled our work as her own, all while we thought she was with us."

"Jesus, Lincoln. I'm sorry."

"Not your fault." He puts a hand on my elbow to steady me as I stumble on the unlit path. "Sorry, not my best idea to go for a walk so close to sunset."

I lean into his hold, feeling emboldened by the dark and drawn to his openness. "I don't mind a bit. I'm used to being out in the dark. Four am is usually my only time to get a run in."

He gives me a long look, and I feel it like a caress on my skin. My body reacts to him so naturally, a sense of rightness between us that catches me off guard. Sex has been transactional for me for years, something I seek when I need release, and never for more than a night or two. But the way this man gazes at me, as though his world has narrowed to me and nothing else? It's intoxicating. Add that to his heartfelt conversation, playful humor, and clear care for his family, and it's like the universe is serving him to me on a silver platter. *Who am I to deny the universe?*

"Anyway," he continues, dragging his eyes back to the path, "Declan has always felt responsible for everything that went down with Anne-Marie. It was his decision to sell my parents' company, his choice to trust her with the investor meetings and strategy conversations. He thought they were aligned, so he wasn't always present. He spent a lot of time with us in R&D, working through the kinks and experimenting."

"I hope you're not making excuses for him and his abysmal attitude," I tease to diffuse the tension, bumping into him again.

His laugh is soft and velvety. "Wouldn't dream of it. Just thought some context might help the next time he puts his foot in his mouth. Because he's going to keep fucking up for a while, I think."

"Do you know why he sees me as the enemy?"

We reach the parking lot, and the light from the street lamps illuminates Linc's wry expression.

"He sees everyone as the enemy right now, Lex." He runs his hand through his thick dark hair. "He's convinced it's all his fault, and he's the only one who can fix it, even though that's the furthest thing from the truth."

His assessment rings true. Though he fought me at every turn, I can tell Declan cares deeply for both his business and his partners.

"This can only work if he gets on board, Linc. With enthusiasm."

He dips his chin. "I know. He knows it, too. He could've thrown in the towel by now, but he hasn't."

"That may be, but I refuse to be the one bearing the brunt of his bullshit." My eyes harden as I look up. "I'm serious, Linc. I won't stand for his insults or attempts to walk all over me."

"Damn straight you won't." His sharp jaw ticks. "Believe me, you aren't the only one holding him accountable."

Even though I know so little about them, I believe him. Something in my gut tells me Lincoln is an earnest, honest man. And I listen to my gut. It's gotten me this far.

Headlights swoop across us before fading into the distance.

"I think that's my cue." I motion to my car.

Linc opens his mouth, then snaps it closed. He purses his lips briefly, nodding once to himself. "We're grateful, Lex. All of us. I know we have a shit ton of work to do, and it seems like Dec isn't doing his share. But he's going to, and we're going to make it work. I know we will."

I study his face for a moment, then reach out to grip his arm gently. My whole body warms at the contact, my nerves practically buzzing. "I believe you, Linc. I wouldn't have made an offer if I didn't."

His hot as sin dimple makes another appearance and, as butterflies take flight in my gut, I know I need to get in my car before I do something I shouldn't. Like wrap my arms around Linc and lose myself in him completely.

I step to my door and slide into the driver's seat. Linc reaches out to close it, smiling at me through the window and patting the roof as I start the ignition. He steps back as I give him a wave, then back out and turn for home. *Going home is the right choice. But why does it feel like a loss?*

Three minutes after I walk in my front door, my phone buzzes with a text message.

UNKNOWN

hey it's linc

i've got your heels and work clothes here

can i drop them off?

I stare at my phone, considering. The thought of Linc in my home after dark, after our intimate conversation and stolen glances, is dangerously tempting. It gives me all sorts of unprofessional ideas, and unless I've completely lost the ability to read people, I'm not the only one with that particular train of thought.

UNKNOWN

just me, no assholes

i can bring food

or wine

or both?

My lips twitch into a smirk. *He's adorable. And ridiculous. Ridiculously adorable.* I save him in my phone quickly, then type out a reply.

ME

Surprise me

I add my contact card with my address, then stare at the screen as anticipation trips through me. I've never engaged in anything resembling inappropriate behavior with a client, never been tempted to cross the invisible line I drew for myself. But there's something about Lincoln and his boyish smile, his infectious energy and earnest gaze. He worked his way under my skin in a whole new way, and I'm struggling to deny him. It feels right to just...give in. *What's the harm? I haven't been this attracted to someone in ages, and I may as well make the most of these three months.*

With the timeline on our partnership and our insane chemistry, it feels almost criminal to let the opportunity pass by. After all, calculated risks are the name of the game for me. And our attraction alone feels worth it, whatever may come.

My phone buzzes again.

LINC

surprises are my specialty

see you in 15

Chapter 8

Linc

S*urprise me.*

I didn't expect her to say yes. Not to going over to her house alone, and not to bringing her dinner and wine. But the moment I saw those two little words, my whole body tightened with anticipation. *I'll always rise to a challenge, gorgeous.* And let's be honest, I've been in awe of her since dinner last night and earlier at the warehouse.

She commands every room she enters, sure, but there's so much more to her than the confident persona she shares with the world. Lex is as quick-witted and playful as she is stunning, but I get the impression she holds most people at arm's length. But when I'd convinced her to get in her gym clothes and go for a walk? *Ugh. Fucking exquisite. Relaxed Lex is my favorite.*

She let me see a whole new side to her while I shared more of our story. Dec was a total shithead, giving her every right to storm out and never talk to any of us again. She would have been perfectly justified in dropping us, but she didn't. She listened.

God, she listens so good. Too good.

I can see myself spilling my hopes and dreams to her

without effort. She's so attentive, the little half smiles and laughs she doles out getting under my skin and *doing* something to me. They make me want to hear what she sounds like at her most vulnerable, most open. I want to drown in the sounds she would make as she fell to pieces for me.

Down, boy. Who knows how tonight is going to go.

My maps app tells me I've arrived. I look up at the architectural monstrosity and whistle.

"Holy shit, Lex, you are living large."

I pull Dec's BMW through the open gate (*she has a fucking gate, and it better only be open because she knew I was coming*) and up to the front door. The place is fucking palatial.

Modern and angular, with more windows than siding, it looks easily three times the size of our place. An attached four-car garage sits perpendicular to the entrance, and I can see a wrought iron gate with an arched canopy covered in green vines off to the side. I crane my neck to look as I slowly roll by, eyeing an expanse of manicured gardens. *Is that an infinity pool? And a fucking pool house?!*

Grabbing the wine and bag of takeout as I park, I climb from the car to walk up the white marble steps. Before I can knock, the door opens.

Fuck. Me. She stands there in an oversized shirt and leggings, her face scrubbed clean and jaw-length dark red hair—which I've only seen straight and parted precisely down the center—mussed.

"Hey Linc." Her playful smile suggests she knows exactly what she's doing to me, standing there looking delectable.

"Lex, you're a goddamn vision."

She laughs and opens the door wider, stepping back to let me in. Her eyes rove over me and my offerings as I step inside and kick off my shoes.

"You have my heels and clothes in that bag?" she teases, knowing I don't.

"Oh, shit. Sorry, here." I hand her the wine and takeout. "I left them in the car, give me a sec."

I hold up a finger and whirl around to jog down the steps in my socks.

Her laughter follows me, and I drink in the sound. "Linc, your shoes!"

"I'm fine!" I call, opening the trunk and snatching her bag.

As I hustle back up the steps, I bask in her grin. Her eyes are sparkling, her rosy cheeks flush. She looks younger, somehow, without all the makeup and designer clothes.

"Here you go. Sorry, trust me to forget the whole reason I stopped by."

Something decidedly naughty enters her eyes as she smirks. "Not the whole reason, though, is it? I don't think my heels need wine or..." she peers into the bag, "Chinese?"

I grin, ignoring the way my cock thickens at her suggestiveness. "Felt like a lo mein kind of night."

She laughs. "Somehow, that's exactly what I'd expect from you. And, to be honest, it sounds far better than the crackers and wine I was planning. Come in."

"To be clear, crackers and wine are not dinner."

She just smiles over her shoulder as she leads me down the hall to her kitchen, where she places the bag and wine on the marbled island. As she opens a cabinet and pulls out some wine glasses, I look around the place, trying not to stare.

It's ridiculously big, almost ostentatiously lavish with its crazy high ceilings and appliances I'm pretty sure cost more than Dec's BMW. But even with the impressive features, it feels almost empty. *She clearly doesn't spend much time here.*

There are no cozy features or photos, only minimalist furniture in neutral colors. For someone so full of fire, her home is surprisingly dull. The kitchen looks toward the back of the house, where the infinity pool is visible amid the gardens through the double sliding doors.

"Is that a pool house?" I squint as I peer through the glass.

"It is. My nephew, Jax, lives out there at the moment."

I blink at her, confused. "How the hell do you have a nephew old enough to live alone?"

She chuckles as she pours a glass of wine. "My brother, Nate, was in high school when he got Jax's mom pregnant. Nate and I are only ten months apart."

"Your poor mom." I grimace.

"You're telling me," she mutters, grinning wryly as she offers me a wine glass.

I accept it and sidle over to her, itching to touch her. Being surrounded by her scent—both floral and fresh, with a touch of citrus—only enhances her gravity, and she effortlessly draws me in. She's fucking gorgeous, that much any idiot could see. Tall, fit, with legs for days and an ass I can sink my teeth into.

But I want more than her body. I want to lose myself in that brilliant mind of hers, wrap myself in the essence of what makes her the most powerful woman in the Bay. *It would be a goddamn shame to work with her for three months and only see her professional side.*

"Linc." Her husky voice catches my attention.

"Yeah?"

"You're staring," she murmurs.

"Yeah." *When did I get so close?*

"Why are you staring?" she presses, her endless green eyes swallowing mine.

She has to crane her head slightly without her heels on, and the angle makes the lines of her neck deliciously inviting. I bend my head, my lips hovering centimeters from her skin. We aren't touching yet, just close enough to feel each other's body heat. I know this is my chance; if I let this opportunity pass me by, I might lose my nerve and never tell her how I feel. *It's now or never.*

"Because I want you," I rasp, fingers skimming over her cheek as I tuck a lock of hair behind her ear. "And I've been thinking about how much I want you since you walked out in those fucking yoga pants."

She shivers as my breath washes over her skin, and I want to groan. My cock is ready to punch a hole through my joggers to get to her. Her chest rises and falls with rapid breaths, and I desperately want to see what hides beneath her oversized shirt.

"May I?" Taking her silence as an opening, I run my fingers along the edge of her shirt, teasing the fabric up an inch.

Her breath hitches. I pull back to see her face and smile when I find her eyes closed.

"May you what?" she breathes.

"Have you."

Her eyes fly open to reveal blown pupils. *Fuck, she's so goddamn sexy.* Those lush pink lips I've been dreaming about part, and it takes all my willpower not to boost her onto the counter and devour her.

"Lex, please—"

"Ground rules," she interrupts, placing a hand on my chest. The heat of her palm burns through the soft cotton of my shirt.

I grunt playfully and lean my forehead against hers, unwilling to let her go. "I hate rules."

She huffs a laugh. "I'm not surprised. But we have to work together tomorrow, so we need them."

"I'm a professional. We can work together fine. Just two consenting adults having some fun."

Lex steps back and grins, the sight of it making my chest swell. "As much as I want to say 'fuck decorum' and take you upstairs, I think we need to take a minute."

"No, no. Upstairs. I choose upstairs. What's upstairs?" I look around. "Where are the stairs?"

Her laugh is a drug. I smile as she settles herself on a stool at the kitchen island, silently telling my dick to *calm the fuck down*. Heaving a sharp breath, I scrub a hand over my face and put the sexy thoughts out of my mind. For now.

"Food, then rules?"

"May as well do them concurrently." Her eyes sparkle. "More efficient."

I groan and drop my head back. "Fuck, don't say shit like that. My blood's all going to the wrong head."

She makes grabby hands at me, ignoring my drama. "You mentioned lo mein?"

"And crab rangoon."

"Ooooh, don't tell the others, but you're my favorite." She digs into the containers I pass over, fishing out the sweet chili dipping sauce.

"For the record, your favorite what, exactly?"

She gives me a sideways glare. "Off the record, you're my favorite client. For this moment."

My eyebrows rise and I puff out my chest. "That's a pretty long list of people, isn't it? You sure I can't tell Dec? He'd be so proud."

Lex snorts, then bursts out laughing at herself, her eyes wide with surprise.

"The venerable Lex Livingston *snorts*?! I did not have that on my Bingo card, ladies and gentlemen. That is truly unexpected."

She's laughing so hard I worry she'll topple right off her stool. As I dash around the island to catch her, she grabs onto the counter and rights herself. Her shocked expression sends me doubling over with laughter, which makes her giggles start right back up. By the time I come up for air, I have no idea where the night is headed. *But I am here for this ride, wherever it goes.*

"So, did you tell me the whole story earlier? Or are there sordid details about Anne-Marie you left out?"

Her expression is teasing, but I feel a twinge of guilt over the one thing I haven't divulged.

"Uh oh," she says, reading my expression. "Oh, don't tell me you were together?" She makes a face like she's tasting something sour.

"Oh god, no. One night, years ago, right when we met." I wave it off. "Once I introduced her to the guys, it was all business between us."

She narrows her eyes playfully as she eats her first rangoon. "Likely story."

I put my left hand up and place my right over my heart. "I swear."

Her indulgent little smile soothes my worry over the confession.

"And how about now...any relationships or situationships?" Her voice is light, but I see a flash of vulnerability in her eyes as she glances up from her plate.

"No, none. Well, other than the one I'm hoping you're about to propose with your list of rules."

"I see." She takes another rangoon. "None for me, either. If you were curious."

"I was. I am. Curious."

She takes a long sip, then sets the wine glass down and slides off her stool. As she walks around the island toward me, my whole body tightens, my fingers flexing with want. She stops a few steps away from me, just out of reach.

"I don't do strings."

Thank god. Her fingers drop to the hem of her shirt, playing with the material. It takes physical effort to drag my eyes back to her face.

"I don't either." *This can totally be just a physical thing. Two consenting adults, right?*

"Good," she murmurs. "What happens between us stays between us."

Ehhhh. "I'm not a good liar, Lex, especially not with the guys. If they ask, I won't stand a chance."

Her mouth curves in one corner, and I want to lick the expression right off her face. "I can live with that. No broadcasting, but no lying."

"Deal. That it?"

"Keep it professional. I won't risk anything happening at Athena or on company time."

My eyes brighten. "So we're talking more than just tonight."

She flushes and looks away, her lips twitching up. "Maybe. We'll see."

She wants me. I fight back the desire to pound my chest and crow at the sky. The fact this incredible woman chose me is worth celebrating, but I don't need to be a Neanderthal about it.

"You done?" My voice is all gravel.

She inclines her head, fingers still toying with the hem of her shirt.

"My turn." I step forward and place a hand on hers, stilling her. "Tell me, Lex. Do you usually take control in the bedroom, or do your partners?"

Those seafoam eyes are almost black, her pupils wide. I love that I'm the one making her feel that desire, the one testing the limits of her control.

"I do." Her voice is unsteady as her eyes search mine.

"I thought so," I whisper. "I know we don't know each other very well yet, but do you think you could trust me tonight? Let me call the shots?"

Her throat bobs as she swallows. "Yes. I think...I think I like the sound of that."

"Good girl." I surge forward and take her face in my hands, pressing my lips to hers.

Her body sways into mine in response, her eyes fluttering closed as she gives herself over to me without hesitation. *Fucking hell, yes. More of that.* I swipe my tongue against her lips and she opens for me with a moan, pressing her body flush against mine as her arms thread around my waist. I can feel every inch of her, and the rush of having her in my arms is overwhelming. My cock is a fucking steel rod trapped between us, straining toward her.

I release her from the kiss slowly. "Two questions."

"No," she whimpers, snaking a hand up around my neck to pull me back down.

Greedy little thing.

I let her direct the kiss for a moment, then reach down and swat her ass sharply. She gasps, and her eyes fly open as she gapes up at me. I look for a hint of accusation or offense but find none.

"Questions," I repeat, pressing my thumb to her chin and holding her in place with insistent fingers. "What's your stance on condoms?"

"Condoms?" She blinks. "Condoms are a yes."

"Noted. Now, where are the stairs?"

"Around the corner—"

I bend and hoist her onto my shoulder, heading in the direction she pointed.

"Linc!" she shrieks, giggling.

"Hush, I've got you."

"Linc, put me down!"

I crack my palm against her ass with more force than the last time and groan when I feel her whole body go pliant in my arms.

"I'm in charge, remember?" I rub a soothing hand over her as I climb the stairs. "If you do as you're told, I promise I'll make it worth it. Can you do that for me?"

Her whimper is barely audible, but I catch the "yes" she gasps out as I turn the corner and stride into the first bedroom I see. I flip her over my shoulder and onto the bed. She looks like a dream, all flushed with her hair in disarray. There's something deeply satisfying about seeing her in such a state, so far from the perfectly put-together CEO.

She shifts on the bed, her thighs pressing together. I tsk and put a hand on her knee, smiling when she freezes.

"That's it," I croon. "When I'm in charge, I'm going to tell you what to do, what not to do...when to come. If you don't listen, there will be consequences."

Her eyes flare at the mention of punishment, and I breathe slowly through my nose to keep myself under control.

"You going to spank me again, Linc?" she asks, her pulse thundering in the hollow of her throat.

I run a soothing hand along her leg as I nod. "Spanking is one method of punishment, yes. But it can also be fun on its own."

She bites her lip and squirms again. I smirk as I kneel on the bed.

"Do you like the sound of that? Does the thought of me smacking that sweet ass make you wet? Do you want to let me have my way with you, Lex?"

She rolls her lips between her teeth and nods. *I fucking knew it.* I reach up and grab the waistband of her leggings, tugging gently. She complies immediately, lifting her hips to make it easier for me to peel her leggings and underwear off her body.

"Before I see how ready you are for me, let's talk safe words."

Her eyes widen. "What exactly are you planning to do to me?"

"So many things, Lex." My chuckle is dark as I stroke my fingers along her bare legs. "I have this feeling you're dying for someone to take control. I promise it'll feel good, when you give in."

I bend and place a wet kiss on her inner ankle. She moans, relaxing back into the mattress once more.

"Let's start easy, okay? We'll use colors." Her eyes find mine as she listens, rapt. *Such a good girl.* "Green means keep going. Yellow means slow down, but don't stop. And red..."

"Stop," she says, her breathing almost ragged.

"That's right. If you say 'red' at any point, I'll stop immediately. Okay?"

"Yeah, okay."

"Now, let's see how wet you are, hm?"

I run my hands from her ankles up to her knees, pushing them apart gently. She resists for a moment, but relents at my pointed look and lets her legs fall open. My cock woke up the second she opened the door, but that was nothing compared to how it reacts to the sight of her pussy spread before me, pink lips glistening with her arousal.

"Fuck, that's a gorgeous cunt," I murmur. "I bet you taste even better than you look, don't you?"

She whimpers and writhes, her fingers tangling in the hem of her shirt. I tsk gently, reaching up to help her. She raises her arms and slips out of the tee to lie back on the bed, naked and waiting. I take her hands in mine and guide them to her knees.

"I want you to stay still so I can enjoy my dessert, beautiful. Can you do that for me?"

Her eyes flutter as she nods, fingers digging into her knees.

"Perfectly still, that's it. But don't be quiet. I want to hear you."

She gasps as I descend on her pussy, roughly sucking her clit into my mouth. *Fucking delicious.* I groan at the taste of her, gripping her hips as I devour her. She whimpers and moans, but keeps herself in place. I hum in approval, my lips vibrating against her clit.

Her legs tremble as she struggles to stay still, but I don't relent. I want to see how much she can take, how long she'll fight her body's need to writhe as her pleasure ramps higher and higher. *How good can you be for me?*

Chapter 9

Lex

I am nothing more than sensation. Linc's face is between my legs, his lips and tongue and teeth at work on my core, teasing at my heated flesh. I've never had someone eat me out with such enthusiasm, never felt so close to falling over the edge from a mouth alone. *How is he so fucking good at this?*

Linc gently scrapes his teeth against my clit, then soothes it with a series of short sucks, and I cry out with the effort it takes not to bow against the bed. The frustration of having to hold still increases the delicious thrum of tension in my body–that sweet push and pull between what he's making me feel and my own physical struggle tugging me to the edge, only to throw me back when I get close.

"I need to move," I beg, my hands shaking against my knees as I battle the urge to tangle my fingers in his hair.

"Not yet," he growls against me, my muscles tensing further.

He licks from the bottom of my pussy to the top, then swirls his tongue around my clit. I moan, sweat beading my forehead, and dig my nails into my skin. The bite of pain has my eyes rolling back in my head, pleasure a tight coil in my belly. Heat flashes through me as he sucks my clit back into his mouth. He nibbles and sucks, nibbles and sucks, until I'm nearly sobbing.

"Please. Please, Linc, let me come, please. Let me move." I'm babbling, but I can't help it. I've never felt anything so intense, never let go enough to let someone else control my pleasure.

All I get in answer is a shake of his head. He reaches out and squeezes my hand against my knee in silent order to stay put, and I sob in frustration. As I open my mouth to beg again, he burrows his tongue inside me. My voice turns into a high whine as I clench around him, desperate to be filled with more.

As though he can read my mind, he brings his fingers up to stroke my entrance, his touch light, teasing. A half sob breaks free and I squeeze my eyes closed, the muscles in my stomach fluttering with pleasure and tension.

"You're so close, aren't you?" he croons, voice husky and low. "But you're not going to come until I say so, are you?"

A thin, desperate sound escapes my throat. I've never made some of these noises before, never felt mindless with need. But that's what I am—a mindless collection of nerves strung tighter than a bowstring. One pluck, one touch of his talented fingers or tongue, reverberates through me with immeasurable force.

"Please," I whisper as his fingers keep stroking. "Linc, please..."

He hums as his lips close on my clit once more, and I lose the battle to stay still. My back arches and I thrust my hips toward him, seeking friction, pressure, *anything* as long as it's more. *More, more, moremoremore–*

"Ah, why'd you do that? You were doing so well."

His fingers fall away as he shifts back into a kneeling position. The heat and dominance in his gaze is intoxicating, and I want nothing more than to please him. *What the hell? When have I ever wanted to please someone in bed? What the fuck kind of sex magic is this?!*

He smirks, as though he can read my thoughts. "I know this is new for you. It's okay, I've got you. I'm going to make this all so worth your while, Lex, I promise."

I can only throw my head back against the pillow in frustration, my jaw almost chattering with the tension that still grips me.

"But I asked you to stay still, and you didn't."

He places his palms on my inner hips, then sweeps them out and up my sides in a long, slow stroke. It isn't pressure or friction where I want it, but it's delicious all the same.

"How should I punish you?"

It's a rhetorical question, and I quiver in anticipation of what he'll choose. It isn't fear, but excitement—hot and thick in my core. I keep my eyes closed, reveling in the feeling of his hands on me, his touch featherlight in one moment, then firm and commanding the next.

"Pick a number between one and five."

I lick my lips as I convince my vocal cords to work. "Three," I croak, my voice rough and thready.

He hums his approval. "Three's a good number. Color?"

"Green," I hiss and he slips his hands down my legs to the ankles, then back up along my inner thighs.

His fingers brush mine, still braced on my knees, as they pass. I shiver at the contact, peering up at him. As I breathe deeply to steady myself, he pulls his hands away completely. His gaze meets mine, his warm brown eyes glittering. I want to ask what he's planning—

Smack.

I yelp as his hand makes sharp contact with my pussy, my body jerking involuntarily in response. It's surprise more than pain that makes me cry out, but the rush of pleasure after has me moaning and fighting not to let my body bow.

"One." His voice is firm, and he smiles broadly at me. "Oh, Lex, you're stunning. Look at that flush. So responsive for me, so good."

He trails his fingers along the redness creeping onto my chest and neck, a look of wonder on his face. I stare up at him, lost in him while he appears lost in me and don't even see the second strike coming. My eyes slam shut as his hand makes contact with my tender flesh, my fingernails digging into the skin of my knees in a desperate bid to obey and be still. *Oh god, why does that feel so good?*

"Two." The throaty satisfaction in his voice has a direct line to my core.

Between the throbbing in my clit, the sting of my swollen pussy lips, and the bite of my nails, I'm untethered. Teetering on the edge of orgasm, poised so close it will take but one gentle press of my clit to send me right over. I crack my eyes open in time to see his hand whip through the air, the momentary anticipation making me flush from head to toe.

"Three," he growls, then descends on me. "You can move. Let me see what I do to you."

I almost weep in relief as I release my knees, my fingers sinking immediately into his lush chestnut waves as he sucks my clit into his mouth once more. He hums, encouraging me, and I grip his hair and thrust my hips forward, grinding into him. Every lick, lap, and suck has me trembling. My breathing shallows and quickens as the wave builds, my pleasure gathering with unfamiliar force low in my body.

"Are you ready to come?" He looks up and I groan at the sight of him, face wet from my juices, eyes glinting with desire and approval.

I nod frantically, and he smirks, dragging his fingers along my entrance again, teasing.

"I want to watch you," he murmurs. "Show me how you come apart. Show me how you break."

His fingers spear into me and I gasp at the intrusion, throwing my head back as pleasure licks fire along my skin. He strokes against the top of my channel, finding that perfect spot with nearly clinical precision, and I cry out as my orgasm crashes through me, wave after powerful wave. I'm vaguely aware of Lincoln praising me as I writhe and ride out my bliss on his hand.

"Again."

The aftershocks continue as Lincoln keeps stroking, then he grazes his teeth along my clit once more. I sob as the pleasure redoubles, almost painfully, and my body locks into one long line of tension—waiting, shuddering, so close. He sucks like a man possessed and a second orgasm comes screaming out of nowhere to rack my body.

Linc slows his pace, then gently pulls his fingers from me. I'm boneless in my afterglow and manage little more than a tiny whimper in response. His lips pave a wet path up my body, then his fingers press against my mouth.

"Taste yourself," he commands, his eyes dark with desire, pupils blown.

I open my mouth and suck his fingers in, moaning at the taste of me overlaid on the warm, clean flavor of him. My eyes lock with his as I grip his wrist, licking and sucking to get every last drop. I've tasted myself before, but it's somehow sweeter on Linc's fingers. His stare goes half-lidded with lust as he groans his praise, and I realize I'm desperate for it.

"That's it, Lex," he murmurs. "You did so good. I'm so pleased with you."

My nipples pebble in response, and he pulls his hand away

to firmly grip my breast, teasing the hard nub between his fingers.

"Such a greedy little thing. Look how your body reacts to me. Wants me." He leans down and closes his mouth around my other nipple, tugging gently with his teeth.

I moan and arch into him, clasping him to me. Two orgasms in, and he's right. *I still want more of Lincoln Wilde.*

"Linc, please..."

He smiles up at me, then leans in to capture my lips in a fierce kiss. I arc up into it and wrap myself around him, pushing at the waist of his gray joggers with my feet. He chuckles as he pulls away and sits back on his heels. He reaches up and grabs his shirt by the neck, pulling it over his head in one smooth motion. *Fucking hell, why is that move so sexy?* His eyes twinkle like he knows exactly what I'm thinking as he shoves his pants off.

"You ready for me to fuck you now?"

"Yes, please." I let my legs fall open, inviting him to take what he wants.

"On your stomach, ass up."

I obey immediately, looking back at him as I settle my cheek against the duvet.

"So fucking stunning," he murmurs, stroking his hands along my ass and thighs.

He pulls a condom from somewhere–probably the pocket of his sweats–and rolls it on. Biting his lip, he strokes his cock through the wetness between my thighs a few times, swirling it over my clit and making me moan. I wriggle my hips to encourage him to *hurry up and fuck me already* and he chuckles.

"So impatient. I love it." He notches the head of his cock against my entrance and pushes in the barest amount. "Hold on, Lex. And don't come until I tell you to."

Before I can protest his order, he slams into me with one

hard thrust. I groan as I feel the stretch, my fingers fisting in the duvet as he sets a punishing rhythm. At this angle, he's stroking over my G-spot with every movement, sending me steadily higher.

"Fuck, you feel like heaven," Linc grits out. "Fucking knew you would."

His fingers bite into my hips as he rails into me, hard enough to bruise. I don't mind the thought of his mark on my skin, don't hate the idea of him claiming some small part of me in this whirlwind of pleasure and release. If I was less dick drunk, the idea might have given me pause. As it is, I close my eyes and let the fire of lust and desire overwhelm my senses.

"I need you to play with that pretty little clit. Want to feel you squeeze me while you come."

I slip my fingers up to my pussy and moan at the feel of his cock sliding in and out.

"That's it. Shatter all over me, gorgeous."

My fingers find a smooth rhythm, brushing soft circles over my swollen clit. Linc keeps his pace up, slamming forcefully into me as stars burst behind my vision. My whole body trembles as my orgasm gathers.

"Fuck, yes, just like that," he gasps. "Come for me, Lex."

He cracks his hand against my ass as I feel myself falling into the abyss. My body tenses as the wave breaks, my pussy spasming around him again and again as my orgasm sweeps through me. I cry out his name, and he shouts his release moments later, his hips stuttering as he works us both through the aftershocks.

As I come down, my legs give way and I flop flat on the bed, Linc a heavy, comforting weight against my body.

"Holy shit," Linc mutters as he slips from me and shifts to my side.

I huff against the sheets in agreement, my eyes still closed.

The bed rises as he stands and walks a few steps away, then dips as he returns. He snuggles up to me, lifting me gently to arrange my body with my head on his chest. I barely help, completely spent.

"I didn't expect cuddling," I murmur.

He chuckles. "Sorry, does cuddling count as a string?"

I shake my head and snuggle against him, taking comfort in his warmth. He may be able to get up and do things, but I'm two minutes from sleep.

"Staying the night does, though." The words feel wrong, but need to be said.

His arm tightens reassuringly. "I figured. Give me a few minutes to catch my breath and I'll be out of your hair."

Lifting my head to rest my chin on his chest, I look up into his eyes and search for any hint of hurt or upset. But Linc looks as content and sated as I am, a small smile on his lips.

"Hey."

"Hey yourself." My smile can't be contained.

"I got one!" He pumps his fist in the air as I laugh in confusion.

"You got what?"

"A new smile. A real one. From you." He grins at me, then pulls me up to meet his lips. "And it was all for me," he murmurs when he releases me.

I can only blink up at him as he kisses my nose, then rolls out of bed to gather his clothes. He dresses quickly, then pauses at the door.

"No strings, no broadcasts, and professionalism. How'd I do?" His eyes glint mischievously.

"Hmmm," I pretend to think, tapping my finger against my cheek. "Six out of ten."

His eyes narrow playfully, but there's a hint of dominance in the look. "Careful, beautiful. I'd hate to have to punish you again."

My pussy throbs, and I bury my face in the pillow. Linc laughs and pats the doorframe.

"See you soon, Lex."

"Bye," I squeak, lifting my head from the pillow, but he's already gone. And I have the sinking suspicion my rules hang by a thread. *That boy is trouble. But I think I like it.*

Chapter 10

Lex

"Whoa, whoa, whoa." Cass holds up a hand. "Hold the phone. You did *what* with *who*?"

Cassandra Thompson, a journalist for the Bayview Bulletin, and I met when she was on assignment to cover a Women in Tech luncheon I sponsored five years ago. We hit it off, and she'd written about the startup community and multiple Athena portfolio launches since. There were roughly ten years between us, but the difference hadn't stopped us from getting close.

I roll my eyes at her dramatics and shake my head. "Keep your voice down, woman."

The redhead bugs her eyes out at me and leans closer, as though that will make her whisper-shout quieter. "I am! You just dropped a bomb on us!"

I open my mouth to protest, but Ruby chimes in from my other side. "She's not wrong. You did."

Snapping my mouth shut, I exhale. We're on bikes at the back of our weekly spinning class three days after Linc broke my...brain. There are few things I manage to keep on my calendar on a regular basis, but this is one of them. Not only do I need the physical outlet, but I need time with my two closest friends. Class was over, and we were using the cooldown as our opportunity to catch up while the rest of the class filters out.

"Okay, fine. I guess this *is* a first."

"Which part? The sleeping with a client, the fact it was at *your* place, or the whole you're-smiling-like-a-giddy-school-girl-three-days-later thing?" Cass hisses.

"All of them really," Ruby chimes in.

I was a grad student when I met Ruby at the library, of all places. She was an undergrad and part-time librarian whose schedule matched up with my late night studying sessions. I was drawn to her dry humor and sharp wit, and we've been friends since.

"Oh my god, I'm never telling either of you anything ever again," I grouse.

They both cackle, drawing our instructor's attention. She gives us a friendly thumbs' up as she throws out goodbyes to the diehard women who sit in the front row. We've been coming to her class for months now, mainly for the relaxed atmosphere and general air of positivity. Our opportunities to catch up are sporadic otherwise.

"He must be something else for you to bend rules for him, though," Ruby muses.

"I mean, he's gorgeous and mind blowing in bed," I concede.

"I don't think I've ever heard you describe a hook up as gorgeous or mind blowing before."

"Ugh, don't make me roll my eyes at you *again*, Cass."

She sits up on her bike so she can throw her hands in the air. "Just saying. You may not call him special, but this one seems different."

She's not wrong. Linc is different from my usual...dates. Not that they're all the same, but they tended to be young, unattached, and enthusiastic about my "no strings" rule. In fact,

I'd only seen a handful of them more than once in at least a decade. I sigh.

"I don't know, girls. It seems like it could be messy."

"Sure," Ruby offers, "but messy seems like a reasonable trade off for, what was it you said? Oh, right, the best sex of your life."

Cass and I stare at her for a moment, blinking.

"What?" Ruby shrugs. "Seemed like it needed to be said."

"Oooh, girl, we're rubbing off on you and I am here for it!" Cass crows, holding a hand up for Ruby to slap.

"Uh, put your arm down. I'm not a frat boy."

Cass giggles. "You crack me up, Roo."

My oldest friend heaves a beleaguered sigh and gives me a look. "Anyway, Lex, you're a grown woman and a complete badass. You work way too fucking hard, and you need to steal every moment you can for the things you enjoy. Who cares if he's a client or, I don't know, the fucking Pope? You're both adults."

Snorting, Cass leans over to peer at Ruby. "When did we start talking about the Pope, again?"

"Oh, whatever," Ruby mumbles. "It's the example I could think of in the moment."

I chuckle. "You made your point, Roo. It's true we're both consenting adults, and I do work too much. Anyway, we did set some ground rules."

"Of course you did."

"Careful, Cass. You keep rolling your eyes and they're liable to get stuck like that."

"Very funny." She sticks her tongue out at me. "So what else is new for you? Any exciting new businesses I need to pay attention to?"

"No, wait, we're not moving on from this topic yet," Ruby cuts in before I can answer.

I don't say anything, looking resolutely ahead as I stretch. My unwavering attention doesn't keep me from feeling Cass and Ruby lock eyes around me.

"Lex," Cass sing-songs. "What aren't you telling us?"

Glancing over at Ruby's self-satisfied smirk, I huff an annoyed noise. "You have to stop using your powers of perception for evil, Roo."

"Hey! I'm hardly evil," Cass protests. "You know this is all off the record, anyway. Well, unless you tell me it shouldn't be. Then it's on the record."

"Not inspiring confidence for sharing with you, you know," I tease.

"No dodging the question," Ruby prods. "Something else happened with Lincoln, didn't it?"

I heave a sigh, resigned. "Yeah, it did."

"And it's the real reason you're still in your head about a hookup that happened three days ago."

Fuck her for knowing me so well. "Maybe."

Cass reaches over and pushes lightly on my shoulder. "Spill, sister. You know we're not going to let up until you do."

"Why are we friends again?"

They both remain silent, waiting me out. *I've really gotta stop teaching my tricks to the people around me.*

"So, Linc might have...showed up on my doorstep again."

"I knew it," Ruby says under her breath while Cass shouts "ah ha!"

"At four the next morning, to be precise."

I peek over to see Cass's mouth hanging open in surprise.

"And," I continue, bowing my head for a moment, "he's been showing up at four every day since."

"Excuse me?!" Cass screeches. "Objection! You buried the lead!"

"This isn't court and you're not a lawyer!" I laugh.

"You told him that's when you run, didn't you?"

I nod at Ruby. We've known each other for so long, I'm used to her uncanny ability to see straight through the people she loves. It isn't unusual for her to know what's bothering me before I do.

"He took me for a walk after my last meeting with him and his partners and it got dark. I mentioned I was used to it, and he's been joining me on my runs ever since."

"No hanky panky?" Cass pouts.

I can understand why she sees it as a letdown, but I'm honestly impressed Linc can keep it above board. *Makes it that much easier to trust him.*

"Only a kiss, admittedly a hot one." I roll my shoulders. "It's been...lovely. Neither of us are morning people, so we don't talk much. But having someone who's just...there...I don't know. It's been nice."

Cass and Ruby exchange another glance.

"Stop it," I say, knowing exactly what those long looks mean.

The two of them staged more than one "find Lex a relationship" intervention in the last few years, and I wasn't interested in another. As much as they mean well, my patience for all things white-picket-fence is non-existent. At the end of the day, some people aren't cut out for marriage and kids, and that's their prerogative. *It's me. I'm some people.*

"I don't want to hear it," I reiterate. "He's a client, and, like you both said, we're consenting adults. I have zero expectations, and I'm just going to enjoy the next three months for what they are. That's the end of it."

"Of course it is," Cass quips.

"Whatever you say," Ruby drawls.

Yeah, yeah. I'm not entirely sure I believe me, either. It feels like I should focus on finishing our workout, so I drop my head and stretch out my legs. Relationships and trust aren't my thing, and I'm not looking to change that anytime soon. My life revolves around my business and the few people I've chosen as family, because goodness knows my worthless blood relatives are either antagonistic or absent on their best days.

The thing with Linc, whatever it is, is temporary. *And the little voice in my head suggesting I'm full of shit can fuck right off.*

Chapter 11

Shane

"Linc, what's up with the early morning runs this week?" I ask.

Declan glances over at me, then to his brother. We sit at the kitchen table scarfing breakfast before heading over to Solum for the day. Linc swallows his bite of cereal slowly, eyes darting first to Dec then back to me.

"Just trying something new."

Someone new, more like. "Who is she?" I press.

He chokes on his bite, thumping his chest with a fist as he coughs. Dec tosses me a wry smile and shakes his head, amused. *Not sure how long you'll be entertained, friend.* I have a feeling I know who it is, and Dec won't be thrilled.

"She who?" Linc coughs.

"I'm surprised you have time for a girl with how much you've been working," Dec muses. "Where'd you meet her?"

Linc looks up at me with panic in his eyes. I raise my brows and tilt my head, waiting for his answer. After a few moments, he sighs and leans back in his chair.

"I told her I couldn't lie to you two."

"Who the fuck asked you to lie to us?" Declan's glare could strip paint off the walls.

"No, no," Linc rushes, raising a hand in plea. "She didn't ask me to lie, sorry. That came out wrong. Fuck."

"Take a deep breath, kid."

He huffs at the nickname, but does as I suggest and fills his lungs with a slow inhale through his nose.

"I've been running with Lex for the past few days."

Declan freezes, his eyes locked on his brother. "Excuse you?"

"Dec, come on, man. Don't be like that."

"I'm sorry I'm worried about getting fucked over by another woman we don't know," Dec snaps.

"Lex is not Anne-Marie, and you know it." Linc's brows draw down. "They're nothing alike."

"How would you know?" Dec taunts, his fear over being betrayed again on full display, whether or not he realizes it. "You having heart-to-hearts on these daily runs?"

"I...no, it's not like that. We barely talk, I just...she mentioned she only has time to run at four in the fucking morning and I hated the idea of her doing it alone. So I showed up the other day, and we went together."

I blink in surprise. Linc's a good man, but I wouldn't call him the most thoughtful person. He's a frat boy through and through, more invested in the fun and games than anything else, especially when it comes to women. Him going out of his way for Lex was telling. *Of what exactly, I'm not sure.*

"Where do you run?" I ask.

He closes his eyes briefly, then meets my gaze. "We do a loop, starting and ending at her place."

"You're fucking kidding me," Declan growls. "Lincoln, tell me you're joking."

"No, I'm not joking."

"Why the fuck do you know where she lives?" Declan throws his arms wide. "Tell me you're not making the same goddamn mistake twice."

Linc levels a finger at his brother. "Hey, that's uncalled for. Nothing about this feels like a mistake. If there's anything I've learned about Lex in the last week, it's that she's an honest, genuine person."

Declan's face falls, consternation crossing his features. "How have you even spent enough time with her to make that determination?" He studies his brother's face for a long moment, then grunts in frustration as he reaches the same conclusion I have. "You're fucking her, aren't you? Shane, did you know about this?"

"Dec, chill." Linc holds his hands out in a placating motion. "Shane didn't know, because it's no one's business but mine and Lex's."

"Oh, right, because she asked you to *lie* to us!"

Linc scrubs a hand over his jaw. "Damnit, man, stop twisting my words. She wanted to keep things between us, and I told her I would be honest if asked. We agreed we wouldn't broadcast it, but I'm not going to lie to you." He meets my gaze. "Either of you."

"Appreciate that," I murmur, processing his confirmation.

I knew Linc was into Lex, that much was obvious from the moment she stepped into the conference room at Athena. And given their easy banter during the facilities tour earlier in the week, I suspected it was mutual. But I'm surprised to hear things progressed so quickly.

"That's all you have to say, Shane? Seriously?" Declan laughs sarcastically. "This is a fucking disaster. I told you going to Athena was a terrible idea."

"Declan, what the fuck? First of all, I'm offended by how little you think of my ability to focus. And second, you have to know Lex is the ultimate professional. Absolutely nothing that's happening between us is going to negatively impact the deal between Solum and Athena."

"You can't know that, Lincoln. This was a reckless, selfish, immature decision. What the fuck were you thinking?"

Lincoln frowns and crosses his arms as he looks down, refusing to meet his brother's accusatory gaze. Having lost his punching bag, Dec rounds on me.

"Are you seriously not going to back me up here, Shane?"

"Linc's an adult, Dec. So's Lex. What they choose to do in their free time is their business."

Dec lets out a shocked breath, his eyes wild and a vein throbbing down his forehead. "I can't believe what I'm hearing. This is bullshit."

He turns on his heel and storms from the room, thundering down the stairs to the basement. Linc sighs and pulls his hat off, running a frustrated hand through his messy curls before resettling it backwards.

"Thanks for backing me up."

"It's the truth. We're all grown ups."

"I know, I just...I wish Dec could see it that way." He looks toward the stairs, then shakes his head. "He's so convinced there's another villain in our story, and somehow it's Lex."

"No, pretty sure he's cast himself in that role."

Linc glances up in surprise, then his expression turns thoughtful. After a moment, he scoffs.

'Yeah, I guess he has. When do you think he'll figure that out?"

"That's the million dollar question, isn't it? Knowing your brother, it'll be right before it's too late and not a minute earlier."

Tilting his head back to face the ceiling, Linc groans. "I hate that you're probably right about that."

He slumps into his chair, then pulls his soggy bowl of cereal closer despondently. Hunched over the table, he looks up between bites.

"You don't have any questions?" he mumbles around a mouthful of food.

"I have all the questions, Linc."

He grins. "Fair."

"Most of them would be a violation of Lex's privacy, though, so...I'll keep them to myself. For now."

His eyes twinkle. "She's something else, man. That's all I'll say."

"She must be, if she's got you up before sunrise and willingly going toe-to-toe with Declan."

He grimaces. "Yeah, it's not my favorite place to be. But I really think Dec's got the wrong idea on this whole thing. Lex isn't the enemy. If anything, she's exactly what I—what we—need."

"I'll take your word for it." I stand, gathering our dishes and taking them to the sink. "I'll go check on our fearless leader."

"Not so fearless these days, is he?"

I chuckle. "As much as I love Bold Lincoln, I gotta counsel you to keep the insightful shit between us."

"I know, I know," Linc says through a shit-eating grin. "He'd fucking deck me if he heard me psycho-analyze him."

"He sure would." I dry my hands on the kitchen towel, then turn for the stairs. "Don't wait up. If you're done, head over. We'll meet you there."

"Sure thing, man. And, Shane?"

I pause at the top of the stairs, looking back at him over my shoulder.

"Thank you."

He has the ghost of a smile on his lips, and I return it before heading down the stairs. The Wilde brothers and I have a pretty smooth dynamic. Dec is our self-appointed leader, Linc the jokester, and I usually try to keep anyone from getting killed or overly pissed off. It works, but we admittedly experienced little conflict to test the model. Then Anne-Marie happened. *Bitch.* Ever since, it felt like everything between us was out of whack. But with Lex and Athena involved, I see an opportunity for us to intentionally evolve into something more sustainable.

I know our time with Lex is temporary, she's been clear on that, but if we can learn enough from her and her team, we'll be able to tackle any future challenge. Though we'll never unlock our potential while Dec has his head in the sand. *Or up his ass.*

"That hole wasn't there yesterday," I observe, walking to stand next to my friend.

He's facing a section of drywall with a suspiciously fist-sized hole punched straight through. His only response is a grunt.

"You want to tell me why punching walls felt like a good idea?"

"Wall."

"Come again?"

He glances my way, his expression pinched. "I punched one wall. Not walls."

"Right," I drawl. "Apologies. You want to tell me why punching this one singular wall felt like a good idea?"

"I just can't believe he's being so stupid, Shane."

"That's an uncharacteristically harsh assessment."

He casts me a side-eyed glare. "I disagree."

"You have every right to disagree. Doesn't mean you're correct."

He grumbles in frustration, then picks up a tape measure and holds it up to the hole. "I'm concerned about the business and the negative impact she could have. The closer Linc gets, the more risk we're exposed to. We all let Anne-Marie in, and look how that turned out."

He can claim it's all about the business, but I have my doubts. Strong ones.

"Lex owns the top VC in the Bay, Declan. Maybe the country. You think she got there by hosing her clients?"

"No, I–"

"Then help me understand. What on earth would she gain from pulling one over on us?"

He scowls at the hole in the wall, stubbornly refusing to meet my gaze.

"And," I continue, "if she wanted to take us down, she could've shown us the door like she did three years ago. It's to our benefit she offered us a deal."

"I know."

"So what's the rub, really?"

"I don't know, Shane," he says, sarcastic exaggeration ripe in his tone, "but the thought of them together is like nails on a chalkboard."

There it is. "Sounds like jealousy."

Dec's jaw clenches. "Fuck off, Shane."

I shrug. "I get it, man. She's intelligent, kind, gorgeous. I've got my own green-eyed monster to deal with over the whole thing."

If Linc and Lex want to have a little something on the side, I won't begrudge either of them. Lincoln deserves something good, and my gut tells me Lex does, too. But it would be a lie to say I don't want an invite to their exclusive little party. *Fuck, we'd be hot together.*

"That's ridiculous. Jealousy is not what's going on for me."

"Sure, Dec."

"It's not."

"I'm not arguing."

"It's a ridiculous assertion."

"Do I even need to be here?" I look around. "Seems like you're carrying this conversation all by yourself."

He flops his forehead against his hand, still braced above the hole in the wall. "You're an ass."

"Sometimes," I agree with a bemused smile. "So are you."

He scoffs and straightens, meeting my gaze briefly. "You're not wrong."

I step up beside him and knock my shoulder into his. "Go easy on Lincoln, yeah? He's trying, and he's not the source of your frustration."

Declan takes a long, slow breath. "I know."

Nodding, I clap him on the shoulder as I turn away. "Come up when you're ready to be civil."

"I'm always civil!"

I snort at the claim and head for the stairs.

Chapter 12

Lex

As I pull up to the house the guys of Solum Technologies share, one week after my night with Linc, I can't help but think it's not what I expected. After touring their facilities and spending what limited time I had with them, I envisioned something modern and sleek. The stunning Mediterranean-style cottage before me is the exact opposite, stately and dripping with old-world charm.

Shane emerges from the front door as I park, barefoot in a fitted white henley with worn jeans sitting low on his hips. *Fucking hell, he has no right to look that edible.* He's tall, lean, and cut—I can see the definition of his abs through the clingy material. A soft smile plays on his lips as he raises a hand in greeting and jogs down the steps to meet me.

"Welcome." He saunters up and tucks both hands into his pockets. "You find it okay?"

"Sure did."

"Lucky us. Come on, the guys are inside."

I follow as he turns toward the door. "Thanks for accommodating the late meeting this week."

He glances over his shoulder, those piercing blue eyes

searing my soul. "It's our pleasure, really. Dec will take any opportunity to show this place off."

I look up to appreciate the ivy-covered stucco. "It's gorgeous."

"Yeah, he'd agree with you." He follows my gaze. "The compliments are wasted on me."

"Not a real estate person?"

He pauses as we reach the door, treating me to the full force of his gaze. "Real estate is fine, but home is about people. I'd happily live in a double-wide if I was with those I loved."

My lips part in surprise at his candor, and his eyes track the movement. There's a fierce glint in his gaze when it returns to mine.

"How about you? Real estate your thing?"

I blink, distracted by the heat I thought I saw, then give myself a shake. "Not so much real estate as architecture and design. I'm an art lover, so I appreciate good lines."

"Plenty of those here." He smirks and opens the front door.

As I step over the threshold, I'm struck by the cozy feel of the place. It's warm and intimate, as though I've stepped into their lives, not just their home. Linc grins as he spots me from the kitchen, hurrying over as I remove my heels. He glances down at them and smirks, no doubt recognizing them from the week prior.

"Hey, beautiful," he murmurs, wrapping his arms around me.

My chest warms at the nickname, and I melt into him. His brief embraces, stolen before and after our runs, were quickly becoming highlights of my week. There's something about being in Lincoln's arms that both comforts and strengthens me.

I smile up at him as he releases me, squeezing his arm gently as we put more space between us. Shane doesn't react to the friendly greeting, and I raise an eyebrow at Linc. His sheepish grin is telling. *So, they all know. Fan-fucking-tastic.*

"Declan's in a great mood, then?"

"He's in a mood alright," Linc mutters, rolling his eyes. "Come on, we cleared the dining table for our meeting."

I follow him over to the large round table and plush chairs. Glancing down, I admire what I assume is the original red tile floor.

"When was this place built?" I muse aloud.

"In the twenties," a firm voice replies.

Declan stalks up to the other side of the table, pulling out a chair and settling in it like a throne, his eyes never leaving mine.

"It's stunning."

He's silent for a beat, then he inclines his head. "Thank you."

I smirk, noting how his jaw muscles ticked before he spoke. "That looked painful. You struggling to hold back an insult?"

"Maybe we should–" Linc starts.

"I'm trying a different approach," Declan interrupts. "Maybe if I keep my mouth shut, you'll dig the hole yourself."

I can't help it; I laugh. *Keep holding your breath, buddy.* "Well, on that charming note, we have a lot to cover. My team came back with the preliminary analysis of your data, and they agree with most of your findings. They have a few suggestions, though, which I sent over via email."

"Thank you. I saw that this morning." Linc glances over at Shane as I take a seat. "There were some good questions in there, and a few angles we haven't fully explored."

Declan frowns but stays silent. *I'll take that as a win.*

"Anyway," I go on, "our main topic for this week is the Summit. We have a lot to do in preparation, and it'll require all of you to be entirely committed."

"Do you have a plan?" Shane asks.

"We do." I pull my laptop out of my bag and flip it open. "The team sent an overview my way just before I got here. What's the wifi?"

Shane reaches out a hand for my laptop, and I pass it over.

"Thanks. Tonight we need to discuss press milestones and launch activities. The team has documented everything, and, if you're aligned, we'll get things in motion."

"Do we get a say in any of this?" Declan looks more worried than hostile. For once.

Mouthing thanks at Shane, I accept my laptop back from him and pull up the presentation. "Of course. Solum is your company, and you in particular are its face. None of it works without your full support."

"So, you're saying you'll partner with us every step of the way?" Linc gives me a little grin.

"Exactly." I smile back, entertained by the lay up.

"And you don't feel the need to be in the limelight?" Declan presses.

"God, no. I hate the limelight, if I'm honest."

"You do plenty of interviews and big events for someone who hates the limelight," Declan mutters.

I study him for a moment as I turn my laptop around so they can see the screen.

"Declan, have you ever had to put your personal preferences aside for the betterment of your business, or the people who work for you?"

He frowns. "Of course."

"I assumed so. It's what we do, as business owners." I tuck my hair behind my ear. "My visibility and press is positive for my business, which means I can take better care of my team and invest more in my clients and community. I might not choose the limelight, but my personal preferences are ultimately immaterial."

Some of the fight goes out of Declan's posture as I speak, and I glimpse Shane's amused expression out of the corner of my eye.

"Anyway, feel free to tab through the overview while I hit the main points." I push my laptop toward them, and they all lean forward to see it. "The press campaign will start in two weeks and will feature three marquee events–a live interview, the launch at the Summit, and the Brightest in the Bay award ceremony when we return."

"Say more about the interview."

There's a frisson of electricity along my spine at the command in Shane's tone. My night with Linc, and the stolen moments with him since, turned on a part of my brain I didn't know existed. I've noticed more dominant behaviors from the men in my life, but none affect me the way Linc and Shane—even Declan–do. They leave me yearning for more.

"You're familiar with Cass Thompson?"

"Hell, yeah. She's dope." Linc's dimple winks at me, and my core aches. *I still want to lick him.*

"She is," I beam back at him, keeping it professional. "She's also a personal friend. I'm working with her to set up an exclusive interview with you, Declan."

His eyes flash to mine.

"She knows the startup community well, the Bulletin has the highest reach in the Bay, and she's experienced in green tech. Even without our friendship, she's the best choice."

"I agree," he admits, sounding mildly surprised. "It would be a huge win to have that kind of attention for Solum."

"It would. You have six weeks to prepare so you can make the most of it."

Declan clears his throat, glancing at his partners. "Will you or your team provide any coaching?"

It's a struggle to keep the smile from my face, but I have a feeling he'd interpret it as mocking, so I lock it up and incline my head solemnly. "Of course."

He jerks his chin in acknowledgement and turns back to the slides on my laptop.

"Interview in six weeks, Summit in ten?" Shane asks.

"That's right. You all have current passports, yes?" At their murmurs of ascent, I sigh in relief. "Good. That's one less thing to worry about. We'll all be going. It'll be impossible to launch Solum without acknowledging the elephant in the room that is Greenstar Labs and Anne-Marie, and I anticipate technical questions Shane and Linc will be best suited to answer."

They nod thoughtfully, and a feeling of accomplishment fills me. We have a short amount of time to make magic happen for their business, and I worried it would be an uphill battle. Declan's attitude and the tension between the three of them is concerning, and I expected the news of Lincoln and I sleeping together to cause more waves. *I might make it through this in one piece, after all.*

———

"Christ, that was a lot," Linc sighs a couple of hours later. He reaches his arms up and laces his fingers behind his head, muscles rippling under his white tee as he leans into the stretch.

I chuckle as I stand, rolling my shoulders and stretching out my arms. "It was. Productive session, gentlemen. Thank you."

"No, thank you," Shane chimes in.

He rises from his seat and walks into the kitchen, moving with almost feline grace. The strength in his lithe form is obvious, especially in that tee.

"Whoa, it's almost nine." Linc frowns, looking at his phone. "Lex, did you eat before you came over?"

"Oh, I'm fine." I wave him off as I pack up my laptop and notebook.

He squints at me. "Lex."

I look up at him with my most innocent expression. "Linc."

"What did you have for lunch?"

It could be a casual question, but from him it's loaded. He's heard too many mentions of missed dinners and snack meals this week during our runs.

My shoulder twitches up. "Cami brought me a quinoa bowl."

"Did you eat it?" Shane calls from the kitchen, picking up on my careful language.

I frown at them both, wondering when Shane joined the conversation. "Not exactly..."

Shane's blue eyes meet mine. "Are you vegetarian? Any allergies?"

Blinking, I shake my head. "No, and no. Why?"

"I'm making dinner. Should be fifteen minutes or so." He looks up at Linc. "Want to head into the living room with some wine?"

"Yeah, sounds great."

Linc jumps up and goes to the kitchen while I look helplessly between the three men. Declan just scrubs a hand over his face.

"What's happening?"

He sighs heavily, rising to his feet. "You're staying for dinner, apparently."

Casting him a sideways glance, I set my bag back on the table. "Does this happen often?"

His green eyes meet mine. "Does what happen often?"

I gesture at Shane and Linc in the kitchen. Declan chuckles, the sound low and rasping. It reverberates through me, and I resist the urge to step closer.

"If you're asking if they make dinner for random people, the answer is no." He turns away, then pauses and looks over his shoulder. "Then again, you're the first random person we've had in this house in the last four years."

"That's either an insult or a compliment. Maybe both."

Something like amusement flashes in his eyes. "I'll leave that interpretation up to you, boss."

My laugh breaks free at the nickname, and his gaze lights up again. There's a pause in the noise from the kitchen, and I look over to find Linc and Shane's eyes on me. When I turn back to Declan, his expression is thoughtful.

"I don't know what I've done to earn that title, but if you're willing to give me a nickname..." I grin, "I'll take it."

Linc whoops his support while Shane smiles before turning back to whatever he's making. Declan's lips twitch, teasing me with the possibility of a smile. He clears his throat, green eyes locked on mine.

"I know I'm not the easiest client," he says quietly, catching me off guard. "I'm still wary after what Anne-Marie put us through. But I...I want you to know I appreciate your team. And you." He looks away, that low, rough sound rumbling through him once more. "To be honest, Lex, I respect the hell out of you. I have for years. I've been shit at showing it, but it's the truth."

My lips part as I blink at him, stunned by the confession. "Declan, I..."

He holds up a hand. "No, please. Let me slink away with some shred of dignity intact, yeah?"

Swallowing, I nod. The moment stretches between us, and I smirk.

"Don't go soft on me now, Wilde. It's not every day I meet a man willing to challenge me at every turn."

Amusement flashes in his eyes as he dips his chin, then steps back.

"Come on, Lex. I've got wine and snacks." Linc lifts a tray laden with chips, veggies, and hummus and tips his head toward the living room.

Glancing at Declan, I smile and tilt my head, inviting him to follow me after his brother. With the slightest motion of his head, he denies my offer, glances at his brother and friend, then turns to walk down the hall.

"Don't mind him. He's going to work out his tension in the basement," Linc explains.

I can't tell if he heard Declan's confession or not, so I respect his brother's ask for dignity and try to recenter myself.

"Do you have a gym down there?" I manage, glancing at the hall one last time.

He chuckles. "No, that would be far too normal for my brother. The basement was a mess when we moved in, so he's remodeling it."

"Oh, wow. Basements are rare around here. Is it a walkout?"

He beams and nods, dropping onto the couch and patting the cushion beside him. "Ridiculous view, too. It's going to be incredible when he's done with it."

"I'd love to see it."

"Next time." His arm settles around me as I sit, tugging me against his body.

I peer over the top of the couch at Shane, then look up at Linc, brow raised.

"Shane's cool," he murmurs, squeezing me gently as he searches my face. "When can I see you again?"

I snuggle into him, tucking my feet under me. "You running with me tomorrow?"

"Of course. But allow me to rephrase..."

He ducks his head to capture my lips with his, reaching up to cup my cheek. I open for him instantly, savoring the taste and feel of him. He slides his fingers into my hair with a claiming touch.

"When can I see you naked and spread out for me again?" he breathes against my lips.

A soft moan escapes me as goosebumps rise on my skin, anticipation filling me. "Tomorrow night?"

He rumbles a pleased sound in the back of his throat, and my clit throbs. "Can't wait."

Shane steps into the living room, three bowls in hand, his icy gaze lingering everywhere we touch. "Dinner is served."

Straightening, I tuck my hair behind my ears. "Oh, wow, that looks amazing."

"Kale caesar with salmon, pretty simple. May I join you?" Shane juts his chin toward the spot on my other side.

"Please."

I glance at Linc to see his reaction, but he just smiles as he grabs two of the bowls and hands one to me. Shane smoothly folds himself next to me as I accept the salad, and I swallow roughly as his firm thigh presses against mine. Being sandwiched between them is an intoxicating experience. They're both athletic and toned, though Linc carries more bulk. I find myself wondering how different they are in other places, and I feel my cheeks heat. *Get yourself under control, Lex. One client situationship at a time.*

Linc flicks on the TV. "Okay, Lex. I have a super important question for you. Do you like *Bake Off?*"

"Um, who doesn't?!"

"Thank goodness," Shane mutters, his tone indulgent.

As Linc pulls up the show, I snuggle into the couch. I'm absently aware of how normal it feels, how comfortable. I don't think I've ever felt as settled in my own home as I do here, in a house I've barely spent three hours in. Being around Linc and

Shane is natural, if I ignore the visceral way my body reacts to theirs. *Both of theirs.*

Fifteen minutes and one stellar signature bake later, I'm the last to finish my salad. I gather up their bowls and take them to the kitchen despite their protests. Shane picks up the appetizer tray and follows.

"I'm glad you stayed," he says softly, standing next to me as we load the sink.

"Well, you didn't give me much of a choice," I tease, "but I'm glad, too. Thank you for the delicious meal."

My hand brushes his as we both reach for the sponge, and electricity crackles between us. His eyes catch mine, those icy blue depths sucking me in, and I stop breathing for a moment.

"It was my pleasure."

I shiver at the low rasp of his voice, and his eyes flare. He swallows, watching me watch his Adam's apple bob. Standing this close to him is the ultimate temptation, and I fleetingly wonder if I'm supposed to feel guilty for eye-fucking this man while the one I submitted to a week ago is in the next room. *All I feel is turned the hell on.*

"I've got this," he says, so calmly I wonder if the lust is one-sided. "Go snuggle with Linc. He needs it."

And then Shane Kelly winks at me. I've never gone weak in the knees from a wink, but I do then. Shane smirks when he sees me sway. *Get it together, Lex.*

Who am I to disobey his order? I pad back to the couch and slip under Linc's arm, cuddling close to finish the episode currently playing. Shane joins us moments later.

As he gets comfortable, he reaches over and grasps my ankle, pulling my foot into his lap. I blink at him owlishly, then look up to find Linc's dimple on show as he watches us.

"Those heels look like they wreak havoc on your feet,"

Shane explains, before digging his thumbs into my arch and making me moan.

"Careful, beautiful." Linc's voice is low and teasing. "Make that sound too many times, and I'll have no choice but to ravish you, audience and all."

I squeeze my eyes shut and try to hold back the whimper his words elicit as my mind conjures an image of me, naked and under Linc while Shane watches. My foot jerks in Shane's hands as he hits a particularly tender spot, and the whimper escapes. Surrounded by their throaty chuckles, I can't stop my imagination from taking that image and running wild. Through the surprise and incredulity at my presumptuousness, all I can think is *yes fucking please*.

Chapter 13

Shane

It's been three days since Lex visited our place, but I still feel her presence like a physical thing. I can't sit on the couch without thinking of Linc's expression as he looked down at her, then up to me. Can't be at our dining table without Dec's eyes lingering on the chair she used, his brows drawing down as his gaze unfocused. Can't stand at the sink without the ghost of her touch whispering against my hand, heat washing through me.

The satisfaction in Linc's eyes is dangerous. He told me about Lex's rules and seemed happy enough with them, but I suspect that won't be the case in three months. He and Lex are tiptoeing through a minefield of potential heartbreak, and Linc is too caught up to realize it.

He isn't the only one. Declan is spending more time in the basement than ever before, his fuse short and volatile. The war he's waging internally is fueled by Linc's moon-eyed focus on Lex. Whether Dec's surliness is because of concern for his brother or jealousy is a mystery I've yet to solve.

"Welcome to Athena Ventures," the same perky blonde from before greets me as I walk into Lex's lobby. She's standing, purse in hand, her day almost done. "I'm afraid the office is closing. Do you have an appointment?"

"No, but Miles said I could come up."

"Oh, excellent. He mentioned you'd be along. You know where her office is?"

"I do."

"Great, I'll buzz you back."

"Thanks, have a good night," I call over my shoulder, mentally mapping the path to Lex's office based on the diagram Miles sent over.

To say Lex's assistant was surprised to receive my call is an understatement. He'd been speechless, which seems to be a rare occurrence, when I announced my intent. Once he gathered his wits, he immediately sent me all the information I needed.

Reaching her office, I peer in for a moment. Lex sits at her desk, focused intently on her computer monitor. Her jaw-length hair, cut blunt and angled toward her face, is done in light waves today, parted precisely down the center as always. I can see she's kicked off her black stilettos under her desk, and I wonder how she'd feel if I crawled under there and gave her another foot rub. *Focus, Kelly.*

I shift to tap on the doorframe, and she looks up in surprise.

"Shane." She straightens, pushing her chair back smoothly. "I didn't know you were stopping by."

"I know." I step into the room, pointing at her couch and raising a brow in askance.

"By all means," she gestures toward the couch and stands, walking over barefoot to join me and fold herself into one plush corner. "Is everything okay?"

"I'm your ride."

She blinks. "I have a driver."

"Do you ever give her a night off?"

"Of course I do." She shakes her head, one hand raised. "I'm sorry, am I in the Twilight Zone? Are you seriously in my office on a Thursday just to drive me home?"

I cough a laugh. "No Twilight Zone. And I might have an ulterior motive, but let's save that for later."

She studies me for a long moment. "Suspense and I aren't friends, Shane. Best you share what's on your mind if you want me to come with you willingly."

Ignoring the way my cock twitches at the thought of tossing her over my shoulder, I pause and meet her gaze. There's an amused tilt to her lips, but I don't miss the demand in her tone.

"You're different here, in your domain, you know. I can see why Linc's drawn to you."

Understanding flickers in her eyes. "I see. I was wondering when this would come up."

She gets elegantly to her feet, walking over to her desk to toe her shoes on and snatch her phone. She's silent, despite the office's employees having long since left. In response to my teasing expression, she tsks.

"I'm sure I don't have to tell you that reputation is everything in this town. Mine is exceptional. I intend to keep it that way."

Nodding, I rise and meet her by the door, pulling her bag off the hook beside it, leaning close as I do. "I can understand that. And I didn't come here to cause a scene, Lex. Just wanted to talk."

"And drive me home." Her eyes sparkle as she ushers me through the door.

"Yes, well, Linc's mentioned your hectic schedule a few times. Figured this would be a good time to catch you."

Her eyes widen a bit as she leads me through the deserted office, surprised at the information. "Has he, now?" She swallows thickly. "Are you out front?"

"I am." I hold the door open for her, waiting as she checks to be sure it's locked before she guides us to the staircase behind the elevator bank. "All he talks about lately is work, and you."

Linc had practically shoved me out the door on my way here, his eyes bright. He's sent three texts already to check in, and I've ignored every one.

She sighs as we traipse down the stairs, pausing on the final landing and meeting my gaze. "I see. Are you here as a client or Lincoln's friend?"

"He's more brother than friend, and I think you know the answer to that." I step out into the cool evening air, pointing to my black Jeep at the nearby curb as she follows me through the door.

"He seems to think you're supportive of...our arrangement."

"I'm supportive of Linc and whatever makes him happy, and you're fitting that bill. For now. But keep using words like 'arrangement' and you might find that changes."

Her brows press together as she walks beside me, her heels tapping a staccato on the concrete. "We've been very clear about what's between us. No strings."

"I know. And I get it. Two attractive people, two consenting adults. It all makes sense, on paper."

She crosses her arms as we reach my car, waiting for me to unlock it. "It's only been a week, Shane. I can't imagine Linc's made any confessions that warrant an intervention."

I face her as I open the passenger door. "You're right, he hasn't. But I know him better than I know myself, and I'm asking you to be thoughtful. And gentle."

She considers my words as I round the hood and let myself into the driver's seat. I'm grateful she's taking the conversation seriously, though I expected nothing less.

Lex drops into the seat with a huff. "Are you asking me not to see Lincoln...recreationally?"

An amused grunt escapes, and I shake my head as I start the engine. "You can 'recreate' all you want. I'm just asking you to take care. This might be all over for you in three months, but if the last week is any indication, we'll all be feeling your presence long past the launch."

"I see. Are you worried about Solum?"

Her eyes are on me as I drive toward her swanky neighborhood. I wish I could look at her, but I'm far more concerned with her safety than solid eye contact.

"Not a bit. We're all professionals. I know we'll make the right calls for the business, no matter what else happens."

She doesn't look away as she mulls over my words. I appreciate her calm and measured response, especially since it's not what I'm used to from Dec or Linc. The older Wilde tends to react first, ask questions later, and his brother only has one energy level: high.

After a few minutes of silence, she turns to me. The air between us shifts, the warm sense of welcome slipping away.

"You clearly care about Lincoln, and that's the frame I'm using for this highly inappropriate conversation that crosses all sorts of boundaries. I don't need to make excuses for myself or him, but to match your energy and openness, I will share that there is nothing about what's happening between me and Linc that I would call normal."

I can feel her fierce gaze burning into me, her relaxed posture against the seat in direct contrast to the firmness of her tone.

"I have never taken up with a client before," she continues, "and I don't do relationships. I have no interest in long-term. Lincoln and I are enjoying each other, but it's new territory for me."

Her voice sharpens, and my cock stirs. I understand why

Linc is smitten. I'm not blind, nor am I immune to her power. Her confidence and control are both admirable and sexy as fuck, and the sheer suggestion a woman like her could be on her knees for either of us is an undeniable aphrodisiac.

"You should also know, Shane, that I am *always* thoughtful. You don't know me, so I'm sharing this with you plainly to make a point. I do not make decisions lightly. I am not a spontaneous person, and I don't do things on a whim. I understand you're concerned about your brother, and I respect it. But please don't come into my place of business and suggest I am anything other than considerate in the decisions I make, professional or otherwise."

She looks out the windshield, giving me her profile as I pull into her neighborhood. "I appreciate the ride, but it wasn't necessary. I'm fully capable of taking care of myself. I've been doing it just fine for the better part of forty years."

I let the silence thicken as I turn into her driveway, then park by her front door. She drops her hand to the handle immediately, but I chuckle and lock the doors. "I think you misunderstood my message."

"Oh? Please, set me right." She twists in her seat, folding her arms.

I'm inordinately pleased she doesn't shrink away. But I can see the subtle markers of a woman with her defenses raised. I lean into her space and plant my hands on either side of her—one on the dash and the other on the center console. She doesn't flinch, her pupils dilating as she inhales sharply, and arousal flashes through me. *Oh, you like that, don't you? It's always the strong ones who want to succumb.*

"You have no idea the effect you have on him, do you?" My voice is low, intimate. "No idea your mere presence calls to him—to all of us—like a fucking beacon. You walk in the room with your own gravity, drawing us toward you the moment we're close enough to feel the pull."

I cock my head to the side as her breathing quickens, wanting desperately to get lost in the building tension.

"You think it's normal for Declan to be tied up in knots, or for Lincoln to give a shit about what his flavor of the month eats for dinner? You said what's between you and Linc isn't normal for you. News flash, Lex, nothing is normal for any of us right now. And the common denominator is you."

Her pulse throbs at the side of her neck, her lips parted as she looks up at me. My nostrils flare as I stare her down, then lean closer.

"I picked you up tonight to make sure you know the power you wield, and I'm glad I did. It's clear you have no idea the havoc you could wreak on Lincoln, the destruction you could cause our family." I take a deep breath through my nose, trying to calm myself. It's a mistake, because her fucking floral scent makes me almost feral. "And you need to realize Lincoln will walk into that destruction willingly, if only for one. More. Taste."

Her eyelids flutter as I growl out the last three words, her eyes nearly black with desire.

"And the most ridiculous part?" I lean another inch closer, struggling to keep my eyes from her lips as I drop my voice to a harsh whisper. "He's not the only fucking one. You have us and our future in the palm of your hand, and you don't even realize it. One week, one fucking dinner at our house, and we're already revolving around *you*."

We're both vibrating, bodies taut and breathing shallow. Pushing forcefully away, I nearly slam into my seat, the Jeep rocking with my movement. No good can come of giving in to my lust tonight. I need to gather my wits, and she needs to decide what to do with everything I dumped on her.

"Have all the fun you want with Linc. Just don't forget how powerful you are."

The shuddering sound of her slow exhale is the perfect exit music as I step out of the car to get her door, my cock hard and my heart beating double time. I didn't intend to give so much of myself away, but I don't regret a word. *Your move, Lex. Let's see what you're made of.*

Chapter 14

Lex

Two weeks had never gone by so fast. Work was wildly busy, but it was the moments in between that were speeding my days, which was a first. After Shane's little visit, I considered reestablishing my boundaries with Linc and going back to just business. But he showed up the next morning with his dimpled grin for our run, and all thoughts of pushing him away fled. I'd leaned into him as he wrapped his arms around me and devoured my mouth in a fiery kiss, then laughed as he slapped my ass and jogged away backwards, arms spread in challenge. I can't imagine letting that side of him go. *Not yet, anyway.*

My phone buzzes with a text, drawing my attention away from my laptop.

LINC

you're distracting

My eyebrows rise. I'm alone in my office at Athena, and I don't have plans to meet up with Linc or his partners until tomorrow.

ME

How so?

LINC

I can still smell you

Heat flashes through me, my clit buzzing with the memory of what we did last night. I shift in my office chair, spinning slowly to face away from the door.

ME

Hmmm, good. We're even.

LINC

even?

ME

I can still taste you.

The three little dots showing he's typing pop up immediately. I roll my lips between my teeth as I smile, imagining him leaning his head back and groaning as he reads my message.

LINC

feeling naughty, are we?

careful, beautiful

I glance over to confirm my office door is closed, then unbutton my blazer and shimmy it open, revealing the black lace crop top beneath. Snapping a quick picture of my torso, from my smirk to my waist, I send it off to him.

A soft knock draws my attention, and I pull my blazer closed before spinning my chair back around to meet Van's amused gaze.

"Am I interrupting?"

"Interrupting what?"

He motions to the phone in my hand as he lets himself in and strides to the sitting area. "Picture time?"

Rolling my eyes, I stand, tucking a hand in my pocket as I walk over to join him on the couch.

"Thanks for stopping by."

"Miles was...insistent."

"I'm sure he was. Contrary to how he might've framed things, there's no emergency."

"Lex, unless I hear otherwise from you or a first responder, I'm always going to assume his urgency is manufactured. He's worse than the boy who cried wolf."

"He's just...enthusiastic."

Van grunts, moving to the bar cart.

"Are we celebrating something?" I glance at my watch. "Feels a bit early for scotch, if not."

"Am I here because of the news about Greenstar Labs and P&L?"

Sighing, I flop into an armchair. "Yes."

"Then no, no celebration. But a drink is called for all the same."

He offers me a tumbler as he takes a seat on the couch.

"Thank you. Though I don't expect this conversation to be difficult."

"Suit yourself." He takes a long drink of his scotch, then looks over at me. "I didn't expect your brother's name to show up alongside Anne-Marie's."

"Neither did I. But it's a dilemma."

The Bulletin published an interview with Anne-Marie this morning, and it featured statements of support for her "revolutionary technology" from the Greenstar board of directors. As the newest member, my brother was quoted.

"What's the dilemma?"

I meet Van's stony gaze. "Whether I should warn him about

what's coming. Greenstar and its board, particularly those who are vocal in their support of Anne-Marie and her tech, are going to be in hot water if all goes as planned. I know Nate wouldn't extend me the same courtesy, but I've long prided myself on having more integrity than the men in my family. It feels like the right thing to do."

"You sound decided."

Shaking my head, I take a sip of scotch. "I'm not objective on this one. Your opinion is valuable to me."

"Lex, you know what I'm going to say."

I did. Van knew more of my history than most. I didn't feel the need to air my family's dirty laundry often, but the context had been important for him to understand before he joined Athena. My father founded one of the largest financial services companies in the country, and I dreamed of being his successor. Unfortunately, I was born with a vagina, and thus became his biggest disappointment instead. The moment he was born, my brother became the heir to P&L.

If that had been the end of it, perhaps a relationship could've been salvaged. But I was a smart, driven kid, and I wanted to earn my place in the family business more than anything. It took my father throwing me out for daring to dream of a life beyond being someone's wife for me to realize there was no place for me to earn. And, though he'd had every opportunity to take my side, Nate had simply sat back and watched it all happen, soaking up the poison my father spewed about me along the way.

"I don't owe Nate shit."

Van leans forward, setting his empty tumbler on the coffee table with a loud thunk. "You really fucking don't. And you're right, he wouldn't offer you the same courtesy. He'd gladly watch Athena burn if the tables were turned."

My eyes close as I lean my head back. "I know."

"And I hate this, but you're also right that it's the right thing to do."

I look over at him, mouth parting in surprise. "Say that again."

He glowers. "No. You heard me."

"I expected you to play Devil's advocate more staunchly than that, Van."

He grunts. "Maybe you've rubbed off on me."

"Me?" I chuckle. "I'd wager it's your wife's influence more than mine."

A soft smile curls his lips, one I only saw when he thought or spoke of Cami. "You might be right."

Sighing, I gather both of our glasses and set them on the lower shelf of the bar cart. "So, I need to set a meeting with Nate."

"Unfortunately. Don't want a paper trail unless you're ready for it to be public knowledge."

"I wish I didn't have to contingency plan for communications with my own fucking family," I mutter, returning to the armchair.

"You deserve better," Van snarls.

"We can agree on that." I roll my shoulders back, physically shaking off the pall of my family. "While we're on a related topic, things are going well for Solum."

Van takes the topic change in stride, swallowing his ire. For now. "I've heard good things from Parker."

"He and the team have done well. They've gone a long way to deepen trust with the partners."

"You'll be comfortable handing the account over after the Summit?"

"Absolutely, Parker's earned it."

While the statement is true, the thought of handing the account over in its entirety feels...wrong. We're only a month in, but I can't quite imagine my weeks without meetings with Linc, Shane, and Declan. It was more than the company on my runs, more than the sex–though that was certainly a plus. The seamlessness of how we worked together had a strong ripple effect. I'd had more proper meals in the last month than in the three months prior. I was sleeping better, and I felt more fit than I had in my twenties.

"I'm glad to hear it." Van's voice draws me out of my thoughts. "I think Parker's going to build our sustainability portfolio, then strike out on his own."

I cross my arms slowly. "Makes sense. Any idea of timeframe?"

"Three to five years."

"Do we have a succession plan? He'll leave big shoes to fill."

"I'm working on it."

"Good." I stand, stretching my arms over my head. "On that note, I'm sure Miles is about to barge in here and send me off to my next meeting."

Van follows and walks to the door, pausing with a hand on the doorframe. "You and Cami may have rubbed off on me, but you still don't owe Nate shit. If you don't want to speak to him, don't."

"I know. I'm sure it won't be a highlight of my week, but I'll sleep better knowing my integrity is intact."

"You want company?"

My expression softens. "No, Van, but thank you. I've been handling Nate since we were in diapers. He doesn't scare me."

Van scoffs. "He shouldn't. But if you think he's going to get nasty without a buffer, I'll be there."

"Nate's liable to be nastier if I bring you," I chuckle. "He's well aware of your disdain for him."

He nods. "I'm glad. Let me know how it goes."

"I will."

As Van heads toward his office, I settle back in my chair. I glance at my phone and am surprised to see far more text notifications than normal.

LINC

fuckkkkkkk

goddamnit

are you busy?

would a quickie in the parking garage violate the rules?

Lex...

you didn't seriously send me that and ghost me

there will be consequences if you don't answer me in the next 5 min

His last text had come through ten minutes before. Smirking, I write him back.

ME

Oops. Had a meeting.

LINC

Pick a number between 5 and 10

Heat flashes through me, starting in my core before suffusing my limbs. My clit tingles with the promise of Linc's punishments, which I've come to covet. They walk this beautiful line between pleasure, pain, anticipation, and excitement I've never felt before. I crave his dominance as much as I crave him.

ME

9

LINC

good girl

when are you free tonight?

ME

10

LINC

I'll be at yours at 10:15

ME

I'll be waiting.

LINC

preferably naked and kneeling

My breath catches as I picture the scene: me, naked and kneeling, facing the bed and away from the door. Linc coming in on quiet feet, trailing his fingers along my bare shoulders as he praises me for my patience. For my obedience. For my willingness to be there, ready for him, knowing a punishment was coming...nine times over. *Holy shit, it's scary how much I crave that feeling of just...letting go.*

ME

Yes, sir.

The three little dots jump for a moment, then my phone rings with an incoming video call from Linc. I start to glance at my calendar, then think *fuck it* and answer anyway. His face fills my phone screen, eyes dark and expression hungry.

"You're fucking killing me, Lex," he growls.

"You liked that, then?"

"You tell me."

He angles the camera down, giving me an eyeful of his hard

cock straining his jeans. As I watch, he palms it, squeezing briefly. I lick my lips, and he groans.

"Fucking temptress. I need to hear you say it."

"Say what?"

I give him my most innocent expression. He smirks in response.

"You know what, beautiful. Tonight."

"Tonight," I agree.

"You're going to be waiting for me? Ready for me?"

"I will."

He makes a guttural sound, his eyes half-lidded. "I can't fucking wait."

"Neither can I." I squirm in my chair, my thighs pressing together, and his expression heats further.

"I'm going to save this for you." He pans back to his lap, hand still on his hard cock, then back to his face. "You do the same. No touching. Your orgasms are mine today, you hear me?"

I nod, my pussy clenching. "I hear you."

"That's my girl," he breathes. "See you tonight."

Before I can say anything else, he's gone. I melt into my office chair for a moment, going boneless as want and desire roll through me. Goosebumps had risen on my arms at his command, excitement pooling in my belly. I know the waiting will only make the eventual release that much sweeter and more powerful. And if it's on the heels of his punishment? I whimper aloud at the thought. *Lincoln Wilde, what are you doing to me?*

Chapter 15

Linc

Lex is wearing a skin tight jacket in light green, a near perfect match for her eyes. She grins at me from her porch as I park, one leg bent behind her as she stretches for our run. I get out of the car and bound up the steps, sweeping her up in my arms as I have every morning for the last five weeks. She laughs and melts into me, smiling into my eyes before kissing me soundly. As I release her, I know the thing brewing between us is different. *And I don't know if I'm more scared or excited about it. Yet.*

"Usual route?" Lex asks, dancing back from me on her toes.

"Whatever you want, beautiful."

Her smile softens at the pet name, and I love that she still reacts to it. Like she isn't used to hearing it, but likes when she does.

We stretch for a few minutes in silence, her concentrating on properly warming up and me focusing entirely on the view in front of me. While still dark outside, her porch light illuminates enough of Lex to appreciate. She takes a long step backward, dropping into a lunge, perfectly showcasing her killer legs and calves.

I have to make myself stop staring before I try to drag her inside for a different kind of cardio. That's not why I show up for these morning runs, though I wouldn't complain if she was game. No, I come to keep her company on the dark, quiet streets. That, and it gives me an opportunity to spend time in her orbit. She might not want post-coital pillow talk, but I'll take what I can get.

"I'm ready. You good?" I ask, as I gesture toward the sidewalk.

"Let's do it!" Lex skips down the steps and begins jogging as we exit her driveway.

I let her set the pace, happy to take her lead. She's incredibly fit, and the run had admittedly been a challenge that first week, but I'd adjusted to the early wake up and conditioning in the month since. *I've never had better motivation.*

Lex clears her throat a few blocks into our route, interrupting my wandering thoughts. "So, I've been wondering. What did you see in Anne-Marie?"

I sputter, completely caught off guard by her question. I struggle for a moment on how to explain my former friend and business partner.

"Huh, well...she was incredibly self-assured, confident. She knew what she wanted and how to go after it. You just knew when she set her sights on something, she was going to get it. That was appealing to me. Introducing her to the guys and bringing her into the business seemed like a no brainer."

"I see."

A long silence passes, the only noise our steady breaths and footfalls against the pavement. I turn my head to peer at Lex's face to try and discern what she was thinking, but her gaze remains on the street ahead.

"And the guys—there was no animosity about you sleeping with her?"

I chuckle at the idea of Dec or Shane caring who I sleep with, and she glances over in confusion.

"Nah, Dec and Shane knew our hookup wasn't anything serious. I didn't–don't–do serious."

"Why not?"

I wipe the sweat from my brow with my sleeve. I'm not sure if it's due to today's pace or Lex's direct line of questioning, but the results are the same. She doesn't beat around the bush when she wants to know something.

"Well, I'm not sure if I've ever put much thought into it to be honest. Shane joined our family when I was a kid, and the three of us did everything together. All the girls I dated would get annoyed that my brothers were always around and would want me to choose. I'm sure you can guess who won every time."

Lex laughs and nods, and I continue.

"And once we started seriously building Procerus, I didn't have the time or energy to think about finding a serious relationship, so I stuck to casual dating that didn't require much effort."

"That I can understand perfectly." Lex steers us into a park, the asphalt trail curving through the trees.

"What...what about Declan and Shane?" she asks hesitantly.

I smirk. *Ah, someone's curious.*

"You'll have to ask them yourself. In the spirit of transparency, I will say this..." I take a deep inhale. "Shane and I have...shared partners in the past."

Lex grinds to a halt.

I stumble, fighting the inertia propelling me forward to turn and gauge Lex's reaction.

She blinks at me, expressionless. "Excuse me? Shared? As in, you've both dated the same person."

Might as well address this head on.

"As in, we've fucked the same person. At the same time."

Lex rolls her lips between her teeth before licking them while nodding absently. In the dimly lit sky, I can see the gears in her brain turning, processing the information.

Evidently deciding on something, she lets out a deep breath before resuming her jog.

What's going on in that brilliant head of yours, Lex?

The silence is going to kill me; I have to know if my honesty snuffed out the fire building between us.

"Do you want to know more about it?" *Do you want us to demonstrate with you?*

Lex swipes her brow, tucking hair behind her ear and meeting my eyes momentarily.

"No. Yes. Fuck, I don't know. That's...a lot to take in."

I laugh on an exhale. "Alright, no details for now. You just let me know when you have any other questions you'd like answered."

We continue in silence for a few minutes, then Lex slows to a walk. She turns to me as I follow suit, a bright flush in her cheeks and her eyes wide.

"Is Shane...like you?" She glances away, laughing softly as though to herself. "I mean, does he like to be in control?"

My weight shifts as my body reacts to her question. "He does, but he's not like me."

Her brow creases as her gaze returns to mine. "What does that mean?"

Chuckling, I shake my head. "He's...hard. There's nothing soft about Shane Kelly."

"Oh, and your pussy slaps and spankings are 'soft'?" She mimes air quotes, her tone teasing.

The corner of my mouth tugs up. "They are compared to him. I'm a total sweetheart, don't you know?"

Her lips part as she stares at me, blinking. After a long

exhale, she rolls her neck from one side to the other, then starts running again. I grin as I quickly follow.

I know there will be more questions, and I'm happy to answer any concerns or curiosities she might have. Shane won't mind me being honest. I can tell he's as attracted to Lex as I am. More than a month of her in our space and I see right through his icy exterior. He's wound so fucking tight it's only a matter of time before he snaps. And now that I've had her? I can only dream of seeing her on her knees for us. *The fun we could have.*

Chapter 16

Lex

"Things are coming together, gentlemen."

Linc smiles, and Shane nods in agreement. We're once again sitting around their dining table for our weekly check in, this time in the early evening. Declan's interview is three weeks away, and we already spent a solid hour aligning on the key points he needs to hit in his conversation with Cass. His eyes flick to me as I speak, then drift away.

"Are we done?" Declan asks absently, eyes on his phone.

I glance at the other two. "That's all I had for tonight. Anything you need to cover?"

"Nothing from me." Declan stands and turns to go, then pauses and looks back at me. "Thank you."

My eyes widen as I nod in response, still taken aback when anything other than skepticism or business strategy passes his lips. Before I can rib him about it, Declan walks down the hall, then disappears through a door I assume leads to the garage. *And there it is.*

"Don't mind him. He's been heading back to the lab most nights, burning the midnight oil. He's usually not home until late," Linc offers, and awareness prickles across my skin. He leans back in his chair, raising his arms over his head to stretch, almost overly casual. "What do you think, Shane? Do we have anything else for Lex tonight?"

You're not fooling anyone, Linc. My eyes track to Shane, feeling something significant gathering in the air between us.

"Nothing business-related." Shane's deep voice rumbles through the room, and I feel it between my thighs.

Linc's words from two days ago reverberate in my brain. *There's nothing soft about Shane Kelly.* Meeting his piercing blue gaze, I have no trouble believing that's true. He may be the quietest of them, but there is a sharpness there that calls to the softest parts of me.

I cock an eyebrow at Shane. "Let's hear it, then."

"How do you feel about sharing, Lex?"

My mouth goes dry as I swallow roughly, heat flaring through me. It had been hard to think of anything other than being shared by them since Shane had leaned over me and asked me to be gentle with Linc. And Linc's revelations during our run earlier in the week only served to fuel my fantasies.

I glance over to find Linc lounging in his seat, smirking as his eyes ping back and forth between us. Shane's gaze never leaves mine, those glacial blues trained on me, as though he can read my every move. I appreciate his directness and reciprocate in kind.

"I'm...open to it." *Please.*

"Have you been shared before?"

I laugh. "Are you asking me if I've ever had a threesome, Shane?"

The ghost of a smile crosses his lips. "Yes."

"Then, no. I've never been shared before."

Linc groans, slumping further in his chair as he tosses his head back. "You're fucking killing me. Both of you."

Shane ignores him entirely. "But you're open to it."

"Under the right circumstances."

"Which are?"

They both watch me intently. Linc had propped his forearms on the table, his hands clasped as he leans toward me. Shane sits kicked back in his own chair, legs wide–the picture of relaxed male confidence. He's wearing a dress shirt and slacks, which I've come to think of as his uniform. While Linc often worked in jeans and tees, both Shane and Declan opted for business casual, and I loved it.

"I'm a practical person, Shane. I'd want to feel safe."

"There's more to you than that," Linc murmurs. "You like it hot."

I smirk at him. "Attraction is a must, of course. And passion."

"What else?"

My eyes fly back to Shane. I'm at an inflection point, like the next words out of my mouth can pave an unknown path. *It's now or never, Lex.*

"I'd want to trust them enough to let them be the ones in control."

Linc crosses his arms on the table and drops his head onto them as he groans. "I fucking told you."

Shane's lips lift into a devilish half-smile. "So you did."

I'm neither surprised nor bothered to hear they've talked about me. The possibility of something...more...had been simmering for weeks. Ever since Shane dug his thumbs into my arch and Linc planted the idea of the three of us in my head. And damn it, I work way too hard not to let myself enjoy something good when it comes along, uncharted as it might be.

"What's on offer, boys?" I tease.

Shane's eyes blaze at the nickname, but I don't take it back. While I might let them take control in the bedroom, I know I will always be the one in charge. And even though my gut tells me I'm safe with these two, it doesn't hurt to remind them of that truth.

"Us." Linc shrugs, like it's simple.

Can it really be that simple?

"Here, tonight. For now," Shane adds.

"Presumptuous of you."

"You might be surprised to learn he's an optimist," Linc quips. "What do you say, Lex?"

I look between them both. "When will Declan be back?"

"Late."

"Hm." I study their faces, ignoring the thrill of anticipation running through me. "If I say yes, what's next?"

Shane straightens, then rises to his feet. "Linc tells me you're willing to obey. Is that right?"

My heart thunders in my chest as my breath stutters. I can feel the wetness gathering in my underwear at the thought of the two of them touching me. Guiding me. Praising me. At the same time. *Is this really happening?*

"I might be."

His eyes glitter with dark promise, his gaze hard. "I hope so. Go upstairs, second door on the right. You have five minutes."

"Five minutes to do what?"

"Get ready."

"Naked and kneeling, Lex," Linc murmurs, his warm brown eyes intense.

I take a deep, steadying breath, my eyes falling closed. The feeling of being poised at the edge of something big, something deep and wide and as exciting as it is terrifying, swirls in my gut. Linc was fun, and sweet, and something I didn't know I'd needed. I suspect Shane's an entirely different animal, and being at their combined mercy will be an experience I'll wear imprinted on my soul. *Am I ready for whatever happens next?* When I open my eyes, I meet Shane's arctic gaze head on.

"You know my rules?"

Shane nods.

"Good."

Linc flashes his dimpled grin, his eyes blazing with want as Shane's lips curve into a tiny, satisfied smile. They can't look more different, a true juxtaposition: one warm and giving, the other cold and unyielding. *Imagine being caught between them.* My belly swoops at the thought.

I rise calmly to my feet, finish the last third of my wine in one long swallow, and turn for the stairs. The faint sounds of low conversation and scraping chair legs reach me as I climb to the second story. Anticipation coils in my gut as I walk through the second door on the right as instructed.

The room's simple, cozy, and modern. *This is so Shane.* A king bed sits on the opposite wall, with an armchair and ottoman off to the right. The gray and blue color palette is masculine and calming, and the military neatness of the space is exactly what I expect from the quiet tech genius. A plush, dark blue bench sits at the foot of the bed, and I step up to it as I slip out of my cashmere sweater. I fold it carefully, setting it aside on the bench as I unhook my bra with my other hand.

After removing my clothing and organizing it in a tidy pile, I move to the center of the bench and take one large step back. Faint sounds filter up from the main floor, but I can't decipher them. Sighing deeply, I lower myself to my knees, then cross my arms behind my back. There's comfort in knowing I'm no longer the one calling the shots, no longer responsible for a million and three decisions. *I'm on my knees, naked, with no idea of what the next few hours will hold...and I have never felt so fucking free.*

Moments after the last of my tension melted away, two sets of footsteps start up the stairs. The hairs at the back of my neck rise in anticipation, my nipples tightening to stiff points. I can hear them enter the room, hear the sharp intake of breath from Linc, but don't turn my head.

"Fucking hell, look at you." Linc's voice is low and reverent, and I smile to myself.

Firm fingers trail along my shoulder, then Shane's feet and legs come into view. I keep my gaze down, waiting. He grips my jaw, lifting my head to meet his gaze.

Shane stares down at me, his nostrils flaring as he takes in my naked body. His pupils are blown, but he's still the picture of calm control.

"Linc, sit."

I hear Linc move over to the cushioned armchair without question, following Shane's order.

"In here, I'm in charge," Shane says. "Do you understand?"

I nod.

"Speak up."

My eyes flash to his. "Yes."

He tilts his head to the side. It's a predatory move, but I read the intent loud and clear.

"Yes, sir," I correct myself.

There's no praise from Shane like I've come to expect, to crave, from Linc. Just a cool, assessing gaze as he looks down at me. He reaches out and caresses my jaw, his large palm warm and his grip surprisingly gentle. I lean into his hand, my eyes fluttering closed as he lets out a soft sigh. It sounds like approval.

"What do you think, Linc?"

"She's stunning. Never seen anyone look so breathtaking on their knees."

Shane's hand slips away with a lingering touch as he makes a soft noise that sounds like agreement, and I open my eyes to watch him step back and sit on the bench before me. His gaze slips to my breasts, lingering on my hardened nipples, then down to my thighs.

"She looks needy."

Linc shifts off to my right, but I don't look away from Shane. "Needy and delicious."

"Are you hungry, Linc?"

"Starving," he growls.

Shane smirks as he reaches for the top button of his dress shirt, undoing it slowly before moving on to the next. "Lift that sexy ass off your heels and spread your knees."

A shiver slips down my spine as I obey.

"Your dessert is waiting, brother."

"Don't have to tell me twice."

I can see Linc rise to his feet out of the corner of my eye, then he's looming behind me. He strokes a warm, firm hand down my side, but before I can turn and melt into him, Shane's shirt gapes open and I see his bare chest for the first time. His toned, muscular, heavily tattooed chest. I gasp as he casually shrugs his shirt from his shoulders to reveal fully inked sleeves on both arms. *Holy fucking hell, and I thought he couldn't get any sexier.*

Before I can comment, something brushes against my inner knees and I look down to find Linc's face beneath me, that damn dimple taunting me as he grins.

"Sit down," he rasps, as he runs his hands along my backside, kneading the flesh.

"Wha—um. What?" My eyes flash up to Shane's as I try to process the inked Adonis in front of me while Linc's warm breath fans right over my pussy.

"C'mon, beautiful. I don't want to punish you right now, okay? Sit on my face, let me taste you."

Shane raises an eyebrow, as though daring me to defy a direct order a second time. As much as I love Lincoln's punishments, I want to see how they planned for this scene to play out. *Something tells me I won't be disappointed.*

Holding Shane's gaze while I lower myself onto Linc's mouth is the single most erotic moment of my life thus far. As Linc's tongue makes contact with my pussy, Shane's eyes darken and we all let out collective groans of lust and desire. He stands as he watches Lincoln devour me, unbuttoning his slacks and letting the fly hang open. I can see the head of his cock peeking out from the waistband of his boxer briefs, and I bite my lip in anticipation.

Linc's grip tightens on my hips as he pulls me down harder and presses his face up, spearing his tongue into my opening. I gasp and slump forward, wishing for something to hold on to. Shane shoves his slacks off and steps out of them, standing before me in his underwear. I look up to meet his gaze, and he smirks at me as he frees himself from his boxers. When I see what else he's been hiding behind his business casual attire, I freeze.

Beneath me, Linc chuckles as though he knows exactly what's happening, the vibration of the sound and soft gust of air from his breath making my pussy clench.

"Holy shit," I breathe, staring at the four barbells winking from the underside of Shane's hard cock. "You have a Jacob's Ladder."

"I do."

"How does that...work?" I stammer, struggling to think straight between Linc's talented tongue and the mouthwatering sight before me.

Shane chuckles as he lazily strokes his cock, fingers playing over the large balls on either end of each bar, teasing me. "Very well. It's better without a condom, though."

I blink. *Context switching is hard.* As though reading my mind, Linc backs off, teasing at my pussy lips instead of attacking my clit. He gives me enough reprieve to focus on something other than how fucking good it all feels.

"Better for who?"

"All of us." The heat in his gaze could melt a glacier. "We have test results, if you want them. We're both negative."

Linc nips at me gently and soothes a hand over my hip and side.

"No pressure," Shane murmurs. "It's up to you."

"I'm negative, too." I press my eyes closed briefly, considering. *Am I really going to break another rule?* The answer's inevitable. "And I have an IUD. Okay, yes. No condoms–"

I gasp, cutting myself off as Linc sucks my clit hard. I rock forward with pleasure, and Shane steps forward, suddenly right there.

"Hold onto me," he commands. By his tone, I know we're back in the scene.

My hands fly to his hips as I steady myself against the onslaught of pleasure caused by Linc's tongue and teeth, my breathing ragged. As my air washes over his straining erection, his cock pulses, and I groan as my mouth waters. *I want him on my tongue.*

"Something you want, Lex?" Shane murmurs, threading a hand into my hair.

"Yes, sir," I manage, nodding frantically through a soft whimper as Linc's teeth graze my clit.

"Tell me."

"I want you in my mouth."

Shane's grip moves to the back of my neck, tightening on my nape. "What does a good girl say?"

Linc circles my clit with his tongue, then sucks it roughly into his mouth as he palms my ass before firmly smacking one cheek.

Pleasure zips through me, my pulse thundering in my ears.

"Please," I manage, thighs shaking as my orgasm dances ever closer.

"You hear that, Linc? Hear how polite she is, even when she's hungry for my cock?"

"Mmmhmm," Linc hums, his lips against that tight bundle of nerves.

I gasp at the vibration and my eyes roll back as Shane's cock taps against my lips.

"Go on then. Be our good little slut and suck my cock while you ride Linc's face."

Our. Good. Little. Slut. A whole body shiver grips me as I open my mouth and greedily do as he asks, my fingers tightening on Shane's hips to steady myself. That commanding hand on my neck remains, grip sharp enough to edge the line between pleasure and pain to drive me wild.

I'm torn between the desire to make him feel good and the pleasure blossoming between my legs, Linc's relentless focus on getting me over that peak severely distracting. I gag around Shane as I try to gasp when Linc's teeth scrape my clit again. He licks long, broad strokes up my pussy as I recover, fisting the base of Shane's cock and hollowing my cheeks around as much of him as I can.

Shane groans in satisfaction, his hips thrusting slightly as his cock twitches in my mouth. The musky, male scent of him invades my senses, heightening my lust. As much as I love being between them, I'm desperate for more, so ready to be filled.

As I find my rhythm and push Shane close to his own release, Linc sucks rapidly on my clit and sends me hurtling unexpectedly over that ledge, a powerful orgasm unfurling through me. I groan around Shane as he slips from my mouth, my body contracting around the center of my pleasure, my thighs squeezing around Linc. He laps up my cum, licking me through the lingering pulses of ecstasy before sliding out from under me.

Breathing heavily and feeling dazed, I look up to find Shane watching me intently as he strokes his cock. Pre-cum drips from the head and over his fingers.

"What do you say to Linc?" he demands, voice ragged. *He's so close.*

I glance back to find Linc kneeling behind me, bare-chested and smirking with a heavy-lidded gaze. He walks forward on his knees until I can lean against him, and I sag against his muscled chest. We fit together perfectly.

"Thank you," I breathe.

Linc's hands smooth down my upper arms as he leans forward to trail open-mouthed kisses up my neck. Shane steps toward us, a feral gleam in his eyes that has my greedy cunt paying attention, even as the effects of my first release sit heavy in my limbs.

"Hold still, baby. I'm going to paint those gorgeous tits before I fuck that pretty pink pussy."

Chapter 17

Shane

It made sense that Linc was a little obsessed with Lex. As I watched that satisfied smile curve her lips while she leaned back in his arms, my cum dripping down her chest and stomach, I got it. Lex Livingston was a goddamn masterpiece. So strong and sure of herself, and yet so willing to obey, to surrender, to let us own her pleasure.

Linc kissed her neck and ear as I came, and after he looked up at me with a smirk, the smug asshole. The unspoken message was clear: *I told you.* And he fucking had. After their run the other day, he sat his ass down at the dining table, and announced to Dec and me: "Lex wants to know more about sharing, and I'm pretty sure she's your dream sub." I just couldn't quite believe how right he'd been.

She didn't give an inch outside of the bedroom. Not a goddamn inch. Even when we negotiated this fucking scene, she remained the picture of calm, controlled poise. Unruffled, unashamed, confident. And to see that woman, that fucking goddess, on her knees and covered in my cum? It made me feral.

"Look at that mess all over you," I rasp. "You love it, don't you? You love being our dirty girl."

Her eyes flutter closed as she squirms against Linc, who's still kissing and nibbling up and down her neck. His hands are splayed on her hips, careful not to smudge my handiwork. Not because he gives a shit it's my cum, but because he knows I have plans for my art.

"Do you need someone to clean you?"

She looks up at me through hooded eyes as I kneel before her, my hands on her toned thighs. Her lower lip folds between her teeth as she hums lazily. Linc and I lock gazes for a moment, then both still. He lifts his lips from her skin, and I remove my hands. Her brows furrow and she whimpers in protest.

"I can't hear you," I say, cocking my head.

Her lust-filled gaze clears a bit as she swallows thickly, then finds her voice. "Yes, please. I need someone to clean me, sir."

"Whose tongue do you want on you?" I demand.

"Yours, please, sir," she moans as Linc licks the hollow of her throat.

Desire pricks my skin and my cock twitches as I lean closer. "You want both our mouths on you at once, don't you?"

She takes a ragged breath as I lick the cum from above her navel with slow, short strokes.

"Fuck, yes." Writhing, she gasps as I sweep my tongue up to the valley between her breasts. "May I touch you, please?"

I growl against her skin, so fucking pleased she asked first. "You really are a good girl, aren't you? Yes, Lex, you can touch me, touch Linc. We want to feel you."

Linc murmurs in agreement as her body relaxes further. She settles more deeply against him, reaching one arm up to loop behind his head and hold him against her. Her other hand slips around my shaved head, her fingernails lightly scraping across my scalp. I groan in appreciation as I run my hands up her sides to cup her breasts, moving to lick the white rivulets off her supple skin.

Lex arches up into my mouth as I close my lips around her nipple, swirling my tongue around her and sucking it into my mouth. The sounds she makes are the sweetest encouragement. *She's so goddamn responsive.* I want to see how she reacts to everything—the sting of my hand on her ass, the little round bruises of my fingertips digging into her hips, the harsh mark of my mouth on her neck.

I move to her other breast, trailing one hand down her body to cup her pussy as I do. My fingers meet Linc's, and we move in unison to stroke her wet lips.

"Oh, god," she gasps, her body tightening between us.

"What is it?" Linc asks, one hand wrapping around her throat as the other teases her pussy lips in time with mine. "Tell us what we do to you, beautiful."

"Fuck," she whimpers. "It's so much, feeling both of you... like that." Her hips buck. "Overwhelming."

I gather her soft breast in my mouth, sucking hard before biting down gently. I don't go too hard, testing to see how she reacts, but my cock jerks at her sharp gasp and long moan. She clutches me to her with desperate fingers, pushing her body against me as she holds me. I take that as an invitation to bite harder next time and grin.

Linc starts to dip his finger into her pussy, and I look up to meet his gaze. He cocks a brow and I dip my chin, before bending back down to lick the last of my cum off her tanned skin. Together, we push one finger each into her pussy, as I bite down again—harder. Lex cries out, her fingers digging into me, and I lap soothingly at the bite mark, my tongue feeling the slight indentations left by my teeth.

"Color?" Linc murmurs, and I flash him an appreciative look.

"So fucking green," Lex gasps, her voice high and thready.

I chuckle as I sit back on my heels to watch her fuck our

hands. It's sexy as hell, watching our fingers disappearing into her tight cunt as she throws her head back against Linc's shoulder and her body tightens in pleasure. I can't help imagining our dicks disappearing into her in the same way, splitting her apart. Linc catches my gaze and I suspect he's thinking the same fucking thing. *Not tonight, Kelly. This is new for her...but someday, yes. Someday, we'll take her exactly like that.*

My cock is rock hard again at the thought, pre-cum leaking from the tip. I want to sink into her tight, wet heat more than I want fucking oxygen. She's close, but I slow the thrusts of my hand and Linc follows suit. Lex whines, her eyes snapping to mine.

"I want to feel you finish on my cock, want you to squeeze me as you come." I pull my hand from her, pushing Linc's away as I do. "Turn around and suck on Linc. Thank him for making you come."

Her immediate acquiescence to my demand makes heat simmer under my skin. I grip the base of my cock tightly to calm my raging erection.

"Ass up. Arch that back and spread your knees."

She complies as she fists Linc's cock and wraps her lips around him with enthusiasm, sucking and licking at his flushed tip. He groans and drops his head back, his hand fisting in her short hair. He doesn't shove her down on him, though, as he typically does in such encounters. His fingers flex and he holds her, then looks down and watches her through heavy lids, his lips parted in awe and reverence. I've never seen him like that. *Like it's her holding him captive, not his pleasure.*

I stare down at her tight ass in front of me, her glistening pussy on display, and push all the dangerous thoughts away. Stroking one hand along her hip, I lean over to kiss and nibble down her spine as I line my cock up at her entrance. This position was intentional; the barbells along my cock will tease at her G-spot with every stroke.

"Don't stop sucking that cock," I demand as I slowly breach her entrance, inching my way into her.

She mewls around Linc and tries to push her hips back to take more of me, but I grab her in an iron grip and hold her still.

"Don't be greedy," I admonish.

After smacking first one pert cheek, then the next–and enjoying her appreciative moans and the way her pussy clamps down on me–I resume my torturous pace. I have to stretch her carefully. She needs to be ready before I can pound into her like I want. Finally, I bottom out, my pelvis tight against her ass. Her body trembles as she holds back the urge to fuck against me, and she channels that energy into swallowing Linc right down.

"Holy shit!" he yelps, his body tensing as she gags, then swallows again. "Fucking hell, that's so good."

She hums in response, and he groans as I start to pull back slowly. Faster than I went in, but nowhere near the pace I'm building to. Lex's tight, soft walls flutter around me as my piercings drag over her most sensitive spot.

"Tell me what she looks like, Linc."

He bites his lip before answering, his gaze never leaving her face. "Wrecked, man. Tears and all. Never looked more stunning."

Lex tightens around me and I moan. "Our dirty girl likes praise, hm? Let's see if she can keep that cock in her mouth until you come."

She pulses around me again, and I brace a hand on her lower back, the other tight on her hip. Without warning, I snap my hips and thrust forcefully back into her, hard enough to send her forward onto Linc. She chokes briefly, pulling almost all the way off of him, then puts a firm hand on his thigh to steady herself.

I wait just long enough for her to settle before I pull out and slam into her again. Linc holds her shoulders, giving me a nod. That, and her pussy tightening around me, is all the go ahead I need to set a punishing pace. I thrust in and out in earnest, biting my lip against the pleasure racing along my spine and settling in my balls.

Lex cries out around Linc as she's forced to fuck him with her throat. Linc's eyes roll and his head drops back, his hips twitching as his orgasm rises. His fingers dig into her shoulders as I continue, relentlessly chasing a collective release. Lex moans long and low as her body shudders, her pussy squeezing as she approaches that edge.

"Fuck, I'm close," Linc rasps.

"Swallow it all, baby. Every. Last. Drop." I thrust in time to each word, slamming her forward as Linc groans his release.

I don't slow as Lex works to obey, her body flush and sweat beading along her spine. When she finishes licking him clean, I draw her hips back to seat her ass against me. I wrap one hand around her throat and snake the other up her torso, pulling her back flush to my chest.

"I can feel how close you are," I breathe into her ear, gentling my movements as she adjusts to the new position. "Do you want Linc to help while I use you like the slut you are?"

She nods, barely gasping out a mewling, "Please!"

Linc needs no further encouragement, surging forward and putting his face between her legs. Her whole body tightens as his tongue meets her, and she throws one hand up to grip the back of my neck while the other grasps his head.

I don't know where she ends and Linc begins, but the fire racing through me rages all the same. Pounding into her, I hold her throat tight in my grasp, just enough for her to feel the pressure. Her fingers grip me as she screams, her tight, hot cunt throttling my dick so hard she coaxes my orgasm out moments after hers.

I pinch and pull one of her nipples as my hips stutter and slow, working us both through the aftershocks. Linc raises up on his knees and pulls her other breast into his mouth, dropping a hand down to caress her clit while she shakes between us.

"Such a good girl," Linc croons around her pebbled flesh. "I'm so pleased with you, Lex, always so pleased."

Even after coming twice, her walls still clench in response to his praise, and I smile as I drop my lips to her neck.

"He's right," I murmur. "You're exquisite."

She sighs, tears still on her cheeks as she melts against me. I turn my chest and put an arm around her as she slides to the side. Linc slowly releases her, and I sweep my other arm under her knees as I get to my feet.

"Wha—"

"Hush, I'm taking you to the bed."

I lay her down on top of the covers and lean over her, staring into her green eyes. "You're something else, Lex Livingston," I whisper, before pressing my lips to hers.

Even though she's sated and coming down from a pretty intense scene, she doesn't hesitate to surge up and wrap her arms around my neck. She gives her all to the kiss, her lips parting and tongue tangling with mine. We break after several long moments and I lean my forehead against hers as we breathe each other in.

"Thank you," I whisper, then stand.

As I turn to the ensuite, I catch sight of Linc buttoning up his jeans. "What the fuck are you doing?"

He blinks at me owlishly. "Uh...well, extended cuddling's a string, and I—"

"A what?" I bark.

"A string," he repeats, as though it'll be clearer the second time.

Lex chuckles lazily. "Cuddling's fine, Linc. It's staying the night that's a string."

My lips thin as I look over at her, stretched out naked on my bed with a wrist over her eyes. I swing my gaze back to Linc.

"No strings, Shane. It's a rule?"

I glower at him, then her. "Whatever. Aftercare isn't a string."

Lex raises her wrist and looks over at me, propping herself up on an elbow. The move makes her tits jiggle, and I want nothing more than to lose myself in her all over again.

"Aftercare?"

Rounding on Linc, I point at his face. "Don't fucking tell me you've been slacking."

He grimaces sheepishly, shrugging a shoulder.

"You're a child sometimes," I grumble, stalking to the bathroom and flipping on the shower to give it a few moments to warm.

I glance back to find Linc leaning over and kissing Lex just as I had minutes before, and a small smile tugs at my lips.

When they part, I slip into the shower and call out to Lex. "Go pee, then get your fine ass in here."

Her eyes widen as she looks at me through the glass. "Excuse me?"

"Pee. Shower. Let's go."

She sits up, then swings her legs over the bed and pads into the bathroom. "Has anyone ever told you you're bossy as fuck sometimes?"

"All the fucking time," Linc laughs as he saunters into the bathroom after her, leaning on the doorframe. "Am I invited, too?"

Lex lets herself into the toilet room and shuts the door. I raise a brow at Linc.

"Are you going to help, or try to get your dick wet again?" He only grins, and I glower. "Get out."

Casting an amused glance at Linc as he laughs and heads for the door, Lex washes her hands then steps into the shower.

"Does he always listen?" she asks softly, stepping close and running her hands over my chest as she studies my tattoos.

"Fuck no," I scoff, trailing my fingers along her sides. "But he knows I take this shit seriously."

"Aftercare?" She looks up into my eyes as she presses her body flush to mine, her arms wrapping around my waist.

I return her embrace, touching my forehead to hers. She's tall but I still have to bend down a bit.

"Scenes like that are intense, Lex. It's important to me that I take care of you and check in."

She smiles, her fingers tracing patterns along my spine. "I'm still very green, if that's what you need to know."

Chuckling, I press my lips to hers, reaching up to cradle her head in one hand. It's a brief kiss, though far from chaste.

"I'm glad to hear it, but I'm still going to help you clean up then give you a rubdown."

She pulls back a bit to meet my eyes, her eyebrows wagging suggestively. "A rubdown?"

I shake my head and laugh, reaching for the shampoo. "A massage, you greedy thing."

She tips her head back into the water to soak her hair, then looks up at me after she clears her face with gentle hands. "I don't know that I've ever been greedy before Linc...and you."

Smirking, I massage the shampoo onto her scalp. "I don't mind causing your greed as long as you let me sate it."

After I rinse the last of the soap from her hair, she looks up at me, her gaze dark and thoughtful.

"You thanked me earlier, and I didn't get a chance to ask you why."

I cup her face, tracing the sharp line of her cheekbone with my thumb. "Being vulnerable is hard. And there's no way to have an experience like we just did without it. Your vulnerability, your trust...it's a gift, and I'm grateful."

She grips my wrist, her thumb brushing the back of my hand as untold emotions swim in her eyes. "I get the sense you and your brothers could change my worldview, Shane Kelly."

"Oh, Lex. You have no idea."

It isn't lost on me that she said brothers, plural. *Baby, it's you who could change everything.*

Chapter 18

Lex

Walking into P&L Capital is an out-of-body experience. It's my first time in the office of the VC firm my brother opened in direct challenge to my business. Though Nate could've taken the opportunity to design a space of his own, he'd mirrored the look and feel of our father's firm (and P&L's parent company) down to the dark color scheme and abundance of leather furniture.

A young woman in a crisp white blouse sits at the palatial front desk, her brows raised as I enter the lobby.

"Ms. Livingston, welcome," she says, slowly rising to her feet. "Do you, um...do you have an appointment?"

I smile. "My brother's expecting me."

Her eyes widen. "Mr. Livingston, right. Let me ring his office."

"No need." I raise my phone and tip it back and forth. "I texted him from the parking garage. And, let me guess...his office is in the back left corner?"

"Yes, that's right. I–"

"Thank you." Stepping around her, I head toward the office that had always held pride of place in our family.

I don't acknowledge the eyes that follow me as I walk through the space. Being recognized was normal, particularly at other VC firms, but there's an undercurrent of tension that comes with being in my family's domain. The media named our relationship a rivalry, and, from what I'd learned from the few former employees in my circle, P&L loved to play into that narrative.

The assistant I'd known would be there looks up in surprise as I walk to Nate's closed door.

"I'm sorry, Mr. Livingston isn't—"

"He's expecting me," I interrupt, opening the glass door and stepping through.

My eyes meet Nate's as I let his door swing shut. He sits at his desk, phone to his ear. The picture of the accomplished businessman, his white dress shirt is wrinkle free, jaw perfectly shaven, and brunette hair immaculately styled. His gaze narrows as I wander over to the windows along the opposite wall, peering out at the forested view.

"I have to go, Reginald. I'll call you when I have an update."

I hear the soft sound of the phone settling into the cradle and turn to him with a knowing smirk. "Reginald, hm? How is our old man?"

"Why are you here, Al–Lex?"

Using my preferred name without correction...huh. It's a start. "It's a shame I haven't gotten a tour of your space yet, Nate. Though it does feel awfully familiar. Did you actually copy the layout of Father's floor at HQ, or...?"

Nate glares. "Spare me. Are you here for a reason?"

"My time is far too valuable to be here without one. You should know that." I gesture to his office and the bustling activity beyond the door. "Looks like you're doing well."

"We manage," he concedes, standing from his leather office chair.

I turn my gaze back out the window. "I'm sure you do."

Nate sighs heavily behind me. I hear him move closer, then glance up as he draws shoulder-to-shoulder with me. He doesn't look my way, just shoves his hands in his pockets and looks straight ahead as I am.

"What did Reginald have to say?"

"If you're wondering if he knew I hung up with him because you were here, he didn't. I've had enough of a headache today."

"I'm surprised you missed the opportunity to put me back on his radar," I muse.

Nate scoffs. "You're always on his radar. He has news alerts set up and everything..."

His voice trails off, as though he didn't mean to share that nugget of information. I look over to find his brows drawn, gaze on the floor.

"I have news alerts for you, too." His gray eyes fly to mine. I shrug. "It's nice to know about your accomplishments."

"You're not just trying to get an edge on us?" he teases, but there's bite to it.

I snort. "I don't need a news alert to keep my edge on you, Nate. Athena's just fine, and you know it."

He huffs. "Dad knows it, too. Drives him nuts."

Grinning, I catch his eye. "Can't say I hate that."

"You shouldn't. I'd be damn proud of it if it were me."

Our eyes meet, amusement twinkling in his. Every once in a while, I caught sight of the little brother I used to know. There was a brief time, as kids, when we'd been inseparable. Before I shared my dreams with my father, before he pulled Nate away to learn the family business, before we were pitted as rivals.

Nate clears his throat, then turns to face me. "So, what can I do for you?"

My lips curl. "Well, that'd be a first. You doing something for me willingly? Whatever would Reginald say?"

He rolls his eyes. "What he doesn't know can't hurt him."

Gasping in false indignation, I put a hand to my chest. "Nathaniel! How uncouth!"

His shoulders relax as he laughs at my exaggerated impression of our mother. "Fuck, how do you do that?"

"Do what?"

"Just...drain the tension. There's so much between us, but most of the time it's like it doesn't even phase you." He studies me, expression open. "Why is that?"

I rock on my feet, hands still in my pockets. "We're family, Nate. Always will be. And I don't have our father in my ear every day, reminding me of all the manufactured reasons I should distrust you. Contrary to what he might think, we're not enemies. Hell, we're not even rivals."

"Oh, come on, there's rivalry here." He gestures between us.

"There'd have to be a threat for there to be a rivalry."

He shakes his head, his expression pinched as though he's warring with whether to laugh or scowl. "You're something else."

"You're not the first to say so."

Nate moves over to lean back against his desk, crossing his arms over his chest. "Alright, then. You're here for a reason. Let's hear it."

I purse my lips briefly as I look down. "I need you to keep an open mind, Nate. And remember what I said–I don't see P&L as a threat. Never have."

His brow lowers. "Okay..."

"We're working with a startup in the green building sector, Solum Technologies. The founders have history with someone in Greenstar Labs' portfolio."

Nate's expression shutters as I explain about Procerus, then

Solum. I'm vague on the details, not fully trusting what he will do with them, though I make the connection between the two businesses clear. When I mention Anne-Marie and her ties to the Solum founders, he straightens and uncrosses his arms.

"I saw the news about you and Greenstar, and—"

"Why are you telling me this?" he interrupts, holding up a hand. "Get to the point."

"I am." I cock a brow at him. "There's a lot you—and I have to assume Greenstar—don't know about Anne-Marie's tech."

"Of course. I don't need to understand the minutiae to recognize a worthy investment when I see one."

"Sure, I feel the same way. But I have reason to suspect you should dig deeper. Take nothing at face value."

His eyes narrow. "What aren't you saying?"

"I can't go into the details, you know that." I sigh, leaning a shoulder against his window. "You might not believe me, but I don't wish you or P&L any ill will. I'm just saying you need to go through things with a fine-toothed comb. Consider bringing in an objective third party for testing."

"You haven't given me anything to go on here. It's just vague speculation."

I give him a hard look. "It's not. I'm telling you—you're missing something. Greenstar is missing something. You need to look closer, and I suggest you do it before the Green Innovation Summit."

His expression darkens. "What do you know about our plans for the Summit?"

Blinking, I straighten. "*Your* plans? Nothing."

"How did you know I'd be there?"

I gape at him. "Are you serious? I didn't know you were going to be there, Nate. This has nothing to do with you or some covert spy operation. I saw the article about you joining the Greenstar board and wanted to do the right thing."

"What, by making vague threats?"

Holding my hands up to placate him, I scoff a laugh. "You're shitting me. I haven't threatened you once. I'm here because I know something you don't, and I don't want you getting caught in a shit situation if I can help it."

"So, what, I have to leave the Greenstar board or you're going to do something?"

Dumbfounded, I shake my head. "Wow. You're just like our father, aren't you?"

He glowers, storming back around behind his desk. "That's not a compliment."

"I didn't mean it as one."

"We're done here."

"Sure. Whatever you say."

"Why are you wasting my time? Was this some kind of diversion?"

For fuck's sake. "I get Reginald has trained you to assume the worst of everyone, especially me, but you need to look past the indoctrination for a minute."

He scrubs a hand down his face. "Unbelievable."

"You can say that again."

"I'd offer to see you out, but I think you know the way," he snaps, throwing a hand toward the door.

Shaking my head, I cross his office and pause at the door, turning back to meet his fiery gaze.

"I'm not your enemy," I say softly. "I never have been."

Something flickers in his gaze before he drops it, hands on his hips as he stands seething behind his desk. "I'll be the judge of that."

"Right," I exhale sharply, centering myself. "Get a third party to vet Anne-Marie's tech. Don't go into the Summit blind."

"I haven't needed your advice before, *Lex*, and I don't need it now." He spits my name out like a curse.

"There's a difference between need and want, Nate. You and our father would do well to learn it."

"Get out!" He slams his palms against the wooden desk.

He looks so like our father, skin flushed red and eyes wild. Reginald Livingston had never attempted to control his temper, at the office or at home. He ruled both with an iron fist, and Nate was his prodigy.

"It's a pity."

Nate's eyes blaze. He can't let me have the last word; his training won't let him.

"What is?" he bites out.

"Even with the distance and freedom to do what you want, be the leader you want to be, create a business you can be proud of...," I gesture around the room, nearly a carbon copy of our father's. "All that opportunity, and you chose to be just like him."

Nate snatches a mug from his desk and hurls it in my direction. I don't flinch, standing stock still as it flies inches from my shoulder to shatter on the floor behind me.

I tsk. "I stand corrected. Father would never miss."

My brother roars in frustration as I open his office door and stride out. His assistant looks wildly from me to the door, then hurries to pull it closed as I saunter away. Even as heaviness and disappointment settle in my gut, I don't let it show.

I'd long since accepted that any relationship with my brother would be strained, at best. He had no interest in removing the blinders our father put on him, no desire to accept the responsibility of thinking for himself. It was a shame because the boy I remembered, the brother who had been my friend and playmate, was full of so much potential.

The Summit is six weeks away. Whether Greenstar realizes the risk Anne-Marie poses or not is up to Nate.

Chapter 19

Lex

Meeting with the guys on the same day I visited Nate was a questionable decision. After returning to Athena and burying myself in work, I texted them to request a change in venue–from their place to mine. My energy was tapped, and I didn't have it in me to trek to Los Altos at eight pm.

There's also a part of me reluctant to be back in their house for the first time since I gave myself to Shane and Linc. The temptation to lose myself in them is strong, particularly after the day I've had, and I don't trust myself to keep it professional. I doubt Declan's attitude will improve if I'm all over his brother and best friend. *And I have no desire to see what happens when it gets worse.*

My phone buzzes on the kitchen island as I pull wine glasses out of the cabinet. I'd grabbed a white and a red from the cellar first thing when I got home. I also perused my fridge for finger foods but came up short. *Whatever Linc and Shane might say, wine can be dinner sometimes.* Setting the last glass down, I snag my phone.

LINC

we'll be there in two

ME

Perfect. Door's unlocked, let yourselves in.

LINC

there's a dirty joke in there somewhere

SHANE

You're a child

LINC

front door or back door?

SHANE

Seriously?

I giggle, shaking my head at their antics. *Wouldn't hurt to play along a little.*

ME

Up to you.

LINC

!!

SHANE

Lex…

LINC

how do you expect me to talk about Solum
when you drop shit like that in the group text?!

DECLAN

Easy. Talk about Solum or you can walk your
ass home.

The faint noise of car doors slamming sounds from out front. Moments later, the door opens and Linc's playful tone fills the hall.

"Given where we are, Dec, that's not really a threat."

I walk toward the three of them as they toe off their shoes. Declan glares at Linc, reaching over to smack him upside the head.

"Knock it off."

"Hey!" Linc ducks away and turns to me, fake-pouting. "You see what I put up with?"

I cross my arms and smile. "Careful, Linc. The vein in your brother's forehead is already out. That doesn't bode well for our productivity tonight."

"Fuck off, all of you," Declan grumbles, reaching up to rub his forehead.

Shane cocks a brow at me as he saunters over. He's wearing dark jeans and a white tee—the first time I've seen him out of a button down...if we don't count the moment he stripped naked and revealed all that gorgeous tattooed skin. My eyes rove over him as he draws closer, appreciating the veins wrapping his forearms.

"He's in rare form tonight," Shane whispers, leaning in to kiss my forehead as he grips my upper arm. "Go easy on him?"

Grinning, I look up at him and shake my head. "Never."

Shane's eyes flash as he chuckles. "Atta girl."

The easy praise from his lips sets off a flurry of wings in my belly. As I'm about to respond, Shane's eyes lock on something behind me and he straightens, stepping back. I turn to see what caught his eye.

"Whoa, am I interrupting something?"

At the sound of the new voice, Declan and Linc freeze, then walk over to surround me, their squabble forgotten. *Wait...are they protecting me right now? All three of them? What on earth...*

I brush off the thought. "Jax, what are you—"

"Well, I know it's a long shot, but I was kind of hoping to

raid your fridge." My affable houseguest rubs his neck and smiles sheepishly.

"There's no chance of you finding anything, man." Linc reaches out a hand. "You must be the nephew. I'm Linc."

Jax grins and holds out a fist. "Nice. Jackson, but I go by Jax."

Linc taps Jax's fist, then turns to me. "Should I order food?"

"Wait, nephew?" Declan glances between me and Jax. "You're her nephew."

"Guilty!" Jax runs a hand through his dark blond waves. "I live in the pool house." He gestures to the backyard.

"How old are you?" Declan presses.

Jax shrugs. "Age is just a number, man." He turns to Linc. "You said something about food?"

I sigh, putting a hand on Jax's back and directing him to the kitchen. The guys follow close.

"Get yourself a glass if you want wine, yeah? We're having a business dinner, so you might be bored–"

"Nah, sounds sweet. But, uh, I'll go grab a beer from mine. Be right back!"

As Jax jogs to the sliding door, the guys crowd around the island. Linc smiles as he pulls out his phone.

"He is not what I expected."

"What did you expect?"

"Nerdy little college kid, not a surfer dude." He looks at his phone. "Pizza work?"

I shrug. "Better than–"

"Crackers and wine," Linc drawls, arching an eyebrow. "I know."

Shane narrows his eyes at me.

"What?" I blink innocently, opening the bottle of red. "Wine?"

"No, thank you," Declan grunts, setting his bag on a stool. "Can we start?"

"Red, please," Shane says.

I fight the urge to smirk at the dismissal of his friend's snarky comment. "You have somewhere to be, Declan?"

I pour a glass and hand it to Shane.

Declan sighs, resigned. "I just want to make the most of the time."

"Oh, we always make the most of Lex's time," Linc teases. He shoves his phone in his pocket, then opens the fridge. "Next time I'm bringing beer."

"I got you," Jax calls as he enters the room. "Brought a six."

"Thanks."

"You got it. So, what business are you all up to this late?" Jax offers a beer to Declan, but he waves him off. "Didn't expect a party when I came over."

"It's a business meeting, not a party," Declan mutters.

"Dec," Shane warns, deep voice calm.

"Linc ordered pizza," I say, moving to take a seat at the dining table near my laptop.

"My man!" Jax offers another fist bump, which Linc returns with amusement. "Tell me you're a pineapple on pizza guy."

Declan scoffs. "He is. No accounting for taste in our gene pool, apparently."

"You're missing out." Jax levels a finger and stern glare at Declan. "That shit's delicious."

"Fruit does not belong on pizza!" Declan protests as Linc and Jax high-five.

Those two are going to be trouble.

Shane takes the seat next to mine. He reaches over and engulfs my thigh in his hand, kneading gently. Never have I been more pleased to be wearing shorts.

"Rough day?" he asks quietly while PizzaGate rages behind us.

I slide my hand over his, squeezing as I relax against my chair. "I've had better."

He searches my eyes with his ice blues. Before he can respond, Declan storms over to the table and yanks a chair back, the legs screeching across the tile.

"Can we please discuss this interview I have in two weeks?"

"Of course." I take a sedate sip of wine. "Have you drafted your recommended questions?"

His forehead bunches. "I thought your team was doing questions."

"You were supposed to draft ones that would help tell the story from your perspective," Linc chimes in, dropping into the chair on my other side.

Jax sits across from me and a couple of chairs down from Declan. He glances back and forth between us, a slight smile on his face as he sips his beer.

"Right," Declan clears his throat. "That makes sense."

I nod. "You met with our media team earlier this week. How'd it go?"

"Fine."

Shane's fingers start tracing light patterns on my thigh, the distraction of his skin on mine enough to keep my temper from rising.

"They mentioned you had concerns about being conversational. Would you like to do some Q&A now to practice?"

I watch, stoic, as Declan breathes deep and forces himself to relax. It's obvious he's nervous, frustrated, and I wish he would put words to the emotions running through him. The last six weeks made it clear that Declan doesn't know how to ask for help. Thanks to insight from Linc, I also surmised Solum's leader carried tremendous guilt for what he perceived as their lack of success. *It kills him that he needed Athena, needed me, to make this dream come true.* If he kept trying to do things on his own, when he had entire teams at his disposal, the failure I suspected he worried about would be inevitable.

Declan glances at me, then Jax. Sighing, he looks down at his hands. "I know how important this interview is."

We all wait for him to go on. Jax catches my eye and winks, then takes a gulp of beer.

"Fine, yes. We can practice."

"Good. I have some of our team's draft questions pulled up. Linc, Shane, our analysts sent a report based on the last round of tests. They had a few suggestions. Why don't you review those while Declan and I work on messaging?"

"Yeah, I saw the email come through on the way over." Linc gets up to grab his laptop from where he left it on the island, then plops down next to Shane.

"I want in! Put me to work, Lexi." Jax quips.

The guys all freeze and look at me in slow motion. Lincoln mouths the name back to me in question, a slow grin covering his face.

"Take notes, Jackson," I order. "Declan, why don't you pull up a doc so he can save them on your machine?"

"Sure...Lexi." Declan raises a brow as he hands his laptop over.

Is Declan teasing me right now?

Jax chuckles. "Tried to call her Auntie once and she nearly killed me. Convinced her Lexi was a decent compromise."

"Under what condition?" I demand.

My infuriatingly lovable nephew rolls his eyes. "Only at home."

"Where no one else would hear it." I give him a pointed look.

"I didn't break any rules, Lexi. We're home. Not my fault you have company for the first time in forever."

My cheeks flush as Linc throws his head back and laughs while Shane chuckles. Declan smirks, his green eyes finding mine and flaring in amusement. I swallow roughly, feeling the weight of his playful attention in my core. Jax smiles and pokes around on Declan's laptop.

"Just take notes, please," I mutter, moving to sit closer to Declan and shoving my wandering thoughts down as I do. "And you're in charge of getting the door when the pizza gets here."

———

Two hours later, I walk the guys to the door. Jax is still in the kitchen, scarfing down the last of the Hawaiian pizza. Declan's gaze lingers on me after he pulls on his shoes.

"Thank you, Lex," he says. "Tonight was...helpful."

I grin, crossing my arms and tracking the dip of his gaze to the hint of cleavage at my neckline. "You've come a long way, Declan. But I'll know you've transcended when you can express gratitude without looking constipated."

Shane pats Declan's arm roughly. "Looks like you've got a ways to go."

"Fuck off," Declan grumbles, turning for the door. He glances back at me one last time, his lips curling into a smug little smile.

Linc steps up into my personal space, crowding his body against mine. "Can we break a rule and allow a string tonight? I don't want to go."

He ducks down and kisses my neck, gripping my waist in his broad hands. I reach up and thread my fingers through his soft curls, pressing my body to his.

"No strings, Linc," I murmur.

Pouting, he straightens and peers into my eyes. He reaches a hand up to cup my cheek, his thumb on my cheekbone. I want to break my rules, want to fist his tee in my hand and drag him right up the stairs. But my nephew is in the kitchen. *And you have rules for a fucking reason.*

"I'll see you soon." I press my lips to his, kissing him sweetly.

He releases me with a lingering look, then squeezes my hand and follows his brother out. Shane is waiting behind him, hands in his pockets. He shaved his head again recently, and I'd admired how gorgeous he looked all night.

"Thank you for being gentle," he says, his deep voice impossibly soft. "He's...invested."

"Who, Linc?"

Shane inclines his head.

Sighing, I lean into him as he presses his lips to my forehead. "I know," I murmur.

"Good night, Lex." Shane grips my arm briefly, then walks out and pulls the door closed.

I sigh, crossing my arms and hanging my head before turning to meet Jax in the kitchen. To my surprise, he isn't in the kitchen—he's standing at the end of the hall, leaning against the wall. I narrow my gaze.

"How long have you been standing there, Jackson Thomas?"

He smirks. "Long enough, Lexi Livingston. Come on, have a drink with me. I know you're not going to bed for another few hours."

Grumbling, I follow him back to the kitchen. "What do you know about my schedule?"

"Aw, Lexi. You wound me!" He winks over his shoulder. "I might be all fun and games, but I pay attention. The lights are on over here until midnight at least."

"Why do you stay up so late?"

He smiles as he hands over my wine glass, pouring the last of the red into it. "My brain doesn't like to shut off."

"Well, sleep's overrated, anyway."

Jax draws back, brow bunched. "Like hell, it is. Sleep's awesome."

Chuckling, I lean against the island and regard him. "If you're so observant, why'd you come over looking for food tonight? You have to know the fridge is usually empty, and I'm pretty sure the pool house has a view of the driveway."

He grins, unashamed. "I've lived here for nearly two years, and you've never had guys over. Not once." He shrugs and chugs some beer. "Had to make sure you were safe."

I glare at him.

"Okay, okay, I was curious as fuck. Still am, honestly." He tilts his head. "You like them."

"Eh, Linc and Shane are pretty great."

Jax just smiles, waiting.

"Declan's a handful."

"Never seen you back down from a challenge," he muses.

I bark a laugh, still surprised by Jax's ability to see through me. "True enough."

Jax studies me. I often got the impression there was far more to him than the sunny, happy jock he seemed to be.

"You're different with them. Free. Never seen you laugh so much, either."

"Are you psychoanalyzing me, kid?"

"No clue. Am I?"

Shaking my head, I take my wine glass to the sink. Jax cleared the table and loaded the dishwasher while I walked the guys out.

"Thanks for your help tonight."

"Of course. Worth it to see you happy."

Is that what I am? Happy? I pause, letting that question and his words sink in. Jax isn't wrong—I do feel free with the guys. Well, Lincoln and Shane mostly. If I'm honest, I don't curb myself around Declan, either. He gets the same version of me the other two do, though his reactions certainly aren't the same. *Aaand, I'm done with this topic.*

"I saw your dad today."

Jax's expression flickers. He glances down with a sigh. "How'd that go?"

"About how you might expect."

"Forget him. Let's go back to your guys."

My guys? I like the sound of that a little too much. "They're not mine."

Jax gives me a "whatever you say" look. "They could be. Pretty sure Shane volunteered for the position every time he served you pizza, brought you water, and topped up your wine tonight. He wasn't playing waiter for anyone else."

Holy shit. Warmth blooms in my chest at the realization he's right, but I push it away.

"I don't have time for a relationship, Jax."

"Bullshit."

My jaw drops. "Excuse me?"

"Look at Van. He's married, kid on the way. Does he still show up for you and Athena?"

"Of course he does." I'm happy as hell for him and Cami.

Jax cocks a brow, then downs the last of his beer. "If Van can do it, you definitely can. You're way more balanced than he is. Like, way more. Anyway, he's never been happier. You deserve that."

He tosses his beer bottle in the recycling bin, then kisses my cheek.

"Night, Lexi."

"Night," I mutter.

He smiles and ruffles my hair before I can duck. Squealing, I dance away as he laughs and lets himself out. As he closes the sliding door, I replay his words in my head. *If Van can do it, you definitely can. The question is, do I want to?*

Chapter 20

Shane

"Hi there, Mr. Kelly," the receptionist at Athena greets. "Go on back."

In the week since we went to Lex's place, Linc and I only coaxed her away from everything else once. Declan glared as we left the house to meet her, jealousy and hurt warring in his gaze. Linc hadn't noticed, though I knew there would be a confrontation at some point. *Today is not that day.*

"Thanks, Ruthie." I toss her a small wave.

Ruthie, and most of Lex's staff, have gotten used to my random visits over the last five weeks. As I walk toward Lex's office, I nod at those who wave. Cami, who I met a few times during lunch drop offs, beams at me.

"Shane!" She pulls her trolley cart to a halt. "Miles mentioned you had her covered today."

"Not as good as yours, I bet."

She laughs. "I'm sure it's delicious. She eats way more of your deliveries than mine. I'm just glad Lex's got someone else looking out for her."

I'm inordinately pleased to hear it. With a smile, I duck my head and continue on my way.

"Shane! Thank goodness you're here." Miles rushes over, cheeks pink. "I've cleared her calendar for ninety minutes today. It's been a doozy."

My brow furrows. "Everything okay?"

He waves his hands around. "It's fine. We're fine. Every-thing's fine."

"Right," I drawl.

Rolling his eyes, he thrusts a hand toward Lex's door in clear demand. I'm all too happy to oblige, letting myself in with a soft knock.

Her office is bright and open, with floor-to-ceiling windows and a comfortable seating area in neutral colors with jewel tone accents. Lex sits at her desk, eyes intent on the screen. She's turned toward me, as though she knows someone's here but can't tear her eyes away from her work.

"Miles said it's been a day," I say as I pull the door closed.

At the sound of my voice, her gaze jerks to mine. "Shane."

She says my name like a prayer, like all she needed in that moment was for me to appear. My lips quirk up as she relaxes into her chair for a moment, then springs to her feet and walks over to me.

"Am I happy to see you." She slides her arms around my neck and draws me to her, pressing her lips to mine.

I sweep one arm around her, crushing her to me, as I devour her mouth. Her lips part and I push my tongue past them, stroking hers, deepening the kiss. She stretches up on her tiptoes and matches my passion, her lips soft and unyielding.

When we part, she sighs happily and looks up at me through her lashes. "How did you know I needed you today?"

My heart squeezes at the idea of being the perfect cure for her neediness. "Linc mentioned you worked late again last night."

She leans away, eyes wide. "I'm sorry, what? Since when does Linc report on me?"

I cock a brow at her. "Did you work late and have crackers for dinner last night?"

"...yes?"

"And how do you feel right now?"

She looks away. "Hungry. Cranky. Annoyed."

I hold up the bag containing her lunch. "Problem solved."

"I don't know how I feel about you two conspiring—"

"Lex, it's for your own good; you're terrible at taking care of yourself." I move over to perch on the couch and unpack lunch.

"I am not!"

"You are. Sit down."

"Shane, I am not a child." Her voice wavers between indignation and confusion.

"No shit, you're not. You're a driven, focused, powerful woman. But I've never seen you put yourself first, so sit your ass down and let someone else step up."

She blinks, lowering herself slowly to the couch next to me. "You're bossy today."

"Linc would argue I'm bossy every day." I hand her a container and a set of chopsticks. "Miso rice bowl with tofu and veggies."

"Thank you."

"You're welcome."

We open our lunches in peaceful silence, Lex stealing glances at me. After she finishes her first few bites, she turns to face me with a thoughtful expression.

"This is divine, Shane. Where did you learn to cook?"

I swallow my bite, then take a sip from my water bottle.

"Dec and Linc's mom. She stayed home and loved to cook." Memories rush up, some less wholesome. "My mom...struggled for a long time. My dad was never around. I learned from Mrs.

Wilde, then I'd make simple things so my mom and I had food at home. When Declan and I went to college, I started experimenting with recipes on my own."

"Let me guess: Linc and Declan weren't as keen to learn?" Her eyes sparkle.

"Not a bit."

"So Declan's the leader at Solum, but you run the house?"

Reaching out, I pinch her side lightly. As she laughs, I move closer to her, our knees knocking together.

"Next you're going to ask me who wears the pants."

She sobers quickly, nodding. "Yes, please. I've been dying to know."

"Haven't you learned by now?" I lean closer, whispering conspiratorially. "We all do."

Heat flashes in her eyes as she chuckles, relaxing back against the couch and regarding me. "Tell me more. I know so little about you, Shane."

"It's not like you give us time for pillow talk."

"Oh, please! You're not the pillow talk type."

"Fair." Taking another bite, I watch as she does the same. "What do you want to know?"

"Everything."

"That sounds like a string."

She glances down at her lunch, swallowing. "Maybe it doesn't have to be. Two people can get to know one another without getting attached, can't they?"

"Can they?" I challenge.

Her nose scrunches. "Some level of attachment is probably inevitable. But...there can be attachment between friends."

Friends, my ass. There's nothing friendly about the way I crave her. "Maybe we start with topics that are already on the table."

"What, work and sex?" she quips as she takes another bite.

"Exactly."

She considers my words. "I can get on board with that."

This should be fun. I wait for her to go first.

"When did you know you liked...being in control? In the bedroom."

"I guess I've always known. I mentioned my mom earlier." Lex nods, focused on me. "She...didn't have a stable source of income, and there was always a new guy around, someone she thought would take care of her. Of us. I didn't know what a healthy relationship looked like until I met Dec's parents."

"I'm glad you had them." Her tone is gentle.

"Me, too. But I'd seen enough with my mom to know I wasn't going to leave my future up to someone else, not unless I trusted them completely. And...that's kind of extended into all aspects of my life."

"I can relate, in a way. On our first night together, Linc asked me if I was used to being in control in the bedroom. I was, but if I'm honest with myself, I used that control as a defense mechanism."

I take her hand in mine. She threads our fingers together and smiles softly.

"For me," I say, "it might have started that way...but I realized pretty quickly I got as much of a rush from being the one directing the scene as I did from participating. Now, it's more about maximizing pleasure—for my partner or partners, and for myself."

Her eyes glaze as she looks off to the side.

"Where'd you go?" I whisper, squeezing her hand.

She flushes. "Just thinking about the other night."

My cock twitches at the memory of the three of us in bed together, the muscles in Lex's back flexing deliciously while she rode me, Linc's fingers between her legs. I clear my throat.

"Which part?"

Her mouth opens on a deep breath, and she grips my hand tighter. "When you told Linc to fuck his hand."

"What about it?" I murmur encouragingly.

"I mean, it was hot, but I was also surprised you were... telling him what to do, too. He's so dominant when it's just the two of us."

"Yeah, Linc's great at reading people. Sometimes I think he knows what the people around him want before they do. He knew I would want to be in control, and you'd want us to take the lead. If we're all enjoying the scene, he's happy."

"So you get off on the control, and Linc gets off on...everyone's pleasure?"

A lazy smile tugs at my lips. "Something like that." I tuck a strand of hair behind her ear. "What do you get off on, Lex?"

Her pupils dilate as she studies my face, that flush creeping up her neck.

"The freedom." Eyes glassy, she sighs.

Seeing she's finished, I take both of our containers and set them on the table. I turn to lean back against the armrest of the couch, my legs spread.

"Come here."

Lex stands and walks over, then sits with her back to my chest. Once she's settled, I wrap my arms around her and hook a leg over hers, snuggling her against me. Her body melts into mine, and I kiss the top of her head.

"Tell me more," I whisper.

She rests her hands on my thighs, thumbs stroking back and forth. "When you first asked if I'd ever been shared before...I'd already been asking myself why I'd never had a threesome. Ever since Linc mentioned it, I'd been...wondering."

"It's not unusual, you know. We didn't have any expectations."

She chuckles. "I know, but...I've had opportunities. Multiple. I've never said yes, not until you and Linc."

I can tell it's not easy for Lex to share about herself. She's used to owning the conversation in a corporate setting, and it's new territory for her to be open and vulnerable. I don't want to push her, but I'm dying for her to truly let me in.

After a few moments of silence, I press my cheek to the side of her head and tighten my arms around her. "Did you think of the answer?"

"I think so? Being with the two of you...it's the most vulnerable thing I've ever done. I've built a business from the ground up, put my professional reputation and entire life savings on the line more than once, but none of that compares." She inhales deeply, her fingers gripping my thighs. "There's never been anyone I was willing to surrender to like that, no one I trusted enough with my body, or..."

Her words trail off, as though there's something else she was about to say and swallowed instead. *Tell me, baby. Don't hold back now.*

"That's why I thank you, you know," I say as I shift slightly. She snuggles closer, hands moving to rest on my forearms. "I don't take it for granted, Lex. Not ever."

"I know you don't," she breathes. "If you did, it would all be over."

The thought of anything being over chills me. Shoving the feeling aside, I drop my lips to her neck, kissing her softly. She tips her head to give me better access, and I press open-mouthed kisses along her flesh.

"Tell me about the freedom," I mumble against her skin.

She squirms in my lap, her thighs squeezing together. I'm desperate to slide my hand into her skirt, relieve the pressure I can tell is building, but her rules stay my advance.

"It's kind of hard with your mouth on me."

I smirk. "I could stop."

As I draw back, she reaches a hand up and clasps the back of my head. "Don't you dare."

Chuckling, I obey, bending back to put my lips on her.

"I just...there's so much I'm responsible for, Shane. Everyone at Athena, all of our clients. And even though it sounds silly, I feel some level of responsibility to the VC and startup communities, female founders, groups of people I care about and want to support. Any given moment, I'm thinking of how to better serve and support them..."

"Sounds exhausting."

"It is. But on my knees for you, for Linc..."

My cock thickens against her backside at the image, burned into my retinas after seeing her in that exact position on my bedroom floor.

"When I'm there, with you...everything else falls away. I'm not responsible for anything. I don't have to make any decisions. I can just be...Lex." Her voice cracks. "I'm not the founder of the most successful VC in the Bay or the sponsor of some event or the mentor of a rising entrepreneur..."

I hold her and breathe her in, feeling the impact of the emotions rolling through her as she takes a shaky breath.

"It's the only time I've ever felt like I'm enough."

Chapter 21

Lex

Am *I crying?* Shane has stilled behind me, his lips on my skin as he holds me and listens. I can't make sense of how I feel. My clit throbs from his sensuous touches, the feel of him hard and warm around me. But my head is a mess, my pulse thundering in my ears. A hot, wet tear curves down my cheek as I put words to something that has simmered unacknowledged for weeks.

"You *are* enough," Shane rasps.

I squeeze my eyes shut, my breath catching as I try to exhale. "I know."

"Do you?"

Nodding, my skin breaks out in goosebumps as he resumes his kisses.

"Say it."

"I'm enough."

"I think you need a reminder." He hums a thoughtful sound. "I'd like to ask you for a favor."

Shane straightens, taking his lips and heat away as I fight the urge to whine. I want his touch on me, want to feel him as he breaks me apart. Sitting up, I turn to look at him over my shoulder.

"What do you need?"

"I want to get rid of a rule. Linc mentioned nothing on Athena property. How strongly do you want to stick to that?"

I lick my lips. "Why?"

He cocks his head, that predatory look heating my blood. "I can feel the tension in your body, can hear the hesitation in your voice when you should be confident in your worth. I want to help, but you've set boundaries and I respect them. It's up to you."

"What do you want to do?"

His chuckle is dark. "More than we have time for, so I'll settle for tasting that sweet pussy properly for the first time."

My core clenches at the thought, my nipples rising. "Properly?"

Shane grins, tapping my hip to encourage me to move. I do, and he slips off the couch, then kneels on the carpeted floor in front of me, his hands stroking my exposed thighs.

"You've kissed Linc after he's had his tongue buried in you, then kissed me. I want more than a secondhand hit."

My skin flushes. The memory of kissing Linc, then turning immediately to Shane, fills my mind and quickens my breathing. I glance at my office door, weighing the risk. Miles blocked my lunch hour, and my door has a lock. *I can keep quiet, can't I?* Shane's grin turns wicked, and I know he's watching me decide to say yes.

He stands, sauntering over to flip the lock on the door gently enough it doesn't click and announce our intent to the office.

Shane walks back to stand on the other side of the coffee table, posture relaxed. "What do you say, Lex? Will you let me remind you that you are enough?"

"Yes," I breathe, feeling one barrier around my heart crumble as I break yet another of my rules.

He reaches up, slowly unbuttoning his powder blue button down to reveal his tattooed torso. The black and gray ink, depicting a mountain landscape, a lighthouse, and a treed forest, stretches across his muscled chest and down his defined, veined forearms.

Shrugging off his shirt, he tilts his head again, eyes narrowed in challenge. *And just like that, he's in charge.*

"Yes, sir."

The weight of my day flows away as I utter those words and give myself over to Shane. Anticipation and desire roar through me as I wait for his instruction.

"Drop your skirt." He speaks softly, respecting my desire to keep what happens next between us.

Standing, I finger the side zip on my tight skirt, drawing it down and stepping out of the material as it falls. I go to draw my thong down, and Shane tsks.

"Do only as I say," he orders, stepping closer. "Sit down on the edge of the couch, thighs spread. Hands on your knees."

I comply, wanting to whimper in protest of the order I suspect is coming.

"Not a sound," he murmurs, kneeling in front of me. "Keep your position, or I stop."

He wants verbal acknowledgement, I know. "Yes, sir."

He hums in the back of his throat as he leans in to kiss my inner knee, his lips soft and tongue wet as he swirls it against my flesh. My heart pounds as I hold back the sounds I want to make as his teeth graze my inner thigh before he nips sharply. I suck my lip into my mouth to stifle the yelp that tries to break free, my fingers tightening on my knees until my knuckles are white.

Shane takes his time getting to the apex of my thighs, biting and soothing my skin in turn. I glance down and want to swoon at the sight of him between my legs, his broad hands engulfing my thighs. His tattoos are on full display, the dark beauty of all that ink on his toned body stealing my breath.

Suddenly, Shane's mouth is on me, licking and teasing through the lace of my thong. I slam my lips and eyes shut, focusing on keeping back the gasp that wants to rip free as he nibbles and sucks. I can feel the wetness gathering, heat and electricity building in my core.

He draws back and I fight the whimper, swallowing it down. I open my eyes to meet his satisfied gaze.

"Let go and lean back. You can move, but stay quiet."

I breathe out an acknowledgement as I obey, resting my shoulders low on the back of the couch, my neck at a sharp angle that almost forces me to watch him. Shane bends back to my pussy, roughly pulling my thong aside and thrusting his tongue into me. My back bows as I thrust my hips closer to him.

He laps at me, then focuses his attention on my clit as his fingers stroke at my entrance. Barely pushing two into me, then retreating, he teases me. His tongue slides around my clit and he pulls it into his mouth, bringing me so close to the brink that my body shudders with tension. Shane hums in approval and I bite down on my lip, a tiny moan nearly escaping.

I writhe against him, unconsciously trying to fuck his fingers deeper into me, but Shane denies me. He keeps barely breaching my opening, then pulling back, and I want to cry out in frustration. *He's testing me.* The second I have the thought, I force myself to drain the tension from my limbs and relax into the couch. If it's a test, I'm going to fucking pass.

The moment my body stills, he shoves both fingers in and bites lightly on my clit. My gasp is inevitable as my body bows in pleasure, my core trembling as my orgasm hovers just out of reach. He strokes the top of my channel as he pulls his mouth away, smirking up at me.

"That was a sound, Lex."

I bite my lip, my eyes rolling back as heat and pressure build in my core.

"I'll let that slide, just this once," he murmurs.

He stares at my pussy as he continues to fuck me with his hand, his eyes dark with want. Gently, he swipes another finger against me, gathering my wetness before sliding it down to my puckered hole.

"Have you had someone here?" He taps against my ass.

I shiver as I nod.

"Did you like it?"

Another nod.

"That's good," he croons, putting more pressure and rubbing his finger in a small circle. "Linc and I can't wait to take you together."

My pussy clamps down on his fingers at the suggestion, my body trembling. He doesn't falter, his touch firm and commanding as he pushes me ever closer to oblivion. I'm torn between the sensations wrought by his hands, my breath ragged as I climb.

"Can you imagine?" he rasps. "Me in your cunt and Linc here?"

Fucking hell, yes, please. I want that. He breaches my tight hole with the tip of his finger, swirling it around in a lazy circle as he speaks. I can picture Linc's hard length in his place, the image so vivid I nearly moan.

"Do you want that, dirty little slut? Want us to fill you at the same time and fuck you until you scream?"

His filthy mouth is going to be the death of me. I can't hold in my reply, the words tumbling free with the delirious force of my need.

"Yes," I gasp. "Fuck, yes, sir. Please."

"Then you better fucking come for me," he growls.

Shane leans forward and sucks my clit into his mouth as he pushes his finger deeper into my ass. My toes curl as my orgasm hurtles through me, sending me into the stratosphere as I clap a hand over my mouth to try and contain the unstoppable moan. He strokes and sucks me through it, wave after wave breaking me into nothing more than a limp, breathless mass of pleasure.

Waiting until I fall still, Shane gently pulls away, his fingers slipping from me and leaving me both sated and wanting. I came hard, one of the most intense orgasms I've ever had, but the idea of the two of them inside me left me feeling almost desperate with desire. *I've never felt so shamelessly greedy.*

Shane stands and adjusts himself, the hard outline of his cock making my mouth water. I reach for him, but he shakes his head.

"This was about you, baby. I'm good," he says, walking over to the bathroom in the corner of my office.

I can hear the sink run, and the vague need to put my skirt back on crosses my mind. Before I can muster the energy to act on the thought, Shane returns.

"You're so goddamn gorgeous when you come," he swears. "Almost made me forget you didn't keep quiet."

I look up at him, blood rushing in my ears. *I can't stay silent enough for a punishment here.* Shane chuckles as my mind conjures the image of my staff staring at my office with wide eyes.

"I think Linc might want in on your punishment. We'll have to put it off until he can join us."

His eyes glint as he watches me realize I'll be carrying the anticipation indefinitely. I swallow roughly and close my eyes, flopping back onto the couch.

"Fuck."

Shane pats my knee. "You'll like it."

"I know, that's the problem," I mumble. "I'm not a patient person."

He laughs, sharp and carefree, and I grin as I push myself upright, then stand. My legs are shaky, making me stumble.

"Here, let me help," Shane urges, sitting on the coffee table and resting a hand on my hip.

I watch as he smooths his fingers along my bunched underwear, settling them gently back over my swollen lips. They're so wet it's pointless to keep wearing them. Shane strokes along my seam once, then looks up into my eyes.

"Do you want them?" I whisper.

His grip tightens on the thin lace. "Fuck yes, I do."

He wastes no time, tugging sharply and ripping them right off my body. Pressing the material to his face, he inhales deeply and groans before shoving them in his pocket. Shaking his head, he picks up my skirt and holds it open for me to step into. I do, and he drags it up my legs, his fingers leaving scorching lines along my skin.

"You drive me crazy," he mutters as he watches me fasten my skirt and smooth it.

"Then we're even."

His expression is stoic as he considers me, then looks down. He seems pensive, almost withdrawn, and I want to know what's going through his head. I wait for him to say something, but he just stands and regards me.

"How do you feel?" he asks.

A soft smile curls my lips as I loop my arms around his waist. "Green."

"Good." He studies me for a long moment, reaching one hand up to cup my jaw. His touch is gentle, almost reverent. "Now, do you remember what you are?"

I frown as I process his question, the sense that there's only one correct answer nagging at me. He watches my thoughts unfurl across my face, expression soft, and I remember our earlier conversation. Letting out a halting breath, emotion wells deep in my chest. *This man.*

"Enough," I say, my voice cracking.

He reaches up to hold my face in both hands. "Never forget it."

Shane crashes his lips into mine. He kisses me like he needs me to survive, like I'm the lifeline tethering him to this earth. I lean into him and return it in kind, our lips and tongues waging a fierce, passionate battle. When we part, he rests his forehead against mine as we both catch our breath.

"Thank you, Shane."

He inhales deeply, then straightens and presses a kiss to my forehead. "You're welcome."

Shane drops a hand down to squeeze mine in farewell before walking away. He pauses at the door and unlocks it slowly, then meets my gaze.

"See you soon, baby."

Chapter 22

Declan

I felt like we were on an unstoppable train, and none of us were in the conductor's seat. Lex and her team had come through at every turn, but I still found myself resisting their help. The responsibility for our business always ultimately fell to me, and the worry over the wrong steps I'd made in the past—and the ones I was sure to make in the future—chafed. I was on edge. *I refuse to be the reason we crash and burn. Again.*

"Feeling ready?"

I clench my notecards tighter and frown at Lex, annoyed at her interruption. I'm in Lex's office, leaning up against the wall by the bar cart, fifteen minutes before my interview with the Bayview Bulletin's reporter.

"I'll be ready if I can review all this in time," I grouse, waving the cards. I'm harsher than I intend to be, nerves flaring.

Her cool expression isn't a surprise as I turn my attention back to the notecards. Doing my best to ignore her presence, I attempt to read the bullet points I wrote. For the third time. But my brain won't focus on the words, my mind tripping over the guilt and trepidation that always rise when I let myself feel an ounce of hope. It's like my handwriting is skittering on the page, each sentence a jumble of nonsense characters.

As I'm about to turn the card over, Lex's hand moves into my field of vision and covers my notes.

"What the hell are you doing?"

"Declan, you don't need notes."

Her voice is firm, but gentle. Placating, almost. I hate it. Hate the suggestion that she has to be the stronger one, the one in the position to comfort and guide me. *I'm the strong one, goddamnit. It should be me reassuring her.*

"I think I can decide for myself what I do or don't need."

If Shane was here, I know he'd tell me to stop acting like a toddler. Linc would roll his eyes and distract Lex, something he's grown proficient at over the last few weeks.

Something fierce flashes in Lex's light green eyes before she closes them briefly and takes a deep breath.

"You don't need them. You know Solum inside and out, not only the spirit of what you're going to accomplish, but the science of why and how. We've gone over your talking points, even role-played the questions. The words as you've written them don't matter," she presses.

Swallowing roughly, I turn away, my body tight. She's dangerously close to seeing right through me, and I'm far from ready to be that vulnerable. *With her more than anyone.*

"Easy for you to say," I toss over my shoulder. "This kind of thing is second nature to you, I'm sure."

She ignores my attempt at deflection. "Speak from the heart, Declan. Tell the story only you can, with the conviction only you have. Smile. Laugh. Be self-deprecating, if that makes you feel more comfortable. But most of all, be honest and let your integrity shine through. Be *you*."

Rounding on her, my lips purse. She stands a few feet away, hands in the pockets of her high-waisted trousers, relaxed and confident. Dressed head-to-toe in deep green, her eyes are almost inhumanly vibrant. So poised, so graceful. My body reacts, swaying toward her, caught in her pull. *Always trapped by her gravity.*

I don't know if I'm angrier that she manages to be so calm, or that I feel so utterly out of control whenever I'm in her presence. *Get it together, Dec.*

"Following my heart sounds like questionable advice," I grit out.

"Does it?"

"Without a doubt. Following my heart got us into this mess in the first place."

She looks at me thoughtfully. "You could look at it that way, I suppose."

Tension gathers in the silence between us. She's so fucking good at letting silence speak for her, letting the thoughts and anxieties of the people across from her build until they can't be contained. I've attempted to wait her out multiple times over the last eight weeks. I've yet to succeed.

"You have another perspective, I take it?" I thrust a hand toward her in invitation. "Let's hear it, then."

"Following your heart brought you, Shane, and Lincoln together. It forged the bonds between you and gave you all purpose. Do you know how rare it is to have close relationships like that as an adult? How hard it is to find loyalty—true, unshakable loyalty that you never have to question?" Her lips quirk into a small smile. "It'd be so easy to say you're lucky, but that's not it at all. Your heart inspired and drove you to build more than a business."

My chest feels tight as I stare at her, my knuckles going white as I grip the index cards. She has no right to see me—see us—so clearly. No one has ever described me as an open book, but Lex fucking Livingston reads me like a grade school primer.

I desperately want to hate her for how it makes me feel. But no matter how exposed and raw I feel, I'm still drawn to her. *How fucking easy would it be to give in?*

"Declan, your vision, your business...it wouldn't have survived the last year without your heart at the center. You let someone in who didn't deserve it, once, and she did her best to take you down." Lex shrugs, taking a step back toward the door. "You haven't let her succeed yet. Hold that line. Show her you're unyielding, and you're still following your heart. Show her she hasn't fucking broken you or your business. Show the Bay what success looks like for Declan Wilde."

She waves a hand at the index cards as she reaches the door, looking up at me with a smirk. "Toss them."

Shane steps into the room as she sweeps out, their eyes locking briefly. The searing look of want that passes between them is staggering, and my jaw clenches. I can't reconcile the emotions raging through me in response to her little speech with the ugly feeling rising in my gut as I witness...whatever that is. *Heartburn. It's just fucking heartburn.*

"She's right," Shane says as he closes the door.

"Of course you were listening."

"You don't deserve a pep talk from her after the shit you've put her through, but she gave it anyway."

"Please. I'm not that bad."

His silence is damning.

"What, you want me to give her a medal?" I grumble, crossing my arms.

He knocks his shoulder into mine, moving to stand next to me as I stare out the expansive windows.

"Listen to her, Dec. Believe her. That'll be the best reward."

I glance at him, hating that I have to look up to meet his eyes. He only has two inches on me, but they fucking count when I feel small.

"Seriously, how are you both so calm?"

"I'm not the one in the hot seat today," he deadpans.

"Fair." I look back out the window. "Your secondary anxiety would take a load off, though."

"Careful, Dec. I might interpret that as you asking for help."

As I turn to roll my eyes at him, he slaps my shoulder.

"I know, I know," he chuckles, "it'll be a cold day in hell when you get your head out of your ass long enough to realize it's not a four-letter word."

"What's not?" My brows draw together.

"Help."

Sighing, I drop my head back and look to the ceiling. "I don't need help, I just–"

"Need a pep talk about how strong you are from a smart, beautiful woman you pretend to hate?"

"Fuck you, Shane," I growl, his words hitting so damn close to home. *I don't hate her. Far from it.*

"Nah, I've got better prospects at the moment. Thanks, though."

I can't remember the last time he was so...flippant. So carefree. We've carried the weight of the world on our shoulders for months, but something is changing for him. And for Linc. Like the longer we work with Lex, the lighter they both get, despite our looming deadlines and uncertain future. *I want that. I want...her.*

Before I can be seduced by my errant thoughts, or the fact I haven't felt carefree in fucking years, I look back at my index cards. Huffing, I chuck them in the bin. *There's no way in hell I'm backing down from her challenge.*

Shane turns and heads for the door. "You've got this."

"Of fucking course I do."

I brush past him, heading for the conference room Lex's

assistant booked for my interview. Shane's bemused chuckle follows me down the hall.

———

"So?" Lex leans against the conference room doorway, arms crossed. "How do you feel?"

She escorted Cass out a few minutes ago, and the guys went to check in with Parker. The only one remaining, I'd taken a moment to gather my thoughts. Lex caught me staring out the window, my gaze unfocused.

I open my mouth to bite out a pithy reply, then stop myself. Shane's words from earlier echo in my head.

Clearing my throat, I opt for the honest answer. "Relieved it's over."

Her eyes widen almost imperceptibly, and she straightens. "Was it that bad?"

Huffing a laugh, I shake my head. "No, it couldn't have gone better. Earlier, though..."

"Ah." She smiles as my voice trails off. "Regretting the attitude?"

"What attitude?" I tease, my lips twitching.

Her laugh is so quick and airy, I could get high on it. "Right, of course. You've reached your self-awareness quota for the day, I take it."

"Pardon me, but I'm very self-aware. Not sure what you're implying."

Those seafoam eyes sparkle as she taps her chin and moves toward me. "You know, you might be charming. If you weren't so completely insufferable."

I step closer, drawn to her like a moth to a flame and meet her in the middle of the room. "Do you always insult your clients?"

"Only the ones who deserve it." She's inches away, the curve of her neck enticing as she looks up at me.

The air thickens between us, and I fight to draw my eyes from her mouth. I'm a compass, and she's true north. I'd never admit it, but I can feel her presence in any room, know when she's close or too goddamn far. It's a constant battle to keep my distance, keep it professional, respect her boundaries...and I'm fucking tired of fighting.

"Do I deserve it?" I rasp, drowning in her citrus and floral scent.

Her smirk softens as her pupils dilate, her gaze dropping to my lips. I'm grateful, because it means I can look my fill without her realizing my gaze is anything but platonic.

"You deserve everything, Declan," she murmurs.

Maybe it's her earnestness or the way we're both leaning toward each other like our bodies are magnets. Maybe it's the high of the interview and the adrenaline still rushing through me. Maybe it's fucking Mercury in retrograde. I don't know what to blame, but I lose all sense in the moment.

"I'll never deserve you," I growl, reaching up to cup her cheek and thread my fingers into her short hair. "But, fucking hell, do I want to."

Ignoring the alarm bells ringing in my ears and hammering in my chest, I tighten my grip on her and pull us together, capturing her mouth in mine. She whimpers in surprise, stiff for a split second, then melts against me as she opens up and gives herself over. My head swims at how readily she succumbs, how pliant this fierce, fiery woman becomes at my touch. *Holy fuck, I want so much more.*

The thought is like a bucket of ice water. I have no business wanting more from her, not after everything I've put her through, everything she's done for us. *Us. Shit, what the hell am*

I doing?! I tear myself away and step back, chest heaving. Lex blinks at me in confusion, her fingers flying to her lips.

"Fuck, Lex, I'm sorry." I run my hand through my hair, turning toward the windows. "Shit. I had no right."

"Declan..." her voice has never been small or tentative, and it kills me that I'm the reason she sounds both now.

I may not have heard them directly from the source, but I'm aware of her rules. Kissing her in a glass-walled conference room in her place of business is a clear violation. And doing it without a conversation about what we both want violates mine.

"I'm a fucking idiot," I snarl, body tight as I glare out the window.

She steps closer, and I can feel her energy calling to mine even with my back turned.

"You are not," she admonishes, voice still softer than it should be.

"I am." I turn to face her. "That was a fucking mistake."

She freezes, leaning away as her cheeks darken. "Excuse me?"

Her eyes are hard, glinting as she stares at me, and I hate that all I want to do is grip her hair, yank her head back, and consume her completely. Now that I've tasted her, I can't think of anything else. My fingers twitch against my thigh, and she tracks the movement. Her gaze narrows.

"I have to go," I bite out, moving to brush past her and escape the room before I do something even more idiotic. *Like lock us both in and ravish her against the door.*

"Sure, of course," she says, her caustic tone stopping me in my tracks. "Go on, Declan. Run away."

My spine stiffens. She's behind me, but I feel her energy shift. The temperature in the room drops, but I don't turn.

"It's a fucking shame." Her voice could cut glass, it's so sharp.

"What is?" I don't know why I'm entertaining this when I know it won't go well. *Maybe I'm desperate enough for a part of her that I'll settle for her rage over nothing.*

"That you're a coward."

My head drops, fingers clenching as I gaze at the floor. "Am I?"

She's silent for a beat. "I didn't think you were, Declan, but what else would you call this? Turn around and face me."

"I can't."

She scoffs. "Can't, or won't?"

"Does it matter?" I mutter, heart slamming against my ribs.

I want to face her, want to turn around and challenge her until we're both vibrating in tension and can't keep our hands off each other. My eyes pinch closed as I imagine slamming her against the wall and burying myself in her. *Not happening, Wilde. Get it the fuck together.*

"It fucking does to me." Her voice is low, controlled. Cold. "You're brilliant, cunning, fucking strategic and talented as hell. You have more potential than most of the people we invest in, if you'd only be willing to reach out and take what you want. *Whatever* you want."

I can't listen to this. If I do, I'm going to make another mistake. I'll do something else to jeopardize more than just our professional relationship. Shane and Linc's faces loom in my mind's eye and guilt flares.

"See you next week, Lex," I say, resisting the urge to glance over my shoulder as I stride for the door.

Before she can reply, Linc and Shane appear before me. Their eyes flit back and forth between my hard expression and Lex's face behind me. They both freeze, Linc's brows furrowing as Shane's smile flattens.

"Everything okay here?" Linc asks.

"I'm fine," I snap. *Fucking idiot, go on and make it worse.*

"Dec–" Shane starts.

"Let him go," Lex interrupts. "We're done here."

I ignore the confusion on their faces as I take the out she offers. Pausing at the door, I can't resist a final glance at her face. I regret it immediately, heart plummeting at the sight of her closed expression. She's put her walls right back up between us, and I'm to blame.

Swallowing my pride, I give her a pleading look. "Lex, thank you for...everything. Today would've been a disaster without you."

Her nostrils flare as she breathes sharply. "It wouldn't have happened without me in the first place, Declan."

The ghost of a smile traces over my lips. *God, I love her fire.* "True enough."

The guys are looking between us in concern, Shane's mouth pulling into a frown. Leaving Lex to share what she will, I turn and head for the lobby to wait for Shane and Linc. If I linger any longer, I'm only going to make things worse.

A cold stone settles in the pit of my stomach as I walk away. From the beginning, I predicted Lex would tear us apart from the inside out. I was convinced nothing good could come of letting another outsider into Solum, into our lives. But today proved she isn't the one to blame. A chasm is opening between me and the two most important people in my life, and I don't know how to close it. *I'm fucking it all up.*

Getting closer to Lex, letting her in? I can only see it leading to heartbreak. She will only be with us through the Summit, anyway. *If keeping her at arm's length is how I keep us all together, so be it.*

Chapter 23

Linc

"How long do you think it takes to fall in love with someone?"

Shane goes still as he bends to pick up another gallon of soft gray paint, his entire body freezing mid-reach. I scrub a hand over the back of my head and clear my throat.

"It's a rhetorical question," I add. *Mostly.*

He scoffs, straightening. "Right. Rhetorical."

"It is. I'm just...wondering."

"You've never been in love before."

It's a statement; he knows I haven't. He's known me nearly my whole life, seen every relationship I've ever attempted. So I don't answer, just splash more paint into the pan at my feet.

When I look up again, Shane's gazing across the hall. Lex is in the next room over, painting. It was Shane's idea to ask for her help on the project we'd been putting off since moving in. He said doing the mundane task of repainting the upstairs bedrooms together could help clear her mind and release some tension.

I don't know if it was us, the looming Summit, or something unknown, but Lex has been in her head for days. She made time for a forty-five minute meeting with the three of us earlier in the week, but even during our daily runs and the one night she cleared for me and Shane, she was distracted. Distant. *I fucking hate it.*

I'd been skeptical she'd go for Shane's painting idea, but then I watched the tension seep from her body as she stood in the middle of the room we'd cleared, hands on her hips. After a deep breath and a nod, she dove right in, torturing us both as she bent in her tight yoga pants to fill her roller with paint. Two hours later, she was laughing again, limbs loose and eyes sparkling as she skimmed the roller over the wall. I've yet to fully process why I felt so overwhelmingly relieved at the sight.

Shane looks back at me, pensive. "I don't think there's a formula, Linc."

We'd left Lex in the other room for a moment to refill the paint trays. I can hear her music drifting down the hall, the hum of her murmured singing a soothing backdrop. I drag my attention back to Shane.

"So you believe in love at first sight?"

I don't. Lust at first sight was one thing, but truly falling for someone? That shit doesn't happen in an instant.

"Yeah." Shane shrugs. "I guess I do."

My eyebrows climb toward my hairline. "You're shitting me."

He chuckles. "I'm not. What, you think I'm too logical for that?"

"I mean, yeah? Kinda." I blink. "You're the stoic one. Grounded, steady. Love at first sight seems like the opposite of that."

"Isn't love grounding?"

My brow creases. "Is it? I've never thought of it like that."

"How have you thought of it?"

"Like...a tempest. A storm. Consuming, but not necessarily

bad. Like that moment when you stand outside and everything's getting dark and even the air is charged and the world feels like it's holding its breath. Waiting for something...atmospheric and dangerous and life-changing."

Shane studies me, then hums an intrigued sound. "I think love can be many things to each of us. You have your storm, I have...safety and a sense of belonging. To me, love is trust and comfort. Warmth."

I can see that, especially for him. "But...how do you feel safe with someone the first time you see them?"

He smirks. "What did you feel that day on the playground when we met?"

"Nah, man. Not that kind of love." I roll my eyes.

"Love is love, Linc. I might not fuck you or Dec, but I love you. Always have, always will. Didn't take me years or even days to figure it out, either. Just one glimpse of Dec's determination and your defiance."

I force myself to swallow down the emotion rising in my throat. He seemed like a superhero to me back then, tall and imposing with his steely glare, even as a kid. I trusted him the moment Declan brought him over, and when he stood up for me? No one had ever been so cool. There'd been no question in my mind—back then and even now—Shane was as much a brother to me as Declan.

"Fuck, man," I rasp.

Shane grins. "What? I've said it before."

"Not sure you have," I challenge, looking up at the ceiling as I blink rapidly, eyes hot. Heart-to-hearts aren't really our thing. *Fuck. Maybe they should be.*

"Hey, did you two lose the paint or something? It's been ages—" Lex sweeps into the room and freezes, looking at me, then Shane. "Um...you okay?"

I want to kick Shane in the 'nads when he laughs.

"Linc's in his feels."

"You said you loved me, asshole," I shoot back, rubbing a hand over my eyes.

Lex's green eyes soften as she smiles. "Of course he does."

I glance at her, raising a brow. She sighs and looks up at the ceiling, as though begging for patience. Stepping into my space, she slips her arms around me.

"Don't be afraid of your emotions, Linc. Don't run from telling the people you love you care about them." Her arms tighten briefly around me as her gaze unfocuses momentarily. "You, Shane, and Declan share something beautiful. And deep. You're family, but it's almost more than that."

Shane smiles at me, stepping up behind Lex. He's not quite close enough to touch her, but she loosens her arms just enough to lean back against him. Her eyes don't leave mine, and she tugs on my waist to bring me closer.

"I've never seen loyalty like yours," she murmurs, eyes locked on mine. "The way you support one another...it's something else. You should celebrate it."

"We do, in our way," Shane offers. He trails his fingers along her arm and smirks up at me. "Dec and Linc have never been free with their deeper emotions."

Before I can tell him off, Lex laughs. Shane's eyes glint as he grins, bending over to rest his chin on her shoulder.

"Gee, that's a shocker," Lex drawls, smile dropping slightly.

"Hey," I protest, gripping her hips gently. "I'm in touch with my emotions." *Sometimes.*

"Oh, yeah, totally," Shane agrees too readily.

"Sure you are, sweetheart," Lex smirks, voice syrupy sweet.

"Fuck off, both of you," I groan.

"No." She pulls me closer, a mischievous grin lighting her features. "Don't wanna."

Tightening my arms around her, I catch Shane's eye as he

straightens to give me more room. I see nothing but warmth and affection reflected back at me as I snuggle Lex, our bodies pressed together. She fits perfectly in my arms, under my chin. *Perfectly in our lives.* My body goes still at the thought, a vision of a future with her playing in my mind. Lex and Shane laughing in the kitchen. The three of us on the couch, her feet in Shane's lap and back against my chest. *Maybe Dec wouldn't complain about us sitting on top of him on the couch if Lex was there, too.*

My eyes widen and my breath stutters at the force with which I want those visions to be real. Shane's lips tip up into a small, knowing smile. He nods slowly, as though he can read the thoughts tumbling through my brain.

Lex leans back and looks up at me, her eyes bright. I struggle to breathe normally as I look down at her, wrenching my gaze from the safety of Shane's.

"If I'd known you were going to abandon me to do all the painting when you invited me to join this little home reno, I would've been harder to convince," she teases, oblivious to my epiphany.

Shane scoffs, saving me from having to answer. Lex turns to look up at him over her shoulder, arms still looped around my waist.

"Something amusing you, Mr. Kelly?"

"We've been gone for five minutes, tops."

"Eight," she counters, looking back at me with a smirk. "Definitely more than five."

Pushing past the overwhelmed feeling swirling in my chest, I conjure a playful smile. "You miss us already, beautiful?"

Something flickers in her eyes, maybe surprise or confusion, before she scrunches her nose and backs away, mischief in the curve of her lips.

"Nah, just needed more paint."

She snags the open gallon from the floor near my feet, turning on her barefoot heel and sauntering away. Shane chuckles as she disappears down the hall, looking over at me with a wry grin.

"You going to tell her?"

I clear my throat, looking down as I pick up the full paint tray. "Tell her what?"

Shane is quiet as he gathers another gallon of paint and some extra rollers. I can feel him looking at me, twin holes boring through my skull as I make for the door.

"Your brother may make a habit of bottling everything up, Linc, but you never have. Would be a shame for you to start now."

My steps slow and I pause in the hall, watching him draw level with, then pass, me. His ice blue eyes meet mine, his chin jutted out slightly in challenge.

"What about you?" I throw at him, deflecting shamelessly.

I need to take the attention, the pressure, off me. My thoughts are tumultuous, ideas for the future tangling with the practicalities of the present.

"We're on our own journeys, brother. Might be with the same girl, and may end up at the same destination, but our pace won't always match."

"Sounds like a cop out," I mutter.

He studies me for a moment, rare vulnerability shining through. "Love's not always enough, Linc."

I watch him disappear back into the guest bedroom, listening to the low murmur of Lex's voice as she greets him. Their tones are playful, and warmth pushes away some of the chill Shane's words sent through me. I'm naive enough to think loving someone is all it takes for a relationship to work, but I want to know exactly what's on Shane's mind.

It's gotta be Dec. Things were tense between the three of us and incendiary between Dec and Lex. The forty-five minutes we spent together on Solum earlier in the week had been heated, neither of them bending an inch for the other. *That's not what Lex is torn up over, is it?*

As though thinking of him summons the man himself, my brother appears at the top of the stairs.

"Linc!" Lex calls, laughing. "Come on, slowpoke–oh!"

Her playful words cut off as she swings out of the room, one hand bracing on the doorframe, and almost runs headlong into Dec. She jerks to a halt just in time and gapes up at him, eyes wide, their bodies barely inches apart.

Dec's nostrils flare as he stares at her, his fingers curling into a fist as heat flashes in his gaze. I catch Shane's eye as he comes into view through the doorway, his expression guarded.

"Hi, Declan." Lex's voice is strangled as she sways toward him, then catches herself. "We're painting."

His eyes trace her face, landing on a spot of gray on her cheek. Without a word, he licks his thumb and swipes it across her skin. Lex gasps at the contact, her body stilling and her eyes locked on Dec's. Her lips part, breath turning ragged as he smears the paint. His eyes flick to hers, pupils dilating as they dip to her mouth.

Holy sexual tension, batman. What the fuck did I miss? I shift, jeans feeling tight, and catch Shane's smirk out of the corner of my eye. Before I can taunt back, noticing he's just as affected, Dec huffs and backs away.

"I can see that," he bites out.

The spell between them breaks, much to my dismay. Lex blinks, shaking her head as though to clear it.

"Right," she sighs, shoulders sagging. I frown as I look between them. "Well, it's good to see you."

Wordlessly, he watches her turn and slip past Shane, expression flat.

"I take it you lost my invite," he grouses, tension bulking his shoulders.

"C'mon man. We thought it would be a good distraction, and you've been an ass to her lately. Didn't seem like an offer you'd be interested in."

"Right." He tsks, glancing at the open door before stepping closer and pitching his voice low. "Is she ever *not* around, Linc?"

Scoffing, I lean away from his aggressive tone. "Fuck you, man. She's rarely here outside of work shit and you know it."

The look in his eyes is feral. My brother is a stern guy on a good day, but something about Lex brought out something... wild in him. I can't tell if it's anger, fear, or lust. *After what I just witnessed, it might be a fucked up combination of all three.*

"I just think you need to be careful–"

I hold my free hand up. "Stop. I'm not going down this road with you, Dec."

I'm so done with his protests about Lex. It's been nearly three months of working together, and his resistance feels more performative than genuine. He's desperate to maintain some semblance of control, and for some reason, he still sees her as a threat.

Declan frowns, his eyes searching mine. He isn't used to me giving him resistance.

"Linc, I just don't want you getting hurt. I–"

"I'm not," I interrupt, backing toward the open door. "Keep pushing her away, Dec, and you might just hurt us yourself."

That wildness runs rampant through him as he watches me go, the vein down his forehead popping. I hold his gaze until I reach the door, challenging him wordlessly to be the bigger man. The better man. The man I know he can be if he puts aside his misplaced guilt and stops trying to control everything and everyone.

My hope is in vain. I know it as soon as he starts to turn

away, but the knowledge doesn't stop my gut from churning as he thunders down the stairs without a backward glance.

Sighing, I shake out my shoulders and muster a smile for Lex. Shane's words echo in my head. *He might not think love's enough, but I'm pretty sure I do.*

Chapter 24

Lex

I*'m fucked.*

I knew a girl's night when I was in a funk would be a terrible idea. The moment I open my door, Ruby's eyes narrow and she hums a determined little noise I've come to dread. It means she'll stop at nothing to unearth exactly what's bothering me so she can try to eradicate it. *Or, in this case, him. Too bad murder is a felony.*

"Not tonight, Roo, please," I mutter, sweeping a hand out to usher her down the hall. "Cass is in the kitchen."

Ruby keeps her eyes on me as she pads by, as though she can glare the truth out of me. When she doesn't succeed by the time she passes, she calls down the hall.

"Status report!"

"Shit's fucked!" Cass hollers back.

With a knowing look over her shoulder, Ruby sighs. Groaning, I rub a hand over my forehead and trudge after her. I'm not ready for her particular brand of disarming insightfulness. *I definitely should've canceled girls' night.*

"I can hear you thinking about throwing us out." Ruby narrows her eyes as I step into the kitchen. I moved so slowly in her wake that she's already sitting next to Cass at the island, wine glass in hand. "It's not happening."

"She's knows it's not." Cass grins over her glass, her eyes flashing in amusement. "She also knows we wouldn't have believed any of her usual excuses, so canceling would've been futile."

"You both suck," I huff, snatching my half-full glass off the counter.

"Trouble in man-sandwich paradise?" Cass coos.

There are no secrets between us. I trust both of them implicitly, even if Cass makes a living by telling other people's stories. I know she'll never tell mine without permission.

"Which one of them is it?" Ruby presses.

"Can we talk about literally anything else, ladies?" I take a sip, watching them watch me. "Please?"

Cass leans toward Ruby. "Is she begging right now?"

Ruby's lips twitch in response to her stage whisper. "Not yet."

"Well, this is fun." Turning, I walk away. If I'm going to endure their shenanigans, I'm getting comfortable. "Bring the wine," I toss over my shoulder.

They mutter to each other as I curl up in the corner of my giant sectional. It's the one piece of furniture in the room I didn't let the decorators pick for me. The soft cushions swallow me as I snag a soft throw from the basket by the arm, tucking it around myself. The lights in Jax's pool house are on, including the twinkle lights he strung up on the porch. He worried they'd bother me, but I find the warm reminder of his presence comforting.

"Cass is ordering Thai."

Ruby sets two bottles of wine on the coffee table as she enters the room, then flops into the big armchair near me. Her sharp gaze never leaves my face.

"Lovely."

"Which one of them fucked up?" Cass asks, walking up with her phone in one hand and wine in the other. She doesn't glance up as she swings up and perches on the opposite arm of the couch, her toes digging into the cushion.

"What makes you think someone fucked up?"

Cass snorts, tapping away on what I assume is a food delivery app. I can feel Ruby's eye roll, but I don't glance over to see it happen.

"We know you," Ruby answers. "You're a reasonable human, and, while you get restless sometimes, you're annoyingly constant."

That gets my attention. "Annoyingly?"

"Yep." Cass pops the 'p' as she taps her screen with her thumb, then chucks her phone down on the couch and looks up. "People aren't constant, Lexi."

"Oh god, not you, too," I groan, leaning my head back. "That fucking nickname."

"What? It's *adorable*."

"It's what my *nephew* calls me. It's not for adults."

"Jax is an adult," Ruby intones flatly.

I glance over at her. "Fine. It's not for *other* adults."

"Whatever. He used it once around me and I loved it, so it's sticking," Cass insists. "Back to the matter at hand. You're the most predictable person I know, and you've been completely baffling for the last two weeks."

"Predictable?!" My lips part as I stare at her. "You're kidding me."

"Don't take it personally." She flaps a hand at me. "You're a brilliant businesswoman and make all sorts of surprising strategic moves at work, you know this."

"But outside of work," Ruby adds, "you're usually very reliable."

"I like reliable more than predictable." I tip my wine toward Ruby.

"Semantics." Cass waves her hand again. "I've known you for years and she's known you for decades and we're both confused as fuck about what's going on with you lately."

"I see."

"This is the part where you spill." Cass perches on my couch expectantly, her expression open and encouraging.

I glance over at Ruby, finding her hawk eyes trained on me. Sighing, I sip from my giant glass.

"I will confiscate that damn thing if you try to hide behind it all night, Lexi, I swear to god."

"Call me Lexi again, and I'll throw you both out."

"Hey!" Ruby protests. "I haven't called you Lexi once!"

"Guilty by association," I insist, gesturing vaguely between them.

"She's on the opposite side of the room and we came in separate cars," Ruby deadpans.

"Whoa, Roo. Stone cold." Cass stares at her with wide eyes.

"What?" Ruby shrugs. "She's my best friend. If I gotta throw you under the bus to help her, I will."

"I'll allow it." Cass raises her glass in salute as Ruby does the same, united in their determination to wear me down. Then the redhead turns to me again. "We're back to my original ask, then. Spill."

"I don't want to." I don't. At all. I'm not sure I've fully processed why I've been in a funk for two weeks. *And processing out loud with these two sounds...painful.*

"We could just get her drunk and try again in an hour," Ruby offers. "Desperate times call for desperate measures." She holds my glare, unflinching.

I've led thousands of negotiations in my career, and no one resisted the full weight of my glaring silence without sweating, fidgeting, breaking, or all three. But Ruby sips her wine, completely unaffected. She'd make a damn fine lawyer if she didn't hate bureaucracy.

"It's silly," I insist. "I'll get over it."

"Stop deflecting!" Cass's tone is indignant as she slides down to the cushion, her back up against the arm. "Lex, you're worrying me. What's going on?"

"Do we need to kick some idiot in the balls?"

Turning back to Ruby, I level a finger at her. "Yes."

"Which one? The tattooed tech geek who brought you blue light glasses last week–I'm still not over how fucking sweet that was, by the way–or the golden retriever runner?" Cass asks eagerly.

"You're both way too invested in this," I sigh.

"It's the brother."

Cass gasps and slaps her thigh. "The brother! Of course!"

Jaw dropped, I stare at Ruby. "How do you *do* that?!"

She studies her nails. "It's a gift. What did the broody asshole do now?"

Over the last ten weeks of working with the boys, I'd kept Ruby and Cass relatively up to date. They knew about Shane joining my fun with Linc, and about the tension between me and Declan from the beginning. I had yet to tell them about the earth shattering kiss on the day Cass interviewed him because I was still grappling with what happened immediately after.

"It's nothing. I need to just woman up and move on."

"Because stuffing your feelings down is definitely the healthy approach to emotional pain."

"Listen to her, Lex. She's brilliant. She's a professor."

Rolling my eyes, I scoff. "Not of psychology."

Cass shrugs. "Still. Smart."

"She is," I concede.

The truth is, I don't know if I even have the words to explain how I'm feeling. How the back and forth between me and Declan has distracted me for weeks. And I have the sneaking suspicion that speaking it aloud will only make it weigh heavier on my mind. There's nothing either of them can do to address what is—or isn't—between us. *And he either has no idea what he wants or has no interest in making an effort.*

"Start thinking out loud, Lex."

My gaze finds Ruby's. Her eyes are dark and soulful, her lower lip caught in her teeth. For as surly as she can be, I suspect no one cares more deeply for others than she does.

"The day you came and interviewed Declan ended poorly." I sip my wine as I look over at Cass.

"What? I thought it went so well. He raved about you and Athena, Lex." She frowns. "He genuinely seemed grateful and couldn't stop talking about you and what Athena's done for Solum. Was he unhappy after?"

I gaze at my hands. "No. He was thrilled. We spoke, and things felt almost natural between us for the first time."

Cass cocks her head in confusion. "I don't understand."

"Neither do I. One moment we were bantering, and the next he was kissing me. And then he was running away."

I glance at them both and chuckle softly at their raised brows.

"He didn't!" Cass is incredulous. "Wait, how are we only hearing about this now? You kissed?!"

"The more important part is that he ran away," Ruby interjects, her tone hard.

"After he called it a mistake."

They both inhale sharply, Cass in shock and Ruby in sheer fury.

"I think he got in his head. Felt guilty maybe?"

"Don't make excuses for him." Ruby's eyes flash. "He's a grown ass man. He should act like one."

"I know. I'm not." I breathe deeply, trying to calm the emotions roiling in my chest. "He clearly wasn't ready for whatever happened between us, and I should let myself forget it happened."

Ruby snorts. Cass ignores her and leans forward eagerly.

"What did you do? Tell me you set him straight."

"Kind of? I called him a coward, then walked out. But since then, I've..." My voice trails off as I consider how much to share. It doesn't take long for me to decide on all of it. "I'm not sleeping well, would've skipped my morning workouts if Linc didn't show up, and I'm running myself ragged at work, glued to a screen eighteen hours a day. And as I've paid enough attention to notice all that, it's opened my eyes to how many people in my orbit take care of me."

I look off to the side, studying the color and textile of the couch. Eye contact feels like too big an ask. "I didn't realize how much you all do, or Miles. Hell, even Cami. And that was before Linc and Shane swept into my life."

Sighing, I slouch deeper into my blanket. "And here I am, with so many people in my circle, and one confusing interaction with a brilliant, beautiful man who is as confusing as he is cunning has taken me offline. That's what it feels like. Like his unwillingness to acknowledge or do anything about our growing tension has derailed my brain. And I don't fucking know why I'm giving him that kind of power."

Silence fills the room as I gulp my wine. After a moment, Ruby goes straight for the jugular.

"You're not angry. You're hurt."

Frowning, I turn to her. "That's not–"

"Whether or not you've realized it, you're invested. Personally. And him keeping you at arm's length is hurtful, especially when he crosses boundaries willy nilly then bolts."

Her words strike a chord, and I mull over them. Of course

I'm personally invested in Linc and Shane, it's impossible not to be. Declan and I, on the other hand, hadn't crossed any lines until he pressed his lips to mine and turned my world upside down. Absently, my fingers brush my lips at the memory, my chest squeezing.

If I'm honest with myself, I'm not the one who wants distance. He's pushed me away at every opportunity ever since he walked out of my conference room. *Do I want something more from Declan?*

"You like him."

Cass is studying me, her shrewd gaze breaking me apart like one of her interview subjects.

"He's...fine." *And infuriating...gorgeous, frustrating, talented as fuck, exasperating. But, yeah, we'll go with fine.*

"You want the full set," Ruby muses.

"Excuse you?" I sputter.

"Oh, come on. You wouldn't be in your head like this if you weren't interested. He's more than a client to you, just like the other two are. You light up every time you talk about them or their business, Declan included."

"Okaaaay, but there's a big difference between being more than a client and being what Linc and Shane are to me." *He'd have to fucking talk to me about something other than Solum, for starters.*

"And you want to bridge that distance. Think about it. What are you really upset about?" Ruby presses.

I frown. Admittedly, I've avoided examining my feelings too closely. Between work and the guys, it felt easier to shove it all to the back of my head and just keep moving forward. It's almost jarring to realize I haven't fully examined the cause of my negative feelings.

"Of course I want him to trust me." The words are more stalling tactic than insight, and we all know it. "But there's also a part of me that wonders..."

"What it would be like to finally let someone in for more than hot sex?" Cass blinks as I stare at her. "What? It's literally my job to be insightful."

"You're usually less blunt about it than she is," I protest, gesturing to Ruby.

"Whatever. Lex, is Cass right? Are you wanting something more?"

Was I? I shake my head. "I...I mean, no, I don't think so." I swallow. "We set ground rules. There's an end date."

A feeling of foreboding flares in my chest at the thought, but I lock it up.

"Do you want there to be?" Cass's voice is tentative, gentle. "An end date, I mean."

"Of course."

Ruby tsks. "Don't give your automatic answer, Lex. Sex may have been something you did to scratch an itch before, but we all know it's a lot more than that with those two. You're basically in a full-on polyamorous relationship. You have been for weeks."

I blink. "They've never used that word."

Both of them roll their eyes, but it's Ruby who speaks. "Do you feel like you're in a relationship?"

Sighing, I close my eyes and consider the question. I see Linc nearly every morning, and Shane drops by multiple times a week. Sometimes he brings me lunch, but there's been other things—an oversized water bottle, the blue light glasses, and even a ring light for my desk after I complained off-handedly about the lighting in my office.

Both of them text me daily, not only to coordinate plans to see one another, but also to simply check in. When something noteworthy happens at work, I want to share it with them before anyone else. And when they have breakthroughs at Solum, I usually get an eager video call before they send the details over to my team. Opening my eyes, I meet Ruby's expectant gaze.

"Yes."

Cass squeals while Ruby just nods back at me. "I thought so."

"Girl, I'm so happy for you!" Cass chirps.

"Yeah," I scoff. "Sure. But it can't go anywhere, even if you were right and I was considering something more. They're a package deal, all three of them, and Declan is definitely not in."

"But you like him," Ruby presses.

Yes. "He's an ass, Roo."

"A biteable ass," Cass offers.

I arch a brow at her.

"What? I have eyes. Dude's a ten."

Ruby snorts while I push right past Cass's comment.

"Hotness aside...yeah, I guess you could say I like him. I'm intrigued by him, I think." I stare off into the distance, picking at the blanket as I try to corral my thoughts. "It's so rare for me to go toe-to-toe with someone and feel evenly matched, you know? When we're not sniping at each other, we're building something incredible."

Heaving a sigh, I swipe my fingers under my eyes. "But I must be making it all up in my head because he went and called me a mistake."

"He called *kissing* you a mistake," Ruby corrects. "He's a shithead for it either way, but let's be clear."

Smiling softly at her vehement defense of me, I incline my head. "You're right. I feel tied up in knots and I don't even know what he wants. That's not how a healthy relationship works."

"And you want that," Ruby presses.

The thought is almost terrifying. I haven't had a long-term relationship in years, not since grad school. My business always came first, and I liked it that way. Attachments are...messy. In my experience, family was a source of pain and weakness, not strength. And while Declan, Lincoln, and Shane seem to have created something that was the complete opposite, it seemed like the exception to prove the rule.

"I can't even imagine what that could look like," I murmur, eyes glazing as my mind whirs.

"Probably a lot like the last few weeks," Cass says. "Except maybe in one house, instead of two."

Before Linc, I would've scoffed at the suggestion of moving in with someone I had a romantic connection with. I couldn't afford that kind of distraction, and I had no desire to weave someone so intimately into my life. Trusting someone to that extent was a foreign concept.

"Lex, stop panicking." Ruby's voice cuts through the rushing in my ears. "You're in control, you know. Pretty sure those two would give you anything you wanted."

"Not if it meant losing Declan." I know it without a doubt—Linc and Shane will never put me before their brother. And I'll never ask them to. I love how they support one another, how they've created the family they want and need. Interfering with it is out of the question, despite what I may want. "He wants nothing to do with me."

"That's not true," Cass exclaims, snatching her phone. "I can prove it."

I glance at Ruby, brow raised. She shrugs.

"Got it!"

"Got what?" I peer toward her phone.

"Voice memo from Declan's interview. He was very complimentary."

He was? It's nearly pathetic how pleased I am to hear it. "I'm failing as a feminist," I sigh, dropping my head back on the couch and closing my eyes.

"Feminism is personal," Cass quips, "and your particular

brand is effective as fuck when it comes to lifting other women up and helping them achieve their dreams, so fuck it. Fall in love with the alphahole if you want. You deserve it. And any feminist who thinks otherwise can get fucked."

She's too intent on her phone screen to notice me staring at her, jaw slightly dropped. "Alphahole?"

Cass flaps a hand as Ruby snorts. "Doesn't matter, listen to this."

She taps the phone with her thumb, and Declan's rough voice fills my living room.

"Honestly, I'm still surprised I'm even here," he says.

"What do you mean?" Cass presses.

He chuckles self-consciously. "Ah, I mean, I'm not surprised we've been funded. We deserve that, our tech is revolutionary. But being here, part of Athena's roster? I have to pinch myself about that one every once in a while."

"Say more." I can hear the smirk in Cass's voice.

"If we were football players, getting signed by Athena is like being a first round draft pick. And having Lex Livingston as our strategic business advisor and personal mentor is like winning the Super Bowl in our rookie year. She's a force."

He huffs, and I can picture him slowly shaking his head. *"I admired her for years, you know. Was so impressed by Athena's rise. It was like they didn't know how to lose, like they didn't even acknowledge it was an option. In a world where it's impossible to play a perfect game, I thought they were the exception."*

"Thought, past tense?"

"Yeah. Then I met Lex, started working with her. And as much as I respect and appreciate the team she's built, Athena's success isn't owed to them." He pauses, and Cass looks at me with tender eyes.

"It's her." He takes a deep breath, soft sounds like he shifted in his chair coming through. *"She's literally the smartest person*

I've ever met, and that's before you realize she actually gives a shit, truly, about the people she works with and mentors."

He apologizes for the swearing. They laugh.

I look up and meet Cass's gaze as he starts back up again, my heart pounding.

"I'm in awe of her. Working with her, benefiting from her perspective and expertise, is a literal dream. I founded Solum because I wanted to build my family's legacy, launch a green building solution that could help address housing insecurity and improve global economies. That was the dream."

Cass reaches out and squeezes my hand.

"Lex Livingston gave me–gave us–a second chance and, in doing so, handed my lifelong dream to me on a silver platter and dared me to dream bigger. Who else in this industry can do that, huh? No one. She's a unicorn."

My friend taps her phone and tosses it back down. "He may do a shit job of telling you how he feels, but he had no problem telling the whole damn world. I don't know what's keeping him from saying those things to your face, but we all have baggage, Lexi. Even you."

I'm so stunned I don't even react to the nickname, my eyes hot.

"The line between love and hate is a tightrope, you know." Cass grins. "And while your broody asshole might be athletic as fuck, he's no acrobat. He's keeping you at a distance for a reason, but clearly a lack of attraction, respect, or admiration isn't it."

The thought warms me through. I almost hate how much I react to the simple idea of something more with Declan. *When did I develop a thing for him?* As soon as I think it, I know it's a silly question. The back and forth between us is an aphrodisiac of its own, given how rarely I find someone to challenge me. And I fucking love how neither one of us can back down when we get into it, each of us pushing the other into something... more than we were before.

"Girl, that man looks at you like he wants to devour you." Cass laughs, filling the silence I let linger.

"And he's mad about it," Ruby adds.

"You haven't even met him!" I accuse, cracking a smile as I swallow back tears.

"But she nailed it," Cass giggles. "Granted, he seems mad about most things."

"He's so hot and cold. I shouldn't even be thinking about this." I drop my face into my hands. "If he can't own up to wanting me, he doesn't deserve me."

"That's fucking true," Ruby agrees. "But the heart wants what it wants, Lex."

"And you think I want him?" I give her a sardonic look, even though she's right.

"I think he's sharp as hell and pushes you, and you fucking love that. And you want all three of them." Cass smiles as I turn to her. "I'm sitting here cheering you on, because you deserve everything. Literally, Lex. Everything."

A thoughtful smile tugs at my lips as I reach out a hand to Cass, gripping hers tightly. That I said almost the same thing to Declan before he walked out doesn't escape me.

"She's right." Ruby arches a brow. "The question is, how are you going to go about getting what you deserve?"

Chapter 25

Declan

"She's pulling up," Shane calls.

It's been eight days since I saw Lex. After she nearly ran into me, I avoided her completely for the rest of Linc's ridiculous little painting party. We haven't been in the same room since our last tense weekly meeting.

Shane jogs down the stairs, no doubt headed outside to greet her. My chest feels tight with discomfort and tension in response. I haven't talked to him or Linc about the kiss, resigned to pretending it never happened. Pretending my worldview isn't forever changed.

"Pretty sure she can find the door on her own," I say as he reaches the foyer.

He replies immediately without so much as a glance my way. "Not doing it for her, man."

The thought of Shane feeling so strongly for her that he can't wait the thirty seconds it'll take for her to get out of the car and walk into the house makes my skin itch. I can see the cracks between the three of us widening and feel helpless to stop the progression. *Just one week to go.* If we can make it through the

Green Innovation Summit in Paris, we'll be back to normal soon enough.

Or, I can try to get her out of our hair sooner.

It's a selfish thought. Being near her, but not with her? It's fucking torture.

"She here?" Linc walks up from the basement in nothing but athletic shorts, a towel slung over his shoulder.

"Seriously? Were you working out?"

He opens the fridge, snagging a bottle of water. "Yeah. What good is the gym you've finally set up down there if we don't use it?"

"You knew we had a meeting."

He rolls his eyes. "Of course I did. I'm up here on time, aren't I?"

"Oh, what? You thought you'd grace us all with your sweaty, smelly ass?"

"Pretty sure no one cares, Dec."

"I care! Have you finally given up all pretenses of professionalism?" The lines between work and home are even more precious to me these days. The murkier they get, the more I worry.

He levels an annoyed glare at me. "Dude. We have business meetings all the fucking time. Hell, the three of us have literally had them *at* the gym. What's your issue?"

"It's not just the three of us anymore, Linc," I point out.

"Lex doesn't mind me sweaty, brother. Promise."

The reminder of the intimacy between them makes my blood pressure spike. "For fuck's sake—"

"There she is!" He calls, cutting me off as Shane opens the door for Lex.

She looks up with a bright smile for my brother, her dark hair straight and parted down the middle. It shines almost red in the fading evening sun streaming through the door, lighting her up. I swallow roughly, trying to ignore the heat flashing through me. I can't look at her without remembering the feel of her body against mine, her mouth parted so willingly.

Her long legs are on display in a tight sheath dress, which stops short of her knees. The smooth black fabric fits her perfectly, showing off the tight nip of her waist and the flare of her hips. My eyes are drawn down the gentle slope of her calf as she toes off her heels before moving across the room toward us.

I hate how much of her I notice, how every little detail burrows its way into my mind. I'll obsess over each one later, unable to banish her from my thoughts.

"Look at you," she teases, smiling at Linc as though I'm not in the room. "Get a good workout in like you hoped?"

She knows his workout schedule? My brow furrows as I watch her walk into his embrace, and he sweeps her into a fierce kiss. They've never really hidden their affections, but they've gotten more brazen about the PDA in the last few weeks. The physical stuff is one thing, but the casual way she makes it clear how close they are lights a fire in my gut as I tear my eyes away.

"Sure did," he says, drawing my eyes back to them as he releases her. "Thanks for being flexible with timing tonight."

"Of course," she murmurs, trailing a hand down his bare arm as she steps away.

It's like I can see the mark of that featherlight touch on his skin, the effect she has on him glaringly obvious as he watches her. But it's not a flash of lust or desire that rises in his eyes, it's affection. Something tightens in my chest as the realization hits me. Turning toward Shane, I find my best friend watching me, a knowing look on his face. As my lips part on the question, he inclines his head, one shoulder lifting as though to say 'what can you do?'

"Well, Declan, I'm glad the time worked for you. We have a lot to cover."

Lex's voice reaches me through a quagmire, my thoughts a frantic jumble of concern, confusion, and sheer fury. *Fuck it, I'm not backing down.*

"Do we?" I answer absently, my voice rough as I turn back to her.

She frowns, searching my face for something. "We do, and we'll be far more productive without your usual attitude."

I chuckle, the sound ugly even to my ears. "This is just who I am, Lex. Take it or leave it."

"God, you're a dick," Linc grouses, glowering straight ahead.

"Declan, I'm this close," Lex holds up her thumb and forefinger, barely a millimeter apart, "to leaving it. Can we focus and leave the bullshit behind, please?"

Sure, Lex. Don't break my brother's heart and we have a deal. "Fine."

I turn to the dining room table and yank a chair back. Lex takes her typical spot across from me, with Linc and Shane facing each other between us. *Always fucking between us.*

"What's on your agenda, then?" I can't keep the bite out of my tone, desperate for distance. From Lex, from my brother and best friend who have no idea how much I want their woman, when I've never entertained joining their bedroom shenanigans before.

My realization about Linc's infatuation has me rattled. I'm not sure what's causing the tension in my body, though I have the sinking suspicion it's fear. Fear for Linc and his impending heartbreak, fear for the relationship between me and the two people I care for more than anything else on the planet. Fear that the woman across from me, with her sharp gaze and sharper mind, is going to herald the end of everything I've worked to build for my entire adult life.

"We're one week out from leaving for the Summit. My team

was expecting the draft of your speech two weeks ago. Have you received their feedback?"

Lex's gaze bores into mine. She knows the answer; it's the same question she's asked for the last two weeks.

"No."

Linc flops back dramatically, heaving an exasperated sigh as he cards his fingers through his hair. Shane is sprawled in his chair, though his typical ease is absent as he stills in response to my short reply. Lex simply sits and watches me, silent. She's fucking brilliant at waiting me out. *I'd admire her for it if it wasn't so goddamn infuriating.*

"I have it under control, though."

For the first time, I watch Lex's cool control break. She can't contain the snort of derision that breaks free, her eyes flashing with an unidentifiable emotion. The most immature part of me wants to cheer at the confirmation that I'm getting under her skin.

"You have it under control?" Her voice is so quiet, so tight.

Linc goes just as still as Shane, his eyes widening as he watches her professional mask crack.

"How do you have it under control, exactly?" Lex's head cocks to the side, her tone sarcastic as her words crack across the table.

"It's my company," I remind her. "I'm the face of Solum, aren't I? It was one of your conditions."

"I'm aware."

"I know what I need to say, I don't need your team to dissect it. It'll be more authentic if I just...speak from the heart. Wasn't that your advice last time?"

"Are you fucking kidding me?" she bites out.

Linc flinches, his wide eyes snapping from Lex to me and back again.

"No." I shrug nonchalantly, desperate to see her let go.

"I know you're not that fucking stupid, Declan."

My pulse doubles at her words, my fists clenching. "What did you just call me?"

"You heard me, you egotistical asshole."

Shane blows out a slow breath, his expression blank as he stares at the center of the table. Linc looks about ready to cry, his expression anguished as he watches it all unfold.

"You're in my house." I slowly rise to my feet.

"And your business exists because of my investment." She stays seated.

She leaned forward as she got angrier, the tension pushing her toward me. I watch as she forces herself to lean back, arms crossed over her chest and one ankle tucked behind the other. *Get up. Get up and fight me, Lex.*

"Is that all you've got?" I taunt her, throwing my arms wide. "The great Lex Livingston, here with her money to make everything better."

"What the fuck, Dec?!" Linc glares at me. "You're out of line."

"Your brother's right." Lex glares. "You signed off on this schedule, on my terms. You deciding to go rogue and wing the most important presentation of your career is not what we agreed to."

She's walling me out again, her professional persona returning. *I hate it. Where's the fire, Lex? Get. Up.*

"Well, I think we're far enough down the path that we can recognize what we really need."

"And what's that, Declan?"

"The three of us," I gesture around the table. "Lincoln, Shane, me. That's it."

Lex studies me, her lips pursed. "I see."

"Do you?" I challenge, frustrated she's eased back into her tight control.

I want to watch those fissures in her perfectly constructed mask widen, want to dig my fingers into the softest parts of her and wrench them apart. I'm desperate for her to mirror the hurricane of emotion thundering in my chest. *I don't want to be the only one feeling so unhinged.*

"I do." Her cold gaze hardens. "You're a fool. And a complete and utter waste of my time."

She stands, finally. Guilt simmers low in my gut. I don't want her harsh words, don't want to hurt her or the men watching us go at each other. But I feel trapped between my emotions and my concern for our future.

"So that's it, then?" I accuse, thinking of her calling me a coward. "All these weeks of work, and you're done?"

Fire flashes in her eyes, fists clenched at her sides, and I want to pound my chest in victory. I can't have her soft affection; she saves that for Linc. I don't get her quiet contemplation; I've seen for myself how she's handed it to Shane. But her anger? Her fight? I crave it. *Give it to me, Lex. Fucking burn me with it.*

"Let me be clear, Declan Wilde. I. Don't. Quit." Her words are sharp, her voice hard as she steps around the table, making a slow path toward me. "I have given you and your dream my all. My team has worked long hours to support your success. And you might feel like the big man standing there belittling me, but I. Won't. Let. You."

She stops directly in front of me, close enough I can feel the warmth of her body seeping into mine. She nearly vibrates with tension, the sides of her neck rigid with it. It kills me she thinks it's still about the business. *This has nothing to do with Solum, boss.*

"You think you're the man, Declan?" she whispers, jade eyes glittering fiercely. "You think you've got it all under control? You don't need anyone's help to succeed?"

I struggle to stare impassively at her, shoving my hands into my pockets to keep from reaching out to touch her. Even though I'm the cause of them, I want to soothe the lines in her brow away.

"I don't."

"Which is why you came to me for help, right? You had it under control."

"I didn't come to you," I point out.

"Oh, right. You needed your little brother to get the help you were too fucking proud to ask for, right?"

I bite the inside of my lip to keep from grinning at her, wanting to seize her face in my hands and kiss her for standing up to me, for calling it like it is. She's absolutely fucking right, I was a prideful idiot and Linc did what needed doing. *I'm terrified of what comes after the business, Lex.* Her gaze searches mine, and she chuckles in surprise, a knowing sound that probably strikes fear into lesser men.

"I see what you're doing."

My lips twitch, but she misses it. Of course she does. "Oh?"

"I'm a threat to you."

You have no idea.

"Oh, Declan," she tuts. "I expected more."

"What are you—"

"They love you, Declan. I can't take them from you. And I don't want to."

Those words feel like a punch to the gut, though I should've known she'd see right through me. I want to look over at Lincoln and Shane to see their reactions, but I can't. She holds me captive, my lips parting as I suck in a ragged breath.

"You're a stronger man than this," she continues, her voice quiet but firm. "Don't let your fear win. Your dream is in reach and it's time for you to take it."

"I will—" I start

"But if you push me away and try to do it alone, you'll push them away, too," she goes on.

Her eyes burn into mine and she's still so close I can feel her breath ghost over my lips. I turn my head and exhale, my shoulders dropping slightly as some of the tension leaves me. Though I don't want to admit it, she's right; Linc and Shane have been telling me as much for weeks. She takes a step back, her arms crossing once more. It's subtle, but it tells me I affected her–one piece of armor she's keeping.

"Are you done?" she challenges, not giving an inch. *God, I fucking love it.*

I simply stare back at her, waiting to see what she'll do next.

"The Summit is next week, Declan. Are you going to work with us to prepare, or are you quitting this partnership?" She gestures to Linc and Shane. "Are you giving up on the team?"

Letting my eyes fall closed briefly, I sigh. "No."

"Thank fuck," Linc mutters, slapping his hands against the table and getting to his feet. "I need a goddamn drink."

He kisses the top of Lex's head as he passes her, brushing her shoulder and arm with a casual hand as he heads to the kitchen. I track the motion and Lex notices, her eyebrow cocking at me in challenge.

"What?" I push, turning back to my chair and giving myself a reprieve from her piercing gaze.

"Green's not your color," she chides, turning to follow Linc.

I stiffen. As my silent and entirely futile denial rises, I catch Shane's eye. His expression is knowing, a tiny smirk on his lips, and I drop my face into my hands as I sit.

"I'm not jealous," I groan, scrubbing a hand over my jaw and turning to look at him.

"Like fuck you aren't." He watches me impassively as I gape at him.

"Seriously? That's all you're gonna say to me."

He shrugs. "Pretty sure Lex said it all. For now."

Scoffing, I slouch back and sigh, looking up at the ceiling.

"For what it's worth, she's right. We love you. She doesn't change that."

I search his face. *Doesn't he see?* "She's changing everything, Shane."

"Not all change is bad, Dec."

We stare at each other for a few long moments until Linc and Lex return with drinks. I'm surprised when Lex hands me a beer, that sardonic look back on her face.

"Consider it an olive branch."

"I hate olives," I reply automatically, mentally slapping myself.

"Declan, take the goddamn beer," Linc barks.

I obey, heart twisting when something like hurt flashes in Lex's eyes. She's quick to blink it away, turning back to her seat.

"Now that we've wasted our first thirty minutes, we should probably get down to business. I'd intended to start with good news: Solum has been selected as one of five finalists for this year's Brightest in the Bay award."

My jaw drops as Linc grins, clapping in victory. Before we can celebrate, Lex continues.

"Yes, it's wonderful news. We'll celebrate when we have time." She gives me a hard look. "Declan, since we're so close to the Summit and I'm unwilling to derail my team's entire schedule to meet your timeline, you get your wish. You have creative agency over your speech. Let's hear it."

Panic rises. "What, now?"

She tilts her head, sipping her wine. "Yes, now. It's the last opportunity for me to hear it and give feedback before we fly to Paris."

"So we'll do it on the plane."

"We'll do it now, Declan. Or I won't be on the fucking plane." Her voice is steely.

"I don't have my notes."

"Just speak from the heart, right?"

I growl under my breath as she smiles at me while she throws my words back in my face. *This is not how I expected tonight to go.* The plan was to push her away, to frustrate her enough that she'd leave it to Linc and Shane to manage me so I got the distance I needed. Not to flounder my way through a speech I've avoided for weeks.

It's not that I don't want to go to the Summit or officially launch Solum, but I'm struggling to put words to what our technology can be. We dreamed of achieving something great for so long, but it had always been an intangible thing on the horizon. In the weeks leading up to the Summit, everything became real. And in my overwhelm and worry over Lex and Anne-Marie—*who is too fucking quiet, I don't trust it*–the inspirational and strategic ideas to rouse a crowd were elusive at best.

"Or we could start with an outline," Lex offers, her voice gentle. "Start there and work up to the full story."

The gratitude is evident on my face. It has to be because her lips curve into the slightest smile when I look up at her.

"We've got this," she says. "We, Declan. The four of us. Together, we've got this."

Shane and Linc are looking at me, but I keep my attention on Lex..

"Together," I say gruffly. I add the next word to mask the emotion welling in my throat. "Fine."

I can almost hear Lex's eyes roll as she sets her wine down and pulls her laptop from her bag.

"Dude," Linc chastises before taking a long pull of his beer.

"At least it's progress." Shane eyes me, a mischievous glint to his expression. "Better than jealousy."

I'm gonna fucking kill him.

Chapter 26

Shane

"Got a minute?"

Declan pauses at the top of the stairs to the basement for a long moment before he turns to me.

"Can I refuse?"

"No." *Come to Jesus time, buddy.*

He rolls his eyes. "Then, sure, Shane. I've got a minute."

I nod. "Great. Let's go."

He frowns as I walk toward the garage. "Where are we going?"

"It's five o'clock somewhere, right?" I say over my shoulder.

"That's what they say." He scoffs as he trails after me. "Just the two of us?"

"Linc's with Lex."

"I see."

I glance over, smirking at the look on his face. "I get it. I'd rather be with her, too."

"I didn't say anything."

"You're a bristly bastard these days, you know that?"

He grunts in response, settling into the passenger seat of my Jeep Wrangler. I eye him as I back out of the garage. He's tense, as he has been for months now. Ever since things ramped up for Solum and Lex became a fixture in our lives, Declan has been a ball of nerves. We have a week before we'll be in Paris, and it's high time he gets his shit together.

"Relax, Dec. It's just me."

"I'm relaxed."

"Right. You're so relaxed you're about to tap a fucking hole in my door."

Dec glances down at his fingers as though unaware he started drumming a beat when he sat down. "Sorry."

I flick on my blinker. "I don't care that you're tapping. I care about why."

"Dunno, Shane. Seems like you have a theory, though."

"Yeah, that's not how this is gonna go."

He scoffs again, and I feel the urge to smack him upside the head.

"I miss my friend," I say in lieu of corporal punishment. "Linc misses his brother."

"I'm not the one who disappears most nights or every morning."

Sighing, I pull into the parking lot of a dive bar near our lab. "Don't get me wrong, Dec, you've been physically present. But that's about it."

"We're all busy, Shane." He climbs out of the car.

"You tired of this?" I follow, closing my door.

Meeting him behind the vehicle, he finally looks at me. "Tired of what?"

"Me and Linc, living in your house. Being around. The three of us being a unit."

His eyes widen. "Fuck, no. First of all, it's our house. Second, why would you think that?"

I walk us both toward the bar entrance. "You've been

pushing Lex away so hard, you've pushed us away, too. Hard not to assume you want us all gone."

"That's the opposite of what I want, Shane. Seriously, the absolute last thing."

"What do you want?"

We slide into a worn booth, ordering a couple of beers when the server stops by. The place is dark and quiet, a few regulars at the long bar and a handful playing pool in the back. The surrounding booths are empty, cracked pleather seats shiny with wear.

"It's complicated," Dec says.

"I'm a smart guy. Try me."

He stares at his hands, lips pursed.

"You know," I drawl, "I've joked about how you consider 'help' a four-letter word, but you seem to need a reminder that getting help isn't a weakness, Dec. There's strength in knowing your limitations and having the wherewithal to get support when you need it."

His green eyes meet mine.

"Seems like your internal processing isn't getting you very far. Let me help you."

He scrubs a hand over his jaw. "I...I kissed her."

I didn't expect him to cop to it so quickly. A smile curves my mouth. "I know."

"Wait, what? How do you know?"

"She told me."

He straightens, his back hitting the booth. "She fucking told you."

I thank our server and pick up my pint glass as she walks away. "We talk."

"You talk about me."

I raise my IPA, inviting him to cheers with me. Hesitantly, his eyes on my face, he does.

"We talk about a lot of things, Dec. Just like you and I do. Or did." I study him as he gulps his lager. "Do you really think it was a mistake?"

"Yes," he answers vehemently. My eyebrows raise, and he groans. "And no. Fuck. I told you it was complicated."

"Break it down for me," I suggest.

"Hang on. You're not mad?"

There it is. "Why would I be mad?"

The crease between his brows deepens. "I kissed your girl."

I chuckle. "Sure did. But I kiss Linc's girl, so."

"And that doesn't bother you?"

Setting my glass down on the worn tabletop, I relax against the seat and drape an arm over the back of the bench. "You've always been pretty tight-lipped about your romantic relationships, man, so forgive me if I'm wrong. But I assume you've never been in a relationship with more than one person at a time?"

He exhales sharply. "No, I haven't."

"But you're interested in it."

"Never was before."

I smirk. "I get it. She's hard to say no to."

"Try impossible. I've been fucking miserable keeping my distance."

Nodding, I watch as he picks at the cardboard coaster, shredding it in his fingers. *Can't say I've ever seen Dec fidget before. This is entertaining as fuck.*

"Why are you keeping your distance?"

He looks up at me through his lashes. "Need to figure my shit out first. And talk to you, Linc."

"That's fair. Talking to us before you kissed her would've been preferable—"

Dec looks down, guilt heavy in the set of his shoulders.

"Hey, man, no. It's okay." I reach out and grip his forearm

through his black henley. "This is new for all of us. I'm not mad, neither is Linc."

"You don't care that I kissed Lex," he says, flat and disbelieving.

"I care. I'm not mad you kissed her." I tilt my head. "I'm a little pissed you told her it was a mistake and pushed her away like a total jackass, but I'm not mad you *kissed* her."

"Fuck," he mumbles, dropping his head onto his crossed arms on the table. "I'm fucking it all up."

"You're sure trying to."

"Gee, thanks for sugarcoating it."

"Not my strength; you know that."

"What the fuck do I do, Shane?"

"About what, exactly?"

He groans. "You're going to make me spell it out, aren't you? You stubborn fuck."

"Guilty."

Lifting his head, he sighs heavily. "I'm...christ, I sound pathetic. I'm scared, man."

I glance at my beer, giving him a reprieve. "You're not pathetic, Dec. What are you afraid of? Linc thinks it's the Anne-Marie shit, but...it's not, is it?"

He chuckles wryly. "It certainly started that way. Now? I...I don't want to drive a wedge between us. But watching you three all cozy feels like I'm on the outside."

"How does that feel?"

"Like absolute shit, Dr. Phil. Thanks for asking."

I laugh, tipping my glass toward him. "I hear you, man. You know you put yourself there, though, yeah?"

My best friend has never been the best at introspection, but he's a smart man. A frown tugs at his mouth as I watch him grapple with himself.

"I mean..."

"Dude. You've done literally everything to keep Lex at arm's length."

Huffing, he hangs his head. "I know I have."

"Except for kissing her. That was a step in the right direction."

His wide eyes snap to mine. "Are you fucking kidding?"

"Nope." I pop the 'p,' because I know it'll get under his skin. "You let your walls down, maybe for the first time, around her."

He looks off into the distance. "They were down, all right. Been a bitch to get them back up."

"So leave them down." I watch him frown at the pile of coaster bits on the table. "You want to tell me why you're jealous of Linc?"

The pensive look disappears from his face. "I'm not jealous."

"You're a terrible liar."

Scoffing, he crosses his arms.

"Tell me, Dec. What is it about Lex that has you in knots?"

"I'm not in knots."

He's dangerously close to pouting, and I have to swallow my smirk. "You are. I want to know why."

"I told you. I'm on the outside."

"Why do you care about being on the outside? Linc and I have shared before and you've never joined in."

He shakes his head. "Not like this."

"What makes this different?"

Fucking say it, Dec. I regard him, waiting it out. He hates every time Lex does the same, but she only does it because it's so effective.

"It's not the same," he finally says. "She's different and you fucking know it."

Nodding slowly, I agree. "She is."

Dec swallows roughly. "He's in love with her, isn't he?"

I hold his gaze. "He is."

He looks away. "I thought so. Saw it all over his face when she was over last."

"I know."

Seeing Dec's realization, and how things unfolded between him and Lex after, was my primary motivation for this little chat.

"He thinks you're still hung up about the business stuff, Dec. That you don't trust Lex like we don't trust Anne-Marie. You get why that's a problem?"

He frowns as he turns back to me.

"He thinks you're making him choose." I give him a pointed look. "Between the woman he loves and the brother he would give anything for."

My words are hard-hitting. Dec dated a few women over the years, though only one came close to lasting. Shortly after their engagement, she grew tired of the time he spent with us, both for work and as friends. She issued him an ultimatum: either he prioritized her and reduced his time with us, or she walked.

The decision had been an easy one because he was never in love with her—not that he'd ever admit it aloud. It happened around the time we started Procerus, and, after he recovered from the shock, he never once looked back.

"Shit," he groans.

"Indeed."

Dec eyes me. "You're awfully calm."

I cock an eyebrow. "All these years together, and that's a surprise?"

He smirks. "No, it's not. You're seriously not worried?"

"Shockingly enough after the last few months, man, I trust you. I know you'll fix it."

His expression sobers, and he nods, looking down as he clears his throat. "Thanks, man."

"I've got your back, Dec. Always. You gotta fix it, though."

"I'm not sure I know how, Shane." Vulnerability swims in his eyes. "Where do I even start?"

"Do you want her?"

He releases a slow breath, shifting in the booth. The bar is still mostly empty, and it's almost like we're the only people existing in the space. The groove between his eyebrows deepens.

"I don't think it matters, Shane. According to her rules, isn't it all over after the Summit anyway?"

"Fuck off, man. Rules are meant to be broken, and you know it." I study him, knowing in my gut he's off base about the Summit. And it matters to me if he wants her, and I know for a fact it matters to Linc and Lex.

"What business do I have wanting a woman like her?" His voice is low, as though he's speaking to himself.

"What business do any of us have thinking we deserve the privilege of loving her?"

Dec searches my face. "You love her, too, then."

I nod. "Yeah, Dec. I do."

He chugs the last of his beer. "I'm happy for you."

Laughing, I reach out and slap his shoulder. "You sound it, asshole. I love you, too. Not like I love her, but I do. And Linc."

He looks as gobsmacked as Linc did the other day. *These fucking Wildes are allergic to emotions.*

"I love us together," I continue. "There's room for all of us, Dec. And as much as you've tried to fuck things up with her, I see the way she looks at you. Linc and I? We want you there. You two are the only family that's ever counted, and I want our family whole. With Lex."

"Jesus, Shane," he rasps, rubbing at his eyes, "I can't fucking cry in a dive bar."

"Sure you can." I say brightly.

His chuckle is low and short, but it's there. *Thank fuck.* I relax into the booth and smile.

"Anyway, Linc and I need your help."

Dec looks up as he sniffs. "With what?"

"Paris. Lex has only ever been for work; she's never seen the city. I got Miles to build some extra time into the schedule so we can play tourist for a day." I give him a small smile. "You're the Paris expert, Dec. Linc set a bunch of stuff up, but he's stumped on what to do for dinner."

"You want me to plan a romantic dinner for the three of you in Paris?"

"For the *four* of us. And share whatever other ideas you have. We're done with the asshole attitude, yeah?"

He barks a laugh. "Being done with the attitude and joining your date day are two very different things, Shane."

"That's not a no."

He sighs heavily as he slides out of the booth. "It's not a no."

I follow him, leaving some cash on the table for the tip. "Thanks, man."

"Don't push it," he grunts, but it lacks bite.

Eyeing him, I can't help but push one more button. "So... you gonna add some big romantic gesture to the itinerary? Apologize for being a sack of shit for months and confess how you feel?"

I laugh as he glares daggers at me.

"Fuck all the way off, Kelly."

Chapter 27

Lex

"Lex, how do you feel about bikes?"

I look up at Linc as he walks across the terrace toward me. "Does spin class count?"

He squints and cocks his head. "Not exactly?"

Pausing to kiss the top of my head, he drops into the chair next to mine with a wide grin. Early morning light fills Paris around us, a warm glow suffusing the lush space outside our suite. It's stunning. *How is this the first time I've seen more of France than my hotel or a conference room?*

"I like bikes of all kinds." I take his hand and squeeze it. "Thank you for this, by the way. I can't believe you conspired with Miles to clear a full day."

I can't remember the last time I truly took a day off. Linc confiscated my phone earlier, promising to give it to me if something urgent comes through, but otherwise adamant about it being off limits.

"Thank Shane for that bit." Linc shudders. "Your assistant is terrifying."

I laugh, not denying it. "So, bikes?"

He gestures grandly toward the city. "There's so much to see and not much time to see it."

Shane appears in the doorway and makes his way toward us leisurely, two cups and saucers in hand. He offers one to me with a gentle smile.

"Where's mine?" Linc blinks big puppy eyes up at his friend.

"Inside."

Pouting, Linc stands and brushes by him. "Rude."

Shane drags a chair closer to mine with an indulgent grin. "Sleep okay?"

He wraps an arm around my shoulders, and I melt into him. He opted for a fitted navy henley today, the top two buttons open and showing a flash of his ink, and dark jeans. I'm tempted to throw Linc's plans out the window and drag them both to my bedroom.

"Yeah." I nuzzle my face into his neck, breathing him in. "It's lonely in there, though."

He snorts. "Your choice, Lex. Linc and I are more than happy to keep you company."

Sighing, I take a sip of coffee. While I recognize boundaries are a good thing, it's getting harder to abide by my 'no strings' rule. And staying overnight with *one* of them feels like a massive fucking string, let alone both.

"Pretty sure Declan would've lost it if we'd all piled into a room together last night," I murmur.

Surprisingly, the flight to Europe was lovely. After Declan scraped his jaw off the tarmac and boarded Athena's jet, we all fell into easy conversation. We took a few hours to go over the presentation plans, refining each of the guys' roles and giving Declan a chance to rehearse until he recited it flawlessly with an easy smile.

Once the business was done, Linc leaned over the table eagerly, a sparkle in his caramel eyes.

"We're going on a date tomorrow," Linc announced. "All day."

My eyebrows rose. "What?"

"Dec did a fellowship in Paris during his MBA, so he hooked us up."

"Did you really?" I turned to the man in question.

He shrugged. "Got to know the city pretty well. Still have some friends there." His emerald eyes bored into mine. "You deserve to experience the city properly, at least once."

My breath had stuttered at the sincerity in Declan's gaze as he delivered that weighty line. We spent the rest of the flight talking about Paris. I shared more about the clients I'd traveled for and, when he wasn't regaling us with memories of the city, Declan listened intently. He asked questions about the people I'd worked with and where they were now. It was the most we'd ever conversed without a biting remark, and something warm and fragile bloomed in my chest.

As we were beginning our descent, talk turned to logistics. Miles had shared the name of the hotel on our itinerary weeks before, but I'd kept the details to myself. I did it partly for the surprise, but mostly because I was a bit embarrassed by my extravagance.

"The hotel looks central." Linc smiled. "Made it easy to plan. How are we rooming, by the way?"

"I had Miles book the penthouse. It has a terrace with the best view in the city. Supposedly."

"Whoa, that's dope. Will you let us crash?"

I chuckled. "The terrace alone is over three thousand square feet, Linc. I think we'll all manage to fit in the same four-bedroom suite."

Shane presses a kiss to my head, bringing me back to the present.

"He'll come around. We were all tired last night, not at our best." His deep voice is soothing as it rumbles through me.

I hum a noncommittal response, unwilling to dig too deeply into the source of Declan's discomfort. The suite is indulgent, excessively so, and I'm typically a conservative spender. I figured our last week together, in Paris no less, deserved a touch of fanfare.

"Is sitting on the terrace the extent of Linc's grand plan for the day?"

Declan's voice cuts through the quiet morning, drawing both of our gazes.

"Chill. We're going out for breakfast after coffee." Linc brushes past him, raising one of the cups in his hands. "I made you one."

Heaving a deep breath after a momentary hesitation, Declan follows his brother to the table. He settles next to Shane as Linc passes his coffee.

"We're starting with croissants, of course." Linc settles back in his chair, bringing his coffee close to his mouth to inhale deeply.

"Of course." I smile, mirroring him.

His hair has grown out a bit in the last few months, the extra length making his curls more pronounced. The light blue button down he wears over his fitted jeans makes his amber eyes pop.

"Then bikes?"

Linc smirks at my attempt to pry. Before he can respond, Declan clears his throat.

"There's a bakery not far from here with the best croissants in the city. It's maybe ten minutes by bike," he smirks at Linc's warning hiss, "and we could go right by the Louvre."

"Sounds lovely." I flash him a small smile, my breath

catching in my throat when he returns it. *Well, damn. Look at that.*

"That's perfect!" Linc grins, tipping his cup to drain the last drop of coffee. He stands as soon as he's done. "Ready?"

———

"Let me get this straight," I tease, "you all give me endless shit for crackers and wine not being dinner, but baguettes and cheese and wine are an acceptable lunch?"

We're in a small park in the shadow of Notre Dame, where Linc insisted we pause during our bike tour of the city. The sun is high in the cloudless sky, a cool breeze making the leaves on the trees dance around us. I lean back against Linc's chest, snuggling against him as he huffs a laugh. The two of us are on the ground, Declan and Shane sitting on the bench behind us.

"There's cheese involved," Shane drawls, winking when I glance back at him.

Declan snorts, taking a swig from our shared bottle of wine. After walking through the cathedral, we wandered to find a rue of quaint little shops. Linc insisted on taking advantage of my basic French, watching in delight as I ordered our simple picnic from three separate vendors.

"What was the guy in the fromagerie asking you?" Linc's arms tighten around me.

I laugh. "He wanted to know if Declan was single."

Linc roars as Declan nearly chokes on his baguette. "He did not."

"He did." I grin at him, coy. "Can't blame him."

Our gazes clash as heat flares between us. Shane claps his shoulder, and Declan tears his eyes away as he shakes his head ruefully.

"You were right," he grumbles to Shane.

"About what?" I look between them as Shane's smirk turns into a grin.

"Told him the leather was a bit much." Shane winks.

I vehemently disagree. When Declan pulled the black moto jacket on as we left the suite, I had to bite my lip to contain my reaction. He'd been hot as hell in his simple jeans and tee, both black, but adding the jacket made the ensemble scorching.

"It's not." Declan's eyes flash back to mine at my comment. "Too much, I mean."

Linc bends to kiss my head, squeezing me. It feels like encouragement, and my stomach swoops at the thought. Ruby's comment about a full set flits through my mind.

"What's next, Linc?" Shane smirks as he redirects the conversation, leaning forward to gently grip my shoulder.

"The bike tour continues! The route is a mashup of high-lights and romantic nooks and crannies, so it's a little...wandery."

"Nooks and crannies?" I giggle.

He flushes. "Yeah. I researched the best routes, and those were the top two. Seemed like combining them would give us the most complete experience. Had to make the most of the day, you know?"

This man. This sweet, adorable man. Placing a hand on his cheek, I smile into his amber eyes. "Thank you, Linc."

"Anything for you, beautiful." He presses a soft kiss to my lips.

Before I can melt into him, he's gone, standing and pulling me to my feet. I can feel Declan's eyes on me as I gather the remains of our lunch.

"Where does it end?" I ask. "The tour."

Linc grins. "You'll see."

Declan rolls his eyes at his brother's giddy teasing, but I

don't miss how his lips tip up in the corner. Linc's enthusiasm is infectious.

"Do we seriously have to use these bikes?" Declan grouses, staring at the two tandem bikes leaning against the bench.

Shane slaps his shoulder as he rights the one he and Linc are using. "You've got this, brother."

"I know I do, I just don't want to."

"Come on, Dec," I taunt, pulling our bike upright. "Has it been so unbearable to be trapped behind me all day?"

His eyes rake over me, heat flashing again as he grunts. "That's not the problem, boss."

"It's not dignified enough for him!" Linc calls, swinging up behind Shane as they pedal seamlessly away.

Laughing, I look back over my shoulder. "Dignity's overrated."

"Right, says the woman who has more dignity in her little finger than half this fucking city."

He pushes off as we both get settled, then starts to pedal, following the guys.

"You know," I muse, fighting the urge to look at him, "that almost sounded like a compliment."

"It was," he calls over the sound of the cars and tourists around us.

"Are you feeling okay? You haven't challenged me once today. I'm getting worried you're off your game, Wilde."

"There's nothing wrong with my game."

We pull alongside Linc and Shane, waiting for the light to change. I take the opportunity to look at him, twisting in my seat.

"Prove it."

Shane's low chuckle brings a teasing smile to my lips as Declan's eyes narrow playfully. The light changes before he can reply, but as soon as we're safely on our way, he rises to my challenge.

"You're good for them."

It's torture not to glance back at him, but I'm not about to risk our safety as we speed through the city. His rich voice is quiet enough not to carry far, keeping our conversation between us.

"It took me a while to see it." He admits. "Honestly, I didn't want to. It's been just the three of us for...a long time."

I stay quiet, listening. My heart pounds as I adjust my grip on the handlebars, steering us steadily along.

"I've been in my head a lot lately. Too much. But you've been there for them, and...I'm grateful."

My feet are still on the pedals, and our bike slows. I steer us over to the side of the path, planting my feet as Dec does the same. Shane glances back and Declan waves them ahead, letting the distance between us widen. Shane jerks his chin in acknowledgement, saying something to Linc as they continue around a corner. I turn back to Declan, my breath strangely loud in my ears.

"Thank you, Lex."

My heart stutters. It's not the first time I've heard the words, but it's the first time Declan has looked at me with such... longing as he says them. "Wha...what?"

"For being there for Linc and Shane when I was too much of an ass to realize what they needed." His gaze holds mine, heavy and earnest. "Thank you."

Swallowing, I stare at him. Is he the same guy who fought me at every turn for three months? He looks the same, but the words coming from his mouth sound foreign.

"You don't have to thank me," I finally manage. "As much as I appreciate you acknowledging all that, I didn't do it for you."

A small smile crosses his lips before he ducks his head. "I know. I'm grateful for that, too."

Heaving a breath, I tilt my head. "Don't take this the wrong way, Declan, but what changed? At our meeting last week, I was pretty sure you hated the sight of me."

His expression is heavy, earnest. "I've never hated you, Lex. You saw right through me, and that's not an experience I relish."

Declan looks off into the distance, his grip on his handlebars tightening. "I care about them more than anyone else in this world." He glances my way briefly. "I like to think I know what's best for them, especially Linc."

I arch a brow. "He might argue."

"Oh, he absolutely would. And in this instance, he'd be right." He eyes me. "*This* instance."

Scoffing, I swing my leg over the bike seat to face him fully. "It's honestly astonishing you're as close as you are. All three of you are stubborn and opinionated as fuck."

He mock glares at me, arms crossed. "You think you know me, boss?"

I shake my head, eyes crinkling in amusement. "No, you haven't let that happen. But I know them pretty damn well."

His chuckle feels like a balm. "That's fair enough." He searches my face for a long moment. "You want to know the truth?"

Please. "Always."

"You scare me."

I still. "I scare you."

He nods. "Yeah, you scare the shit out of me."

"Why?"

His look suggests I know exactly why. *But I don't. Why did you kiss me?*

"I don't want to drive any wedges between you, Declan." My voice is impossibly gentle.

The breath he draws is ragged, his expression softening. "I know, Lex. I've finally let myself believe it. Being here, seeing them..." He sighs, carding his fingers through his dark hair. "Seeing you, the way you are together. I could pretend not to realize it before, but it's obvious now."

"What is?" I'm barely breathing, vaguely aware of the city bustling around us.

"You care about them."

"Of course I do." I frown. "Why would that scare you?"

He swallows, his Adam's apple bobbing as he shifts on his feet, eyes intent on mine. It takes him a moment to speak.

"It's not you I'm worried about driving us apart." He exhales sharply. "It's me. I shouldn't have kissed you like I did, not without a conversation with you and them, and not...not like that."

"Declan..." my voice trails to nothing as my heartbeat pounds.

"No, Lex, I mean it," he interrupts gently. "You deserve bike rides in Paris and picnics in the shadow of Notre Dame. Someone who shows up for you, even in the small moments. And so much more than an asshole losing control and attacking you in a fucking conference room."

I laugh as he smirks, his brows raised.

"But what if I liked what went down in that conference room?" I tease.

Desire sizzles between us, his sparkling emerald eyes drinking me in. "To be clear, Lex, kissing you wasn't the mistake. I never should have let you think it was."

My breath catches as I grin, goosebumps rising on my arms in response to the intensity of his gaze. "Thank you, Declan."

He inclines his head, shoulders relaxing as he sits back against the bike seat.

"To be honest, I've never found caring for people easy," he

admits. "Shane says I often mistake control for kindness, and he's not wrong. But you make it look effortless."

"Because it is, Declan. Caring for them is the easiest thing I've ever done."

Silence stretches between us as he searches my face. "You mean that."

"With all of me."

"Fuck, I'm an asshole," he mumbles.

I gaze at him, still processing his confession. Declan glances at his watch, then tosses a small smile my way, looking at me through thick lashes. Butterflies dance in my belly.

"Linc's going to kill me if we miss our reservation. We should go." He swallows, looking down. "If you want to. Go with me, that is."

Reaching out, I place a hand over his, still gripping the handlebar. "Of course I do, Declan." *Linc and Shane aren't the only ones I care about.*

The reservation Lincoln would've killed us for missing is at the Eiffel Tower. When we finally pull up, Linc grins and embraces us both, then leads us to the ticket counter. We cram ourselves into the elevator with other visitors, smiles passing between us. Declan's eyes find mine a few times, as though he can't tear his gaze away for long. I try to ignore how I respond, goosebumps rising on my arms and the small hairs on the back of my neck standing up.

The view from the top of the tower is spectacular. The city sprawls before us, the clear weather giving us visibility for miles. Pink light casts an ethereal glow as the sun begins to set, light glittering on the Seine.

Shane walks up behind me on the viewing platform, caging

me against the railing with his warm, hard body. He buries his face against my neck, wrapping an arm around my upper chest and pulling me close. I latch both hands onto his forearm, eyes falling closed as I hold him against me.

"Can you believe this view?" he murmurs into my skin.

"Not for a minute," Linc replies, just as quiet.

I glance over to find him staring at us, a content smile on his face. Reaching for him, I grip his hand in mine. Declan walks up next to us on the other side, leaning his arms on the railing as he looks out. He's close enough to brush against me and Shane, the heat from all of them warming me through.

"Well, it's confirmed. Paris is magical."

Shane smiles his agreement against me, his arm tightening before he looks up to take in the city skyline. Declan glances over his shoulder, the fire in his eyes lighting me up from the inside out.

"Wait til you see where Dec's taking us for dinner." Linc squeezes my hand, tugging gently. "Come on, beautiful. Your day isn't over."

Chapter 28

Lex

Dinner is a dream. Linc and Declan sped ahead of me and Shane, then welcomed us to a stunning private rooftop with views to rival our suite. The Eiffel Tower stood so close it felt like a painted backdrop, not real life.

Gentle twinkling lights illuminate the small, intimate space, canopied in greenery. Candles on the table provide enough light for us to see, setting an impossibly romantic ambience.

"My friend's family has owned this space for years. They run the restaurant on the ground floor and rent this out for private events," Declan explains. "We're lucky it was available."

"I'm sure it's luck we should thank," Shane muses, giving his friend a pointed look.

Declan rolls his eyes, but I don't miss the slight darkening of his cheeks. My heart speeds up at the idea I bore witness to Declan Wilde blushing, and I swallow down my giddy response.

Course after course of stunning authentic French cuisine is served. I'd eaten at some of the top restaurants in both Paris and the Bay, and none held a candle to the delicious comfort of the evening's meal.

As the city darkens around us, soft music reaches us from the rue below. A band is playing on the corner, romantic instrumental tunes floating through the air. I smile and let myself relax in my chair, my last glass of wine half-gone as I swing it in time to the music.

"Dance with me."

I look up at Linc, returning his wide smile as I rise and accept his hand. There's barely any space, but Declan and Shane make quick work of moving the table carefully to the side. Linc presses his forehead to mine as he wraps his arms around me, pulling us flush against one another. My eyes flutter closed as I raise one hand to cup his nape, the other flat against his muscular chest.

"I never want this day to end." His breath washes over my lips and I hum in agreement.

We sway comfortably together for several long minutes before Shane steps up and gracefully cuts in. Linc happily hands me over, his touch lingering on my waist. Shane wraps one arm around me, holding my hand on his chest between us.

"Thank you." His deep voice is so quiet I barely hear him.

Searching his gaze, I smile softly. "For what?"

His arm tightens as he draws a long breath. "Being gentle with Linc. Being in the moment with us today."

I rest my head against his shoulder, squeezing his hand as emotion wells in my chest. "It's been perfect, Shane. Enlightening, even. I should be thanking you."

He kisses the top of my head. "Thank Linc and Dec. They need it more than I do."

Chuckling, I look back to meet his piercing blues. "I see you, Shane Kelly."

"Oh?"

"You're their glue. You're our glue." I tighten my arm around his waist, my thumb stroking along the small of his strong back as we move to the music. "I don't know everything you've said and done to keep Linc grounded or urge Declan to open up, but I'm grateful. We wouldn't be here now without you."

"I'd do anything for them, Lex," he murmurs.

"I know."

His gaze searches mine. "I'd do the same for you."

It isn't a declaration of love, but for Shane Kelly, it's damn close. I can feel the tears gathering in my eyes, hot and insistent, faint panic rising through me at the thought of our perfect day being the last we spend together like this. The four of us, bantering, laughing, and experiencing somewhere–and something–new.

Before I can collect myself enough to respond, Shane looks behind me and motions someone over with a jerk of his chin. Declan steps up a moment later as Shane slowly releases me, his gaze knowing. He presses his lips to the back of my hand, then leaves us staring at each other across the meager dance floor.

Declan clears his throat, his Adam's apple bobbing as he grips the back of his neck. He looks young, almost boyish, as he glances up at me through long lashes.

"I'm not much of a dancer," he mumbles.

"Neither am I, Wilde."

His eyes flash at the nickname, some of his nerves falling away as he steps up to take me in his strong arms.

"I saw a new side of you today, Lex." His broad hand is firm on my back, the heat of him searing through my thin sweater.

"I could say the same about you."

"This version of you..." his voice trails off. He takes a long breath, as though steeling himself. "You're just so much more, Lex. I admired you when I only saw the business side of you, but I realize now that it's just one of your many facets."

My chest pinches at the sincerity in his words. His expression is open, his eyes shining with a vulnerability I've never seen from him.

"I understand why Linc and Shane want more of you," he murmurs, "when there's so much more of you to experience."

My breath catches, my head swimming with the possibilities. It's easy for me to envision life as the four of us, even though I've only ever imagined a future alone before now. The prospect is as exciting as it is panic-inducing.

"I'm pretty fond of this version of you, too, Declan," I demure.

He huffs a laugh. "Thanks for giving me a chance. Even though I didn't deserve it."

His self-deprecating grin holds an edge of truth that makes my heart clench.

"You deserve everything, Declan. I won't let you try to convince yourself otherwise."

We're no longer swaying along with the melody. We stand frozen on a rooftop in Paris, drowning in tension. Declan's emerald eyes drop to my mouth, and I'm painfully aware of how close he is. If I press myself up the slightest bit, our lips will meet. My pulse pounds in my ears as I wonder if I'll survive a second kiss from Declan Wilde.

As I lean a fraction closer, Declan stills. Frantic eyes meet mine, then shutter as his hands drop away and he steps back, clearing his throat. Disappointment settles in my gut at the loss of him.

"It's, uh...the night's not over," he croaks, turning to Linc and Shane. "We have to go, right?"

Linc's brows furrow momentarily before they smooth with his easy smile. "Sure, let's go."

Chapter 29

Shane

Lex steps to the table, raising her wineglass to her lips, hand trembling. As I leave Linc to soothe Dec, she finishes it in three long gulps. She sets the glass down and presses a hand to her mouth as I move behind her. I place a hand on her hip and she melts into me, leaning back without hesitation.

"Don't give up." I press a kiss to the hollow of her throat, my words for her ears only. "You want him?"

She freezes. When she told me about their kiss before, she didn't seem ready to answer the question, and I couldn't blame her given Dec's behavior. After a day together, the want between them is obvious, but I still want to hear it from her.

"Relax, Lex," I croon, smiling in her skin. "I'm not mad. Linc either. But...do you?"

Her eyes close and she nods almost imperceptibly. I groan, pressing myself more firmly against her, my cock hardening in my jeans. Her soft gasp tells me she can feel exactly what the thought does to me. I grip her waist tighter and kiss her again to make it perfectly clear.

"I'm so fucking glad, baby. Can't even tell you how hot it is to think of you with all of us."

I watch her chest rise and fall more rapidly with smug satisfaction, hoping she's envisioning the same myriad of filthy scenes marching through my brain.

"Promise me you won't give up on him," I urge, my grip tightening. "If you want him...want all of us...don't let him pull away again."

Letting out a shaky breath, she whispers words that are equal parts vow and damnation. "I promise."

"Good girl."

She shivers at the praise, and I bite back another groan. After the day we've spent, we're all on edge. I'm desperate to bury myself in her, to lose myself to the lust and desire only she can ignite. But I'm equally needy to watch her come apart for Linc. Even for Declan. *There's nothing I've ever wanted more.*

Breathing deeply through my nose, I force myself to think of anything other than Lex laid out for all of us. It feels within reach, but Declan is clearly going to fight it to the bitter end. *Stubborn dick.*

"Come on." I step back, adjusting myself, and take her hand. "Fancy a walk?"

Lex's eyes shine with anticipation and a hint of nervousness as she turns to face me. "With you three? Always."

Chuckling, I press a kiss to her temple, then pull her toward the stairs. Linc and Dec disappeared through the doorway a minute before, and we find them waiting on the street. Paris comes alive in the dark, bright streetlights and the sparkling Eiffel Tower almost overwhelming.

Lex releases me as she steps out into the cobbled rue, the musicians who inspired our impromptu dances filling the block with romantic music. There isn't a car in sight, and she walks right into the middle of the rue, arms outstretched as she throws her head back and twirls.

"*J'aime Paris!*" she calls, laughing.

Cheers and hollers from pedestrians and the street band rise in response, and she grins our way. She's a vision, her cheeks flushed and eyes bright as she giggles. Linc can't resist, rushing out to sweep her into his arms, lifting her off her feet and spinning them both. Lex squeals as she flings her arms around him, her legs swinging wide.

I watch Dec as he takes them in with a look of intense longing, a smile playing on his lips. *You can join them, brother. You can share in their joy.* I know he won't, not yet. Dec glances up as I step next to him. His smile doesn't falter, and I take that as a good sign.

"He'll stay out there with her like that all night if we let him." Dec's eyes flash with good humor.

"Nah," I disagree. "He wants inside her as bad as we do. Can't do that in the street, even in the City of Love."

Dec chokes on air, coughing as I laugh and slap his back.

"Fuck, Shane," he croaks.

"That's the idea, Dec," I tease, waving Linc and Lex over. "That's the idea."

"You're ridiculous."

"Maybe. She's into me, though. Must be doing something right."

Lex grips Linc's face in her hands, kissing him soundly as he slowly lowers her to her feet. When they part, they smile at each other, so clearly in love I can't help but chuckle. Warmth washes through me as they tear their gazes from one another and run back over to us. Linc grins as he steps onto the sidewalk, his hands in his pockets. Lex loops an arm through mine, then Declan's, and starts walking briskly toward the hotel.

"Come on, boys!" Lex casts me a sideways look as she grins and Dec scoffs at the nickname. "Linc, what else are you planning?"

"You'll see!" he sing-songs, dancing ahead of us on the path.

Lex beams back at him, steps light and quick.

"Best day ever," she sighs, leaning her head on Dec's shoulder.

He looks down at her with wide eyes, then glances up at me. I can see he's at war with himself, struggling to give in to what he so clearly wants. Cocking my head at him in challenge, I send him a silent plea. *Don't fuck it up now, brother.*

Chapter 30

Lex

The moment we walk through the doors to our suite, I am overwhelmed.

There are roses *everywhere*. Vases of red roses are on nearly every table in the living area, a trail of petals leading to the entrance on one side and to the opulent primary bedroom on the other. A tray of chocolate-covered strawberries and éclairs waits for us on the coffee table, along with two bottles of champagne.

"Linc!" I gasp, frozen in the doorway.

He grins, taking my hand and pulling me forward. "You like it?"

I laugh, tears threatening. "Like it? This is insane!"

"But, like, in a good way, right?" He teases, fingers tightening on mine.

"Of course, in a good way!" I launch myself at him, smiling as he laughs and catches me.

He doesn't spin me like he did in the street, instead staring up into my eyes as I twine my legs around his waist.

"I figured showering you in roses on a normal day counts as

a string. But it's Paris, and maybe the rules don't need to exist here. At least today."

My heart melts as I stare down at him, threading my fingers through his hair. Hope and a touch of fear war in his gaze, and I want to erase every last trace of the latter. Leaning down, I press my lips to his urgently, needing to feel him. He groans into my mouth, holding me more firmly against him.

Tearing my lips from his is a struggle, but I manage it. "No rules. Not tonight."

His smile is incandescent as he walks over to the couch, sitting with me still wrapped around him. I can sense Shane and Declan still hovering by the door, watching, but I'm not ready to look away from Linc. I wave at the others, gesturing for them to join us.

"Sit your asses down, both of you!"

Linc chuckles, shaking his head as he stares at me in wonder. "Yeah, guys. What she said."

Giggling, I kiss him again, sinking into his body as he reaches up to cup my head in one hand, the other gripping my ass. Losing myself, I open my mouth the second his tongue touches my lips, eager for him to invade my senses. We'd been touching all day, though wary of letting the PDA go too far. Our kiss in the street in front of the restaurant was the most salacious we'd gotten. *I am so ready for more.*

The sound of a champagne cork popping breaks us apart abruptly. I yelp, then collapse in laughter at Linc's wide-eyed look of surprise. Slipping off his lap, I snuggle against his side as I take in Shane on the opposite couch. He's smirking, legs spread with an arm thrown over the back. His eyes flick to Declan before he raises a brow in question.

Biting my lip, I look up into Declan's fiery gaze. He's holding the foaming champagne bottle, filling the first glass. He offers it to me, our fingers brushing as he does. Electricity shoots through me at the touch, my breath catching as his pupils dilate.

"Thanks, man," Linc says, interrupting the tension as he takes the champagne bottle from Declan's loosening fingers.

Linc fills the remaining glasses, holding one out to Shane before passing the last to Declan.

"Any more surprises, Linc?" Declan asks, his voice gravel.

"Nope."

"Good." Declan sits heavily next to Shane, gulping half his champagne with a wince.

My gaze rakes over him, catching on the clear bulge in his black jeans. He shed the moto jacket at the door, leaving his toned arms on display. Linc shifts next to me, setting his champagne down so he can roll up his sleeves. I bite my lip as I watch. *Why does something so innocent feel so pornographic?*

Linc catches my eye and smirks. He knows exactly what he's doing to me. He leans forward to give me a quick kiss, then grabs a strawberry and holds it to my lips. I open my mouth immediately, taking a bite of the sweet confection. Juice drips from my mouth and I laugh, reaching up to cup my hand under my jaw.

"Let me."

I look up, surprised to see Shane lowering himself to his knees in front of me. He leans forward and presses a kiss to one corner of my lips, then the other. When he licks the last of the juice from my chin, my pussy quivers in want. Linc groans next to me, watching with hungry eyes.

Across from us, Declan clears his throat, drawing my attention. Shane gives me a pointed look. *It's now or never, I guess.* Reaching forward, I grab a strawberry from the tray, then step over to Declan.

"Strawberry?" I offer, tilting my head.

He swallows roughly, then nods once. "Alright."

Not giving him a chance to react, I crawl up on the couch on my knees and straddle his lap. He grunts in surprise, arms raising out to the side as though he doesn't know what to do with his hands.

"Relax, Declan. I don't bite."

"She prefers to be on the receiving end." Linc winks as I glance over my shoulder and scrunch my nose at him.

Slowly, Declan settles his hands on the seat cushion, fingers twitching as they brush my calves. I tsk at him as I hold the strawberry out for him to bite, trying not to let the distance he's putting between us get to me.

I half expect him to ask me to get off him, but he leans forward and gently bites into the fruit. He grunts as the juice bursts from his mouth, leaning forward automatically. I reach up and swipe it off his chin, keeping eye contact as I suck the redness from my thumb.

Declan's nostrils flare as his pupils blow. I slowly remove my thumb from my mouth, shifting slightly in his lap. His hands fly to my hips to keep me still, but the damage is done—I feel how he's reacting to me.

"So you do want me," I murmur, strawberry forgotten.

His fingers flex against me, digging in almost harshly. I try to steady my breathing, the thought that he could be just as dominant as Shane and Linc nearly making me whimper with want.

"You two clearly need a minute."

We both look over at Shane. He and Linc are standing by the hall to the primary bedroom, matching smirks on their faces.

"We'll be in the bedroom when you're ready," Linc adds.

As one, they turn and walk away. Declan's body goes still beneath me. I lean over and deposit the partial strawberry on the tray, then rest my hands on his shoulders.

"In case you missed it, Wilde, that was an invitation."

"I...what?" He swallows roughly, grip fierce and eyes wild.

Using my hold on his shoulders as leverage, I roll my hips forward to drag my core along his erection. He groans, his head dropping back as he makes a feeble and delayed attempt to still my hips. I pause. I can feel him throbbing against me, but if he really doesn't want me, I'm not going to push it. If he's resisting out of some misplaced sense of fear or duty? *All bets are off.*

"Do you want me?" My voice is quiet, controlled.

His expression is almost blank as he regards me. Almost. I can see the nearly frantic energy in his eyes, creasing his forehead. Raising a brow, I rock my hips back and forth again, waiting for him to either answer or deny me.

"You see, Declan," I murmur, continuing the slow roll of my hips when he doesn't try to stop me, "there's one rule I won't bend for Paris. Not even for you."

I can feel his length, hard as steel, under me. My underwear is a lost cause, wetness slicking almost through my jeans. His cock twitches as I press myself more firmly against him, riding him through our clothes. I moan as the angle and pressure push the seam against my clit just so, pleasure coursing through me.

"Wha...what's the rule?" he bites out.

While his fingers grip tight enough to bruise, he still isn't trying to control my movements. I lean forward slowly, dragging my core over his cock and my breasts along his chest. When our faces are almost close enough to kiss, I drop my lips to his ear.

"I want you, Declan," I tell him, sliding back and forth along his hardness. "I want you to finish what you started in my fucking conference room." I increase my pace, twisting my hips and grinding down on him at the end of each stroke. "I want you to do what you threatened: lose control and attack me."

I lean back slightly to find him staring up at me with impossibly dark eyes, lips red from his teeth as he holds himself back.

"But I only fuck men who want me out loud."

Stilling, I relax my hands on his shoulders. Declan's gaze

turns stony, his fingers still digging into my skin. His cock is hard and pulsing between us, and there's a bead of sweat trailing from his hairline.

"This is it. Choose me and join us, or don't and miss the chance. For good."

I smoothly extract myself from his lap and stand. His chest is heaving, his cock straining against his jeans as he scrapes a hand over his jaw. Fingering the hem of my sweater, I tug it over my head, dropping it to the floor. Declan blows out a sharp breath as I discard my jeans, standing before him in nothing but my lacy black bra and thong.

"Your move, Wilde."

Without another word, I turn and saunter toward the primary bedroom. As I leave, I barely catch his muttered reaction.

"Fucking hell."

Chapter 31

Declan

I considered myself strong. Sitting on that couch after Lex walked away in her goddamn fucking underwear? I was weak. So fucking weak.

My cock is still rock hard, pulsing uncomfortably against my jeans. As if her slow torture wasn't enough, I can fucking hear them. Can hear the murmur of voices and the hint of soft gasps and moans.

You can't do this, Wilde. As much as you want to, you can't. You're already too invested and she doesn't do long term.

The more I hear, the more I question why I can't. *This is fucking torture, I swear–*

A loud smack sounds, followed by a yelp. Then Shane's voice, louder than before.

"You like that, don't you? Our dirty little slut."

Our dirty little slut. All the blood in my body goes straight to my cock. Another smack, accompanied by a loud moan. I groan, standing to alleviate the pressure and pressing a hand against my dick. In a daze, I move toward the bedroom, those four little words on repeat in my mind.

As I near the door, I realize it's cracked. *Motherfuckers.*

Panting, I pause outside it. I know I shouldn't be listening. *Lex said it was an invitation to join. Listening is joining, right?*

Leaning my arm against the wall, I drop my head on it. Lex's moans are coming more rapidly now, wet smacking noises filtering out the door. Linc groans something incomprehensible, and I'm faintly surprised the sound of my brother's voice does nothing to calm my raging dick.

"Do you need to come?" Shane's deep voice is hoarse, like he's close. *That shouldn't be such a fucking turn on.*

"Yes, sir," Lex gasps, and my knees buckle. "Please."

Yes, sir.

Dirty little slut.

Please.

I grip the base of my cock, shuddering as I hold back the urge to barge into the room. *Fuck, she's going to be the death of me.* Lex's moans and gasps increase, my body shaking as I listen.

"Now," Shane commands. "Come for us."

I almost convince myself to go back to my room when she screams.

My head snaps up, everything in me wanting nothing more than to witness what she looks like when she makes that exquisite fucking sound.

Fuck it.

I push open the door.

Holy fucking shit.

Chapter 32

Linc

Lex was on her knees choking on my cock, Shane buried in her pussy with his fingers in her ass, when Dec walked in.

He freezes, like his brain short-circuited, and then I have no idea what the fuck he's doing because Lex's mouth is goddamn magic and I'm going to come any fucking second.

"Lex, don't you stop." Without looking away from the goddess pinned between us, Shane points at the chair by the bed we're on. "Sit down, Declan," he barks. "Not a word."

Lex moans. I half expect her to pop off my cock and look toward Dec, but she doesn't, too deep in subspace to come out of the scene. The scent of roses is thick in the air thanks to the petals we didn't bother to sweep off the bed, and the dozen vases full of them throughout the room. The sweet floral undernote to the sweat and sex is intoxicating. Lex pulls back to swirl her tongue around my head, then dip it into the slit to lap at my pre-cum, sending shocks of pleasure straight to my balls.

I gasp, eyes rolling back as she dives forward with Shane's thrust and swallows my cock, nose bumping against me. "Fuck!"

"Touch yourself."

Lex immediately obeys Shane's order, fingers dipping to

her clit as she continues to suck me like a pro. *Ugh, so hot. Such a good fucking girl.* She whimpers as her fingers brush where her and Shane's bodies join, her eyes falling closed. I shudder at the sight, cock throbbing in the hot, wet haven of her mouth.

"Are you going to come again, Lex?" My voice quavers as I reach out to cradle her head in my hands, thrusting lightly in time with Shane's pounding.

Tears stream down her flushed cheeks as she nods, her whole body trembling.

"Not until I tell you," Shane bites out.

He grips her ass cheek roughly, his fingers digging in hard as he continues his assault of her tight hole with his other hand. Her lips and tongue are working me frantically, one hand between her legs while the other plays with my balls, tugging gently. She's destroying me bit by bit, and I groan as I feel that telltale tingle in my spine.

"You close?" Shane asks.

I dip my chin, eyes glazed.

"You get her ass next."

Oh fuck. The mere thought is enough to push me over the edge, my hips stuttering as my orgasm violently rips through me. I groan as I erupt into Lex's mouth, holding her head in place as I pump down her throat. She's shivering, her hand barely moving between her legs as she fights to hold back her own climax and still obey. *So fucking good.*

"That's it," Shane rasps, his hips losing rhythm as he tips over the edge. "Look at Dec, look at what you do to him."

Lex's eyes flash to the side as I slip from her mouth, biting her lip on a moan as her pupils dilate.

"You see that?" Shane croons, wrapping a hand around her neck to haul her up, flush against his body. "Do you like him watching you?"

"Yes," she moans, clutching his arm as he slowly thrusts into her.

His eyes flash to mine, and I snake a hand out to seize a nipple, teasing it before I twist it sharply. She gasps, writhing in his hold.

"Yes, sir," she babbles, "sorry, sorry, yes."

Her jaw drops as he increases his pace, her perfect tits bouncing with each harsh snap of his hips.

"You want him?" Shane asks, and Lex's body convulses.

"Fuck, yes," she pants. "Please, sir."

Her skin is flushed red and blotchy, her hips trying to counter his movements as she resists her orgasm.

Shane kisses the sensitive hollow of her throat, making her moan as he drags his tongue up the side of her neck to nip at her ear. "Then you better fucking come for me, you perfect slut. Now."

Lex's eyes close as her body bows, her low moan turning into the sweetest scream. She leans her face against Shane's neck as she whimpers and shakes, her body sagging. Shane bands an arm around her chest to hold her up as he works them roughly through their mutual climax. The only sounds in the room are our heavy breaths and the slowing slap of Shane's hips meeting her ass.

Still breathless from his orgasm, Shane looks up at Dec. "Enjoy the show?"

Dec doesn't answer, and I can't tear my eyes off Lex to see his reaction. She's flushed from head to toe, skin slick with sweat, mascara streaked down her cheeks. *A masterpiece.* Shane eases back, causing Lex to moan as he slips from her. He looks down as she falls forward onto her hands, his blue eyes darkening as he stares at the evidence no doubt dripping down her reddened flesh.

"You're missing one hell of a view," he mutters distractedly, reaching down.

A soft gasp from Lex, followed by a languid writhe of her hips, tells me he's pushed his release back inside. He's fond of doing that, and judging by the way Lex's fingers dig into the duvet as she exhales sharply, she doesn't mind one bit.

Shane leans forward and kisses the base of Lex's spine, his eyes closing briefly as he does. I know the look, know how he feels. He's worshiping her, thanking her, reveling in the fact we are here together and she deigned to let us in. *She is utterly and perfectly destroyed.* I meet his gaze as his eyes open. *So are we.*

"Relax, baby." Shane smooths a hand over her lower back, pressing slightly.

She gives in to him immediately, molding herself against me where I half-lay propped up on my elbows and frozen in awe. Nuzzling against the sensitive skin above my cock, she looks up at me with heavy lids as she wraps her arms around my waist. I smile down at her, still catching my breath, and tangle my fingers in her hair. *This is heaven.*

Dec clears his throat, drawing all of our attention.

"Lex mentioned an invitation," he rasps.

My eyes wander over him, smug amusement rising in my chest. *The man is wrecked.* His hair stands in every direction, the button on his jeans popped and doing nothing to hide his arousal.

"She's the boss," Shane drawls.

Lex huffs, still relaxed against me. "No I'm not. Not here."

Her complete comfort with us makes my heart squeeze. *Does she even realize how intense that level of trust is?* Lex presses a kiss to the inside of my hip, and my cock stirs.

"Careful, gorgeous." I smooth her hair back, cradling her face in my hands. "You sure you're ready for all of us?"

Her pupils blow as her lips part, her gaze going hazy with lust. "Please, sir," she breathes. "Yes, please."

"Fuck," Declan croaks.

I glance over to watch him draw a trembling hand over his jaw.

"Can you follow orders, Wilde?"

Shane's voice is sharp, commanding. He's in full dom mode, protective as fuck over his perfect sub. *Our perfect sub.* Dec nods in my periphery.

"We'll see," Shane grunts. "Strip. You know the color system?"

"Yes," Dec answers, rising from the chair to shed his clothes.

I can't decide if I'm surprised or impressed at how seamlessly he follows direction.

"She says red—"

"We stop." Dec confirms. "I know." His gaze softens as he looks at Lex, who is still draped over me, surprisingly calm. "She calls the shots."

"Are you three going to fuck me, or talk about me like I'm not here?" Her tone is playful, her eyes flashing as I look down at her with raised brows.

"I'm sorry, who is this brat and what have you done with my good girl?" I tease, grinning down at her.

She giggles, then squeals as Shane leans forward and sinks his teeth into her ass cheek. The sharp sound quickly turns into a thready moan as he licks the sting away, the soft rush of her breath against me waking my dick right up.

"Up." Shane taps Lex's hip, and she complies immediately, kneeling between my legs and waiting for the next instruction.

"Linc, up against the pillows."

I can feel my brother's eyes on me as I move back, partially propped up. My cock is hardening rapidly, anticipation rushing hot in my veins. Memories of the few times Shane and I have taken her together fill my mind, making my cock bob as I shudder out a slow breath.

Shane shuffles up behind Lex, shifting her hair back with gentle fingers and making her shiver. He drops his lips to her ear.

"Look what you do to him," he murmurs.

He grips Lex's jaw firmly, making her stare at me. I answer his pointed look with a long, slow stroke of my dick, biting my lip at the feel. Lex whimpers, her fingers twitching as though she wants to touch herself, or me. *Or both.*

"You want him here?" Shane asks.

Lex's body stiffens as she mewls and nods. His fingers are probably toying with her ass again. Pre-cum gushes from my dick at the thought.

"Turn around, dirty little thing. Back that ass up and sit on his cock."

"Christ." Dec's harsh mumble is loud in the room.

Lex scrambles around, ignoring everything but Shane's order. She straddles me backwards, moving back until her ass bumps into me.

"Spread your cheeks."

I go lightheaded when she graces me with that perfect view. Her tight hole is shiny with lube from Shane's fingers, so fucking sexy and inviting. Shane hands me the lube, and I work a liberal amount over my dick.

"You ready for me, beautiful?"

"Yes, sir, please." Lex presses back against me, my dick slipping between her cheeks.

We both groan as I slide against her hole a few times, relishing the slick feel. Shane slaps my foot, a clear signal to hurry the fuck up, and I almost roll my eyes as I notch the head of my cock against her.

"Come on, gorgeous. Relax for me, yeah? Come on and let

me in," I soothe, stroking my hands along her sides as we press together.

There's resistance, that delicious tension as her tight little hole attempts to deny me entry. She mewls softly at the stretch, stiffening. Shane glances at Dec.

"Distract her," he commands.

Dec moves forward slowly, kneeling next to Lex on the bed. She turns to him, the side of her cheek red and damp from tears. My cock is throbbing, every little move sending jolts of pure bliss through me.

"We've got you," Dec soothes Lex, leaning forward to kiss her neck.

Her little gasps turn sensual, her body relaxing as the pain recedes. Dec's head moves down her chest toward her nipples, and she moans deeply as she starts to bear down. I groan, eyes shutting as she eases herself back inch-by-inch. We're both panting by the time I'm fully seated in her ass.

"Fuck," I moan, leaning back to look down at where we're joined as I stroke her sides. "You feel so fucking good, Lex. So tight."

She clenches around me at the praise, doing her damn best to unravel me completely.

"Lean back and spread those legs," Shane commands before she can respond.

As she does exactly as Shane asks, Dec shuffles back to give them room. His eyes are locked on Lex, drinking in every reaction.

"You're not done," Shane mutters.

Dec's brows fall as he swallows roughly.

Wasting no time at all, Shane eases his way into Lex's pussy, the barbells on the underside of his cock stroking us both in a blaze of fiery pleasure. Lex cries out at the stretch, hands scrabbling to grasp onto something. I catch one, holding tight as her fingers thread through mine.

My pulse increases when I realize Dec has seized her other hand, his white knuckles matching hers. *This is it. No going back now.* I can see the tension on Dec's face as he reaches down between Shane and Lex.

"Breathe," he murmurs, shuffling closer, his hand still between her legs. "You can take them. I know you can. You're made for them. Just let go. Give in."

Her body tightens, drawing twin groans from me and Shane as her hips shift. *Oh, dear god, he's playing with her clit.* Dec leans in, kissing her throat again, as Shane presses forward once more.

Shane exhales sharply as he stills, Lex finally impaled on both of us to the hilt. I can see the flush on her shoulders creeping over her chest and up her neck as she pants between us.

Lex turns to Dec, a lazy little smile barely visible from my vantage. She moans and bites her lip, her body nearly suspended between us. Dec's gaze is intent, a flush to match Lex's darkening his cheeks.

"Feed her your cock."

Dec's eyes flick from Shane to Lex and back again. Lex moans a little as she leans her head toward him eagerly, and I watch his brows climb.

"C-color?" he asks, as though he needed reassurance.

Lex shudders all over as Shane and I both shift minutely, her answer turning into a soft gasp. "Green."

I have the vague thought I should feel some kind of way about being so fucking close to my brother's hard dick, but all I feel as Lex descends on him is ecstasy.

Shane and I rock gently, hardly moving, as Lex finds her rhythm with Dec. She doesn't hesitate to pull him into her mouth, winding one arm around his thigh and gripping my hand to anchor her other side. I tip my head back and close my eyes, losing myself to the sensation of Lex's ass gripping me, and Shane's piercings sliding against me with the slightest shift.

"Look at you taking all of us," Shane growls, slowly increasing the pace and intensity of his thrusts. "We're filling you up, every hole. You love it, don't you? Our dirty slut."

Lex moans around Dec, and I look over to watch his hips twitch. Her ass tightens around me, Shane's dirty talk working her over as it always does.

"Hold on."

That's the only warning Shane gives before he starts pounding into Lex in earnest. He surges forward as I pull back, one hand latched on Lex's hip to help guide her between us.

"Don't you dare come off Declan's cock, Lex."

Lex whimpers, her hand squeezing mine impossibly tight. I grunt as her body constricts around me, already so close to exploding from the sensations racing through me. Holding myself back, I try to focus on the steady give and take with Shane, the sound of us nearly overwhelming in the huge room. Lex's whimpers and moans urge me on, and I thrust my hips up more forcefully, planting my feet on the bed for leverage.

"God, your mouth..." Dec's voice is ragged, his breaths sharp as Lex sucks him down, sloppy and desperate.

"Fucking talented, isn't she?" I grunt, mildly amazed at my ability to form coherent words.

"So good," he breathes.

"Our perfect girl," I agree, my fingers sinking into her flesh sharply as she shudders and grips me impossibly tight.

I teeter on the edge, Lex's incredible tight heat combined with the delicious glide of Shane's pierced cock through the thin wall of tissue between us pushing me toward an epic climax.

My hips start to stutter as I groan, clenching my teeth as I try to hold it back.

"I'm right there," I bite out, squeezing Lex's hand as she bucks against us.

"You hear that, baby?" Shane rasps. "Hear what you do to us?"

He snaps his hips sharply, tunneling into her with a force that vibrates into me.

"So fucking powerful on your knees."

The rare praise from Shane has her shivering, her movements getting more stilted as she sobs around Dec's cock. She's desperate to come; I can feel the telltale tremors in her legs and core.

"You're waiting, aren't you? Such a good little slut. Our perfect whore. Come. Come for *all* of us."

My vision nearly whites out as I come with Lex, both of us crying out. Pleasure bursts from the base of my spine through my limbs, and I tear my hand from hers to wrap an arm around her waist and clutch her to me. I bury my mouth against her neck, my teeth biting into her shoulder as pulse after pulse of my orgasm rocks through me. She moans and quakes in my arms, every sound and movement heightening my pleasure.

I'm vaguely aware of Dec's hoarse cry as he follows us into oblivion. Shane finishes moments later, the feel of him pulsing against my overstimulated cock through Lex making me tremble.

"Holy fuck," Dec groans, dropping roughly to the side of the bed. His wild eyes meet mine. "Is it always like that?"

Lex chuckles weakly, her body lax against me. Shane surges forward to claim a harsh kiss, both of them moaning into each other. I hiss as she clamps down around me, forcing me from her as she responds to him. It doesn't matter how many orgasms we drag out of her, she always wants more. *Greedy fucking goddess.*

Shane finally releases her, climbing off the bed and heading for the bathroom to start the shower. Dec watches him go, his brows drawing down.

"Aftercare," I offer in response to his questioning glance.

I collapse against the pillows, Lex's back plastered to my chest. She turns with an exhausted groan, slipping off me to settle into my side, head on my shoulder. She gazes at Dec as she tangles our legs together.

"Yes," she mutters, voice hoarse. "It's always like that. I'm pretty convinced it's not just Paris that's magic."

My pulse jumps as I swallow roughly, my arm tight around her. I look up to find Dec's loaded gaze on us both. *He knows. Of course he fucking knows. He couldn't possibly let me tell the woman I love how I feel before he tells* **me** *how I feel. With nothing but a look, no less. Bastard.*

"You good?" I ask, in lieu of sharing my news with Lex and destroying the mood. *Would she run? Fuck, I hope not.*

He smiles slowly with a deep sigh, his whole frame more relaxed than he's been in months. "I'm good, Linc."

Shane walks back into the room, reaching over the bed to smack Lex's ass. "Let's go."

Lex leans up to kiss me, her lips lingering for a long moment, before she slides out of my hold and off the bed. She pauses by Dec, stepping up between his knees and threading her fingers into his hair.

"I'm glad you accepted my invitation, Wilde," she murmurs. "Consider it an open one."

He stares up at her, expression soft as he drinks her in. His hands settle on her hips, then slide around her waist. "I'm a fool for letting it take so long for us to get here."

My brows rise as I glance at Shane, but he just smirks. *Sneaky fucker. Of course he's not surprised.* Lex leans down and kisses Dec, and the sexual tension in the room explodes.

Dec growls, sounding so like Shane I almost do a double take, and surges to his feet. He crushes her against him, and Lex meets him in kind, winding her arms around his neck and going up on her tiptoes. They kiss like they argue, each fighting for dominance before Dec finally gives in and melts into her touch. It's so different to how she is with us, little trace of soft edges and willing surrender.

She's the one to release him, pulling back with his lip between her teeth in a move so hot I'm nearly ready to go again. *Who am I kidding? My refractory period is fucking nothing around her.*

"No more running. Deal?" She steps back, a twinkle in her eye as she reaches a hand toward Shane, eyes on Dec.

"Deal," Dec growls.

I level a finger at my brother as the love of my life saunters off with our best friend. "You're fucking trouble."

Shane snorts as he leads Lex away. I choose to interpret the sound as agreement. Dec watches them disappear into the enormous bathroom, then turns to me with wide eyes.

"I know, man," I answer his unspoken exclamation, moving off the bed to find my boxer briefs.

"Linc..."

"Don't," I toss over my shoulder, pulling on my underwear. "Get out of your head."

"I'm not in my head," he grouses unconvincingly.

"Sure, Dec. Whatever you say."

He clears his throat as I turn back to him. He's gotten his own boxer briefs on, and it feels like we might be able to have a somewhat normal conversation now that we're both semi-clothed.

"You love her." His voice is soft, quiet.

I fight the urge to scrub a hand through my hair. "That obvious, huh?"

"Pretty obvious, brother."

I sigh, eyes flicking toward the bathroom. "I thought falling in love was supposed to be hard. Everyone talks about how relationships are work, but it's never felt like that with her. Loving that woman is like breathing, Dec. Easy."

His lips purse briefly, something flashing in his eyes. "I'm glad for you, Linc."

I eye him. "You sound super stoked."

He groans, dropping back into the chair by the bed. "There's a lot to think through. What about her rules?"

"Nope." I shake my head. "This is Paris, and Paris is magic. Rules aren't magic."

"Linc..."

"I'm serious, Dec. Not now." I'm not ready to think through the what-ifs of whether Lex will walk away from us after this. *Let her fucking try.*

He searches my face for a long moment, no doubt tracking my hard jaw and steely eyes. Finally, he ducks his head and nods.

"Okay. I'll follow your lead." A smile curves his lips as he looks back up at me. "Never thought I'd see the day I let you three call the shots. And all at once, to boot."

Laughing, I walk over to shove his shoulder. "You're a controlling asshole on a good day, man. We're good for you. Stick with us, you'll see."

Dec turns thoughtful eyes toward the bathroom, Lex's laugh reaching our ears. He looks back at me, something indecipherable in his gaze.

"You might be right."

Chapter 33

Declan

"You ready for today?" Lex eyes me from across the elevator, a soft smile on her lush lips.

I already found myself staring at her mouth a dozen times since breakfast, the vision of my cock disappearing into it warring with one of her flushed and needy, impaled between Shane and Linc. *I can't decide which I prefer.* Absently, I shift to adjust myself.

"Ready as I'll ever be."

She smirks, Linc rolling his eyes at my short reply. Lex doesn't need me to elaborate; she knows I'm ready, she just wants me to admit the same. *I'm ready, thanks to you.*

Sex could be clarifying. In the aftermath of arguably the best sexual encounter of my life, I had a few revelations. As I railed against Lex and my own feelings, I failed to celebrate something monumental—we'd been funded. Startups were a dime a dozen, but startups with prominent VC backing? Those were in a far more exclusive group. Shane and Linc were right— we should've been celebrating the last three months.

Looking back, it's laughable that I tried to liken Lex to

Anne-Marie for so long. Our conniving former business partner didn't have a compassionate bone in her body. She looked out for number one–herself–and didn't give a flying fuck what happened to anyone around her. She sold an inspiring story of trial and error, a bright young woman making it in a cutthroat industry, but it was all smoke and mirrors.

Lex was the antithesis of Anne-Marie. Cunning, direct, and invested in the people around her as much as she was in their professional success–more so, even.

"Greenstar's on the schedule for this morning." Linc stares at his phone with the Summit schedule pulled up on the event app.

Lex nods. "Right before you. We might run into her. Are you worried?"

Am I? I don't want to be, but I can't deny the thought of coming face-to-face with her is unpleasant.

"No." Shane answers before I can, stepping through the elevator doors as they open.

He looks as relaxed as ever, hands tucked in the pockets of his dark gray suit pants. A small smile lifts Lex's mouth as she glances from him to me, and I want to kick myself for missing so many similar moments over the last few months. Paris Lex is playful, unguarded. She's quick to smile and laugh, and seems happiest when touching one of us. *Is this what she's like at home, too?*

"She'll try to unsettle you, Declan." Lex pitches her voice low, her hand on my shoulder as we walk toward the registration desk. "Don't let her. She's the one who stands to lose everything today, not you. Remember that."

I dip my chin as she grips me gently before moving to greet the event organizers with a smile. They're clearly pleased to see her, several of them rushing over to take her hand. She's relaxed and warm in response, one hand in the pocket of her wide-leg pants. *So fucking effortless.*

"You good?" Shane steps over, holding out my badge.

Taking it, I run a thumb over the bold green 'Presenter' banner along the top. It's simple, but seeing my name and title over 'Solum Technologies' is something else. We'd never invested in business cards, so the opportunity to see my name in something more official than an email signature was rare. Everything suddenly feels *real*. I'm struck with the weight of the moment, years of pressure and strain fading as fragile hope settles in its place.

"You did it." Linc joins us, gripping my shoulder.

I look from him to Shane, my Adam's apple bobbing. "We did."

Lex wanders over, a soft smile on her lips as she regards us. Linc offers her a badge, which she loops over her head without hesitation. My eyes drop to the bold black letters under her name.

"It says Athena Ventures."

She glances down. "So it does. Should it say something different?"

"I...no. I suppose not." It feels wrong for her to be here representing Athena and not Solum. *She belongs with us.*

The thought catches me by surprise and I blink rapidly, overwhelmed with emotion.

"Solum's yours, Declan. I'm just here to celebrate your success."

Clearing my throat, I stare hard at the badge in my hands. "Thank you," I manage, voice raw.

"Don't thank me. Thank yourselves."

Linc grins as Shane ducks his head, hiding his smile.

"No, Lex," I press, meeting her gaze. "We wouldn't be here

without you. And whatever happens in there today..." I swallow roughly, my voice trailing to nothing as nerves and hope and wicked want momentarily overwhelm me.

Lex grips my forearm. "Declan, don't–"

"I'm grateful." Her expression softens at my insistent words. "I'm so fucking grateful, Lex. For your team, for Athena. But mostly for you."

Silence falls in our small circle as warmth gathers in my chest. Lex's fingers on my sleeve may as well be a brand for how they sear straight to my soul.

"Wow, brother. Paris really is magic," Linc quips, breaking the growing tension.

Chuckling, I take a deep breath to ground myself, staring once again at the badge in my hands. I'm vaguely aware of Lex saying something to Linc and Shane before walking away, leaving the three of us in the welcome lobby.

"We should go catch the opening ceremonies," Linc suggests, stepping toward the main theater of the Palais des Congrès.

"Yeah," I mutter absently, draping the lanyard over my head as I follow him and Shane. Lex's touch lingers.

The convention center hums, the crowd lively with first-day energy. As we move toward the main theater, a familiar grating laugh breaks out just ahead. Linc's spine snaps straight as he glances toward the noise. The crowd parts, and there the bitch is.

As though aware of our presence, Anne-Marie Townsend turns to look over her shoulder, harsh brown eyes zeroing in on me. Surprise flickers in her gaze before it sharpens to determination, and she turns back to her small audience.

"That didn't take long," Linc mutters, moving to go wide of Anne-Marie.

I assume she won't let us by so easily. A second later, she proves me right.

"Lincoln Wilde," she calls, one hand on her hip. "Fancy seeing you here."

Of course it's my brother she targets first. His shoulders are tight as he turns to give her a flat look. He doesn't speak, and the small group around her exchange raised eyebrows as he regards her stonily. Anne-Marie cocks her head, then turns to Shane.

"Shane, I'm surprised to see you. I thought you would've slunk back to Seattle with your tail between your legs long before now."

"Why? We've been on the agenda for months."

She blinks, seemingly taken aback by his cool response. It's further proof she never paid attention to anyone other than herself–Shane's retort is laughably on-brand. Her lips part, then purse, her gaze finally landing on me.

"Declan."

"Anne-Marie."

"I'm looking forward to hearing more about your tech. Pity you're going after us, though. I'll just be stealing your thunder." Her eyes flash with triumph at the chuckles from her audience.

"There's certainly something to be said for first mover advantage," I concede, "though I've always focused more on results. That was the key difference between us, wasn't it?"

Anne-Marie crosses her arms, waiting for me to go on. I give her a wolfish smile, tamping down the fury I've felt since her betrayal. Faced with the opportunity to dress her down, I find I don't want to waste the energy. I want to eviscerate her company, yes, but *she* isn't worth my time. When I look at her, all I feel is pity.

"You might be seduced by speed, but I'll always put functionality first. You'll give me the perfect lay up, Ms. Townsend.

You can share all the lofty promises you're so fond of, get the ball ready, but it'll be Solum who sends it through the net." *I'm looking forward to it.*

"You think you're hot shit now, huh? Got a little funding and think you can waltz in here and play in the majors." Anne-Marie spreads her arms, like she owns the Summit and everyone attending. "What even is Procerus without me, Declan? The three of you couldn't make it happen then, and you can't now."

"Well, Ms. Townsend." Lex steps up next to me, poised and nonplussed. "I'd say it was a pleasure to see you again, but we both know that would be a lie."

Shocked murmurs start up in Anne-Marie's crowd, a tall man in the back glaring daggers at Lex as he steps forward. Lex had mentioned she saw Anne-Marie at Bay events here and there. From what I understood, they'd always been civil.

"I didn't realize we had history, Lex." Anne-Marie's careful mask slips as she glances back at the people behind her. "I assure you I wish you nothing but the best."

Lex cocks her head, a patronizing smile on her lips. "This is the fourth–no, fifth–opportunity you've missed to right your past indiscretions, Ms. Townsend. One must wonder whether you're truly that calculating, or simply oblivious. In our line of business, I know which is worse. Do you?"

Anne-Marie gapes. I've never seen her at a loss for words. *Point, Lex.*

"That's enough." The tall, dark-haired man scowls, and Shane moves to intercede.

Lex holds up a hand, bringing Shane to an immediate halt. "It's good to see you, brother. Despite the company you keep."

Brother? I glance at Shane and Linc, but their expressions are stoic. I knew Lex had a brother in the business, everyone in the Bay did, though I'd never met the man.

"Are you seriously here just to stir shit, Lex?" Her brother's voice is low as he leans in, clearly wanting to keep the conversation between them.

"I'm here to celebrate the launch of one of Athena's most promising clients," she answers, her voice firm and clear. "Why are you here, Nate?"

"You know damn well why I'm here," he snarls.

Shane is a solid wall next to me. Linc shifts, gripping his arm tightly and shooting me a concerned look. Despite the tension, Lex laughs. She shakes her head, smirking at her brother.

"I don't, actually. I've been focused on my client. I suggest you do the same; seems she could use the coaching."

Anne-Marie's cheeks pinken. "I do not need coaching," she protests. "I'm perfectly prepared and looking forward to sharing Greenstar's revolutionary technology later today. You may have been fooled by those three and their pathetic last ditch effort to get attention, but I'm the one–"

"Do not mistake my professionalism for leniency," Lex sneers. "I can look past your insolence and lack of preparedness three years ago, Ms. Townsend, though I won't forget it. But I will not allow you to stand there and make baseless claims about my clients."

Lex takes a step forward as Anne-Marie tries to back up, but the people behind her aren't about to move away and miss the show.

"The three businessmen behind me have given their all to Solum Technologies, and they've built something remarkable. You might be good at selling an idea, but I suspect your ability to deliver is as nonexistent as your professional courtesy."

"Lex, that's enough." Nate's nostrils flare as he stares his sister down.

Lex tsks, her eyes on Anne-Marie, who is white as a sheet. "You're right. It is. Ms. Townsend isn't worth another second of my time." She turns to Nate, dismissing Anne-Marie.

Nate's eyes narrow as Anne-Marie's gaze pings back and forth between the siblings.

"Anne-Marie."

I turn to Shane in surprise as he calls to her, his deep voice deadly and soft. Her gaze flies to his, her lips pinched in frustration.

"You asked what we even have without you." Shane slides a nonchalant hand into his pocket, his expression hard. "Nothing you gave to Procerus made a difference, so why would you possibly think we ever needed you? You did us a favor when you walked out the door."

Anne-Marie's brow furrows. "Listen here, Shane–"

"Is Reginald here?" Lex barks at Nate, ignoring our former partner entirely.

Anne-Marie steps back abruptly, eyes wide as she notices the attention of the crowd. Swallowing roughly, she spins and hurries away, shoulders hunched.

"He is," Nate bites out, glaring daggers at his sister.

Lex sighs. "That's a shame. I'm sure you were hoping he'd let you do something on your own for once."

His jaw clenches so tight I'm surprised we don't hear his teeth crack.

"Anyway," Lex continues airily, turning toward us, "we have places to be, don't we?" With a pointed look at Nate, she starts toward the theater as she tosses the final word over her shoulder. "Good luck, brother. Make good choices."

I turn wide eyes to Linc and Shane as we follow her. Shane's scowling, no doubt still frustrated at Nate's treatment of Lex, but Linc is grinning ear-to-ear.

"That was hot, right?" Linc whispers. "Really fucking hot. Fuck, she's something else."

"Get it together," Shane deadpans.

Linc grins and I fight a smile. Of course, my brother catches it.

"Dec even agrees with me! Look at that smug grin." Linc jostles me with his shoulder. "Bet you're as turned on as I am."

"Fuck off, Linc," I groan as Shane rolls his eyes. "Time and fucking place."

No need to tell him he's right.

Chapter 34

Lex

"Who's ready for the city of the future?!" Anne-Marie cries, clearly hoping to incite an enthusiastic reaction. Wearing black slacks and a turtleneck, she looks like a tech founder cosplayer.

To the crowd's credit, they offer a polite round of applause. It isn't the most energetic response of the day, but it isn't the most subdued, either. As expected, Anne-Marie's presentation is more aspirational than informative.

All three guys are backstage while I wait in the audience. I sit near the front, close enough for Declan to find me if he needs an anchor in the crowd. As Anne-Marie bows a final time and turns to exit stage left, Nate rises from his seat a few rows away. He looks back at the crowd, a satisfied smile on his face—until he sees me.

"Come on, brother." I wave him over. "Join me."

There's an empty seat to my left. Nate looks like the last thing he wants to do is be in my presence. I watch him war internally before his curiosity wins out. Grumbling, he makes his way over and takes the open seat.

"Don't be so disappointed in yourself," I tease, knocking my shoulder against his. "I'd have taken the offer, too, if it'd been you asking."

"Father's going to be displeased." He sighs and pinches his brow, his body slumping minutely.

"Trouble in the ranks?"

Nate's off-handed comments about our father, and the thinly veiled references to how close they were while I was kept on the outside, used to eat at me. Years of focus on my business, and a small fortune in therapy, had worked wonders. I no longer feel a pang of jealousy for the position my brother happily stole.

Nate grunts in response to my lighthearted question. "He's pushing, per usual. He questions whether we should even focus on this sector."

"Ah, yes. He's still in deep with oil and gas, I assume?"

He eyes me as though the answer is obvious. I chuckle, glancing up at the stage as the emcee returns.

"Pay attention, Nate," I urge, looking meaningfully toward the three men on stage.

Nate's brows furrow as he looks at me, then the guys. The crowd claps as the emcee steps away, Declan moving toward the middle of the stage. His hands are in his pockets, his posture confident and relaxed. In a tailored black suit and crisp white shirt, his maroon tie accenting his glittering green eyes, he cuts an impressive figure in the spotlight.

Shane and Linc stand further back, flanking the modest display of prototypes we brought. Linc fidgets with his sleeve while Shane is poised and calm, stoic as ever in his gray suit and black shirt, open at the collar.

"Thank you." Declan smiles at the crowd, his voice amplified through the mic clipped to his lapel. "It's an honor to be here."

As Declan introduces himself, the guys, and Solum Technologies, I can't help my grin. He's come so far in the last few weeks; he owns that stage. His eyes flick to mine and he smiles, ducking his head. *Fuck, he's cute when he's not a raging asshole.*

"What's the story, Lex?" Nate urges, leaning toward me.

Keeping my eyes on the stage, I shake my head minutely. "Just listen."

He huffs, but takes my direction. Linc winks at me as my eyes wander to him and Shane. Smirking, I wink back. Declan gestures toward them both as he describes the early history of their business, and they raise their two earliest prototypes.

"Three years ago," Declan explains, "we were close. We thought we were ready. But we weren't willing to compromise on the quality of our product. After all, something that failed in high heat or wind, both increasingly common conditions across the globe, wouldn't do."

Nate finally has a sense of where Declan's story is going. His knuckles are white as he clasps his hands together, leaning forward to plant his elbows on his knees.

"We suffered a significant setback, it's true. In the end, it was all worth it because it brought us here, to this Summit, with the best news we could offer."

Shane and Linc are building a small structure on stage with the latest prototypes.

"Today, we launch Solum Technologies' first product: Terra. This versatile material combines all the best qualities of its traditional counterparts. It's flexible like steel, strong like brick, and acts as a natural carbon sink like wood."

Nate glances sharply at me, his lips pursed. The single prototype Anne-Marie had shared was almost a more modern brick and mortar—a small block paired with a special adhesive mud. Though it was carbon neutral to develop it, the guys hadn't quite figured out the composition to take it to the next level before she made off with their formulas.

"To accommodate everything from single family homes to

multi-story office buildings, pre-made pieces interlock for a clean, dry construction. For increased durability, it can be poured in a custom mold like concrete, with reinforcing materials that could support up to thirty stories."

A low murmur spreads through the crowd as Declan grins.

"And that's just based on last week's test, which showed a 15% improvement in durability over the week prior." His tone turns teasing, "At that rate, we'll be building entire cities with Terra by the end of the year."

Soft chuckles surround us. The smile feels etched into my face; I couldn't wipe it away if I wanted to.

"How is this possible?" Nate mutters, brows drawn.

"I told you to dig," I whisper.

Shane and Linc had finished their structure. The small wall was my idea, though the next part was all Linc.

"Watch this!" he cries, his enthusiasm ramping up the crowd with just two words.

He goes to the opposite end of the stage, then runs toward the wall, which Shane was bracing from the opposite side. I tense, knowing what's coming, as the crowd gasps. When he draws close, he launches himself at the structure and plows straight into it. With a loud grunt, he bounces lightly away. The wall slides slightly, pushing Shane back, but it doesn't flex. Not a single block out of place.

Immediately, the crowd cheers. Nate scoffs, running a rough hand through his hair as Declan explains how the materials would save installation time and reduce maintenance costs.

"This is bad, Lex," he mutters, glancing over his shoulder. *Likely looking for dear old dad.*

"I can see how you'd see it that way. Tell me, Nate...did you get the school contract from the State?"

He stares at his hands, his body stiff. Drawing a hand over the stubbled lower half of his face, he nods once.

"Did you test it in heat and wind, like Declan mentioned?"

"Of course we did."

"With a third party?"

His eyes search mine. "I...I don't know."

"Find out. The product Anne-Marie stole was flawed. After three months of targeted development, this one isn't." I gesture toward the stage where Declan is thanking the audience.

He turns and bows to Shane and Linc, hands pressed together in gratitude. The crowd goes wild, several in the rows surrounding us rising to their feet. The guys are beaming, arms around each other, as they bow together.

As one, they look at me. I stand and clap enthusiastically.

"Bravo!" I call.

Their answering grins and laughter fill me with an overwhelming sensation of warmth and joy. My smile wide, I turn to Nate as the guys leave the stage. They'd be heading out to our meeting place near the press room before they host a Q&A session on the secondary stage.

Nate reaches out and grips my arm as I go to move past him. "Lex, I...what do I fucking do with this?"

"I tried to warn you." I keep my voice low, aware of the crowd settling in preparation for the next presentation. "Nate, I don't care if P&L becomes the best VC in the country. If you and Reginald make fifty times the fortune I do, it won't bother me. But that product is dangerous."

I clutch his wrist, squeezing to make my point. "You build schools with that and you're taking responsibility for the people who use them every day. One heat wave, one high wind warning, and you could find blood on your hands. It could happen in two years or not for twenty—"

"It doesn't matter," he insists. "I know it doesn't matter. The outcome is the same."

Nodding, I search his gaze. "No payout is worth someone's life, Nate. Would Reginald agree?"

He steps back, his hand sliding slowly off my arm. Resting my hand on his shoulder briefly, I sigh.

"Good luck, brother. Do me a favor?"

Dazed, he blinks. "Uh, sure. Yeah. What is it?"

Gripping him firmly, I look him square in the eye. "Do the right thing. Whatever it takes, no matter how hard Reginald pushes you to take the easy way out. Even though it'll be hell... do the right thing."

"I will." His jaw clenches as he swallows, eyes fierce. "Lex, I promise you I will."

Outside the press room, three gorgeous men wait. As one, they turn to watch me approach. They look so happy, so full of joy. I can't help but smile in response, laughing as Linc rushes forward to sweep me into his arms.

"We did it!" He swings me up and in a circle, releasing me with a soft sigh. "Lex, thank you. I can't fucking believe it."

"I can," I tease, smoothing the rumpled shoulders of his navy suit coat.

"How'd we look?" Linc couldn't have reminded me more of an eager lap dog if he tried.

"Competent."

Linc grunts at my teasing, rolling his eyes. Shane laughs, the sound so free and unrestrained it dazzles me. Ever the gentleman, he reaches out and squeezes my hand, though his eyes rake over me with blazing want.

"Linc's right," he says softly. "Thank you."

"That was all you, gentlemen," I insist.

Turning to Declan, I step into his personal space under the guise of straightening his lapels and tie.

"You were magnificent, Mr. Wilde," I murmur, looking up at him through my lashes. "How did it feel?"

He rests a hand on my hip, the other tucked into his pocket. "Unbelievable. I can't...I don't have the words—"

"I'm proud of you, Declan."

He stills, his fingers flexing against me as he searches my eyes.

"You've overcome so much, worked so hard." I step back, heart aching at the loss of his touch, but needing to include all of them. "I'm so incredibly proud of each of you. What you've accomplished...it's astonishing. I feel fortunate to simply witness your rise."

"You need to stop talking," Linc chokes. "I don't think it's in the PR strategy for me to bawl my eyes out in front of the press."

Laughing, I hug Linc tightly. Truth be told, tears are threatening for me, too.

"Go on." I lightly push on Linc's shoulders, pointing him to the press room. "Go bask in their attention."

"All downhill from here, huh?" Linc grins.

Chuckling, I shake my head. "Oh, sweet summer child. This was the easy part. We get home and the real work begins."

In tandem, their grins stutter. They glance at each other, then back to me.

"Don't think of that now." I flap my hands at them. "We're still in Paris for two days! Keep basking, keep basking."

Declan tosses me a wry grin. "I don't know whether to be excited or scared."

"Both," I answer sagely. "Definitely both."

Chapter 35

Nate

"I fail to see the issue, Nathaniel."

My father sits in his suite, a tumbler of bourbon in hand. His salt-and-pepper hair, short on the sides and smoothed back along the top, is perfectly styled. He attended exactly two sessions of the Summit that day–Greenstar's and Solum's–before busying himself with other Paris-based clients.

"You can't be serious."

He gives me a hard look, straightening the lapel of his red and black smoking jacket. "I saw you sitting with your sister. Is she the one filling your head with ridiculous notions?"

"This has nothing to do with Lex."

His gaze narrows. "*Alexandra* chose this distance between us. She chose to leave the family, and she's eager to tear us down. You're a fool if you listen to a word she says."

Two years ago, I would have agreed with him. I'd never understood why Lex ran away from our family, from everything our father offered her. She'd seemed like a spoiled little princess who threw a fit when she didn't get what she wanted. At least, that was how our dear father referred to her. *And I lapped it right up.*

"Again, she's immaterial to this conversation."

Reginald huffs. "Oh, she's immaterial alright."

Frustration flares. For years, I'd gone along with his critical narrative. When I moved to the Bay to open P&L, I relished the opportunity to put 'Alexandra' in her place. I wanted to flaunt my knowledge, my professional success. But my sister, with her thriving business and immaculate reputation, thwarted me at every turn.

She never once displayed any of the negative traits my father so vehemently extolled, no matter how intently I watched for them. The Lex I'd met at galas, during business dinners, and through industry happy hours was poised. She was elegant, smart, and so well-respected it almost felt like a personal joke. As though her meteoric rise to the upper echelon of Bay society was something she'd accomplished solely to fuck with me.

"What are you so worried about, Nathaniel?" Reginald's shrewd gaze assesses me, measures me, and—no doubt—finds me wanting. *He always does.* "Are you going soft on me?"

"We can't move forward with the contract with the State. If there's anything the Solum Technologies presentation proved, it's that Greenstar's product is flawed."

"So theirs was a bit more sophisticated. What of it? We got to the State first. The contract is signed. It would be more than foolhardy to renege now. It would be ruinous."

"Were you listening?" I press, incredulous.

"To what?"

"Declan Wilde, the CEO of Solum."

He takes a long drink of his bourbon. "I heard enough."

"Father, their product failed extreme condition tests as recently as three months ago. That's *after* Greenstar Labs acquired Anne-Marie's technology."

"How are these things related?" he sighs, as though the conversation is beneath him.

I yell in frustration. "Because they're the same! Anne-Marie's tech and their tech are the same!"

"Calm yourself, boy," he snarls. "Don't you raise your voice at me."

Scoffing, I grab a tumbler and aggressively splash bourbon into it. His hypocrisy is rich. He'd ripped into me far more severely too many times to count.

"Anne-Marie stole the tech *from* the team at Solum before Greenstar bought it. It's flawed."

"I've seen the reports. Everything looks to be in order."

I turn to him, eyebrows raised. "You've seen the reports?"

"Why wouldn't I?"

"I'm on Greenstar's board. They're not a P&L client. Where did you even get access?"

He sniffs. "Don't question me, boy. I have my ways."

I rack my brain, trying to connect the dots. My father is, and always has been, overly involved in every move I make at P&L. Part of the reason I was so keen to join Greenstar's board was the opportunity to do something on my own.

"Ugh, it's painful watching you attempt to figure it out," he grumbles. "Your incompetence yet again makes me wish Alexandra had been born male."

"Is she immaterial or your preferred heir, Father? Pick your position before I get whiplash." Scowling, I sit roughly in the chair opposite him, kicking my legs out in a sprawl.

"Stop acting like a child, Nathaniel. I know one of the other board members, and I suggested he nominate you for their open seat."

I squint. "Cooper?"

He tips his glass toward me with an exasperated huff. "In exchange, he keeps me informed."

"In exchange for what?"

"My business dealings are none of your concern."

"But mine are yours?" I snarl.

He stands, ruddy cheeks shaking as he storms toward me. "You are nothing without me, Nathaniel! I've made you, given you a career! You owe me everything and you'd be wise to remember that."

Seething, I look away, dismissing him. I've heard it all before. We have the same conversation every time we see each other.

"Don't push this thing with Greenstar, boy. The deal is done and you need to let it be. That's an order."

"Father, I can't just—"

"You can and you will!" he roars, spittle flying.

Disgusted, I slam my tumbler down on the side table so hard the glass cracks. Reginald sputters, stepping back as I surge to my feet.

"I may be your son," I growl, "but I am not your whipping boy or your fall guy. Not anymore. I'll make my own decision on this. Your input is neither required nor welcome."

"You listen here, you—"

"No!" I bark, turning my back on him. "I'm done listening."

"Don't be stupid, Nathaniel."

Ignoring his final volley, I storm from the room. My father raised me to listen and obey, to value money and success over all else. The Livingston name and the legacy he'd built at Price & Livingston Financial were to be revered and protected at all costs. For decades, I'd fallen in line. I'd played his game, pleased with the rewards: a successful career and the style of living most people could only dream of. From the outside looking in, I had everything. *Or so I thought.*

Being in the Bay had taught me I had next to nothing. My professional reputation was inextricably tangled in my father's. Hell, it was even tied up in Lex's. It felt like I didn't have an independent identity, though each of them did.

The people who surrounded me at P&L were just as driven by greed and monetary gain as my father was. They weren't the type to be recognized by charities or industry organizations for their contributions. No one would point to one of my colleagues as a pillar in the community. *Lex certainly is.*

I could buy anything, anyone, but what did I truly have? An empty penthouse and a nagging suspicion that things were far worse behind the scenes of my father's company than I could imagine. And I'd bet my trust fund that if anything nefarious ever came to light, I would be set up to take the fall. My father might talk a good game in public about how proud he was of his son and heir, but I knew he wouldn't hesitate to throw me on the flames to save himself.

My promise to Lex weighs heavily on my shoulders. She's right; I can't stand by and put other people's lives in danger. *How far will I have to go to do the right thing?*

Chapter 36

Shane

"Shane, Linc, I'd like you to meet Dr. Jasper Still." Lex waves us over to a tall, thin man with glasses half the size of his face. "He leads research and development for the Earthware Institute."

"Oh, wow," Linc eagerly takes the man's hand for a vigorous shake. "I've been following your work in renewable energy storage for a while now. Real pleasure to meet you."

Lex's eyes sparkle as she watches Linc gush over Dr. Still, her gaze flashing to mine. She leans closer, her voice low.

"I'm not sure you'll get a word in edgewise," she teases.

I chuckle. We're at the Summit's closing happy hour, the marbled foyer full of people. Several bars and hors d'oeuvres tables are set up around the edges. Lex had been weaving us through the crowd all night, introducing us to business leaders and technology visionaries along the way.

"Do you know everyone here?" I whisper, smirking.

"These communities are small, when it comes down to it."

"There are two thousand people here."

She shrugs. "Sure. Half are investors like me, about a

quarter are established companies looking to acquire or recruit, and the rest are hopefuls. Those lines get blurry when you've been in the game as long as I have; lots of the same faces show up."

I scan the crowd. "Where'd you leave Dec?"

"I introduced him to Morris, the Greenstar Labs CEO."

My eyebrows rise. "That's...an interesting move."

"They see the potential in your tech, even if they invested in the wrong person. Seems like a valuable connection for you all to have." She glances over my shoulder, as though scoping out her next target. "Uh oh, look sharp. Livingstons incoming."

"Livingstons? You mean–"

She sighs deeply, the corner of her mouth quirking into a rueful smile. "Well, hello again, Nate. Reginald."

Anger settles in my belly as I turn to regard Lex's family. Her brother made an impression the day prior, and not a good one. I can't imagine her father will be much better, especially after the crumbs Lex had dropped about her childhood.

Nate and Reginald Livingston are moving as though they intend to walk right past us. It's Nate who acknowledges Lex first. He slows, clapping a firm hand to his father's shoulder to stop him as the older man attempts to ignore her completely. *Fucking prick.*

"Lex. How has the Summit been for you?" Nate asks.

I can't imagine a more uncomfortable family dynamic than the one taking shape before me, and I grew up with an absent father and a desperately ill-equipped mother. Anxious energy emanates from Nate, while Reginald quietly seethes. Lex's talent for remaining calm suddenly makes sense. *Caught between these two, it'd be more survival technique than strategy.*

"Enlightening," she quips, her eyes glinting with equal parts mischief and challenge. "And for you?"

He nods slowly. "I'd say the same."

Their father huffs. "I don't have all day, Nathaniel. I'm sure you aren't stupid enough to bring me here in an ill-fated attempt to facilitate some sort of..." he waves his hands aimlessly, "reconciliation."

Lex laughs brightly, drawing the eyes of most folks around us. They answer her mirth with smiles before turning back to their own conversations.

"I wouldn't dream of a reconciliation with you, Reginald. That ship sailed long ago, didn't it?"

The words could've sounded pleading coming from someone else, someone less...composed. From Lex, they're teasing and confident. Whether the men in her family can see it or not, Lex holds the power.

"And where's Anne-Marie?" Lex asks, her expression suggesting she knows something I don't.

Nate tips a brow at her in warning. "She caught an early flight home."

Lex tsks, eyes sparkling. "Such a shame. I wanted to go a second round after Declan's presentation. Would've been fun."

I can see Nate fighting a smile. *Maybe he's not a lost cause.*

"Forgive me," Lex says, putting her hand to her heart briefly. "Shane, please meet Nate and Reginald Livingston. Gentlemen, this is Shane Kelly, lead engineer at Solum Technologies."

Acting as though Lex didn't speak, Reginald harrumphs. "Nathaniel, I must insist we go."

"Shane, it's good to meet you. You're the one who led the R&D for Terra?" Nate turns to me, ignoring his father completely.

Reginald's cheeks redden as he sputters.

"I am."

"Yesterday, you mentioned heat and wind in your presentation–"

"Not this again," the elder Livingston barks. "There's no use in talking to them about any of this, Nathaniel. The deal is done and the tests are sound."

My gaze narrows. "What deal?"

"None of your concern, boy."

What an absolute asshat. I glance at Lex, a few pieces of her story falling into place.

"Reginald." Lex's tone is firm and full of warning. It isn't lost on me that she doesn't protest his crass regard toward her or Nate, but the second he lashed out at me, she was quick to admonish him.

"With the State–" Nate starts, Reginald spluttering and attempting to interrupt.

I hold up a hand to silence him, keeping my focus on Nate. "You won the deal for the schools?"

"We did," he confirms. "In the presentation yesterday, your CEO mentioned concerns with test results involving high heat and wind."

"That's right. We only recently found the right combination of form factor and organic composition to solve for them." My eyes flick from Lex to her brother. "Has Greenstar changed the formula they bought from Anne-Marie?"

Nate's lips purse. "Nothing significant. But the test results we have don't show any issues."

"Nathaniel, it is highly inappropriate to be sharing any of this with a competitor." Reginald tries to physically insert himself into the conversation, moving to step between me and Nate.

"We're not a competitor," I snap, holding an arm out to keep him at bay. "Greenstar is peddling our stolen tech, and a flawed version at that. If you plan to build schools with it, you're as criminal as you are foolish."

"Excuse me?!" Reginald booms.

He's loud enough to pull the attention of the people around us, confused expressions flitting before landing on our small group to watch.

"Maybe we should—" Nate starts, looking around as though seeking a more private place for us to continue the conversation.

"Shane's right," Lex insists, her gaze hard on her father. "This issue is bigger than intellectual property theft. Fulfilling that contract without serious changes to the product is dangerous."

"Watch your tongue, Alexandra. You will not talk down to me."

While he oscillated from blustering to dismissive before, Reginald's demeanor turns icy and threatening when he confronts Lex. His eyes narrow, mouth turned down at the corners. As I watch him face off with the woman who was arguably more successful than he'd ever be, I realize something. *Reginald Livingston sees his daughter as a massive fucking threat. Maybe he's not a complete idiot.*

To her credit, Lex just stares back at him impassively. "That look might've worked when I was a child, Reginald, but it has no effect now. I don't know how you operate things at Price, but at Athena we put the safety and good of the community before all else."

Reginald's eye twitches as she references his company by his partner's name. I attempt to fight a grin. *Fucking savage.*

"I'm not sure what you're implying—"

"I'll spell it out for you, then, shall I?" Her head tilts predatorily, making my blood sing. *She's a goddamn queen amongst peasants.*

"If, knowing what you know, you don't counsel Greenstar to reconsider their deal with the State, you'll not only be grossly negligent, you'll be criminally liable. Now, you never let me know much about what was happening at Price, but I assume the legal team and board are both still fiercely conservative when it comes to risk? You know, since the argument about dying children doesn't do it for you."

"You little bitch, how dare–"

I stiffen, my lip curling up in a sneer as I take a half step forward, putting my body between Lex and her father. *I don't fucking think so–*

"That's enough," Nate barks, hauling Reginald back by the collar as he aggressively steps toward Lex. "I told you I would handle this."

Nate physically turns his father away as Lex watches, her expression stoic and body relaxed. She didn't flinch as Reginald attacked her.

"Your input is not required, Father," Nate presses. "I'll catch you up when we're both back in the States."

"You will not dismiss me, Nathaniel, I–"

"Respectfully," Nate bites out, eyes hard, "if you can't deescalate the situation, then I will. I told you last night I'd handle this. I fucking meant it."

The two men stare at one another for a drawn out moment, Reginald's flush gradually darkening.

"We will have words–"

"I'm sure we will. Good night."

"In case you were looking for an exit, Reginald, that was it." Lex regards the older man coolly, one hand in her pocket and the other relaxed by her side.

I think Reginald is going to demand to get the last word, but Lex doesn't give him the opportunity. Turning to Nate and giving her father her shoulder, she places a hand on her brother's arm and urges him toward the bar.

"We should get a drink. I'm sure you have questions for Shane."

Reginald's lips part, his eyes darting between his children

with an unreadable expression on his face. Nate goes willingly, and Reginald licks his lips as his brow creases and he turns to me. I smirk. *Here we go.*

"Shane," Lex calls, "it's not worth it."

Tilting my head in deference, I step back and turn to follow her and Nate. Before I go far, Dec's voice sounds behind me. *Where'd he come from?* Slowing to a halt, I tip my ear toward them to listen.

"Reginald Livingston, right?"

"That's right. And you are?"

"Someone who can see what you're too willfully ignorant to acknowledge."

"I beg your pardon?" Reginald blusters.

"That woman is smarter and more driven than any man here, you included. You could've handed her your business and watched it flourish." Dec's voice is low, rough. "But you didn't, did you?"

"Listen here—"

"No. For once in your life, Reggie, you need to listen," Dec seethes. "I hope your regret over letting someone as cunning and brilliant as Lex slip through your fingers eats at you every moment of every day. I hope you look in the mirror and are ashamed of the fool you were when you tried to hold her back."

Glancing over my shoulder, I see Reginald blow out an aggravated breath, his eyes wide and flush creeping down his neck. Dec stands close, jaw set and fist clenched at his side.

"You know what?" Dec leans back, regarding the older man with disdain. "Lex is right. You're not worth it. Just another pompous asshole grasping for scraps of power. You? You're nothing."

He chuckles, low and menacing. "But her? She's everything. I hope you enjoy watching her build a legacy in spite of you, old man. And I hope it fucking kills you when you realize the world has already forgotten your name."

Looking down, I smile. *Atta boy, Dec.* My friend slaps his hand against my shoulder as he reaches me, steering us both after Lex and Nate without a backwards glance. Chuckling, I shove my hands in my pockets. *Now if you can be as good a man to her as you are for her, brother, we'll get somewhere.*

Chapter 37

Lex

Tension ratchets between us the second we step into the elevator at the Le Meurice. Linc crowds me, pushing my body toward the wall as he cups my face in his hands.

"You're fucking stunning, you know that?" he breathes before crashing his lips into mine.

I gasp against him, giving way to his tongue as I grip his shirt. He turns me as he ravages my mouth, pushing me roughly into a warm, hard body. Declan's scent surrounds me as soft lips descend on the juncture of my throat, licking and teasing my skin. The elevator sounds as it reaches our floor, but they don't release me.

"Come on, Lex," Shane's deep voice breaks through the haze of lust, his fingers tangling with mine as he draws me toward the door.

Linc and Declan move back reluctantly as I follow Shane, heart beating double time. They crowd close to us as we move into the suite, Linc snagging my free hand as Declan lays a hand on my nape. I feel like I'm burning alive with the three of them so close, each claiming part of me.

"You want us?" Shane asks, slowing as we reach the living room.

"God, yes." I nod, feeling dazed. *Is this really my life?*

Linc steps up against me, pressing his lips to my neck as he draws my coat off my shoulders and lets it slip to the floor. Shane takes my bag, moving to set it somewhere I don't see because Declan is gripping the back of my head and pulling me in for a searing kiss.

Whimpering, I anchor myself on his biceps, my core clenching in want with every swipe of his tongue. Fumbling hands work at the zipper of my trousers, jerking it open and shoving both pants and underwear down my legs. Declan bands an arm around my waist, crushing my heated flesh into the soft, cool fabric of his tailored suit.

Strong fingers tease at the hem of my blouse, rucking the fabric up toward my head.

"Buttons," I gasp, leaning back from Declan.

"Fuck the buttons," he growls, gripping each side of the silky material and yanking.

The soft ping of buttons hitting the table and floor is drowned out by my yelp and Shane's husky laugh.

"Jesus, Declan!" I huff, glancing at the ruined material hanging from my shoulders.

Declan smirks as he runs his big palms under my breasts, framing the lacy cups of my black bra with his thumbs.

"What?" he mutters, looking at me through his thick lashes. "I'm impatient."

"You're a brute, is what you are."

Resting my hands on his shoulders, I look into his emerald eyes and suck my lip between my teeth as his expression darkens.

"Brute, huh? I'll show you brute."

Before I know what's happening, he hefts me into his arms.

Giggling, I wrap my legs around him and hold his face in my hands. He grins up at me, his eyes bright and laugh lines appearing in the corners. I lean down and press my lips to his for a long moment, then pepper his face in gentle kisses. As I do, he turns and moves us toward the couch.

Linc and Shane wait by the largest sofa, both down to their boxer briefs. Shane's gorgeous ink is on display, the intricate black and gray scenes mesmerizing as ever.

"Give her here and strip."

Declan glares at Shane as he complies, setting me on my feet. "You always like this, man?"

Glancing up as Shane wraps his arms around me from behind, I nod. Resting his chin on my shoulder, he reaches up to tweak my nipple—gently at first, then finishing with a harsh twist. I gasp as I arch back against him, electricity zapping straight to my clit at the brilliant flash of pain.

"That a problem?" Shane asks, teeth scraping along my ear before he nibbles on the lobe.

I shiver in his hold, body going languid as I watch Declan strip.

"No, just takes some getting used to," Declan answers as he drops his slacks.

Shane's warm tongue laves the sensitive spot at the hollow of my neck, drawing a moan from my lips as I squirm in his hold. Declan's pupils dilate more the longer he watches me with his friend, his cock already tenting his boxer briefs. Licking my lips, I stare at the hard length, remembering the heft and flavor heavy on my tongue two nights before. I want to drop to my knees and swallow him down again, but don't dare without Shane's direction.

"Sit," Shane orders, pointing toward the couch.

Declan's lips twitch before he obeys. My belly swoops at the ease of the expression, craving more intimacy from them.

Always more. When Declan is seated, Shane releases me and steps back to regard us. Linc gestures toward his brother with a mischievous grin, amber eyes dark with want.

"Your throne, m'lady," he teases, tapping Declan's thigh.

I comply, stepping forward before turning and settling my ass on his lap. His cock nestles against my cheeks, my pussy throbbing at the hard, hot feel of him.

"Hold her knees for him, yeah?" Linc suggests.

Declan spreads his knees, pushing my legs apart as Shane watches with ravenous eyes. When he stops, Declan reaches down to grip my inner knees and open me further. I'm on display for Shane, bare and dripping, wide open and completely at their mercy. Sighing, I feel all the tension seep from my body as I lean back against Declan's bare chest, my head lolling on his shoulder.

"That's right," he croons in my ear. "I've got you."

"Look at you, baby," Shane murmurs, kneeling between our spread thighs.

Reaching out, Shane runs teasing fingertips along my calves, goosebumps rising in their wake.

"You're soaking wet, Lex," Linc groans, watching from the chair opposite. He's lightly stroking his cock, eyes half closed and briefs pushed down his bulging thighs. "God, you're so hot like that, all spread out and needy."

"Isn't she?" Shane bends and licks along my seam, his tongue barely delving between my lips before he draws back. "So fucking sweet, too."

I whimper, my whole body reacting to the weighted stares of the three men surrounding me. Heat settles in my core, a slow fire building with every look, every touch. As I let out a shuddering breath, Shane takes my hand from my thigh, drawing it toward my pussy.

"Touch yourself," he orders.

Closing my eyes and losing myself to the scene, I press a finger to my clit and gently swirl. My breath catches as pleasure explodes through me, nerve endings raw under their attention.

"Two fingers, all the way in."

My channel is slick as I work two fingers inside, dropping my shoulder as I try to reach my G-spot. Just before I find a rhythm, Shane wraps his fingers around my wrist. I want to whine as I still and he pulls my hand back, my fingers slipping away.

"Let Declan taste you, gorgeous," Linc rasps.

Oh, fuck me. My lips part as I reach up to do as he asked, twisting so I can watch Declan lean forward eagerly and suck my fingers into his mouth. His mouth is soft, wet, and blazing hot, more wetness gathering in my core as his tongue works me over. Those green eyes meet mine as he sucks noisily, a low rumble of approval vibrating his chest.

Before I can catch my breath, Shane leans forward and buries his face against me, sucking my clit into his mouth. Crying out, I arch back against Declan, my knees starting to close.

"Ah, ah," Declan admonishes, gripping me tighter and wrenching me open even further. "Don't you dare interrupt his feast."

Panting, I look over to Linc. He's watching with a hooded gaze, cock rock hard and weeping in his fist. Licking my lips, I close my eyes and shudder, overwhelmed with the desire rushing through me. Shane nips at my clit, then soothes it, winding me up with every swipe of his talented tongue.

As my orgasm builds, Declan leans down and sucks hard on the soft skin between my neck and shoulder. Gasping sharply, I writhe between them, the sensations working to build me up and make that peak more elusive at the same time.

"Needy, greedy thing," Declan breathes against me. "Look

at how you react to us, how you flush and whine. I bet you're covering Shane's face in your cum, aren't you? Dirty little whore, so ready for us to fill your holes."

"Oh god," I moan. *The mouths on these men, I swear.*

"I bet you're coating his tongue in your sweet taste, aren't you? Gushing for your men."

Shane growls in encouragement, the vibration making me twitch with pleasure. He teases two fingers along my pussy lips, stroking me, as he circles my clit with his tongue.

"If I let your knees go, will you keep yourself open for him?" Declan rasps.

"Yes, sir," I manage, voice thready.

"Good girl," Linc murmurs. "I'm watching, Lex. Don't close those legs an inch."

Declan tightens his grip on my knees before releasing them. He wraps one hand around my throat, the other dropping to pluck at my peaked nipple. I arch into the touch, straining against his hand, my pulse thundering in my ears. Shane slips two fingers into my pussy, stroking along my upper wall, finding my G-spot with ease. My orgasm swells as I tremble against Declan, teetering on the ledge.

"What's going to push you over, huh?" he asks, twisting my nipple to the side, then tugging it forward. "Will it be Shane's fingers in that tight cunt?"

Shane presses more firmly against me, circling his fingertips right where I need him.

"Will it be my hands on your perfect tits?"

He grips one breast firmly, kneading the flesh hard enough to bruise, as I moan.

"Or will Shane's mouth be to blame?"

On cue, Shane nips my clit roughly, teasing it with his tongue before sucking in sharp pulses. I cry out, my legs twitching but staying splayed.

"Or," Declan draws his nose up my neck as I shudder against him, the sensation almost too much, "does our little whore like to be choked?"

He tightens his grip, thumb stroking along my jaw as my breathing grows harsh. My head is swimming, my skin on fire. Declan plucks at my other nipple as Shane strokes and sucks, strokes and sucks. I'm vaguely aware of a low keening noise as warmth blooms in my core. *Is that me?*

"Don't hold back, Lex," Declan growls, "I want to fucking hear you."

My orgasm is a detonation. Arching my back, I scream as it explodes through me, my hands gripping onto Shane's head as my pussy clamps around his fingers. He keeps sucking, keeps stroking as I writhe, anchored by Declan's hold on my throat and chest. Wave after wave bursts through me, my skin flushing as my body quakes.

"Holy shit," Linc groans in the distance. "Fucking hell."

I slump against Declan, my fingers loosening as Shane's ministrations slow. He draws back as I twitch through the aftershocks, pressing wet kisses to my mound and inner thighs. I shiver when he kisses my clit, flicking it with his tongue before he sits back on his heels with a smug grin.

Declan's fingers loosen around my throat and I gasp a clarifying breath, my body buzzing with adrenaline. He soothes his thumb along the side of my neck as he gently massages my breast, caressing where his fingers bit.

"Color?" he rumbles, lips against my shoulder.

"Green," I breathe, a lazy smile curving across my lips.

I reach up and pat the arm wrapped under my chest, my eyelids heavy as I gaze at Shane and Linc. They exchange a glance, then both rise to their feet. Declan shifts behind me to watch them.

"You want more?" Shane draws a featherlight touch down my jaw.

My greedy pussy clenches. "Yes, please, sir."

He leans forward, gripping my chin between his finger and thumb. "You want us all?"

"Yes, sir. I do."

Shane's eyes slip to Declan. "You up for it?"

I feel him breathe deeply. "Up for what, exactly?"

"You in her cunt, me in her ass," Shane deadpans.

"And me in your perfect mouth, gorgeous," Linc pipes up. "If you want a taste of this."

He grips his bare cock, smirking as I lick my lips and hum in anticipation.

"If it's what Lex wants, I'm in," Declan rumbles.

I flush hot with anticipation. "Yes, sir."

Declan clears his throat. "We haven't talked about protection."

Blinking, I mentally shake off the lust enough to sit up and turn to him. I wince as my legs finally close, my hips mildly protesting how long I'd been in the extreme position.

"You're negative?" I peer up at him, searching his gaze.

He dips his chin. "Got tested after my last thing ended a while back. Results are in my email somewhere."

Reaching up to trace his cheekbone, I smile softly. "I trust you, Declan."

Something flashes in his eyes as he searches my gaze. "I trust you, too, Lex. You know that, right?"

Exhaling haltingly, I dip my chin. "I do now. Thank you."

He shakes his head, eyes never leaving mine. His lips part, then close as he swallows. I smile, turning around in his lap to face him as I thread my fingers into his hair.

"It's okay, Wilde. We're here now. That's what matters, yeah?"

I lean forward and kiss him, taking my time as I tease his mouth open and slip my tongue inside. He grips my hips, one hand snaking up my back to fist in my hair. A moan breaks free and he groans, crushing me against him as he fights for control. We clash, rocking back and forth, as his cock stiffens between us. Breaking apart, I nip at his lip as I release him.

Shane and Linc press up behind me to kiss either side of my neck, hands moving to stroke along my breasts and sides. Declan lifts his hips and shoves his underwear down as they draw me back. He kicks the material away and resettles on the couch, his back propped on pillows against the arm.

"Come here," he commands, legs spread and hard cock straining toward his muscular abs.

As I obey him, crawling onto the couch, I take a moment to appreciate him. The shortest of the three guys, though still over six feet, he's bulkier than Shane but leaner than Linc. His abs are cut and defined, the dark hair dusting his chest gathering into an enticing trail that leads to a delicious V. *I want to lick every groove.*

"Are you going to fuck me with your eyes or get your ass over here and sit on my cock?" he rumbles.

Smirking, I sit back on my heels, raking my eyes over him. "I haven't decided yet."

Linc chuckles behind me. Declan glances at him, then narrows his eyes on me.

"Don't make me say it again."

My stomach flutters, the hard edge to his voice striking a chord deep in my psyche. "Yes, sir."

Dropping back to my hands, I crawl up into his lap and straddle him as he steadies my hips. Staring into my eyes, he reaches down and slides two fingers along my pussy, slipping through the wetness.

"Are you ready for me?" He shoves two fingers into my channel firmly, making me gasp at the sudden intrusion. "Look at that, our little whore is still dripping. So ready to be fucked, aren't you?"

"Yes, sir," I moan, thrusting against his hand.

"You're desperate, aren't you? I bet you'd beg for it."

His fingers dig into my hip as he pushes a third finger inside, and I grab onto his shoulders as I squirm. He slows his pace, teasing, as I pant.

"Do you want to come?"

"Please, sir." I nod, trying to ride his hand.

"Look at you trying to steal your pleasure," he croons, staring down at where his fingers disappear inside me. "Do you need a cock?"

"Yes," I breathe.

He hums under his breath as he teases me, fingers plunging in only to retreat as my hips move to work them deeper.

"How about two?" he growls, pulling his hand away.

He trails his fingers to my ass, painting my wetness along my puckered hole. A bottle cap cracks, and I turn to see Shane standing behind me, stroking lube along his pierced cock. Declan cracks his free hand against my ass, bringing my attention whipping back to him.

"Eyes on me," he commands, eyes flashing.

My body relaxes against him as he breaches my tight ring, his finger slipping into me. He rumbles his approval, circling his finger inside me before gently adding another. Moaning through the slight burn, I reach out blindly for something to hold on to. Smooth, hard flesh meets my seeking hand, and I bite my lip when I wrap my fingers around Linc's cock. He groans as I grip him, stroking over the head and back down.

"Dec," Shane barks.

"Okay, okay," he grumbles, freeing his fingers. "You can suck him now."

Linc steps closer, tapping the flushed red head of his cock against my lips. I smile up at him as he reaches down to cup my face, his thumb stroking my cheek.

"I know tonight's new," he murmurs, amber eyes warm and comforting, "but I'm going to need you to wait to come until we tell you, okay? Can you do that for me?"

Anything for you. I answer him by taking him into my mouth, my lips and tongue teasing at his silken skin. He sighs, hips tilting as I grip his base in my hand before sucking him down. As I draw back, slicking my hand over his shiny head, Declan presses his cock against my pussy and strokes it through my folds.

My eyes roll back in my head as Declan stretches me, working his way in inch-by-inch as Linc fills my mouth. I can feel jostling behind me, the heat of Shane's body seeping into mine as he draws closer. Working Linc with my hand and lips, I moan against his dick as Declan pulls me down harshly, slamming home. I hollow my cheeks and bob my head as I whimper. Tears leak down my cheeks and I swallow around Linc, determined not to lose my focus on him.

"Fuck, Lex, the mouth on you," Linc grits.

He's holding himself back, hips and legs stiff with tension as he fights the urge to thrust into me. I pop off him with an audible sound, breathing deeply before looking up at him.

"Fuck my face like you want to, sir. Please."

His eyes flash, pupils dilating. Declan groans as my pussy clenches around him when Linc pushes himself back into my mouth. He sinks a hand into my hair, holding tightly as he buries his cock in my throat. My nose bumps against him, and I gag once before I force myself to swallow.

"Here goes, gorgeous."

I hold his thigh as he draws back and thrusts into my mouth, breathing sharply through my nose. Shane's fingers slip down my back and to my ass, stroking my hole firmly. Squeezing my eyes shut, I give myself over to them, all three of them. I want them to use me, fill me, and break me. Utter devastation feels like it's a stone's throw away, but I'll gladly run headlong toward ruination if it's at their hands.

"God, you look fucking fierce right now, Lex," Linc grits out, his hips snapping forward.

Moaning, I shudder as Shane adds another finger while Declan starts to move. He drags his cock out of me, almost all the way, then shoves back in forcefully. Jolting between them, my body suspended by theirs, I'm floating. My heart swells and pulse thunders, my clit throbs. Limbs tremble as my eyes close. As I am systematically torn to pieces, I've never felt more whole.

"I'm close," Linc warns.

His thrusts stutter and I focus enough to swallow as he comes, his warm seed spilling down my throat. I hum in pleasure as he groans, cock twitching in my mouth as I suck every last drop down. He twitches, hypersensitive, as I lick him clean before pulling back.

Linc drops to his knees, pulling me in for a desperate kiss. His tongue strokes along mine as he holds my head in his hands, his lips soft and warm against mine. I whimper in surprise as I feel Shane notch his cockhead against me, then slowly push his way inside. Pulling back from Linc with a gasp, I squeeze my eyes shut at the burn.

"Relax, beautiful, you've got this. You can do it, I know you can," he soothes, pressing kisses to my parted lips. "I know it stings, gorgeous. Bear down. Let him in. Let them fill you up, okay? It'll feel so good, I promise."

His voice washes over me and I submit to the effect, tension bleeding from my muscles as I bear down and take Shane deeper into my body. Linc presses his forehead to mine, eyes closed as he praises me.

When they're both fully seated, Shane's piercings little nubs of white hot pleasure within me, we let out a collective groan.

"Fuck, you're so hot," Linc murmurs. "Can't wait to see you shatter."

He draws back, eyes hungry, as he watches me rock between Shane and Declan. Linc's cock is already half mast again, bobbing as Declan pulls back. I moan as he surges forward, Shane retreating. Burying my face against Declan's chest, I melt into him.

He wraps an arm around me and braces his foot against the couch, using it as leverage to thrust his hips up. I'm so full, my body stretched deliciously as they find their rhythm. Rising pleasure skitters across my skin the longer they pound into me, my chest tight as I try to catch a full breath. It's impossible, the feeling of being torn in two and reformed with every hard movement warring with the need to breathe.

"Fuck," Declan grunts.

I moan in agreement, walls tightening around them as Shane curses, rhythm breaking.

"Ready for my cum, Lex?" he rasps, fingers bruising my hips.

"Yes, sir," I manage, sweat trickling down the side of my face as a tidal wave, powerful and deadly, gathers in my core.

Declan slows as Shane's hips jerk, the warm rush of his cum in my ass making me heady with want. He drapes himself over me briefly as he softens, pressing gentle lips to my spine before he pulls out. I can feel his presence behind us, watching the cum I can feel trickling down my skin.

"So pretty painted in my cum," Shane mutters, swiping his fingers through the mess and rubbing it into my flesh.

Squirming, I try to release the building pressure rising in me. Declan huffs, pulling us both more upright so I'm sitting up in his arms.

"I want you to ride me," he commands.

I nod, eyes slipping closed as I start to move. His palm cracks against my ass and I shiver, nipples pebbling almost painfully in response.

"Eyes on me," he growls.

As much as he's willing to share, Declan is clearly a possessive man. My pussy squeezes at the thought, relishing the idea of being his. I curl my hands around his neck, looking into his fiery green eyes as I lift myself until just his tip rests at my entrance.

Declan grabs my hips and roughly yanks me down. I cry out, fighting to keep my eyes open as he urges me up and slams me back down again. My thighs burn, muscles trembling as I try to match his pace and intensity.

He slips a hand between us, finding my clit with his thumb. My mouth falls open as I gasp, my eyes widening as pleasure blooms and coils through me. His eyes flash in satisfaction as I tighten around him, my body shuddering as the first wave of my orgasm crests. Pressing hard on my clit, he surges up and captures my mouth with his, teeth sinking into my lip. The spark of pain sends me hurtling into the abyss, my body tensing as I gasp and quiver, mouth open on a silent scream.

Declan leans back as he starts to come, his thrusts slowing as our eyes meet. Emotion clogs my throat at the vulnerability in his gaze. I cup his face in my hands, kissing him desperately as we rock together, trembling.

My eyes fall closed as we part, and I bury my face against

his neck. Declan holds me, soothing gentle hands along my back.

"Thank you," he breathes. "I didn't know...I've never felt..."

His voice trails off as his arms tighten, but he doesn't need to finish his thought. I feel it, too. *Complete. Whole.*

As I huddle in Declan's arms, emotion welling deeper than it ever has, fear lurks. *If I'm not careful, I'll never survive them.*

Chapter 38

Lex

Our last morning in Paris dawns bleak and gray, matching my mood. *Ugh, it's way too early to be this maudlin.* Pushing the dark thoughts away, I sit up and scrub my hands over my face. My phone pings with an incoming text.

ROO

don't miss your flight

CASS

😶 girl, she took the jet

ROO

so? It has a flight plan

ME

I'm up, ladies, thank you

Enjoying your Friday night?

CASS

i talked roo into going out!!

ROO

it's not a big deal

> **CASS**
>
> she's in a dress!!!!

Cass sends a photo next, of Ruby in a little black dress, her expression droll. I giggle. She looks gorgeous and exasperated, exactly what I expect for a night out without me, her typical buffer for Cass's enthusiasm.

> **CASS**
>
> she's having fun, i promise

> **ME**
>
> looks it

> **ROO**
>
> cass insists i tell you that i am, indeed, enjoying myself

> **ME**
>
> Very convincing, Roo. Well done

> **ROO**
>
> enough about me. Have you talked to them?

I slide out from under the covers and pad over to the ensuite bathroom. The space feels cavernous and empty without Linc, Shane, and Declan. They'd surrounded me in their warmth the night before the Summit, waking me up the next morning with languid touches and long kisses. It had felt like a taste of something forbidden and elusive, which could only exist in the bubble of the Paris we'd claimed for ourselves.

After Declan shattered my defenses and laid me bare the night before, he'd slipped away to wash up while Shane bundled me into the shower. Linc had wandered into the room with a wolfish smile, offering to keep me up with orgasms all night so we didn't break any rules. Shane came to my rescue, shooing him out and placing a chaste kiss on my brow. As he'd left, guilt twisted my gut. I could barely sleep, the flash of hurt in Linc's eyes before he laughed it off replaying on a loop in my head.

I regret it fiercely while sheer terror over the implications of my regret grips me.

> CASS
>
> uh oh
>
> she didn't
>
> ROO
>
> Lex.

Staring at my phone, I sigh. I splash water onto my face, trying to wash away the feeling of loss I can't shake.

> ME
>
> We go back to reality today
>
> Time's up
>
> ROO
>
> do you want it to be?

I can't answer her. *Okay, I can, but I don't want to.* Admitting it out loud, or in text, is too much.

> ME
>
> I don't know how to handle the alternative
>
> CASS
>
> oh, lexi

I send a thumbs down reaction. *That fucking nickname is going to haunt me forever.*

ROO

you're capable of a long-term relationship, lex

a healthy one, even

promise

Exhaling a slow, shuddering breath, I lock my phone and turn it face down on the counter. As much as I value Ruby's insights–and fear her preternatural powers of deduction–I'm too raw to process her message.

Seeing my father the night before took more out of me than I thought it would. Shane had praised me when we'd gotten back to the hotel, had kissed me all over as he whispered sweet nothings about my strength and power. In his hands, naked and kneeling, I'd felt it.

In front of my father as he'd done his best to reduce me to nothing, I'd felt anything but. All the therapy in the world couldn't eliminate the last remnants of the little girl who desperately sought her father's approval. When I was small, I thought Reginald Nicholas Livingston hung the moon, sun, and stars, all for me. As a grown woman, I know the only thing he's ever given me is my name.

"Alexandra Regina Livingston," I murmur, staring at myself in the mirror. "Look how far you've come."

Even though he refused me as his heir, shunned me from his business, my father had still saddled me with an ode to himself. As a young entrepreneur, I'd abhorred him and the injustice of his actions, his misogynistic preference for my younger brother. After years of forging my own path, I felt neutral about him more often than not, but I'd be a lying fool if I claimed his words and actions had no impact.

Long-term relationships lead to families, and–in my experience–families are nothing more than inescapable pain and disappointment. I don't want more of that hurt, and I can't imagine subjecting Linc, Shane, or Declan to it, either.

Discarding the dour thoughts, I flip on the shower. I have a few hours to get ready and check my email, perhaps make myself a coffee, before I bundle the guys and our luggage into a car.

As I step under the warm spray, I resolve to keep my insecurities to myself. The three men in my suite have an incredibly bright future ahead of them, and a long, busy road to get there. Today marks the first day of a new chapter for Solum, and for them. I won't let myself sully it.

"Man, Lex, you've ruined me."

I glance over at Linc in surprise, a smile crossing my lips in response to his ready grin. "Do tell."

He spreads his arms wide, settling back into the plush leather seat. "This jet is ridiculous. Flying commercial will feel like torture now."

"Hm. I might have a few ideas on how to solve that problem."

"Solum will never have a private jet," Declan interjects. "Commercial is better for the environment."

His eyes meet mine across the small table between us, his brows drawn. He's been brooding all morning, stealing glances at me without saying a word.

"Air travel in general isn't very eco-friendly," Shane points out.

As Declan opens his mouth to launch into what will, no doubt, be a spirited debate, I raise my hand. "As much as I'd love to hear your opinions on the matter, we have some business-related topics we should cover. Our opportunities to discuss them as a full group will be...limited, moving forward."

I suddenly have three pairs of eyes on me. Linc's warm amber ones are reserved, almost anxious. Reaching out, I squeeze his hand briefly in mine.

"When we get back, I'll have a formal handoff meeting with Parker to bring him up to speed. As we discussed back in February, he'll handle your account moving forward."

"We'll still see you, though," Linc insists. "At Athena, and...around."

"Of course you will." I swallow, choosing my next words carefully. "I hope you'll stop by when you come to the office to meet with Parker."

Linc blinks and looks down. Across the table, Declan's scowl is deepening by the minute. Shane is silent and stoic beside me, though I can feel his piercing blue gaze boring twin holes in the side of my skull.

"I know you all know this, but the Summit was a resounding success. It couldn't have gone better, from my perspective." I glance at each of them, smiling encouragingly. "How are you feeling?"

Linc glances at Declan, then Shane. His Adam's apple bobs before he speaks up.

"It was amazing, Lex. I mean, not only did Declan kill it on stage," he says as he leans over to bump his shoulder to his brother's, but Declan's stony gaze doesn't leave my face, "but we also made so many incredible connections. Thanks to you."

"Thank you." Shane reaches over to grip my thigh gently. "None of this would've happened without you."

Their gratitude will be the death of me. "No, guys, don't you see? I was just your...emotional support investor."

Linc laughs, the sound buoying my mood despite Declan's glower.

"Seriously," I continue. "You are responsible for your success. Athena may have provided a catalyst, but the three of you are the ones who got Solum onto that stage and made the most of the opportunity." Deciding to confront the bull head on, I turn to Declan. "Did you have anyone approach you about sales?"

He glares at me long enough for Linc to fidget. I wait him out. *Don't play this game with me, Wilde. You can't win.*

"Honestly, Lex, I don't want to talk about sales at the moment," he rasps.

My eyebrows rise. Shane rubs a hand over his forehead in the most overt expression of frustration I've seen from him.

"Tell me something. How can what happened last night not be the only thing on your mind? You trembled naked, nearly sobbing, in my arms for twenty minutes, and you want to talk about handing us off to Parker?"

I glance around the table, fighting the urge to worry my lower lip with my teeth. *I haven't done that since undergrad, for fuck's sake.* The tension around the table is palpable, Linc and Shane both eyeing Declan with a mixture of concern and wariness. Clearing my throat, I decide to deflect. *For now.*

"Declan, I'm not sure where your frustration is coming from. This conversation is just another business meeting. What we do in our personal time—"

"What we do in our personal time?" He sits back, expression incredulous. "Are you kidding me? We spend a fucking day and two nights like *that*, and it's just business as usual? You're handing us off to Parker and that's it."

"If you want to have a conversation about what's between us—"

"What *is* between us, Lex, huh?" Declan presses, eyes wild as he leans across the table.

Linc and Shane look at each other, but I keep my gaze on the visibly angry man across from me.

"This is neither the time nor place to have that discussion." My tone is cool, firm. I can barely breathe past the lump in my throat and tightness in my chest, but I lock it the fuck down.

"Why do you get to decide that? There's three of us—"

"I don't know what the fuck is going on right now, Declan, but keep me out of it," Linc protests, throwing both hands up in surrender. "You do not speak for me. I agree with Lex; this isn't the time or place."

Declan's jaw clenches as he turns wide eyes to his brother. "You're kidding."

"I'm not."

"Dec, take a beat." Shane's deep voice carries a hint of command.

"I am *not* your sub." Declan levels a finger at his friend before turning back to me. "Though maybe that's what I need to do, hm?"

He cocks his head to the side, expression harsh. Discomfort writhes in my gut, a frisson of fear for what he's planning tripping down my spine. For the first time since I started things with Linc, I'm nervous about what will happen next.

"Will you only give us the time of day when we're making you come? Do I have to threaten you with punishment to get what I want?" Declan's voice is dripping in sarcasm, his words ugly and cold.

I can't look away from him, emotion gathering hot and wet in my throat. My lips part on a tentative breath as Declan continues, Shane rigid beside me.

"How many spankings will it take to get you to change the subject and talk about 'what's between us'?" He throws up air quotes as he speaks.

"Declan—" My voice is hoarse, thready.

Linc's eyes fly to mine, his hand shooting out toward me. His face crumples when I draw away. I'm desperate for his touch, his comfort, but I know I'll fall apart if I give in to him.

"Or is it just about the business now? You had your fun for the last three months, but hey! Time's up. You have rules, right?"

"Dec, stop," Linc snaps, eyes on me.

"No. Do I need to get you naked and kneeling, *baby*?" Declan spits the pet name out like a curse, and I flinch.

"That's enough." Shane surges to his feet, tension racking his body as he leans over the table.

"Please," I gasp.

My blood is rushing in my ears so hard I don't know what I sound like, but it makes an impression. All three of them freeze, turning to me in unison. I lift my eyes from the table, taking in Linc's haunted expression as I do. Shane is a vague shape to my left, body still strung taut. Declan's brow falls, his lips tugging into a frown as his mouth opens, then closes.

"To borrow Shane's phrase, I think we all need to take a beat." My voice sounds hollow, tinny. *I don't sound like me.*

It's as though I'm watching the scene happen from the sidelines. I rise slowly, Linc and Declan scrambling to their feet as I step out of my seat and turn to address them all with a detached look.

"Thank you for this week, gentlemen, I...I don't have the words to express what it meant to me."

"Lex..." Linc looks like he wants to reach for me again.

I can't decide if I'm pleased or devastated when he restrains himself.

"I meant it when I said you and Solum have a bright future. I'm proud Athena will be part of it."

"Lex, I didn't–" Declan starts, his eyes filling with regret.

"Doesn't matter, Declan." The thinnest smile crosses my

lips. "It's clear nothing productive can come of this conversation. I'll go back to the bedroom so you all can have some privacy. We'll connect soon when we're back in the Bay, I'm sure."

I'm trembling when I turn and walk away. My body sways, my hip catching the seat behind Linc's as I shakily make my way toward the back of the plane. I can feel someone's eyes burning into me as I go, maybe all of them, but something tells me it's Shane. He'd been too silent, too still. *Oh god, what happens now?*

Shoving the thought from my mind, I slip into the small bedroom and slide the door closed, locking it gently. The soft click feels final somehow, as though I'm closing the door on something more than just a room. As I sag against the door, a soft sob works its way up my throat.

Holding my phone unsteadily, I pull up the messages app.

ME

everything's fucked

The reply is quick. *Thank god.* They must still be out.

ROO

whatever happened, it's not

CASS

we'll meet you at the airport

ME

bring wine

maybe vodka

CASS

oh shit

ROO

Lex, nothing is fucked

deep breaths, yeah?

you're safe

CASS

you are safe, yes?

Declan's angry scowl and bitter words fill my head, the memory of my fear a sour taste in the back of my throat. I'm not scared for my safety, though.

ME

i'm safe

The tears rush faster, my vision blurring as I continue to type.

ME

they're not

CASS

what?

ME

cuz of me

i'm breaking them

i don't want to

CASS

oh, honey

ROO

you haven't broken shit, lex

ME

i hope you're right

I'll give anything for her to be right.

Chapter 39

Linc

"We got an email from Parker. He wants to meet Wednesday. That work for you two?" I look across the dining table, my phone in hand and a bowl of cereal in front of me.

Shane grunts, intent on his avocado toast.

"If we must," Declan mutters.

He's been morose since we got back from Paris, but he's done literally nothing about it. *Not a goddamn thing.*

"You know what, Dec?" I snarl, leaning back in my chair. "Fuck you and your shit attitude."

He turns to me, eyes wide. "Whoa, Linc. What the fuck?"

"She told us from the beginning he'd be taking over," Shane cuts in, his tone calm and even. "Everything's going to plan."

"Everything." My brother rolls his eyes. "Really? Everything's going to plan."

Shane looks up at him with just his eyes, brows raised. "Yes. Want to say it one more time?"

"Fuck off, Shane."

"Pretty sure you're the one who needs to do that, Declan."

Dec shoves his chair back. "Okay, we're doing this. What the fuck, guys? We need to clear the damn air."

"We do." I stand, taking my bowl to the sink and tossing it in. "Downstairs."

Dec's brows draw together. "Why?"

"Because if I don't have something to hit while we have this conversation, I'm going to hit you."

Shane snorts and gets to his feet, dumping his plate in the sink before trailing after me.

I pause at the top of the stairs, looking back at Dec's bewildered expression. "You coming?"

Without waiting for an answer, I jog down the stairs. Shane is hot on my heels, the aggravated energy running through him since our disastrous flight back from Paris a tangible thing between us.

"You good?" I ask under my breath as we reach the landing.

"No." His sharp blue eyes meet mine. "I will be, though." He gestures to the punching bags. "Which one you want?"

"Speed bag."

Jerking his chin in agreement, he turns to the freestanding heavy bag and rolls up the sleeves of his black button down. As Dec appears on the landing, Shane throws a vicious punch. It lands with a satisfying thunk. Dec pauses, his eyebrows inching toward his hairline, then continues.

"That for me, Shane?" Dec's voice is gruff.

"Yep."

We both freeze at his response. Shane is our peacekeeper. Even if we don't talk about it, we all know it. He understands the two of us better than we understand ourselves, and he navigates conflicts between us with ease. Part of his technique, though, is keeping his own emotion out of it. He plays a mean Switzerland, but it seems he's breaking with tradition. *Aren't we all?*

"Out with it then." Dec sounds resigned.

"Why don't you unload what's in your head." Shane lands another punch as I step up to the speed bag.

"Of course," Dec mutters, rolling his eyes. "Since I'm the only one who apparently doesn't feel the need to be violent, I'll just take a seat."

He gestures toward the weight bench, seemingly looking for some form of acknowledgement. When he gets none, he huffs and slumps onto the bench. Like Shane, he's already dressed for work, his business casual attire clashing with the gym equipment.

"Okay, I'll start," Dec announces. "I'm pissed."

"No shit," I grunt, my shoulder muscles bunching under my white tee.

"I don't get how she can just turn it off. That day in Paris was...fuck, it was magic. And on the plane back she's all business? What the fuck?"

"Explain something to me."

I stop hitting the bag, the harsh tone of Shane's voice grabbing all of my attention.

"Explain, Dec, how you're so fucking smart and so goddamn dense at the same time."

"Hey!" Dec protests.

"No, listen. How many business meetings did we have with Lex over the last three months?"

"I–I'm not sure..."

"I don't need an exact count, Dec. But it was a lot, yes?" Shane's whole body is a hard line as he turns to Dec, arms crossed.

"Yes?" Dec looks askance at me, confused.

"Right. A lot. And how many of those meetings happened while Linc or I were fucking Lex?"

I flinch. He's making a point, but it still feels wrong to call what we have with Lex nothing more than 'fucking'.

"Uh, most of them?"

"Right. And how many of those meetings revolved around our goddamn personal relationship?!" Shane's volume steadily increases to a dull roar.

Dec sits roughly against the wall behind the bench, his eyes wide. "None of them."

"Fucking. None. Of. Them," Shane bites the words out. "What gave you the right to assume your relationship with her was so goddamn special she needed to change the dynamic we've had for the past three months?"

"I...I didn't think of it that way, Shane, I–"

"You didn't *think*," Shane snarls. "Period, Dec! You didn't fucking think! You think Linc and I weren't in our heads on that flight, wondering how the next few hours were going to go? You think we hadn't talked about how we wanted to approach her about something more than just the three months she negotiated at the beginning?"

"You did?" Dec looks at me.

I spread my hands, palms up. "Of course we did. In case you missed it, we're in love with her. Not like we're just gonna shrug and say bye because an arbitrary clock ran out."

"You didn't talk to me."

"You haven't exactly been forthcoming about where you stand," Shane deadpans. "And you've treated her like shit for three months. Explain to me how that puts our relationships on the same level?"

Hurt flashes in Dec's eyes, but Shane punches the bag again before he can say anything.

"It's not about you, asshole! Of course we want you involved. We fucking invited you in. We've opened the goddamn door for you and put out a red carpet, but you've never told us if you're in! And you've certainly never fucking talked to her about it!"

Dec's mouth opens and closes soundlessly. If I wasn't so stressed out by all the yelling, I would laugh. The glimpse of humor dries up, however, when Dec's gaze falls.

"You're right," he says, his voice small. "Fuck, Shane, you're right."

He scrubs his hands over his face, then leans forward to prop his elbows on his knees. "I was scared on that plane. Scared of losing what I got a glimpse of with Lex, with both of you. And worried as fuck about you two getting hurt."

"Not your call," I say.

They both turn to me, Dec with a frown and Shane a picture of exasperated rage.

"It's not your call, Dec. Worry about you, okay?" I glance between them, heart pinching. "I can't watch more of this, so I'm gonna go."

I can hear Dec get to his feet as I start up the stairs, but Shane must stop him because I don't hear any footsteps behind me. As I reach the kitchen, I pull my phone from my pocket.

ME

still up for that run?

LEX

Yes, please

ME

usual route?

I tap my foot as I wait, hoping she says yes. She canceled on me a couple of times over the last week, and she asked me to meet her in different locations more than once. I suspect she's keeping her distance, but after what happened on the flight, I don't blame her.

LEX

Yeah. It's already been a day.

ME

we could stay in instead

i have some ideas for how to relax you

LEX

Cute. I'll see you at 6:15?

ME

so is that a no on the sensual massage, or...?

LEX

See you soon, Linc.

She hearts my massage text. I take it as a good sign. Before Dec shot all our plans to hell in a blaze of fiery glory, I wanted to tell Lex how I felt on our first run back from Paris. My brother dropped a bomb on us all, though, and the opportunity hasn't presented itself. Yet. *Good things come to those who wait, right?*

Chapter 40

Shane

"Hey Miles."

Lex's assistant looks up with a wide grin above his purple bowtie. "Mr. Kelly! How was Paris? I'll be honest, I was expecting the boss to be a bit more...relaxed when she got back. Everything go as planned?"

"For the hundredth time, it's Shane. And Paris was perfect." I pause, jaw ticking. "The flight home could've been smoother."

His eyes narrow. "Turbulence?"

"Of a sort."

"I see." He regards me. "Is she going to be happy to see you?"

"I hope so."

"Is she expecting you?"

I cock my head. "We had a meeting with Parker."

"Uh huh." He nods, then sighs. "Fine. You can go in. But if you–"

"Hey, Miles?" I interrupt as his voice takes on a hard edge.

He raises an imperious eyebrow, crossing his arms over his chest.

"I fucking love the woman in that office. Save the threats for someone who needs them, yeah?"

He grins. "You got it, Mr. Kelly."

"It's Shane."

"Whatever you say, honey."

As I turn to Lex's office, I catch sight of her business partner, Van. He juts his chin toward Miles, then shakes his head with a knowing expression. I return it, my lips curving into a smile. *Yeah, we could be friends.*

I tap lightly on the door, then let myself in. Lex looks up from her computer and smiles, her shoulders dropping.

"Shane Kelly, you are a sight for sore eyes."

"So's the sun."

"Hm?" she tilts her head, a soft smile on her lips.

"Have you been outside today?"

She glances at the window, then scrunches her nose. "Not exactly."

"Come on. I'm taking you for a walk."

Chuckling, she toes her shoes back on and gets to her feet. She snags her bag from the hook by the door, leaning into my space as she does. I slip my arms around her, and she melts into me. I want to sigh in relief. Giving her space for the last week has been torture.

"You've been avoiding us," I murmur, staring into her seafoam eyes.

She threads her arms around my waist, resting her head on my chest. "Seemed like a good idea after the flight home."

"Lex, look at me."

She obeys, straightening to peer up at me. Her voice sounded so small, nothing like the warrior I know her to be. I want to chase away the thoughts making her feel like that, want to lift her up and help her see herself the way I do. *My fierce, savage queen.* I cup her jaw in my hand, soothing a thumb along her cheekbone and wanting to lock the door when her pupils dilate.

"I know we have some shit to work through. That flight was...well, it was terrible. For all of us, but especially for you." I stroke her cheek again, my other arm tightening around her. "But if we're going to work through the shit, we need to be together, yeah?"

"Yeah," she whispers, nodding. "You're right."

I press a grateful kiss to her forehead, taking her hand in mine. "Parker's our guy now, so I'm going to hold this on the way out."

Her breath stutters as she stares down at our joined hands. "Okay. Speaking of Parker, how'd it go?"

I open her door and draw her after me, ignoring Miles's smirk as he looks up from his desk. It takes more than I want to admit not to celebrate her easy acceptance of my affection. *Look your fill, folks. This one's all mine.*

"Seems like he knows his shit. He honestly might know more about the technical side of things than Dec does."

Lex chuckles. "Sounds like Parker; he's talented. More importantly, though, he's a stellar human."

"You seem to surround yourself with those," I observe, glancing her way as we enter the elevator.

"Stellar humans?"

I nod.

The corner of her mouth lifts. "Yeah. I'm pretty lucky."

"It's not luck, Lex. It's you."

"Oh, I don't know about that..." Her voice trails off as she follows me into the foyer.

"You get back the energy you put into the world." I hold the front door open for her, then fall into step with her on the side-walk. "Your energy is powerful."

She moves closer, slipping her hand from mine to wrap it

around my waist. I tuck her against me, leaning over to press a kiss into her hair.

"Thank you for getting me outside," she sighs, tilting her head up toward the sun.

"I'm here for you. Always will be."

She peers my way. "Always, huh?"

I incline my head. "Always."

"Feels like a string," she murmurs.

"Yeah, about that..." I steer her toward a bench by a small park.

She follows my direction easily, sitting and turning to me. Her hand grips mine where it rests on my thigh.

"I'm done with your rules, Lex."

Her eyes flash up, widening in surprise. I cock an eyebrow at her meaningfully.

"Pretty sure we did away with them a long time ago."

She clutches my hand, looking down as her fingers tremble.

"I don't do long-term, Shane."

"Why?"

She huffs. "Not my thing. Marriage and kids have never been part of my dreams."

"Who said anything about marriage and kids?"

Blinking, her gaze meets mine. "Isn't that what most long-term relationships lead to?"

I shrug. "Don't know, don't care. It's not what I want, either."

"It's not?"

I shake my head. "Not big on the institution of marriage, if I'm honest. And kids?" Looking off into the distance, I try to picture myself as a father. "Not part of my dreams, either."

"Why? You'd be a great dad, Shane."

I shoot her a wry look. "And you'd be a great mom. Doesn't make either of us want them, does it?"

She chuckles. "I suppose not." Her gaze searches mine. "What do you want, then?"

I look out at the park, lush with spring green in the bright afternoon sun. We're surrounded by new life, but all I can see is the woman beside me.

"Love and commitment. I want us to support each other and be loyal to our relationship, whatever it looks like."

"Whatever it looks like, hm?" It's her turn to look into the distance. "Like if there were four people involved, not just two?"

My heart swells at the number, relief rushing through me. I feared Declan fucked everything up on the flight home, worried she'd be unwilling to try again after the awful things he said. *I should've known she wouldn't back down. My warrior queen.*

"Yeah, Lex. Like that."

"You trying to tell me something, Shane?" She peers up at me through her lashes, her expression guarded.

"I've been trying to tell you I love you for weeks, Lex. I'm not great with the words, but I'll never stop showing you."

Her lips part on a faint gasp. "Shane..."

I wrap my arm around her shoulders, needing to anchor her. "Don't tell me you're surprised."

"I...shouldn't I be?"

"No." I press another kiss to her head, letting my lips linger. "I need to do a better job of showing you, apparently."

"Shane, no, you're perfect, I–"

Smiling, I cup her cheek, drawing her to me for a slow kiss. I wipe the sheen from her lips when I release her.

"I'm not perfect, Lex, and I don't expect you or our relationship to be."

She bites her lip, looking away. Anxiety flares in my gut, my arm tightening around her shoulders.

"Talk to me."

"It's just," she bursts, looking out at the park, "we have such a good thing going the way it is. I don't know...I don't know if something formal is a good idea."

She's scared and I suspect I know why, but I need to hear her say it.

"Why?"

She rubs a hand over her face. "Someone's going to get hurt, Shane. If we're in a relationship, then we're a family, and...families..."

Her voice trails off and my heart clenches for her, for the pain she experienced at her family's hands.

"Families hurt each other, disappoint one another. I can't imagine doing that to you or Linc or even Declan."

"Lex, each family is different. Do you see me hurting and disappointing Linc and Dec, or them doing that to me?"

Her eyes drop to her hands. "Not before. But on the plane..."

Fucking Declan and his temper. "Every family has conflict, Lex. The healthy ones communicate and work through it."

"Have you three talked and worked through it?"

My lips tip up. "We're working on it." She starts to roll her eyes, but I squeeze her against me again. "I'm serious, Lex. We are."

I can tell she's not convinced. She's been self-reliant for so long, carrying the burden her asshole father heaped on her shoulders. Though I know she has friends, I also know she's never let anyone help carry her burdens. Lex spent nearly four decades keeping people at arm's length, and now she had three demanding assholes forcing themselves into her life. *Anyone would be overwhelmed.*

"I know you're not a patient person," I say, "and I'm not, either. But if you can be patient with me, with us...I think we have something worth fighting for."

She looks up and I let her see the earnestness in my gaze.

"You're not worried about what happens when it all falls apart?"

"First of all, it's 'if it falls apart', not when," I tease, then sober. "I'd be a fool not to consider the negative possibilities, baby. We'd also both be fools not to consider the positive ones and, from where I stand, they far outweigh everything else."

Sighing, she leans her head on my shoulder. "I don't have an answer for you today, Shane."

"I don't need an answer. I just need you to know I'm all in, and I'm not going anywhere."

She tangles her fingers with mine. "I don't deserve you, Shane Kelly."

"You're wrong. You deserve far better than me, but I'm just selfish enough to keep you for myself. And my two best friends, of course."

She giggles and sniffles, burying her face against me. We sit on the bench for another thirty minutes, laughing and snuggling. By the time I escort her back to her office, it's the best hour of my entire week.

Chapter 41

Lex

"Yo, Lexi!"

I pause on my way up the stairs, leaning down to peek through the railing. My nephew stands at the threshold of my sliding door in board shorts and a tank top that shows more skin than it covers. He grins and waves enthusiastically, lifting a pizza box in one hand.

"Hey, Jax." I trot back down the steps, walking over to give him a hug. "You alright?"

"Can't complain." He raises the box again. "Figured I could use some help devouring this bad boy. Haven't seen your guys around lately, so I also figured you had your usual tonight."

Glaring at him, I walk toward the kitchen. "They're not mine."

"I'll ask you again...do they know that?"

Handing him a beer from the fridge, I gesture toward the island. As I reach up for a wine glass to go with the bottle of white, he glances at the beer.

"This is my beer."

"The kind you seem to prefer, yes."

He perches on a stool, placing the pizza box on the island. "You bought my favorite beer."

"I did."

I hold out a plate, but he rolls his eyes. Chuckling, I pop them both back into the cabinet before settling onto the stool next to him and dragging over the paper towel holder.

"Awful nice of you, Lexi," he says around a mouthful of pizza.

"It's just beer, Jax. You've lived here long enough I should stock more than your favorite drink."

"Nah," he shakes his head. "You're the busiest person I know. Yet you still made time to get something just for me. Last person to go out of their way for me like that was my mom."

"We're family," I answer automatically, but the moment the words pass my lips I pause.

Jax notices. He always notices. He's only been living with me for six months or so, but I suspect he could rival Ruby with his insightfulness.

"Why does talking about family make you go all frozen and stone-like?" He asks innocently, his blue eyes wide and inviting.

"Well, Jax, I do believe you've met my brother."

"Once or twice," he quips.

There's some truth to the statement, and it makes me angry at Nate all over again.

"Have you ever met Reginald?"

"Can't say I've had the misfortune."

I laugh. "Good. Probably best to keep it that way."

Jax looks down, and I curse internally.

"I'm sorry, Jax, I shouldn't be so flippant. The way he ignores your existence is abhorrent and not something to joke about."

He grins lazily. "Aw, Lexi, you're sweet. I'm okay, promise. After what little I've heard from you and Mom, pretty sure I'm better off never meeting dear ol' Grandpa. Did you see him in Paris?"

I grimace. "Unfortunately."

He sighs. "I'll never understand these people, will I?"

Huffing, I look up at the kitchen cabinets, my gaze unfocused. "I grew up with them for seventeen years and I still don't understand them, Jax, so...no. Though I'm certain that's not a bad thing. All they've given me is emotional trauma and thousands of dollars in therapy bills."

He chuckles before his gaze goes pensive. "So you left home right around..."

Setting my pizza down, I grab a paper towel and wipe my hands, then squeeze his shoulder.

"Just before Nate found out about you. If I'd been there when it all happened..." I trail off, sighing. "Well, there's no sense in postulating what might have been, but I'm sorry I wasn't there to try and make it better."

"Thanks, Lexi." He leans into my side briefly, then goes back to his pizza. "Though, if what I've heard is true, I guess I should be glad Grandpa paid Mom off."

I gasp, then cough, nearly choking on my pizza. "He did what?" I croak.

Jax reaches over and thumps my back. "Damn it, sorry. Thought you knew. Mom didn't make it a secret."

"I've never met your mother, Jax."

"That's a shame, too. She's a peach."

He smiles as I compose myself, taking a long pull of wine to wash everything down.

"Anyway, when she went to Dad to share the big news, she ran into Grandpa first. He scared her pretty good, made some threats, then offered her a million bucks to move to the west coast and never contact the family again."

I stare, my lips parted, then blow out a harsh breath. *That asshole.* "Fuck, Jax. I'm sorry. I had no idea."

"What was Dad's story?"

"He said your mom wanted to move to LA and he couldn't do anything about it, that Reginald kept him from seeing you until he moved out here."

"Grandpa's a wily one, eh? Spinning stories to get what he wants."

I huff, downing more wine. "That's an understatement."

Jax eyes me as he takes a drink. "Why are you in your head about family tonight, Lexi?"

He may be nearly two decades younger than me, but Jax is wise beyond his years. His casual surfer dude persona puts those around him at ease, and he seems to genuinely care about people.

"You've probably gathered or guessed the gist of it." I give him a gentle smirk.

He nods. "Your guys want to stick around for good, I take it."

Swallowing to give myself a moment, I look down at the paper towel in my hands. I pick off a corner, worrying the stiff material until it goes soft.

"Shane told me he loved me today."

Jax grins. "He's a straight shooter, that one. I like him."

"I do, too." The pile of power towel pieces grows before me.

"You don't feel the same?"

"I...fuck." Dragging a hand down my face, I lean my head back and stared at the ceiling. "I don't know."

"Don't lie to me, yeah?" Jax's voice is gentle but firm.

"You and Ruby should be friends," I huff, looking away from his earnest gaze. "You're the only people on the planet who can read me like a book."

The ghost of a smile crosses his mouth. "We aren't talking about me, Lexi."

"Fine. I...I've never been in love before. The way I feel about Shane, though...I can't describe it."

"What do you feel when you're with him?"

I pick at the paper towel, heat in the corners of my eyes. "Seen. Cherished." A ragged breath shudders through me. "Safe. He makes me feel both untouchable and powerful, like he can give me this shot of confidence while also clearing away anything trying to hurt me. Even when it's me doing the hurting."

Glancing up at Jax, I blink in surprise to find his eyes swimming with tears.

"Sounds like love," he rasps with a laugh.

"It does, doesn't it?" I murmur, sniffling. "Which is confusing, Jax, because it's nothing like how I feel with Linc or Declan."

Jax snags a tissue from the box on the island. "Do them next. Start with Linc; he's wicked on a surfboard."

"That doesn't surprise me." Taking a moment to consider the question, I smile. "Linc's...god, he's fun personified. I've never laughed so much with another human, ever. And while Shane keeps me safe, Linc makes me feel like I can do anything, like no dream is out of reach. He's playful and thoughtful and kind."

I laugh wetly, surprised by the tears on my cheeks. "We have entire conversations with little looks and glances when we run."

My breath catches and my eyes squeeze shut, my voice dropping to a whisper. "He's the first person I've let myself be truly vulnerable with. I...I don't know if I ever fully trusted another person before him."

"Fuck, Lexi, why are you here in this kitchen with me?" Jax gasps. "You should be with the guys you love."

"Is that love?" I ask him, voice shaky.

Dabbing his eyes, he turns to me and grips my hand. "You know what I've learned about love?"

"Tell me."

He smiles. "Love is a choice, Lex. One you make every day. There's lust and passion wrapped up in it, but ultimately it's you deciding you're willing to give yourself to someone, to put them first, regardless of what you get in return."

He looks down, breathing deep. "People call it falling in love, right? I think it's more like taking a swan dive without knowing what's beneath you. It's crazy and could definitely go sideways in a heartbeat, but you climb that cliff and dive into the abyss every day anyway."

"It's a choice," I whisper.

"Yeah, Lexi. It doesn't just happen. Love is something you weigh, consider, and decide."

"I'm pretty good at decision-making." My lips lift through my tears.

He chuckles. "I know you are."

"I can just choose to love them. All three of them, if I want."

"You can." His hand tightens around mine. "You didn't tell me how Declan makes you feel."

"Fucking murderous."

Jax laughs so hard, he snorts. I laugh with him, leaning against the counter as I double over.

"He..." I sigh, dipping my chin. Despite the emotions warring inside me since the flight home, a smile still pulls at my mouth. "He challenges me, Jax, and that's not something I've gotten outside of work."

"Yeah," he scoffs. "You're intimidating as fuck."

I blink. "I am not."

"Uh, yes. You are. I'm the one who had to ask you for a job the first time we met."

"And look how that turned out for you, hm?" I smile.

"Anyway, go on," he prompts. "More about Declan. He challenges you."

"And infuriates me." I hold up a finger. "But he's also disarming. In Paris, there was this whole new side to him. He was...vulnerable. There was this promise of something deep and overwhelming just under the surface. Something consuming."

I sigh, gripping my neck. "He reminds me of me. When I was constantly railing against the world because I was scared it would realize I didn't belong in the places I forced my way into. It's probably why we can be so volatile."

"You like the volatility, though?"

"I think I love it, Jax," I murmur.

He grins, eyes shiny. "So what's stopping you from letting them love you?"

My mouth opens, then closes. I look at the pile of paper towel shreds on the counter.

"When I think about family, I...I get scared. I've seen what a family can be at its worst."

"Yeah, Lexi, but what about when it's at its best?" Jax grips my hand again. "What if you create a new family with the people you love, and leave the old one behind?"

Tears fill my eyes. "Is that...can I do that? Is that real life?"

"It can be." A tear spills over, slipping down his cheek. "You don't have to keep the people who want to love you at arm's length, Lexi. Let us be your family. Let us love you."

"Is it weird that sounds as terrifying as it does wonderful?" I whisper.

"Pretty sure that's why it's worth it."

Chapter 42

Declan

"Are you ready to get your head out of your ass?" Shane barks.

I swing away from my latest basement project—tiling the shower in the guest ensuite—and frown. "The fuck is your problem?"

"You." He stalks over, his black jeans and henley matching the dark expression on his face.

"The fuck did I do now?"

"It's what you haven't done, dipshit."

I rear back, eyes wide. "Shane, brother, I'm going to need a fucking shred of context," I bite out, wiping my hands on my ratty tee.

"Lex Livingston. That enough context for you?"

My gaze narrows. "I haven't spoken to Lex since we got back."

"I'm fucking aware."

"Then what's the problem?"

"The problem, Dec," he growls, "is that you're going to ruin everything."

"How?!"

"By completely fucking it up with Lex!"

"She doesn't want me!"

"How would you know if you haven't. Fucking. Talked to her?" he growls, hands up to emphasize each word.

"Ugh!" I throw my hands up in frustration, turning away. "I'm tired of this, Shane!"

"Wow, we actually have something in common."

"God, I hate being on your bad side," I grouse, glaring.

"Pretty sure I hate it more."

Lincoln thunders down the stairs in his running gear. "And I hate it the most. What are you two yelling about now?"

He glances between us then sighs, hands interlaced on top of his head as he stares at the ceiling. "Not sure how much more of this I can take, guys. This shit is toxic."

"No kidding," I mutter.

Glowering, I cross my arms and lean against the wall. Shane closes his eyes, taking a deep breath through his nose before exhaling it sharply.

"Okay." His blue eyes shoot straight to mine when they open. "Let's start with why you're icing Lex out, yeah?"

I shift uncomfortably, glancing between them. "It's a recipe for disaster, isn't it? She set her rules."

"You don't want to get hurt." Shane's tone is blunt, matter-of-fact.

"I don't want *you* getting hurt," I challenge, gesturing to them both. "It's what I've been most concerned with from the beginning, when Linc first announced their little arrangement."

"Hey, Dec," Linc pipes up. Sitting on the floor, he has his back to the wall and his arms draped over his knees. "One problem with that."

"What's that?"

"It's not your call, man. You don't get to decide what risks I take with my heart."

"Doesn't mean I don't want to protect you," I grumble.

"Sure," he nods affably. "I get that. I hate seeing you hurt, too. But you haven't even asked us what we think, you know?"

My lips purse. "What do you mean?"

"If we think she's worth it."

I study his expression. He's calm, collected, almost relaxed. My eyes flick to Shane, finding his shoulders dropping minutely and his eyes intent on Linc's. They both seem surprisingly comfortable with the topic at hand.

"Do you?" I ask. "Think she's worth it."

"Without a doubt. One hundred percent. That woman could turn around tomorrow and tell me she never wants to see me again, shattering my heart into a million tiny pieces, and I'd still do it all over again. In a heartbeat."

Shane nods. "It's the same for me. She's it."

"You..." I swallow. "You mean that."

"Fuck yes, I do," Linc vows. "I *love* her, Dec. I'm not holding onto the fear anymore. I've let it go. Did I worry when I first realized how wound up I was in her? God, yes. I was scared shitless."

Shane chuckles, glancing down. "Me, too, man."

"I know!" Linc cries, throwing a hand toward Shane. "I know. You fucking said it: love isn't always enough. And it's not, not always. I get that. Love looks different for everyone; it's a personal fucking journey."

My little brother gets to his feet as I wonder when the fuck he got so wise.

"When we were in Paris, it fell into place for me. That day..." He trails off, looking into the distance before a smile curves his lips. "Lex called it magic, and it was, but it wasn't Paris. It was us. The four of us, how we laughed and talked. How we loved."

His amber eyes slowly meet mine. "How we made love,

because that's what it fucking was. The magic wasn't because we were in France or on vacation. It was just us. Who we are, together."

Shane steps closer as Linc talks. He claps a hand to his shoulder and touches their foreheads together for a moment, eyes falling closed. Linc grips his arm in return, and they just stand there. Their eyes lock as Shane straightens and moves back, unspoken words heavy between them. *They're closer than ever.*

The realization strikes me dumb. *And I worried she'd tear us apart. I'm a goddamn fool.*

"You both deserve magic." My voice cracks. "So does Lex."

My best friend turns to me. "You're part of the magic, Declan. It doesn't work without all four of us. But you have to be all in, and you have to get over what's holding you back."

Looking down, I consider his words. I've been reacting for weeks, too afraid of what it could mean to truly examine what I feel and why.

"You deserve her," I rasp. "The both of you, you deserve everything."

"So do you, Dec," Linc insists.

"I don't know if that's true, little brother."

Shane glares. "Why don't you deserve her?"

My jaw ticks.

"Come on, Dec," he goads. "Spit it out. What's holding you back, huh?"

I scrub a hand over my jaw, chest tight. "I don't know."

"Try again. What are you worried about?"

"I don't know!"

"You do!"

I yell, throwing my hands in the air. "She could have anyone!"

"Yeah, so what?" Shane challenges.

"Anyone, Shane! Fuck, what can I offer a woman like her?" I grip my hair, tugging sharply. "She's a goddamn billionaire. The strongest person I've ever met. I mean, fuck, look at her!"

Linc and Shane are watching me, but I don't glance toward them.

"She's the most beautiful thing on the fucking planet. What the hell gives me the right to think I have a hope in hell with her?"

"What about us?" Linc's voice is quiet, gentle.

I whip toward him. "Linc, you are everything good in this world. I see the way she lights up around you, how you make her smile. She has a laugh she only does around you, have you noticed that?"

Searching his gaze, I smile. "Her eyes get soft and she bites her lower lip. It starts out as a little chuckle, but then she throws her head back and she's completely lost to it, and it takes my breath away. And that's all for you."

Linc's lips part as he blinks. Shane knocks a shoulder into his.

"It's true," Shane mutters.

Linc scoffs, swiping at his eyes.

"And you," I look at Shane. "I think she trusts you more than she trusts herself. You're her safe place. Every time she's on uneven footing, she gravitates toward you. You walk in the room and she breathes easier."

"I know." Shane dips his chin.

"She's got everything she needs."

"She doesn't have you," Linc presses. "Not yet."

"She doesn't need me."

Silence settles between us, heavy and uncomfortable.

"That scares you, doesn't it?" Shane's deep voice scores straight through me.

I raise my gaze. "What good am I to the woman who has everything?"

Linc clears his throat. "She might not need you, Dec, but what if she wants you?"

Shaking my head, I grip my neck. I can't answer Linc's question out loud. *Why would she?*

Chapter 43

Lex

"You running off to an early meeting, or can we take our time to cool down today?"

I glance over at Linc and smile. "I've got some time."

"Thank fuck," he breathes, slinging an arm over my shoulders.

We're both sweaty and breathing hard, having just ended our run. It's been a week since Shane told me he loved me, and a little over two since Paris. Linc steers us onto the sidewalk to loop around the block again.

Linc's in a white tee and black athletic shorts, his typical running attire. I'd opted for a black sports bra and matching leggings, which he'd run his hands all over under the guise of helping me stretch.

"How are things going with Parker?"

Linc chuckles. "Ask what you really want to ask, gorgeous."

I sigh. *Am I that easy to read now? And why don't I hate it?* "How's Declan?"

"Oh, he's still a stubborn asshole, but we're working on him."

"It's been...strange. Not seeing him."

Linc kisses my hair. "I know. He's got some shit to work through, though. Can you be patient with him?"

"Not much else I can do, is there?"

It feels like I need to let Declan come to me. I'd mentioned it to Shane a few days prior, and he'd agreed, saying his friend needed to reach some of his own conclusions before he'd be ready for the conversation we needed to have. I suspected Shane was helping those conclusions form, if the glint in his eyes had been any indication.

"Hey." Linc draws us to a stop, taking my hands in his. "I know this is hard, Lex. It's certainly not how I envisioned things going after Paris."

"That's an understatement," I mumble.

He reaches out and taps underneath my chin with a knuckle. I look up into his amber gaze, threading my arms around him and pressing my body to his. With a gentle smile, he reaches up to cup my face in his big, warm hands.

"Shane and I? We're not going anywhere. And Dec will come around, beautiful. I know he will."

"I trust you, Linc." I do. There was a time when the realization had thrown me for a loop, given how few people I've let into my life, but my desire to trust Linc, Shane, and Declan feels natural. Right.

"I'm so grateful for that, gorgeous. I trust you, too." He presses a kiss to my forehead.

Leaning back, he smiles down at me, his thumbs brushing along my cheekbones.

"You should also know I love you, Lex," he whispers, tone almost reverent.

My lips part as I stare up at him, pulse thundering in my ears.

"Shane and I, we've been loving you quietly for months. It's way past time for me to love you out loud, don't you think?"

His expression is so open and earnest, no trace of hesitation or fear in his gaze. My heart swells in my chest as I rise to my tiptoes, gently pressing my lips to his.

I intend for it to be a sweet kiss, gentle, but the moment Linc groans and drops an arm around my waist, it's anything but. He teases my lips with his tongue, diving between them without hesitation when I open for him. A quiet whimper escapes as I wind my arms around his neck, clinging to him. Emotion claws its way up my throat as we devour each other, tears welling.

I gasp when we part, and stare up at Linc with glassy eyes. "Linc, I…"

"I know," he whispers, kissing the tears as they spill down my cheeks. "It's okay. You don't have to say anything."

My gut twists, the thought of him not knowing how much he means to me repulsive. I reach up and cup his cheek in one hand, smiling through my tears.

"I think it's time I love you out loud, too."

The sweetest smile breaks over his face, his perfect dimple appearing to taunt me. I swipe my thumb over it, biting my lip.

"Yeah?" he whispers, voice cracking.

I nod. "Yeah. Someone told me recently love is a choice. And loving you is one of the easiest choices I've ever made."

Linc surges forward, capturing my mouth in a searing kiss. Then he's squatting down, wrapping his arms around me, and lifting me into the air. I squeal, giggling as he spins me around, just as he did in Paris. He throws his head back and shouts up into the sky as I laugh.

"I love you, Lex Livingston!"

———

The intercom on my phone beeps right before Miles's voice comes through.

"Uh, Lex? You have a, um...visitor."

I blink, looking toward the door. Miles isn't a person I'd describe as hesitant or timid, but his tone suggests both. Rising to my feet, I slip on my heels and walk to the door. Before I can open it, a sharp knock sounds.

"Sir, please be patient!" Miles barks.

My gaze narrowing, I pull the door open. As I meet the stony gaze of the tall man on the other side, my eyes widen.

"Nate."

"Lex." He nods. "Can I come in?"

Miles shoots me a nervous look over my brother's shoulder, hand raised in an ok sign. I give him a smile, then turn to my unexpected visitor.

"By all means. What brings you to enemy territory on a random Thursday morning?"

Nate makes his way to my couch, unbuttoning his navy suit coat as he sits. He leans forward, resting his elbows on his knees as he glances up at me.

"I wanted to thank you."

My eyebrows rise as I shuck off my heels and fold myself into the armchair opposite him. Nate watches the move, his lips curling.

"Still hate shoes, I see."

Chuckling, I tuck my feet underneath myself. "Some habits can't be left in childhood."

"Can't say I've seen you this relaxed around me since then, either."

He isn't wrong. Seeing him stand up to our father, as calm and professional as it had been, had gone a long way toward helping me see him in a new light. I eye his body language, comfortable in my space.

"I could say the same for you, brother."

He grunts, smile spreading. "What a pair we are, hm? The Livingston siblings, together again."

Tilting my head, I hum. "Are we, Nate? Together?"

His expression sobers. "I'd like to be, Lex. If you'll have me."

"Is this a business proposition or a family one?" I ask softly.

He stares off into the distance, then turns to me. "It started as a business one, but I'd rather it be both."

I smile gently. "Why are you here, Nate?"

Sighing, Nate slumps back on the couch. "Two reasons. I'd like your advice on how Greenstar should handle next steps with the State, and..." He takes a deep breath, expression turning sheepish. "And I'd like to get to know my sister again."

"Ah."

He studies me, his steely eyes gentle. "I've had a lot of time to think since Paris."

"Come to any realizations?"

"I did. Namely, that I've followed our father blindly for long enough. His refusal to see reason despite the evidence your client shared..." He exhales sharply. "It has me wondering where else his decision-making has been flawed."

"I see."

Nate clears his throat. "I've been an ass to you for years."

"Decades," I correct.

He doesn't laugh it off. "You're right. Lex, I'm sorry."

I huff. "Nate, if you think you can erase–"

"I don't," he interrupts, raising a hand. "I'm sorry. I mean it, and I want to prove it to you."

Taking a steadying breath, I push the topic to safer waters. "Are you still running P&L?"

He cards a hand through his hair. "Yes."

"I see."

"For now."

I cock a brow at him. "For now."

He smiles, head ducking. "I told you I've done a lot of thinking."

"Seems like you have," I murmur, studying his face. "What can I help with?"

"I want to suggest the State contract with Solum instead of Greenstar."

"How does Greenstar feel about that?"

Nate chuckles wryly. "They weren't thrilled, but they also didn't have a better answer. We had a third party run some tests, and the results...well, they weren't what we'd been promised."

"I'm sorry to hear it."

He smirks. "Are you?"

I shrug one shoulder. "I'm thrilled you ran more tests. It's disappointing when an investment fails, though. I know that pain and I'm sorry you're experiencing it."

He watches me, eyes searching mine. "Father has no idea who you really are, does he?"

"You know the answer to that, Nate," I whisper.

"He's a fool."

I nod. "So I've said."

"You have. I might finally be ready to listen."

Humming, and not ready to go down that path, I adjust in my chair. "You mentioned needing advice."

"Yes, right. Maybe I can schedule time with your lovely assistant," he smirks at the door, "to get into those details."

"Sure, Nate. Happy to help."

"You might be pleased to know Anne-Marie has lost her position with Greenstar."

I chuckle. "Far be it for me to wish for someone's career to go up in flames. But if I was ever going to put a target on some-one's back, it would've been hers."

"It would've been a well-deserved target. The woman is

insufferable and crossed several lines in her attempt to salvage her career."

A frown tugs at my lips. "Maybe I'm too harsh, but I would hope there's nothing left to salvage."

Nate's gray eyes twinkle. "You've always been a little cutthroat when someone wrongs your people, Lex. It's served you well. And, in this case, she's honestly getting off easy. Your guys could sue, especially after all the shit she tried to say in the press after Paris."

After we landed in the Bay and I buried myself in work to escape my emotions, several reporters had reached out for commentary on a wild story Anne-Marie concocted to save her reputation. It took little more than a few targeted phone calls to kill the headline before it saw the light of day.

My chuckle is dark. "I probably took too much pleasure in refuting her claims. But when the only publication willing to run your story is a tabloid...well, that's statement enough, isn't it?"

We laugh, and for the first time in decades, I think it might be possible to know my brother as more than a passing acquaintance or business rival.

"You looked happy in Paris, Lex. It seemed like more than just the Summit."

"Bold of you to assume you have the right to gauge my happiness," I tease.

He chuckles. "Fair."

"You're right this time, though. I was very happy in Paris." I smile, glancing down at my hands as my thoughts turn to Linc and Shane, even the possibility of Declan. "I'm happier now."

Nate's grin lights the room. "I'm glad. You deserve happiness."

"Took me a while to realize that, you know. After everything."

His grin falls away. "I can imagine. Our father...he's always been cruel, but especially so to you. I hope...Lex, I hope you don't let him sabotage the future you deserve."

Reginald wasn't the only cruel one. "Say more, please."

He shifts, turning to face me. "I don't think Reginald is capable of loving another human being, but that doesn't mean you aren't. And it doesn't mean you don't deserve to be loved. You do."

I take a shuddering breath, looking away. *I'm not ready to cry. Not to him.*

"Thank you," I croak, clearing my throat. "By the same coin, Nate, I hope you realize you don't have to keep a family who has only ever ordered you around in their own self interest. You can build your own."

His chuckle is self-deprecating, almost hollow. "With who?"

"Me," I offer. "Your son."

Nate's eyes bore into mine. "Jackson."

I raise a brow. "He goes by Jax."

He huffs. "Right, Jax."

"He lives in my pool house, not sure you knew."

His brows raise. "I...I should've known."

"Probably," I concede. "Do you want to hear the story? From my perspective, at least?"

My brother searches my face, his expression torn. "Yes, Lex. Please."

I smile. "He walked right up to me in the lobby downstairs and introduced himself as my long lost nephew, then gave me this sheepish little smile and asked if I wanted to get to know each other. I took him to the coffee shop across the street, and we talked for an hour." Chuckling, I look out at the redwoods. "Miles was ready to kill me for messing up my schedule, but I couldn't walk away. And when Jax asked if we were hiring, I gave him a job on the spot."

Nate huffs, shaking his head. "Bold of him."

"No, you don't get it," I insist. "He's so...genuine. I don't know that I've ever met someone so real and open about who they are. I couldn't abide the thought of sending him somewhere else to find work, not when I could keep him close and get to know him. And when I found out he was sleeping in his sprinter van in my parking lot, well. It was a no-brainer to offer the pool house."

His jaw drops, and I laugh.

"I know. That was my reaction, too." I smile, thinking of the lights Jax strung up when he moved in, and how their very presence is soothing. "He's special, Nate. You should be proud. I am."

Nate swallows roughly. "How is he?"

"Too insightful for his own good," I chuckle. "You've met him."

"He's a surfer. And I think he mentioned modeling?"

"He still works in my mailroom, too. He wears the surfer persona well, though you'd be smart not to underestimate him. There's a lot more to him than his easygoing nature would suggest."

Nate swallows roughly. "Does he...does he want a relationship with me?"

I unfold myself from the chair and move to the couch, perching next to my brother. Reaching out tentatively, giving him the opportunity to put his boundaries back in place, I grip his hand in mine.

"That's something you should ask him, Nate. I know your son better than I know you, you know."

"Yeah," he grunts, voice raw. "How weird is that?"

"What even is normal in this family?" I counter, expression wry. "I know him well enough to know he'll give you all the chances you want, Nate. He's got the biggest heart. I love him fiercely."

Nate's eyes widen as he watches me. "You do?"

"He's my family. And I'll protect him with everything I have." I tilt my head, raising a brow.

"I hear you, Lex. I do. I...I don't want to hurt him any more than I already have."

Searching his face, I tighten my fingers around his. "What's done is done, but it's not too late, you know. To build a family of your own, with me. With Jax."

Nate lets out a shuddering breath. "You sure about that?"

"Without a doubt. Not saying it'll be easy." I smirk, squeezing his hand again. "You still physically incapable of not rising to a challenge?"

He chuckles. "You could say that."

"Good. I have high expectations, little brother."

"I'd expect nothing less." Nate grins.

Chapter 44

Declan

"**G**uys, it's starting!" Linc hollers.

I pause my workout, stepping back from the bag. Shane's footfalls sound overhead, followed by Lincoln's thundering stomps. My brow furrows as I pull off my gloves, breathing hard.

Shane came home late from a meeting at Athena the day before with the news Lex would be on TV again. Apparently, she had an interview with a local morning show about startups in the Bay. Linc had eagerly put a hold on our personal and company calendars, blocking the time so we could all watch together.

"Declan!" Shane roars.

Sighing, I swing a towel over my shoulder before jogging up the stairs in nothing more than my black athletic shorts. When I reach the living room, Shane aggressively gestures to the gap on the sofa between them before turning his attention back to the screen.

"I won't fit," I grouse, crossing my arms. "And I'm sweaty, I'll–"

"Shut the fuck up and sit down," Linc barks.

I blink while he just grins at the TV. *Asshole.* Grumbling, I squeeze myself between them.

"How do neither of you understand the concept of personal space?" I complain, shoulders hunched.

Shane pats my knee. "Get used to it."

My brows rise. "What makes you think I'm going to get used to it if I haven't—"

"Shhhhhh," Linc interrupts, holding his hand over my mouth. "There she is!"

Breathing is suddenly difficult. I tear Linc's hand away as Lex smiles graciously at the morning show host, her jaw-length dark auburn hair styled in soft waves. She's wearing a burgundy pantsuit over a silky black camisole, her light green eyes popping against the rich colors. I want to reach through the television and press myself against her, inhale her very essence.

"How's your no-contact strategy working out for you right now?" Linc asks good-naturedly as he shoves his shoulder into mine.

"Fuck off," I mutter, eyes glued on the woman of my dreams.

I've been a coward, just as she accused me of those weeks ago, more comfortable wallowing in my own self-loathing than trying to fix things. Seeing her again, so close and yet so far, makes me think I've been a fool to wait.

"We're so glad to have you join us for our Bay's Brightest Startups segment, Lex!" The brunette host smiles brightly at her guest before turning to the camera. "Lex Livingston is the founder and CEO of the Bay's most successful venture capital firm, Athena Ventures. She's also on the board for Brightest in the Bay, and will host the upcoming annual award night. Welcome!"

"Thank you, Amanda. It's a pleasure to be here."

Her voice is an arrow to my heart. I practically vibrate with tension, my fingers digging into my knees. Avoiding her for the last three weeks was torture.

Lex talks about a high-tech startup making headlines for their compression algorithm, discussing the potential impact for the entertainment industry. I'm barely listening to the words as I bask in her voice and drink up the simple sight of her. *I'm in fucking trouble.*

"Let's talk about green tech," the host gushes. "You were in Paris a few weeks ago, weren't you?"

"I was," Lex nods. "The Green Innovation Summit is an incredible annual event gathering the most promising innovators in the sustainability space. It was an honor to attend."

"You were there to help Solum Technologies launch their first product?"

"More to cheer them on," Lex demurs. "You should've seen the crowd during their presentation—they were hanging on every word. And after? The team at Solum has been busy."

"What's the secret to their success?"

Lex's lips tip into a smile as she glances down. Linc reaches across my shoulders to grip Shane, shaking him lightly.

"I know," Shane chuckles. "I see it."

I glance between them. "See what?"

"That look." Linc gestures at the television.

"What look?"

"Shut up and listen, asshole," Shane urges.

I fall silent as Lex chuckles.

"There's no secret formula to success in the startup world. If there was one, though, the three men behind Solum Technologies would have cracked it."

My eyebrows climb. It's high praise, particularly from someone who has personally coached some of the highest-valued startups in the country.

"Between them, they're well-equipped to bridge their strategic, impactful ideas with the practical skills required to bring them to life. Shane Kelly and Lincoln Wilde are an impressive engineering team; Terra, the product they created, is the first of its kind. I suspect we'll see a lot more from them, faster than you might expect."

"You've been known to remind us that a business is more than its tech. How does that factor in here?"

Lex inclines her head. "I appreciate the question. Many successful startups flourish with innovative tech and strong direction, whether it comes from their internal leadership, a board, or investors. The ones with the highest potential, however, have leaders who possess something...intangible. A passion, a drive to motivate their team and achieve something great, paired with the business acumen to turn their vision into reality."

She smiles again, the same as before, and Linc smacks my shoulder.

"Solum is lucky to have one such leader in Declan Wilde. He's an innovator, an incredible businessman, and as fiercely passionate about the company's potential global impact as he is their product."

My chest tightens. I'm not sure I'm breathing. *She's talking about me. Me. The asshole who turned keeping her at arm's length into a goddamn Olympic sport.*

"I'm confident we've only seen the tip of the iceberg in terms of what Declan is capable of," she continues. "Solum is a company to watch, to be sure, but if you're smart, you'll keep a close eye on Declan Wilde."

Linc slaps my chest, gripping my shoulders and rocking me back and forth. "Did you hear that, you asshole?! Did that get through your thick skull?!"

He grins as he releases me, reaching up to high-five Shane over my head.

"I don't....what just happened?"

I glance to the screen, where Lex is answering a new question, the conversation moving into another sector. Her expression is friendly and professional, but the warmth that had suffused her while she talked about Solum—*talked about me*—is gone.

"Were you listening?" Shane asks.

Turning to him, I scoff. "Of course I was."

"You heard her, but did you listen?" he presses.

Frowning, I think back to what she said. "I can't believe... after everything..."

"Yeah, asshole," Linc goads me, punching my shoulder.

"Would you stop hitting me?" I bark, slapping his hands away. Surging to my feet, I start pacing in front of the television.

"Why do you look so pissed?" Linc asks, turning to Shane. "He's seriously mad right now?"

"He's guilty."

If he sounded smug, I would completely lose my temper. He knows it, too, and his voice is flat, matter-of-fact.

"Ohhh." Linc slumps back into the couch. "Sure, yeah. That tracks."

"Did you tell her to do this?"

Shane snorts. "Right, because that would work with Lex."

"She listens to you." I protest.

"Oh, come off it, Dec." Linc rolls his eyes. "No one told her what to say."

Stopping in the middle of the room, I plant my hands on my hips. "What was the look you two kept making eyes at each other over?"

They lock gazes, Linc grinning as Shane blows out a breath.

"It's her Declan smile," Shane says.

My whole body stills. "Her what?"

"The smile she gets when she talks about you," Linc explains.

"What do you—"

"When we were in meetings with her and the team, and she'd talk about you, or when she was introducing us to people in Paris. It's this warm, proud, kind of sultry look she gets when her focus is on you."

I gape at my brother. "She doesn't have a Declan smile."

"She does," Shane cuts in. "You were always too busy scowling at the table, or your laptop, or one of us to notice."

"I wasn't scowling at the Summit!"

"You were also meeting people and shaking hands, bro. You weren't watching Lex introduce you to people like we were."

"You're telling me she's been looking at me in a specific way for weeks?"

"Try months," Shane cuts in.

I lower myself to the ottoman, jaw slack.

"Holy shit," I breathe, dropping my head into my hands. "Oh god, what have I done?"

Linc launches forward, arms spread wide. "Fucking finally!"

I can only gape at him. Shane's look is knowing as he leans his elbows on his knees, hands clasped.

"How do I fix this?"

"You ready to keep listening?" he retorts, lips quirking.

"Yeah," I rasp. "Yeah, I'm ready. I can't believe...that was real, right? She just said all that shit about me on public television."

"Yeah, Dec." Linc grins. "You going to tell her you don't deserve her after that?"

Nodding slowly, I start to plan. "Actually, yeah, Linc. I just might."

My brother jabs his fist in the air. Shane chuckles, shaking his head.

"You better grovel, brother," my best friend warns.

"Oh, I will," I answer absently, mind whirring.

If Lex is willing to lay it all on the line, who am I to deny her? As though he can hear my internal dialogue, Shane smirks.

"It's time to stop fighting the inevitable, Wilde. Go get our fucking queen."

Chapter 45

Lex

"Got a minute?"

My head snaps up to find Declan standing in my office doorway in a dark green suit, crisp white shirt open at the collar. *Holy shit, he looks good.* Lips parting, I move to stand. He raises a hand to stop me as I grapple with the fact that he's within reach for the first time in weeks.

"Please, sit. I'll only be a minute." He glances back as he steps in and closes the door. "Miles said he'd throw me out if I made you late for your next meeting, anyway."

I stare up at him, brows drawn, then give myself a little shake. *Focus.* "Declan. This is a surprise."

He grips the back of his neck. "Yeah. I've been...well, I had some shit to figure out. I'm sorry I've been MIA."

Leaning back in my chair, I study him. "Did you figure it out?"

"Hm?"

"The shit. You figure it out yet, Declan?"

He straightens at the hard edge in my tone, broad shoulders squaring. "It took me longer than it should have, but yes. I did."

Silence settles between us. My eyes dart to the slim black

object in his hand, then back to his face. He glances down, then reaches out and places the picture frame on my desk, facing me.

My breath catches as I pull it closer, cradling the frame in my hands. It's a photo from Paris, one he took from the back of our tandem bike. I was laughing as I looked over my shoulder at him, Linc and Shane in the background as they rode in front of us. We were all grinning, cheeks tinged pink from the cool breeze. My fingertips hover over the glass as I huff a soft laugh, emotion clogging my throat as memories rush to the surface. *I didn't know I could be so happy.*

"I've caught myself getting my phone out to stare at that photo every day for the last three weeks," Declan murmurs.

"I can see why." I clear my throat, sniffing.

He moves around my desk to crouch next to me. I frown, setting the frame down to stand and take us both over to the couch, but he seizes my hands as I start to rise. Electricity crackles through me at the touch, my whole body stilling at the force of the reaction.

"I've made a lot of mistakes in my life, Lex." He speaks earnestly, a small wrinkle appearing between his eyebrows. "None of them hold a candle to how I fucked up on that plane."

I tighten my grip on his fingers, exhaling softly. It feels as though I've been waiting a lifetime to hear his truth, and it only feels right to give him mine.

"It tore me in half to go to bed alone that night in Paris, you know. I had to psych myself up all morning to try and keep my composure."

His eyes fall shut as he leans his forehead on our joined hands, his voice rough. "I came back to your room to find Shane escorting Linc out. The look on his face…"

My chest constricts as Linc's look of hurt fills my mind's eye. "I wasn't trying to hurt him, or you. What we shared…Declan, it was so intense. I don't think I've ever felt closer to another person, but with the three of you..." I swallow, my throat dry and eyes burning. "I was overwhelmed, and I fell back on my rules to protect myself."

He raises his head, gaze darkening as he sees the tears welling. "When you acted like nothing had changed...Lex, I was devastated. And so confused."

Oh god, this man. I'm desperate to soothe him, want nothing more than to ease the ache and hurt he finally lets me see.

"I'm so sorry, Declan." I tighten my fingers again, silently begging him to believe me. "The last thing I ever want to do is hurt any of you."

Blinking away his own emotion, Declan clears his throat. "Thank you, Lex. I know...I know giving you a photo doesn't make up for the awful things I said, for the boundaries I crossed."

"It doesn't," I agree, a hint of teasing in my tone to lighten the heavy mood.

A ghost of a smile flickers across his lips. "I hope you make me work for your forgiveness."

Scoffing, I pray my voice doesn't quaver. "Bold of you to assume forgiveness is on the table, Wilde."

He sobers. "It is. I know, and I'm not here to ask you to forgive me."

"No?"

"No. Not now. Not when I haven't earned it."

His words resonate in my chest, fragile hope blooming to life. "Why are you here, then?"

"To apologize." He soothes his thumbs along my hands, a gentle caress. "I'm sorry for being an insufferable asshole on the flight back from Paris."

Unable to resist, I arch a brow. "Just the flight?"

He huffs a laugh, jade eyes blazing. "I've been pretty awful for months now, haven't I?"

"You have."

He releases my hands and rises to his feet. Moving slowly, watching for any signs of denial, he reaches out to trace a finger down my cheek, his touch featherlight. My skin flames in his wake, the fine hairs on my nape rising.

"That forgiveness I mentioned?" he rasps, tone low and full of promise.

"Hm?"

"I'm going to earn it, boss. Whatever it takes."

Breathing deeply to control the fine tremble in my limbs, I stare up into his dark gaze. "You think that's what I want?"

Declan's chuckle is rough, gravel in his throat, as he leans down and braces his hands on the arms of my chair, crowding me.

"I know it's what you fucking deserve, love. I meant what I said in Paris. You deserve someone who shows up for you in the small moments, like Linc and Shane have for the last few months. It's not much," he nods toward the photo frame, "but something tells me flashy gifts won't cut it when you could buy yourself a private island."

A soft chuckle escapes before he leans forward and kisses my cheek, his lips lingering. The loss of his heat leaves me shivering when he withdraws, my pulse spiking as I fight to catch my breath. When I look up, Declan is back at my door.

"I hope the photo makes you smile, like it has for me." He pauses, lips parting on a slow breath. "I'd never dream to claim I'm worthy of you, Lex, but I'd like to start being there for you in all the ways I haven't."

"Yes, please," I murmur, chest tight.

Declan's eyes flare before he dips his chin, tapping his fingers against the door. "I'll see you soon."

His words are a promise, carving themselves into the connection between us as he starts to leave.

"Thank you," I call, making him stop and look back over his shoulder. "For the photo, Declan, it's...I love it."

He smiles, bright and full, his laugh lines appearing at the corners of his eyes to strike me dumb. By the time I gather my wits once more, he's gone.

———

When I emerge for my run a day later, Linc's BMW is parked in a different place than usual, and it isn't Linc leaning casually on the hood in a black tank and shorts. He has stubble on his jaw, his dark hair–typically swept back to perfection–flopping charmingly over one eyebrow.

"Uh, hi," I greet, jogging down my front steps. "What are you doing here, Declan?"

"Linc had a...thing."

My lips twitch. "Was the thing being a decent brother and not fighting when you asked to take his place?"

He squints and looks away, feigning nonchalance. "Maybe."

"I see." I eye him. "You a runner?"

His grimace is answer enough. *Oh, I'm going to enjoy this.*

"Tsk. Maybe Linc *wasn't* being a decent brother."

Declan's brows rise as I start to stretch. "What does that mean?"

"Hope you can keep up," I taunt, stepping into a lunge.

"Don't worry, boss. I'll be a gentleman and match your pace. Wouldn't hurt to take it easy." The edge of bravado in his voice is as entertaining as it is delicious.

"Of course, Wilde." I roll my eyes. "Can't leave me in the dust, can you?"

"Wouldn't dream of it," he grins.

Something flashes in his eyes at my sharp smile, but I don't stop to analyze it.

"Alright then, Declan. Let's see you earn it."

I take off down my driveway, Declan's thundering footsteps hot behind me. Unwilling to give an inch to the cocky asshole, I set a brutal pace. When Linc had first joined me, I'd slowed down a bit until he got used to things, then ramped back up to my usual. For Declan, I step it up a notch.

Halfway through our route, Declan is breathing hard, face red and dripping with sweat. I slow, smirking as he stumbles back to a walk, hands on his hips.

"Fuck, Lex. Linc actually does this with you every day?" he gasps.

I shrug, jogging lightly on my toes. "Just about, yeah."

He side-eyes me. "He never used to run."

My heart swells as I grin. "I know. He's a willing convert now, though. You planning to join him?"

"Fuck no," he barks, shaking his head. "This was a onetime deal. Back to your regularly scheduled Linc tomorrow."

"Aw, not having fun?"

He chuckles, smile sardonic. "I'm with you. That's a plus."

I snort. "Cute."

"Hey, I could either give a good answer or an honest one."

"What would you rather do, then, Wilde?"

His breathing has calmed somewhat, enough for him to pick back up into a light jog.

"You want to work out with me, Lex, come to the house. You know how to hit or kick a bag?"

Big, broody asshole likes to hit things. Shocker. "I love kickboxing, but I've never tried it outside of a class. The kind without props."

He glares. "Learning to use the *equipment* is half the fun."

"I see."

Clearing his throat, he coughs. "I could teach you."

"Think that's a good idea, do you?"

His eyes burn blazing tracks across my skin as he takes in my sports bra and running shorts. "Yeah," he grunts, "I think it has its merits."

Caveman. I shouldn't find him blatantly checking me out quite so charming. Or maybe it's the return of the easy banter between us buoying my spirits for the first time in weeks.

"We'll see. You still have to make it back alive today."

He huffs. "I'm fine. Nothing to it. Could keep this up all day."

Challenge accepted. "Great! Look lively, then–let's go."

I increase pace again as he curses, laughter bubbling through me. The smile feels plastered to my lips for the rest of the morning.

———

"You're not Shane."

Declan scoffs as he enters my office in slacks and a black button down, takeout bag in hand. "I certainly am not, though I'll thank you for sounding surprised rather than disappointed."

I chuckle at his easy smirk, rising to greet him. He pauses, setting the bag on the end table, and slips his arms around my waist as I go up on tiptoes to hug him. The cropped hem of my blouse rides up as I do, his hands slipping onto bare skin as he returns my embrace.

"I'm glad it's you," I murmur.

His arms tighten, and I can feel the hot press of him against my belly. I bite my lip, pleased at his ready reaction, and want to pout as he steps back. He reaches out and tugs my lip free, his eyes dark with desire.

"None of that, please. I'm under strict orders to feed you, then escort you to your car."

"Really, now?" I hum, folding myself into one corner of the

couch. "Since when do you follow Mr. Kelly's orders outside the bedroom?"

"Since I started prioritizing the person his orders are intended to serve over my personal need for authority," he answers easily.

"Ah," I mumble, swallowing roughly. "I see."

He hums as he pulls the containers from the bag and sets the coffee table. "I think you're starting to."

Why do I suddenly feel exposed? I clear my throat and smirk. "Did you steal Shane's food along with his lunch plans?"

Declan glowers at me with playful eyes. "I offered to make it."

I fight to hide a grin as I read between the lines. "He kicked you out of the kitchen, didn't he?"

"He asked me to leave," he grumbles, "and I went willingly."

"Right," I drawl, unable to hold back the giggle.

Declan growls and drops onto the couch next to me, reaching out to tickle my sides. Laughing, I bat him away and knock against him with my shoulder, reaching for what looks like a quinoa bowl topped with salmon.

"I see how it is," he teases. "I'm just your food delivery service. Is this how it goes with Shane, too?"

I scoff, digging into the bowl. "Shane wouldn't dream of distracting me from eating."

"He's a little intense, isn't he?"

Glancing up, I find him watching me as though he's trying to memorize every inch. My lips curve into a smile.

"You all are."

"Even Linc?"

I raise a brow, cocking my head. "Seriously?"

"What? He's a total goofball."

"Not all the time," I muse, smiling as his eyes narrow. "Did you come here to fish about Shane and Linc, or...?"

Declan sighs exaggeratedly. "No, I didn't. Mostly, I wanted to see you." He pauses, fidgeting briefly with the napkin under the bowl in his hand. "I missed you."

My fucking heart. "Is it so hard to admit?"

His eyes meet mine. "No, I...I'm getting used to saying that shit out loud. It doesn't come easy."

"What, communication?"

Declan scoffs, setting his bowl down and leaning back against the couch. "Vulnerability. It's foreign territory, but I'm... I'm trying to get comfortable with it."

As I take another bite, I study him. He's more relaxed in my presence than he's ever been, even in Paris. After he brought me the photo and apologized, he started cropping up in the group text for the first time since well before the Summit, bantering with all of us. He even started texting me to check in or share little wins as he and the team work through the rush of interest after their grand debut.

Bit by bit, Declan is fitting himself into my life as seamlessly as Shane and Linc fit into his. *Almost like a family.* For the first time in my life, the thought of having one of my own doesn't fill me with dread.

"I am and always will be a safe place for you, Declan," I murmur. "Just like Shane and Linc."

He looks up and holds my gaze. "I know."

"Good." Taking the remnants of our dinner to the waste bin, I turn. "Will you come over with them tomorrow night?"

Since they had both laid my rules to rest, Shane and Linc made a habit of stopping by a few times a week for a sleepover. We had spent little time at their house since Paris, letting Declan dictate his boundaries.

"Not this time," he says gently, walking over and sliding a hand along my jaw to grip the side of my neck. "I have to pick up our tuxes for the Brightest in the Bay award ceremony on Friday."

I frown and lean into his touch, hands resting on his chest. "You could come after, if you wanted to."

"I do." His fingers flex against my throat with intent, the command in the subtle move going straight to my clit. "More than you know."

"Then you'll be there?" I try not to plead as I toy with his buttons.

He leans his forehead against mine, breathing deep. "I want to do it right this time. Be patient with me for a little longer?"

My eyes fall shut. "Okay," I whisper.

"Thank you." He lifts his head, pressing a long kiss to my brow. "Come on, love. Let's get you home."

He says it so casually, but my heart flutters at the name. It's the second time he's used it, and my reaction is the same each time. I grab my purse, then lean into him when he wraps an arm around my waist, his fingers gripping me tight. *Just a little longer, Wilde. I'll hold you to it.*

Chapter 46

Lex

"Holy shit, look at this place."

I chuckle to myself as Linc's voice wafts up the stairs, full of awe. My house has been transformed in the hours since he and Shane left that morning, protesting my order and kissing me senseless on the porch. They'd only stopped when cars started pulling up behind them, a small army of event staff pouring out to prepare the grounds. As finalists in their category, the guys would be in attendance to hear whether they'd be walking away winners.

Pausing by the mirror at the top of the stairs, I study my reflection. My stylist and his team left moments ago, sweeping out of my glam room in a cloud of hairspray and air kisses. Massimo called the look modern sophistication, my hair slicked back with my makeup minimal. The dress is royal blue silk that wraps around my neck, leaving my left shoulder bare to hug down my figure and flare at the knees, a long swath of material hanging to the floor over my right. I turn, eyeing the plunging back. *They're going to lose their minds.*

"Gorgeous!" Linc yells. "Where you at?!"

"Lincoln," Shane tuts.

I chuckle, picturing his frown.

"Patience!" I call, turning the corner toward the stairs.

As I start down, my breath catches in my throat. *Dear god, they should wear tuxes more often.* They are tailored to perfection, black pants fitted perfectly over muscular thighs. Shane sports all black, his jacket a luxe velvet with satin lapels. Linc's dark green jacket shines, silky all over with a black bowtie and white shirt. And between them, a teasing smile on his lips, Declan topped his black shirt and tie with a jacket in a shade of cream so rich it looks gold. *Could they really all be mine?*

When I finally catch their attention, they freeze. Shane recovers first, desire darkening his icy gaze as he settles a hand in his pocket and watches me with predatory intent. Linc gapes like a fish before coughing a muttered curse into his fist. Declan moves toward me as I draw closer, taking my hand the second I'm within reach. He draws me out into the foyer and leads me into a spin, a pleased sound rumbling from his throat as he catches sight of my back.

"Boss, are you trying to distract me?" he rumbles.

Smirking, I pat his chest. "You're a big boy, Declan. You'll manage."

His eyes burn at the challenge, squeezing my hip as he kisses my forehead before stepping back.

"I'm glad you're all here." I reach out to take Shane's hand. "Nate mentioned something the last time we spoke, and I wanted to hear your thoughts. All of you."

Shane's fingers tighten around mine. "Let's hear it."

"He suggested you could go after Anne-Marie, sue her for damages to your company, and to each of you personally. He's even willing to help us build a case, if that's what you want. And you know I'll support you, whatever you decide."

Linc and Shane look to Declan. He smiles softly, and my heart twists in my chest.

"Honestly, Lex, we've given her enough of our time and energy. Anne-Marie is in our past, where she belongs. I, for one, would much rather focus on something brighter." His emerald eyes flash as they flit to his brothers and back to me. "Our future."

"I couldn't agree more," Shane murmurs, while Linc nods with a wide grin.

"Very well." A smile tugs at my lips. "Happy hour started a few minutes ago. Why don't you go get a round and find Parker?" I kiss Shane, then Linc. "I have to greet the rest of the board before things get underway."

"We'll see you after, then?" Shane asks.

I nod, then hold up my hands, shooing them away.

"Now who's the distraction? Go, begone with you, guests of honor. And good luck!"

They obey, Linc walking backwards with his lip between his teeth as he rakes his eyes over me. I laugh as Shane stops him from crashing into a side table, turning him around by the shoulders with a firm tug.

"Lex! This place is ridiculous!" a bright voice calls behind me as they disappear around the corner.

I turn to the front door, smiling as Preston Brooks steps through in a bold red chiffon gown with a high neck and a slit to mid-thigh. I'd asked all the Brightest in the Bay board members to use the front entrance, while the majority of the guests are being sent through the lavish side gate to the gardens.

"I'll take ridiculous as a compliment," I laugh, embracing her.

"You should! I've never seen so much marble. You could make this a wedding venue, for fuck's sake." She looks around, brown eyes wide.

I chuckle. "It's so good to actually see you. You've been dialing in for most of the board meetings the past few months."

Her smile falters, almost imperceptibly. "I've been on the East Coast a bunch."

"I see." When she doesn't elaborate after a moment, I smile, letting her keep her secrets. "Shall we? The rest of the Board is either in my study or still on their way."

She loops her arm through mine as I lead her down the hall, eyeing my dress. "This color is divine. Are we both arriving fashionably late to our own party?"

"Is there any other way to do it?" I whisper conspiratorially.

Her answering laugh announces our arrival as we reach my study, faces turning towards us with matching grins.

"Welcome, everyone," I say, bowing my head briefly. "Thank you for being here."

Preston snorts. "I think we should all be thanking you for this stunning venue you so kindly donated, Lex."

"Nonsense," I protest over the chorus of agreement. "It's my pleasure. Enough about that. Let's go celebrate this year's Brightest, hm?"

———

As much as I love the Bay's startup community, I'm ready to send them all home. The winners are all deserving, and I am beyond pleased to be celebrating their successes, but my eyes keep drifting to Linc, Shane, and Declan. The manicured gardens, sparkling lights, and impeccably dressed crowd melt away as I watch them, my mind wandering to inappropriate places.

Nate arrived shortly after things got underway, making a beeline to greet me. We've found time to reconnect roughly once a week since he showed up at Athena, and he helped us fully navigate the intricacies of taking over a government contract. I can't call him a friend yet, but we are certainly on our way to something...more.

The program wound its way through various categories, recognizing the Brightest startups by industry, special interest, and community impact. We're finally coming to the headline award of the evening, known simply as the Brightest, celebrating the startup with both an impressive debut year and significant community impact potential.

I clap along with the crowd as Preston takes the stage to announce the nominees for the Brightest, which includes Solum and four other startups. My eyes dart to the guys, who stand in a tight group across the space. We managed to avoid each other most of the night, the anticipation making me more anxious for things to wrap up.

Flashing her winning smile to the crowd, Preston rips open the gold envelope.

"I'm delighted to announce this year's Brightest in the Bay, fresh off their spectacular debut at the Green Innovation Summit in Paris–Solum Technologies!"

The audience roars with applause and cheers as the guys embrace and Linc claps his brother's shoulder. Declan grins back at him, such joy in his expression I can't help but smile in return.

"Accepting on behalf of his business partners, Lincoln Wilde and Shane Kelly, is CEO and founder Declan Wilde!"

Preston grasps Declan's hand for a firm shake, his eyebrows rising slightly as she passes him the award. He walks up to the podium with his eyes on the engraved glass, a broad smile on his face. He sits it carefully on the edge and chuckles, shaking his head.

"It's an honor to be here," he says, looking out at the audience. "If you'd asked me four months ago if I could see myself here, I would've scoffed in your face."

Gentle laughter sweeps through the crowd.

"Our road here was rocky. It was paved with betrayal and challenges, some out of our control, and more than I want to admit my own damn fault." He glances down at the podium, voice raw. "As I stand here tonight, I feel compelled to confess."

The crowd is quiet, rapt. Something flutters in my gut, my heart rate picking up.

"I didn't win this," Declan proclaims, raising the award in one hand.

What the hell? My brows knit in confusion. I try to seek out Linc and Shane, but their attention is glued on Declan.

"This award, and the successes that brought Solum here, are all owed to one person. A beautiful, brilliant, talented woman with endless patience and a will so strong she could carry this entire community on her shoulders." He chuckles, cocking his head. "If I'm not mistaken, she has."

My heart is in my throat, my hand trembling as I touch my fingers to my lips. Declan's eyes snap to mine across the crowd, as though acutely aware of where I am.

"Lex Livingston, this award belongs to you. You saw what no one else could, believed in three bumbling idiots–"

He smirks at the soft gasps and chuckles from the crowd, then continues.

"You believed in us based on nothing more than your intuition and commitment to doing what's right. I punished you for your belief for months. Because I was afraid."

Declan stares into my soul. People are glancing between us, whispering to their neighbors. I'm vaguely aware of Van drawing closer, Cami at his side. He places a reassuring hand on my shoulder, but I can't look away from the man on the stage.

"You okay?" Van mutters.

"I don't know," I whisper, reaching up to grip his fingers in mine.

"I told myself I was afraid to trust someone else, afraid to risk being betrayed all over again. But I've recently realized it was another lie I told in a misguided attempt to protect myself." Declan pauses, breathing deeply.

"Oh, I was afraid of you, alright. I was afraid of how you could see straight through me. How you challenged me, forced me to confront every flaw I knew and hated. It took far too long for me to recognize you were coaching me, driving me, helping me overcome things I thought would always hold me back."

Declan's voice goes hoarse. "While I was too busy lying to myself, you were daring me to dream bigger than I ever thought possible. And making sure every goddamn one came true."

My breath stutters as I try to control it, chest constricting with the weight of my emotions. Van steps away, Linc and Shane surrounding me in his stead, anchoring me with a hand each to my hip and shoulder.

"And the best part? I could see how it wasn't just me you were pushing to be more...it wasn't just my dreams you cared about.You've had the same effect on all three of us from the beginning. We're sharper businessmen, better engineers, more conscious community members because of you."

The first tear spills over, sliding down my cheek. Linc and Shane shuffle closer, bodies touching mine on either side as I grip Shane's hand at my hip and Linc's on my shoulder.

"You make me want to be a better man, Lex. I can't imagine living my life without you, let alone running Solum without your counsel. Every opportunity you had to claim ownership of our success, you turned right back on us. I won't let you do it tonight."

Declan tears his eyes from mine and I feel the loss like a physical ache. My knees go wobbly, Shane's arm around me tightening to hold me up.

Declan gazes out at the audience. "I don't think any of you

will disagree. No offense to the well-deserving startups recognized tonight, but no one shines brighter in the Bay than Lex Livingston."

The applause is thunderous, cheers sounding across my expansive yard. Smiling faces turn to me as I dab at the tear tracks on my cheeks, laughing in disbelief.

"Thank you, Lex," Declan calls, sparkling eyes finding mine once more. "You never once gave me an inch. I love you for it."

My mouth falls open as the world narrows to nothing but the two of us. In a daze, I watch him step off the stage, walk through the crowd as they part seamlessly for him, giving him a straight path to me. Then he's here, taking my face in his hands and holding my gaze so fiercely I think I might combust.

"I've never seen you speechless," he murmurs, lips twitching into a smile.

I laugh wetly. "What the hell did you just do, Wilde?"

His expression softens, turning more serious. "Can we go somewhere?"

Breathless, I reach up and take his hand, leading him away. I'm vaguely aware of Preston and the other board members onstage to close the ceremony and say farewell to the audience. I'm supposed to be up there with them, but I know Preston will cover for me. After Declan's very public speech, I doubt anyone will hold my absence against me.

The security guard pulls back the velvet barrier when we reach the landing, standing still and stoic as we slip past and make our way up to my bedroom. I open the door and lead Declan in, heart beating erratically in my chest. He pulls the door shut as I watch, his fingers curling around mine.

"Scotch?" I ask, voice shaking, as I turn to the decanter on my wooden side table.

"Alright," he rumbles.

My hands tremble as I pour the liquor into matching

snifters, stepping close to Declan to hand it over. He accepts it gently, eyes on mine as he takes a slow slip. I follow suit, gulping the smoky alcohol down and turning to set my glass back on the antique brass tray. Declan steps up behind me, setting his glass down before trailing his fingers down my arms.

"Breathe, love," he whispers, pressing his cheek to mine over my shoulder.

"There's that word again," I manage, voice little more than a croak.

"Love?"

Dipping my chin, I swallow roughly. "Do you mean it? Did you...did you mean it?"

"Every word."

I gasp a laugh, turning to face him. "And you couldn't tell me before?!"

His brow creases as he reaches out to grip the side of my neck. "I wanted to raise the stakes. It felt...I felt like I needed to do something more. To earn your forgiveness."

"You don't need a stage to prove yourself, Declan. This, right here," I wrap my fingers around his wrist, leaning into his claiming touch, "this is what matters to me. Us."

Sighing, he presses his forehead to mine. He grounds me, calms some of the anxious energy skittering through my body. I let my eyes fall shut and relax into him, dropping my arms to rest my hands on his waist.

"I'm not always going to get this right," he whispers. "Like I have for months, I'm going to make mistakes, going to fuck up. But I promise you, I'll love you through it. I won't stop trying."

He straightens, stroking a thumb along my jaw.

"I don't want perfect," I vow. "I just want you."

His eyes flash as he steps closer, pressing himself flush against me. I can feel all the strong, hard planes of him through the thin silk of my dress, feel his arousal push against me as his cock thickens.

"What do you want?" he demands, pressing his thumb to my lower lip.

"All of you," I whisper. "No more keeping me at arm's length, Declan."

"No more," he intones, mouth inching closer.

I lean into him, ghosting my lips against his. "I've missed you," I breathe.

"I'm here now, love, and I'm yours."

My heart sings. "I love you, Declan Wilde."

His name is barely out of my mouth before he hauls me into his arms and slams his lips to mine. I moan into the kiss, clinging to him as I give him everything he asked for. Groaning, he reaches down and swings me up into his arms.

"What do you plan to do with me?" I tease, running my fingertips over his jaw in wonder. *He's mine.*

"Everything," he growls playfully, eyes sparkling. "If I'm honest, though, there's something I've been dying to do since well before Paris."

He takes me to the bed, gently laying me down before shrugging off his jacket and stepping out of his shoes. Then he crawls up into my pile of pillows and gathers me in his arms. *Well, I'll be. Declan Wilde is a snuggler. Who would've guessed?*

Chapter 47

Linc

"I fucking love this room." I lean back on my hands on Lex's bed, looking around at the inviting space.

It's huge–because, duh, mansion–but it's also the only space in the whole place that feels...warm, cozy. It's full of soft touches of luxury, a plush cream rug underfoot and a fireplace on one wall. The furniture is lush, all shades of white with brass accents.

Lex peers at me over her shoulder, smiling. "Me, too. I let the decorators do whatever they wanted in the rest of the house...well, except for the sofa."

"That thing is fucking magic. Good call."

She laughs. "Why, thank you. But, yeah. I was pretty specific about this one."

"It suits you." I eye her. "Only part of this place that does, really."

"I know." Her nose scrunches as she shrugs on a thick gray cardigan. "Shall we join them?"

I grin, stepping into her space and looping my arms around her waist. She gives in immediately, rising to her tiptoes to meet my kiss. *God, I can't get enough of her.*

The night before, we gave Declan an hour. One hour after he spewed his heart all over the Brightest in the Bay award ceremony before we let ourselves into her room. We found them curled around each other on her massive bed, both still fully clothed, gooey smiles on their faces as they talked.

Lex was the first to scramble up, rushing over to wrap her arms around me and Shane. Dec followed, pulling us both into rough, back-slapping hugs as we laughed. Somehow, we'd all ended up back on the bed in a puppy pile, talking deep into the night.

Then we needed to get ready for bed, and the sight of all that blue silk pooling at Lex's feet, revealing miles of smooth skin, went straight to my dick. Dec and Shane apparently felt the same, and we ravished Lex for hours before finally falling asleep together. *Pretty sure I'll never be able to think of last night without getting emotional.*

Lex pulls back, breathless, and giggles when I try to chase her with my lips.

"Linc! Come on, they're waiting for us."

She twines her fingers in mine, pulling me toward the kitchen.

"Fine," I whine. "I just want you all to myself."

"You've had me all to yourself since the shower."

She tosses me a wicked smirk over her shoulder, and the memory of her on dripping wet knees for me makes my dick twitch. *Okay, so add the bathroom to the list of rooms I love in this place.*

"Face it, gorgeous. I'll never get enough of you. I'm a lost fucking cause." I clutch at my heart dramatically.

"What are you whining about now?" Dec looks up as we enter the kitchen.

"Apparently, your brother wants me all to himself," Lex says airily, settling herself on a stool at the island.

Shane and Dec both freeze, turning to me with matching expressions, all hard and threatening.

"Can you fucking blame me? Look at her!" I gesture toward the siren, looking delectable in her lounge pants, tee, and oversized cardigan. *Casual Lex is still my favorite.*

The guys exchange a loaded glance, then shrug.

"Yep, can't blame him," Dec quips, turning back to the pancakes on the griddle.

Lex giggles as Shane walks around behind her and sets a coffee cup in front of her, leaning in to kiss her neck as he does. She sighs and leans back against him, gripping his forearms after he wraps them around her upper chest for a standing cuddle. *So fucking natural.*

"Can every Saturday morning be like this?" she muses, eyes falling closed.

I glance at Dec, then Shane. We have a quick silent conversation, then nod.

"Must suck to rattle around in this giant place every weekend," I mutter.

Lex pops one eye open, arching a brow as she peers at me. "I mean, I'm hardly here."

"Expensive place to have if you never use it," Shane drawls.

"Questionable financial choice," Declan adds.

Lex sits up, swiveling on her stool to look up at Shane, then me. "Okay, what's going on here?"

"Do you really want every Saturday to be like this?" Dec asks, still facing the griddle.

"Yes?" She looks at his back sideways, then to me and Shane.

"This neighborhood...all this space. That important to you?" Shane questions, walking over to pull plates down from the cabinet.

"I mean, the neighborhood's nice enough. The house is definitely too big–Linc's right about that. Having Jax here helps."

Dec nods absently, pulling his phone out of his gray sweatpants. Lex produced three pairs that morning with a slight flush, mentioning she'd had her personal shopper pick up a few things for us on their last trip. What she meant, apparently, was we now had a fully stocked closet in her bedroom. *Billionaires are something else.*

"Three weeks from today should work," Dec announces.

"I'll make sure Miles blocks Friday night through Sunday," Shane murmurs, reaching for his phone.

"What the fuck is going on?" Lex demands.

I lean over and kiss her temple. "Move in day."

"Excuse me?"

"You. With us."

She gapes. "You want me to move in with you?"

I pick her hand up off the island. "I planted a rose bush out front for you. It might take it a while to bloom, but it's an old French varietal with these dark petals with a light edge. Reminded me of Paris."

"What Linc's trying to say," Shane interjects with a smirk as Lex stares, her eyes wide and swimmy, "is we'd love for you to move in with us, and we've already started getting things ready for you."

She squeezes my hand. "Thank you for the roses. I can't wait to see them. You're very sweet, Linc."

"You're welcome!" I grin.

"To be clear, gentlemen, this is my decision." She arches a brow. *Cute.*

"Of course it is." Dec flips another round of pancakes before passing a steaming plate to Lex.

"I'd like to point out that none of you have actually asked the question."

"Hey, baby?" Shane calls from the fridge, where he's pulling out the milk. "Want to move in with us in three weeks?"

She stares in his direction, dazed, then scoffs. "Fuck it. Yes."

I straighten, turning to her with a grin. "Wait, really?"

Dec is no longer paying attention to the pancakes, his arms crossed as he watches her with dark, hungry eyes.

"Yes, really. Were you expecting—"

Lex can't finish her sentence because Shane has marched over and seized her throat, pulling her in for a rough kiss. She moans, her body going lax as she succumbs readily to his commanding touch. My cock stirs as the energy in the room changes, anticipation tingling through me.

"I fucking love you, baby," Shane growls, releasing her.

She licks her lips, blowing out a sharp breath. "I love you, too." Glancing around at the three of us, she smiles. "I love all of you."

"Love you forever, beautiful." I lean over and peck her lips, knowing I risk derailing Dec's breakfast plans if I linger too long. "So, we're really doing this?"

"Yeah, I think it makes sense to consolidate households," she agrees, unable to resist talking through the strategy. *There's a reason Dec calls her boss.* "You and Shane have been staying here more often than not, and—"

"No, I mean the *bigger* this," I interrupt. "Us. All four of us, all in."

"Oh." Lex smiles, looking around the room. The way her eyes soften and cheeks flush does things to me. "Yeah, Linc. I am."

"We all are," Shane confirms as he sets places at the island for him and Dec.

I can't contain my excitement, jumping to my feet and punching the air. "Fuck yeah!"

Lex giggles, shaking her head as she takes a bite of pancake.

Shane doctored the short stack Dec handed her, adding bananas, strawberries, and a dollop of whipped cream.

"So, what are we, though?" I ask the question I've been batting around for weeks. "Are we the Wildes? The Livingstons? The Kellys? The Kelly-Livingston-Wildes? Because I gotta be honest, that last one is a bit of a mouthful."

Shane chuckles, knocking his shoulder into mine as he sets down a bowl of fruit. "I think we can wait on that answer, Linc. One thing at a time."

"Sure, yeah. Totally," I agree, diving into the fruit. "Thanks, guys. This is awesome."

Lex glances at each of us, smiling down at her breakfast before taking another bite. "It really is."

Epilogue

Declan

6 months later

"You look stunning in red, love."

I trail my fingertips across Lex's calf, lingering over the small indentations where the wide ribbon bites into her skin. Her body bows as she tries to get closer to me, desperate for my touch. She attempts to shift, her ankles straining against her binds.

"Declan," she whines, sweat beading between her breasts and trickling down her stomach to darken the swath of ribbon across her torso. "Please, sir. Touch me."

"Hm. I do love it when you beg for me."

I want her vocal, and she knows it. Linc likes to push her in the bedroom, challenge her in ways she struggles to obey so he can exact the punishment they both crave. Shane demands nothing less than her complete submission, wanting her putty in his hands so he can wring every drop of pleasure from her. Me? I want her mindless, love her babbling, won't stop until she screams.

As much as I love sharing her with them, revel in the pleasure of breaking her apart together, I live for the moments I get our queen all to myself.

Lex is stretched out on my bed, bound from wrists to ankles in silky red ribbon. I stole it for just this purpose from the pile of gift wrapping supplies she stuffed under our bed. The moment I saw it, I couldn't strike the vision of her wearing nothing else from my mind. *It's even better than I imagined.*

She pulls on her wrist bindings, trying to twist her hips and thrust them toward where she felt me last. I'd tripled the ribbon over her eyes, needing to hear the little gasping sounds she makes when my mouth descends on a new part of her without warning. It's been twenty minutes since I wrapped her up like my own Christmas gift and started toying with her, stirring her up.

"What do you want, hm?"

I kneel between her spread legs. She keens when she feels the bed dip, lifting her hips toward me.

"Fuck me, sir, please," she pants. "Need you."

"You need me?" My lips press to the inside of her ankle, then trail up her inner calf.

"Yes, sir," she breathes.

My cock is rock hard beneath me, pinned against the sheets. It twitches every time she calls me 'sir', every time she submits willingly. What I want most, though, is for her to be desperate enough to forget the honorific.

"Where?"

When I get to the curve of her inner thigh, I suck hard, making her cry out at the sting. I soothe it with my tongue, kneading the same spot on the opposite side with my hand. She tries to squirm, her muscles trembling, as I kiss, lick, and nip my way toward her glistening pussy.

She's dripping, a wet spot already spreading beneath her. I

groan at the sight, pressing my face against her to languidly lap up her cum. Pleading, almost babbling, above me, her hips jerk as she tries to get the leverage to push herself against me.

I'd avoided her pussy until that moment, had kissed and teased every other inch of her. She almost sags in relief when I stroke her entrance with two fingers, a ragged sob tearing from her throat.

"Shhhh," I croon. "It's almost seven."

"Declan, please," Lex gasps. "I need to come, sir, please. Don't let me...don't leave me...fuck..."

Her voice trails off as I slide two fingers inside her and circle her clit with my tongue. I know what she's worried about. We're hosting a holiday party soon, and several of our guests are known to be chronically early. As punishment last week, Linc had wound her up until she was nearly in tears, then left her tied up for an hour. Even though she'd come so hard she passed out when he was done with her, she wasn't ready to go through that torture again.

"I won't leave you wanting, love," I murmur against her flesh, licking long stripes up her pussy lips. "Don't worry."

Burying my face back against her, I suck her clit into my mouth, pulling it gently between my teeth. I roll it with my tongue, sucking lightly before releasing it. She's gushing, her cum all over me as her body trembles.

I hook my fingers against the spot at the top of her channel, pressing and stroking in short bursts. Her body stiffens, a telltale sign she's close, and I smirk.

She yells in frustration when I pull away completely, dragging my fingers slowly out of her.

"No, Declan, don't, please, don't do that, not again," she pleads, tears streaming down her cheeks.

The ribbon over her eyes is almost completely darkened by her tears, her mouth open in anguish as she gasps.

"There you are," I hum, stroking my hands along her thighs to her sides, then up to her nipples. I tweak them both, then trail my fingers back down across her lower belly.

She jerks and shivers, oversensitive and ticklish, her lower lip starting to quiver as her chest heaves with sobs.

"My desperate, needy little whore."

I push my hand against her opening right as she whimpers in response, her arousal leaking through my fingers as I work them inside.

"You're ready for me, aren't you?"

"God, yes, please, I need you, need your cock. Fuck me, Declan, please. No more–"

I still. "No more?"

"No! Nonononononono, please no, don't–"

Shushing her again, I lean over her, bracing on my elbow, to tease the head of my cock against her tender, reddened flesh. The moment it slides against her, she moans, straining against her binds to try to curl toward me.

"Fuck, you feel so good," I groan, burying my face against her neck as I thrust against her at a leisurely pace.

My cockhead catches against her for a moment, then pops free and slides forward. Her chest heaves against me as she groans, trying to thrash her head from side to side. Turning her jaw with one hand, I crush my lips to hers, stealing a harsh kiss before I push back to my knees.

"I think you're ready, love."

"Yes, please, yes," she chants mindlessly, licking her lips.

Getting off the bed, I unhook the spreader bar her ankles are tied to from the fastener on the footboard. Lex whimpers as some of the tension keeping her in place is released. I hold the bar as I climb back up to kneel before her wide open pussy, the cool metal across my chest keeping her ankles suspended in the air.

"I've got you, Lex. Deep breath, okay?"

She obeys immediately, breathing sharply through her nose as I curl an arm under the bar, holding it in the crook of my elbow. With my other hand, I line my cock up with her entrance, barely pushing in.

"Give me another," I command.

As she follows my order, breathing deep into her belly, I thread my other arm through the bar. The position gives me the leverage to pull her up and toward me with every thrust, hitting the deepest parts of her. Lex begins to exhale, and I yank the bar, snapping my hips toward her at the same time. Her greedy pussy sucks me in and clamps down so hard I curse, closing my eyes against the pleasure rushing through me.

Her scream as I bottom out, hips smacking against her ass roughly, is fucking music to my ears.

"That's it, little whore," I pant, jerking the bar in time with my hips, bringing us together forcefully with each aggressive thrust. "You know what I want."

"Oh god, Declan," Lex gasps, voice hoarse. "You're so deep, fuck."

I shift, changing the angle of the bar slightly, and she cries out. Brow furrowing in concentration, I hold her in that position, pounding relentlessly into her G-spot as she starts to tremble. The walls of her pussy tighten around me, the slick sound of us coming together nearly overwhelming.

"I'm so close," she pants, core clenching. "Fuck, don't stop, Declan, please..."

Reaching down with one hand, I swirl my thumb roughly against her clit as she starts to come. She screams as her body contracts, cunt tightening fiercely as she rides out wave after wave. I pump through it, sweat beading as I fight to hold my own orgasm at bay.

As she melts back into the bed, I slip the bar over my head.

It braces against my shoulders as I lean forward to drive her into the mattress. Mewling, body still trembling with aftershocks, Lex tries to meet me thrust for thrust.

"That's it," I grit out, my orgasm building in the base of my spine. "Fucking love your tight little cunt, Lex."

Dipping down, I kiss her savagely, all teeth and tongue. She moans, kissing me back, as her pussy tries to drag my orgasm from me.

"Fuck," I groan, hips stuttering.

Leaning my head against her neck, I lazily work us both through the aftershocks. Lex is hypersensitive, her breath catching with each slow press of my body against her where we're joined.

"I fucking love you, boss," I mutter, pressing a kiss to the hollow of her throat.

She gasps a laugh, boneless and sated. "I fucking love you, Wilde."

"And while I fucking love you both, you need to hurry the fuck up."

I push to my knees and look over my shoulder at Linc. Leaning up against the open doorway in black slacks and a pale green button up, he's already dressed for the party.

"Fine," I huff, reaching up to release Lex from the ankle cuffs on the bar. "How long were you standing there?"

"Walked up around the time Lex started to come."

"You asshole. You heard her getting close, didn't you?"

He chuckles as I climb off the bed and grab my boxer briefs, pulling them on. His eyes drift behind me, his pupils blowing as he catches sight of my handiwork.

"Holy fuck, you actually did it."

My naughty Christmas ribbon fantasy may have come up once or twice in the last few weeks.

"Hey, sweetheart," Lex calls, her voice rough.

"Hey, gorgeous. You look...goddamn. We're buying a metric fuck ton of ribbon this weekend, okay?"

She giggles, breathy and soft, as I untie her wrists. Wincing slightly as she draws her arms down, she bites her lip and groans as I massage her reddened skin with my thumbs.

"Don't just stand there, asshole. Come help."

"Don't have to tell me twice," Linc quips.

He pulls the door closed and goes to the other side of the bed, working on her other wrist. As he does, his eyes rake over our lover, his gaze lingering on the wet mess between her thighs and the purpling marks on her breasts.

"Shane's gonna skin you alive for not leaving enough time for proper aftercare," he mutters, glancing at me sideways. "You two might need to be fashionably late."

"Was already planning on it, Linc."

"That's enough, you two," Lex sighs, her lips tipping into a smile. "I would like to see your faces now, though."

"Oh, shit." Linc reaches for the ribbon on her head.

"I got it." I wave him off, pulling the end of the bow on the side of her neck.

Linc watches as I unwind the ribbon from her face, his brows raised. "I gotta admit, man, this shit is impressive. I didn't know you were some kind of...rope master."

Lex grins up at me as I release her, reaching out to cup my cheek in her hand. "Love you."

Smirking, I peck a quick kiss to her lips. "Love you."

She turns to Linc as she slowly sits, the ribbon loosening and sliding away the more she moves. Linc's gaze turns hungry as he watches her free herself.

"As much as I love seeing you like this, gorgeous, your brother will be here any minute."

Lex's eyes widen. "Shit, what time is it?"

"Almost half past."

"Seven?" she shrieks, scrambling off the bed. "Declan!"

"Don't yell at me, woman. You came so hard I have to change the fucking mattress protector."

Lex flushes, her scowl morphing into a mischievous grin. "You owe me for making me late."

"Oh, I owe you, do I?" I launch toward her.

She squeals, turning tail and running toward the ensuite, trailing ribbon in her wake. I take off after her as Linc laughs behind us.

"Twenty minutes, you two!" he calls.

I ignore him, intent on wringing one more epic orgasm out of Lex before she gets into her party dress.

"Oh, you better run!"

———

"I hear you're negotiating a new contract with the State," Van Costa says, stepping up to join me and Parker.

His arm is slung around his wife, Cami, who has a tiny sleeping baby somehow strapped to her chest with a colorful piece of cloth. It looks complicated as fuck.

"We are," I answer, clasping Van's extended hand before taking Cami's for a brief squeeze. "It's good to see you, Cami. How's Bea?"

Cami beams, peering down at her daughter. "Conked out two minutes after we got here!" she laughs, rubbing the infant's back through the intricate wrap.

I gesture toward the stairs. "You're welcome to take her up to one of the rooms if you want to try and lay her down."

"Nah," Cami shakes her head. "Thanks, Declan, that's sweet, but she'll sleep better like this anyway."

"Alright, well. You let us know if you need anything, okay?"

My lips thin as I watch her sway from side to side. The woman is constantly in motion. *Looks exhausting.*

She touches my arm, her smile warm. "Thank you, really. Oh! There they are." I follow her gaze, spying Parker's fiancé and twin by the bar. "I'll find you in a bit, Gio."

After his wife kissed him and walked away, still swaying, Van gives me a nod. "Thank you."

"Of course." As Parker launches into an explanation of Solum's latest government bid, I take a long swallow of my drink and let my eyes scan the crowd. *Our house has never been so full.*

Lex settled into our space like it was made for her. She brightened it and made it cozier at the same time, filling gaps I didn't even know we had before her. Little touches of hers are everywhere, from the sofa she refused to give up to the luxe blankets tucked in hiding places in every room.

When she told us about her annual holiday party tradition, Linc lit up like a kid on Christmas morning. He went out and bought a massive live tree at the earliest opportunity, setting it up in the living room. It swallows a good third of the space, but it makes him happy and none of us have the heart to deny him.

Linc and Nate walk up to join us, easy laughter between them fading as Nate and Van regard each other.

"Van." Nate inclines his head, tipping his glass toward him.

"Nathaniel." Van responds coolly as Nate's jaw clenches.

Linc smiles good-naturedly as he claps Van's shoulder, eyes bright with mischief. "Nate here was just telling me about Jax's latest escapades. Something about your coffee machine?"

With a long-suffering sigh, Van launches into the story I've heard eight different ways over the last month. My attention wanders, finding the culprit of the drama across the room. He's chatting with Lex and her friends, Cass and Ruby, probably telling the same story if their expressions are any indication.

As Cass laughs with abandon, Ruby chuckles and slowly shakes her head, eyeing Jax out of the corner of her eye. He smiles at her, appearing to launch into another story. Lex catches my eye as I start to pull my attention back, her lips quirking into a knowing smile.

She's wearing red, a simple silk shift I've tried to ignore all night. The mere sight of it reminds me of where we were just two hours ago, a similar silky red material leaving marks on her skin.

As though she can read my mind, Lex's lips part, her tongue darting out. Eyes on me, she takes Cass's hand and points toward us. The other woman nods, then they both turn and say farewell to Ruby and Jax. I'm vaguely aware of them continuing the conversation before my attention is stolen by the vixen working her way toward me.

"There she is," Shane mutters, coming up on my other side.

Linc turns to watch, leaving Parker and Van to chuckle at the lot of us. As men in love, they understand the command Lex holds over us. Nate shifts, chatting easily with Parker while Van refuses to engage. I suspect Van won't ever forgive Nate for his past choices and their impact on the woman I love. But if Lex is willing to try with Nate, I'm certainly not going to make it any harder for her.

"Nate, I'm glad we finally caught you." Lex leans up and kisses his cheek, squeezing his arm. "I wanted to introduce you to my good friend, Cassandra Thompson."

"Cass," the redhead insists, smiling warmly at Nate.

"Nate." He takes her hand, shaking it firmly. "You're the reporter."

"Yes, that's me. I'll be honest, I asked Lex to introduce us. I was hoping to run an idea by you, if you don't mind."

He inclines his head as she beams.

"Great. Shall we?"

As Nate follows her to a quiet corner of the room, Lex slips her arm around my waist. I press a kiss into her hair, draping an arm around her. Shane steps up behind her to rest his chin on her opposite shoulder. Van and Parker turn and filter back through the crowd, no doubt looking for their women.

"If we're having a standing snuggle fest, I demand to be included," Linc announces, stepping in front of her and closing our small circle.

He cups her face in his hands as she hums a sigh, melting into all of us.

"When can we make our escape?" Shane murmurs, lips against her neck.

She frowns, but Linc smirks and smooths it with a finger.

"He just wants you naked, beautiful," he whispers. "We're all enjoying the party."

Shane and I make noises of agreement, putting her concerns to rest. She presses up on her tiptoes and kisses Linc, slow and sweet, then smiles.

"Soon." She glances at me over her shoulder. "Maybe we can recreate earlier."

My cock stirs at the thought, Linc's eyes darkening. Lex smirks as Shane looks askance between us.

"Poor Shane missed it," she murmurs, kissing him lightly. "Don't worry, sir. We'll give you an encore."

Shane's eyes flash at the honorific, his fingers digging into her waist before she slips away with a mischievous look over her shoulder. Linc groans as she goes, shoving his hands in his pockets.

"I could cut the power," Shane offers, nonchalant, eyes on Lex.

"No need," I mutter. "Keep your distance, but don't take your eyes off her. She'll clear the place out when she's ready to succumb."

Lex turns to us as she reaches Ruby once more, lips parting as she takes in our hungry gazes. She flushes, turning to her friend. I smirk.

I never knew life could be so full.

What happens in Paris when Lex and her boys head back to celebrate one year since the Summit? For those of you looking for a little more HEA or bit more spice...get the bonus scene free when you sign up for our mailing list!

GET THE BONUS SCENE
http://bit.ly/succumbed-bonus

Also by Ashley Jacobs & S. S. Rich

South Bay Billionaires
Contemporary romance

Arrived (Parker & LB)
Reserved (Van & Cami)
Succumbed (Lex & her boys)
Exposed–*Coming soon*
Schooled–*Coming soon*

———

Sinister Empire Mafia
Dark Bratva romance

Sins of His Father–*Coming soon*

———

Learn more at shelfindulgences.com.

Acknowledgments

Y'all, Lex and her boys put us through it in the best possible way. Their story literally birthed the Bay–after we met Lex and learned where she wanted to take us, the rest of the universe unfolded. We wanted to do her justice, and we hope Linc, Shane, and Declan did just that.

If there's anything we've learned since beginning our author journeys, it's that stories like this one take a village. We're incredibly grateful for ours.

To our husbands, who kept water bottles full, wrangled fur kids and children, and weighed in on spicy scenes and tech details–thank you.

To our alpha reader, Júlia, thank you for helping us whip Declan into shape and build his story arc with Lex–your insights were invaluable!

To our beta team, Abbey, Anne, Ashly, Brittany, Clary, Courtney, Dorien, Kazia, Kelsey, Kimberley, Lo, Natalie, Nicole, Nicole, Paige, Sara, and Zoë–thank you for your recommendations, support, and love for these characters. We're grateful they entered the world in your hands.

We have so much more in store for the Bay...just take a peek at the previous section for a taste of what's to come for friends of Athena (Dorien, your intuition is spot on 😊).

On to the next! Which might just take a turn into a darker world, on the opposite coast...where a certain Bay darling has been spending a suspicious amount of time. 😊

If you want updates on our stories or opportunities to join

our beta and/or ARC teams, join our Facebook reader group, Ashley Jacobs & S. S. Rich's Billionaire Babes.

'Til next time!

xoxo

ashley & s.

About the Authors

Ashley Jacobs is a contemporary romance author. She loves to write alpha billionaires and the strong women they fall for. She lives in the United States with her golden retriever husband and goldendoodles. When she isn't spending time with fictional characters, she's busy hunting for the perfect croissant.

———

An avid reader from an early age, S. S. Rich grew up on old school sci fi and fantasy. Now, she enjoys creating strong female characters and the growly alphaholes who melt for them. When she's not writing, you can find S. chasing her children and dogs, enjoying the Pacific Northwest, obsessing over special edition books, or feeding her wanderlust.

———

Find out more and sign up for our newsletter at shelfindulgences.com.

9 781962 441056